POE

POE

19 New Tales of Suspense, Dark Fantasy, and Horror

Inspired by Edgar Allan Poe

Edited by Ellen Datlow

SOLARIS

First published 2009 by Solaris
an imprint of BL Publishing
Games Workshop Ltd
Willow Road
Nottingham
NG7 2WS
UK

www.solarisbooks.com

ISBN-13: 978 1 84416 595 7
ISBN-10: 1 84416 595 7

Designed & typeset by BL Publishing
Printed and bound in the US.

CONTENTS

INTRODUCTION

EDGAR ALLAN POE (January 19, 1809—October 7, 1849) lived a relatively short, unhappy life but during it he produced some of the world's most recognizable poetry and stories. Orphaned before the age of two, he became estranged from his foster father in his teens and became an alcoholic who had difficulty keeping a job. He married his thirteen-year-old cousin Virginia Clemm (who probably inspired much of his fiction and poetry), only to see her sicken and die of tuberculosis in her twenties. His drinking was exacerbated by her death, and only two years later he himself died in Baltimore, four days after being found wandering the streets, delirious and in clothing other than his own. His first book, *Tamerlane and Other Poems*, was published anonymously in May 1827. Although his first love was always poetry, he wrote stories, reviews, essays, and commentaries, in order to support himself and Virginia. He worked as assistant editor for the *Southern Literary Messenger* in Richmond, Virginia, then at *Burton's Gentleman's Magazine*, and finally in 1841 was appointed assistant editor of *Graham's Magazine*, both in Philadelphia. Some of his work was collected in the two volumes of *Tales of the Grotesque and Arabesque* in 1840. It was during this period that he wrote what many consider the first detective story, "The Murders in the Rue Morgue." Both "The Pit and the Pendulum" and "The Tell-Tale Heart" were also written while Poe was living in Philadelphia. The publication of his poem

"The Raven" in the February 1845 issue of *The American Review* and subsequently in *The Raven and Other Poems* the same year finally brought him the recognition he had long desired.

For the reader unfamiliar with Poe's work, one can't go wrong picking up a copy of *Tales of Mystery and Imagination*—it can be purchased in inexpensive editions with or without illustrations.

In honor of Edgar Allan Poe's Bicentennial in 2009, I commissioned our intrepid contributors to write stories inspired by Poe. I only specified that I did not want pastiches. I asked each writer to tell me in advance what work of Poe's was to be riffed on and then write an afterword discussing his or her choice. Although I discouraged Poe being used as a character in the stories, a couple of writers came up with such ingenious *uses* of Poe within their stories that I was delighted to include them.

So we have nineteen stories and novelettes that have been influenced by Poe's work ranging from "The Tell-Tale Heart," "The Fall of the House of Usher," "William Wilson," and "The Masque of the Red Death," (three of the latter, all quite different from each other) to one of Poe's essays, his poetry, and even an unfinished fragment of a story. The periods, styles, and backgrounds are varied. The subject matter and themes sometimes address contemporary concerns and fears. The contributors are from the United States, Great Britain, Australia, and Canada, and just about evenly split male-female (all inadvertent).

I've always been a fan of Edgar Allan Poe's prose and poems and have appreciated the movies made from his work—as dumb as some of them have been. Kim Newman starts off the anthology using his immense filmic knowledge to create a tale "celebrating" these mostly cheapie efforts to take advantage of public domain fiction. John Langan finishes with a story that includes, among other things, a postmodern exegesis of one of Poe's most famous stories.

Each author contributes an afterword explaining from which of Poe's works they've taken inspiration. Although the reader can check out these afterwords in advance, I urge you not to. It may spoil the surprise, the shock, and, yes, the horror these authors have in store for you.

KIM NEWMAN was born in Brixton (London), grew up in the West Country, went to University near Brighton, and now lives in Islington (London).

His most recent fiction books include: *Where the Bodies Are Buried, The Man From the Diogenes Club,* and *Secret Files of the Diogenes Club* under his own name, and *The Vampire Genevieve* as Jack Yeovil. His non-fiction books include: *Ghastly Beyond Belief* (with Neil Gaiman), *Horror: 100 Best Books* and *Horror: Another 100 Best Books* (both with Stephen Jones), and a host of books on film. He is a contributing editor to *Sight & Sound* and *Empire* magazines and has written and broadcast widely on a range of topics, scripting radio documentaries, role-playing games, and TV programs. He has won the Bram Stoker Award, the International Horror Critics Award, the British Science Fiction Award, and the British Fantasy Award. His official website, "Dr Shade's Laboratory," can be found at www.johnnyalucard.com.

I chose this story to start the anthology because although its tone is lighter than most of the other stories, it serves to introduce the reader to many of the filmed versions of Edgar Allan Poe's work... until it gets a little... weird—even for Poe.

ILLIMITABLE DOMAIN

By Kim Newman

OKAY, YOU COULD say it was my fault.

I'm the one. Me, Walter Paisley, agent to stars without stars on Hollywood Boulevard. I said, "Spare a thought for Eddy," and the Poe Plague got started...

It's 1959 and you know the montage. Cars have shark fins. Jukeboxes blare The Platters and Frankie Lyman. Ike's a back number, but JFK hasn't yet broken big. The commies have put Sputnik in orbit, starting a war of the satellites. Coffee houses are full of beards and bad poetry. Boomba the Chimp, my biggest client, has a kiddie series cancelled out from under him. Every TV channel is showing some Western, but my pitches for *The Cherokee Chimp*, *The Monkey Marshal of Mesa City*, and *Boomba Goes West* fall on stony ground. The only network I have an "in" with is DuMont, which shows how low the Paisley Agency has sunk since the heyday of *Jungle Jillian and Her Gorilla Guerrillas* (with Boomba as the platoon's comedy relief mascot) and *The Champ, the Chimp, and the Imp* (a washed-up boxer is friends with a cigar-smoking chimpanzee and a leprechaun).

American International Pictures is a fancy name for James H. Nicholson and Samuel Z. Arkoff sharing an office. They call themselves a studio, but you can't find an AIP backlot. They rent abandoned aircraft hangars for soundstages and shoot as much as possible out of doors and without permits. At the end of the fifties, AIP are cranking out thirty–forty pictures a year, double features shoved into ozoners and grindhouses catering to the

Clearasil crowd. They peddle twofers on low-budget juvenile delinquency (*Reform School Girl* with *Runaway Daughters!*), affordable science fiction (*Terror From the Year 5,000* with *The Brain Eaters!*), inexpensive chart music (*Rock All Night* with *The Ghost of Dragstrip Hollow!*), cheapskate creatures (*I Was a Teenage Werewolf* with *The Undead!*), frugal combat (*Suicide Battalion* with *Paratroop Command!*), or cut-price exotica (*She-Gods of Shark Reef* with *Teenage Cave Man!*). When Jim and Sam try for epic, they hope a marquee-filling title—*The Saga of the Viking Women and Their Voyage to the Waters of the Great Sea Serpent*—distracts the hot-rodders from sub-minimal production values and a ninety-cent sea serpent filmed in choppy bathwater.

The AIP racket is that Jim thinks up a title—say, *The Beast With a Million Eyes* or *The Cool and the Crazy*—and commissions lurid ad art which he buries in hard-sell slogans. He shows ads to exhibitors, who chip in modest production coin. Then, a producer is put on the project. Said producer gets a writer in over the weekend and forces out a script by shoving peanuts through the bars. *Someone* has to direct the picture and be in it, but so long as a teenage doll in a tight sweater screams on the poster—at a monster, a switchblade, or a guitar-player—no one thinks too much about them. Sam puts fine-print into contracts which makes sure no one sees profit participation and puffs cigars at trade gatherings.

Roger Corman is only one of a corral of producers—Bert I. Gordon and Alex Gordon are others—on AIP's string, but he's youngest, busiest, and cheapest. After, to his mind, wasting half his budget hiring a director named Wyott Ordung on a 1954 masterpiece called *The Monster from the Ocean Floor*, Roger trims the budgets by directing most of his films himself. He seldom does a *worse* job than Wyott Ordung. Five critics in France and two in England say Roger is more interesting than Cukor or Zinnemann—though unaccountably *It Conquered the World* misses out on a Best Picture nomination. Then again, Mike Todd wins for *Around the World in 80 Days*. I'd rather watch Lee Van Cleef blowtorch a snarling turnip from Venus at sixty-eight minutes than David Niven smarm over two hundred smug cameo players in far-flung locations for three or four hours. You don't have to be a contributor to *Cayenne du Cinéma* or *Sight & Sound* to agree.

After sixty–seventy films inside four years, it gets so Roger can knock 'em off over a weekend. No kidding. *Little Shop of Horrors* is made in three days because it's raining and Roger can't play tennis. He tackles every subject, within certain Jim-and-Sam-imposed limits. He shoots movies about juvenile delinquent girls, gunslinger girls, reincarnated witch girls, beatnik girls, escaped convict girls, cave girls, Viking girls, monster girls, Apache girls, rock and roll girls, girls eaten by plants, carnival girls, sorority girls, last girls on earth, pearl-diver girls, and gangster girls. Somehow, he skips jungle girls, else maybe Boomba would land an AIP contract.

The thing is everybody—except Sam, who chortles over the ledgers without ever seeing the pictures—gets bored with the production line. Another week, and it's *Blood of Dracula* plus *High School Hellcats*, ho hum. I don't know when Roger gets time to dream, but dream he does—of bigger things. Jim thinks of bigger *posters*, or at least different-shaped posters. In the fifties, the enemy is television, but AIP product *looks* like television—small and square and black and white and blurry, with no one you've ever heard of wandering around Bronson Cavern. Drive-in screens are the shape of windshields. The typical AIP just lights up a middle slice. Even with *Attack of the Crab Monsters*, *The Amazing Colossal Man*, and *The She-Creature* triple-billed, kids are restless. Where's the breathtaking CinemaScope, glorious Technicolor, and stereoscopic sound? 3-D has come and gone, and neither Odorama nor William Castle's butt-buzzers are goosing the box office.

Jim or Roger get a notion to lump together the budgets and shooting schedules of two regular AIP pictures and throw their all into one eighty-five minute superproduction. Together, they browbeat Sam into opening the cobwebbed cheque book. This time, Mike Todd—well, not Mike Todd, since he's dead, but some imaginary composite big-shot producer—will have to watch out come Oscar season. So, what to make?

In England, they start doing horror pictures in color, with talented actors in starched collars and proper sets. Buckets of blood and girls in low-cut nightgowns are included, so it's not like there's art going on. Every other AIP quickie has a monster in it, so the company reckons they're expert at fright fare. There's your answer. Roger will make a classy—but not *too*-classy—horror. Jim can get Vinnie Price to star. He'd been in that butt-buzzing William Castle film for Columbia and a 3-D *House of Wax* for Warners, and is therefore a horror "name," but his career is stalled with TV guest spots on debatably rigged quiz programs or as fairly fruity actors touring Tombstone on Western shows. After Brando, well-spoken, dinner-jacketed eyebrow-archers like him are out of A pictures. What Jim and Roger don't have is a clue as to what their full-color, widescreen spooktacular should be *about*. They just know *Revenge of the Crab Monsters* or *The Day After the World Ended* won't cut it.

Enter Walter Paisley, with a Signet paperback of *Tales of Mystery and Imagination*. No, it isn't altruism—it's all about the client.

Boomba's out of work and eating his weight in bananas every single day. Bonzo and Cheetah have a lock on working with Dutch Reagan and Tarzan, so my star is unfairly shut out of the town's few chimp-friendly franchises unless he's willing to do the dangerous vine-swinging, crocodile-dodging stunts those precious primates want to duck out of. Therefore, I'm obliged to scare up properties suitable as vehicles for a pot-bellied chimpanzee. I ponder a remake of *King Kong*, with a chimp instead of a gorilla, but RKO won't listen. I pitch a biopic of Major Sam, America's monkey astronaut, but that goddamn Russian dog gets all the column inches.

In desperation, I ask an intern who once had a few weeks of college about famous, out-of-copyright stories with monkeys in 'em, and get pointed at "Murders in the Rue Morgue." Okay, so, strictly, the killer in that yarn is an orangutan not a chimpanzee—but every film version casts a guy in a ratty gorilla suit, so Boomba is hardly wider of the author's original intent. I know of AIP's horror quandary, and a light-bulb goes on over my head. I dress Boomba up in a fancy suit and cravat and beret for the Parisian look and teach him to wave a cardboard cutthroat razor. I march the chimp into Jim and Sam's office just as Jim and Roger are looking glumly at a sketch artist holding up a blank board which ought to be covered with lurid artwork boosting their break-out film.

Tragically, Boomba compromises his employment prospects by crapping his velvet britches and grabbing for Sam's foot-long cigar, but my Poe paperback falls onto the desk and Roger snatches it up. He once read some of the stories, and thinks he particularly liked "The Fall of the House of Usher." Sam objects. The kids who go to AIP pictures have to study Poe in school and will therefore naturally hate him. But Jim remembers Universal squeezed out a couple of Poe pictures and racked up fair returns back in the Boris and Bela days. Then, Sam—who gives every appearance of actually having *read* "The Fall of the House of Usher"—says you can't make a horror movie without a monster and there's no monster in the story. "The house," says Roger, eyes shining, "the *house* is the monster!" Jim and Sam look at each other, thinking this over. Boomba is forgotten, chewing the cigar. Then, management buys Roger's line. The house *is* the monster.

Important issues get settled. Is there a part for Price? Yes, there's someone in the falling house called Roderick Usher. Is there a girl? Roderick has a sister called Madeline. Paging through the paperback, they discover Poe doesn't say Madeline *isn't* a teenager in a tight sweater. I suggest the thin plot of the eighteen-page story would be improved if a killer chimp escaped from the Rue Morgue and broke into the House of Usher to terrorize the family. No one listens.

Jim and Roger run with "The Fall of the House of Usher." They happily read out paragraphs in Vinnie Price accents. The sketch-artist covers his board with a falling house, Vinnie lifting a terrified eyebrow, a buried-alive babe in a tight shroud, coffins, crypts, skeletons, an atomic explosion (which gets rubbed out quickly), and slogans ripped from Poe prose. "He buried her alive... to save his soul!" "I heard her first feeble movements in the coffin... we had put her living in the tomb!" "Edgar Allan Poe's overwhelming tale of EVIL and TORMENT!"

I see my slice of the deal vanishing along with Sam's cigar. Eddy is dead and long out of copyright, so there's no end for him. This cheers Sam up, since he'd been all a-tremble at the prospect of having to buy rights to some horror book from some unwashed writer.

So, just when it would take a steam-train to *stop* AIP making *The Fall of the House of Usher*, I mention I am the agent for the Edgar Allan Poe Society of Baltimore and can easily secure permission—for a nominal fee—for the use of the author's name, which they have registered as a trademark. For a few moments, the room is quiet and no one believes me. Sam is skeptical, but I tell him the reason Poe's middle name is so often misspelled is to evade dues payable to the EAPSoB. He mulls it over. He swallows it, because it makes sense to him. He's ready to argue for going with *Edgar Allen Poe's House of Asher* as a title before Jim and Roger shout him down. Sam doesn't care about critics, but little slivers of Jim and Roger do, so they're ready to strike a deal on the spot. I have a pre-prepared contract, which needs crossings-out as it's for a monkey as actor rather than an august body as trademark-leaser, but will still do.

As soon as I'm out of the office, I *found* the Edgar Allan Poe Society of Baltimore and start paperwork on trademark registration. It turns out I'm not even the first in the racket. Edgar Rice Burroughs and Mark Twain, or their heirs, have beaten me to it. The deal may not be 100% kosher, but AIP's check clears. Probably, they just want to shut me up, since I'm theoretically responsible for bringing them the property. Hey, it's my drugstore paperback. They offer me an "associate producer" credit, but forget to include it on the film. Maybe it's lost in the five minutes of swirling multi-colored liquids tacked on after the house has burned down and tumbled into the tarn. But, from then on, I'm part of the Poe package.

The Fall of the House of Usher—or *The House of Usher*, as it is called on the posters to save on lettering—is made in a comparatively leisurely fifteen days. Vinnie shaves his moustache, under protest as if he were Cesar Romero, and wears a white wig, which he likes enough to model in his off-hours along Sunset Strip. There are only three other people in the speaking cast, so the star gets first bite of all the scenery available for chewing. On set, Vinnie objects to the line "The house lives, the house breathes!" Roger tells him "The *house* is the monster," and Vinnie sells it with eyeball-rolling, velvet-tongued ham. In my capacity as "ass. prod.," I have Boomba pose for a portrait as a degenerate Usher ancestor. Floyd, the camera genius, doesn't get a good shot of it so you can't see the chimp's cameo in the picture.

This is how it plays. In some earlier century (no one's sure which), a brooding youth with a Brando sneer and a Fabian haircut travels through burned-out wasteland to a painted-on-glass mansion where Vinnie twitches at the slightest sound and rolls his eyeballs as if they were marbles. He has extra-sensitive senses, which are a perpetual torment to him, and looks severely pained whenever anyone drops a fork or lights a lamp. Our hero is searching for his missing girlfriend, Vinnie's sister. She flits about, showing cleavage, then faints and is buried alive in the basement. Girl claws her way out of crypt, irritated, and scratches out Vinnie's eyes as if he were making a play for her date at the record hop. A candle falls over and the House of Usher catches light like Atlanta in *Gone With the Wind*—indeed, some of the burning building stock footage might *be* offcuts from David O. Selznick's day. Vinnie and girl get crushed and/or burned. Our hero makes it out unscorched and broods some more—presumably his agent has just told him how much he's getting paid and he's resolved to quit acting and become a producer so *he* can wave the foot-long cigars some day. A caption runs: "'…and the deep and dark tarn closed silently over the fragments of the House of Usher'—Poe." Just to make sure you know, Eddy's name pops up several more times during the swirly credits.

Against expectations, *Usher* is a monumental hit, boffo boxo, molto ducats in the coffers. Roger makes money. Vinnie makes money. Sam and Jim make more money than they can imagine, and Jim at least has a great imagination. Edgar Allan Poe, or the Baltimore Society in his name, makes money. Even Boomba gets residuals for the use of his unseen likeness. There actually *are* residuals and Sam has to find out how to pay them. The matter never came up with *Voodoo Woman* or *Phantom From 10,000 Leagues*. Naturally, being Hollywood, this means only one thing—sequels.

The first pass runs to pitches like *Return to the House of Usher*… only there's a stinking tarn where the old homestead used to be, so few dramatic possibilities not involving expensive underwater photography present themselves. I spin a story out of my head in which Roderick Usher's ghost crawls out of the tarn as a green monkey with flippers. Jim sees straight off that I'm angling a star role for Boomba and nixes the approach. It would be easy to take offence—after all, the chimp is a better actor than the ducktailed hoodlums AIP put ruffs, doublets, and floppy-tasseled hats on in subsequent movies.

Skipping through my now dog-eared and broken-spined *Tales of Mystery and Imagination*, Roger gets excited about "The Pit and the Pendulum." The slavering sketch artist, about whom I'm starting to worry, draws a teeny-bopper in a tight sweater strapped down in a pit while Vinnie swings a blade over her bazooms. Jim and Sam love this, and are disappointed when Roger looks up the story and finds it's a *guy* in the dungeons of the Spanish Inquisition. Never mind, he says, the *pendulum* is the monster. By this, he means the torture angle is grabby enough without the added distraction of bazooms. The artist rubs out the bosomage, and puts in a manly chest—revealed through pendulum-slashes in a frilly shirt.

So, *Pit and the Pendulum* gets a greenlight. Even Sam sees one picture for the price of two is a better deal if it hauls in ten times the gross of the average four old-style AIP creature features. He quietly squelches Bert I. Gordon's *Puppet People vs. the Colossal Beast* project and Alex Gordon's long-cherished *She-Creature Meets the Old-Time Singing Cowboy* script, and pours added shekels into *Pit*. It's AIP's big hope for 1961.

Only problem is, "Pit and the Pendulum" *isn't* a story—just a scene. Guy in pit. Nearly sliced by pendulum. Escapes. Even Roger can't spin that out to feature length with long shots of dripping walls, gnawing rats, and Vinnie licking his lips. The problem is solved, unusually, by the writer. Dick Matheson takes his *Usher* script, changes the names, and drops the climactic house fire in favor of Pit/Pendulum business. This time, brooding youth—not the same one, though you'd be hard pressed to tell the difference—is looking for his missing *sister*, and she's married to Vinnie. But she's still buried alive—twice, as it happens. The *Usher* sets are back, with new painted flats and torture equipment to bump the House up to a castle. The establishing shot is a bigger glass painting, with crashing waves included. Vinnie keeps his moustache—which saves behind-the-scenes drama—and wears tights, always a big favorite with him.

One morning, I wake and find I've grown a moustache too. Plus I'm thinner, paler, and more watery-eyed. And my wardrobe—once full of snazzy striped threads—runs to basic black. I don't think much of it, because the times they are a-changing. *Pit* is, if anything, bigger boffier boxo than *Usher*, and the walls start closing in.

Tales of Terror gets through *its* remake of *House of Usher* in the first reel, and calls it "Morella." Then, it runs through "The Black Cat" and "A Cask of Amontillado" (Peter Lorre and Vinnie compete in a face-pulling contest) for a second act, finishing up with "The Facts in the Case of M. Valdemar" (bad-tempered Basil Rathbone turns Vinnie into a "nearly liquid mass of loathsome—of detestable putrescence"). Since most of the pages are now torn out of my book, I venture the opinion we're using up doable Poe at an alarming rate, especially since AIP are cranking out more than one of these pictures a year. I try to get "Rue Morgue" back on the table, determined Boomba will have his comeback before the well runs dry. After only one and a half remakes of *House of Usher*, everyone is bored again—the curse of success in this business, if you ask me—and trying to break out.

First, Roger sneaks off to do *The Premature Burial* at another outfit, with Ray Milland playing Vincent Price, but Sam and Jim buy into the deal, so Roger is sucked back in. *Premature* isn't quite as much of a remake of *Usher* as *Pit* and "Morella," but it *is* a remake of the scheme-to-drive-the-husband-crazy subplot Matheson padded out *Pit* with. Roger wants to hop-frog off and make, I don't know, socially significant movies about segregation. He winds up buried alive in Venice, California, in those standing Danny Haller sets. Decaying mansions with stock furniture. Tiny soundstage exteriors with false perspective stunted trees. Dry ice mist pooling over bare floor.

Piqued that Milland is daring to usurp his shtick, Vinnie hares all over the library, doing *Master of the World*, *Confessions of an Opium Eater*, *Twice Told Tales*, *Diary of a Madman*, and *Tower of London*. In Vinnie's mouth, Verne, de Quincey, Hawthorne, de Maupassant, and Shakespeare somehow turn into Poe. Brooding youths. Velvet jackets. Buried alive girls.

Vinnie a-flutter. Crypt in the basement. House burns down. Swirly credits. The Shakespeare (*Tower of London* is *Richard III* translated into English) is directed by Roger, who swears he can't remember being on the set. He admits it's possible the film got shot during a blackout he had during a screening of a Russian science fiction film he was cutting the special effects out of to fit around rubber monster scenes shot by some kid to see release as *Rocket Voyage to the Planet of Prehistoric Women of Blood*. Meanwhile, Vinnie is *muy fortunato* lording it over the castles of AIP, hawking Sears-Roebuck art selections and cookbooks on the side.

Even the critics start noticing they get the same picture every time. Recalling that this happened before, I propose an ingenious solution. When Universal got in a rut with Frankenstein, Dracula, and Mummy pictures, they had the monsters meet Abbott and Costello. Comedy killed off the cycle. Once you've laughed at a horror, it's never frightening again. Since Lou has passed away, we can't get the team back, but I suggest it would at least triple the hilarity if Bud's new comedy partner is a rotund, talented chimpanzee... and AIP can launch a new series with *Abbott and Boomba Meet the Black Cat*. It'll slay 'em in the stalls when Boomba starts tossing loathsome, detestable putrescence at Vinnie Price's moustache. We can bill Boomba as "The Chimp of the Perverse."

Before I sell Jim, Sam, and Roger—not to mention Bud Abbott—on this, Matheson dashes off a *funny* remake of *House of Usher*, purportedly based on "The Raven." It breaks my heart to tell Boomba he's been benched again, but the "ass. prod." gig is still live and EAPSoB dues are pouring in. *The Raven*, for comedy value, casts Vinnie as the brooding youth in tights, makes the buried alive chick a faithless slut and has Boris Karloff play Vincent Price. The castle still burns down in by-now scratchy stock footage, which almost counts as a joke. Lorre is in it too, driving Karloff nuts making up his own dialogue. The juve is some piranha-toothed nobody who lands the job by spreading a false rumor he's Jim Nicholson's illegitimate son. When it comes out that he isn't, Sam swears the grinning kid will never work in this town again, though it's too late to cut him out of *The Terror*, yet another remake of *House of Usher* that Roger shoots in three days because he still has Karloff under contract. The twist here is that the house is washed away rather than burned down.

After sending the cycle up with *The Raven* and cynically hammering it into the ground with *The Terror*, there's no way this perpetuation of Poe can persist. So, relief all round, and a sense everyone can move on to better—or at least new—things in 1964. Jim thinks H.P. Lovecraft could be the new Poe, and buys up a ton of his stories. Yes, AIP lays out for film rights! Banner headlines in *Variety*. Having missed out with Verne, Hawthorne, de Quincey, and the other bums, I found the Howard Phillips Lovecraft Society of Providence. I pore through *The Outsider and Others*, determined to find a tale with a good part for a chimp—the best I can manage is a rat with a withered human head in "Dreams in the Witch House," which should be close enough. But first up on AIP's Lovecraft schedule is *The Case of Charles Dexter Ward*. Only it's going to be *The Curse of Charles Dexter Ward*—*Curse*, which sounds like swearing and violence, is a better movie title word than *Case*, which sounds like measles and bed rest.

For some reason no one can fathom, Roger wants the non-bastard Nicholson to play Charles Dexter Ward. He thinks up this scene where Chuck is possessed by his evil wizard ancestor and smashes an axe through a door to get to his terrified wife (Debra Paget) while shouting something from *The Tonight Show*. I know that will never work, but keep quiet. Vinnie, meanwhile, happily breezes off to play Big Daddy in *Sweet Charity* on Broadway, intending to conquer a whole new career as a musical comedy star. The velvet jackets go in storage. The burning building footage goes back in the cans. As per HPL, this time, the *monster* is the monster.

Though I don't live anywhere remotely near a Witch House, I'm tormented by dreams—not of human-faced rats or green monkeys, but an angry Eddy. In my restless slumber, Poe comes at me with a long list of grievances which, in my official EAPSoB capacity, he wants presented to Congress, the publishing industry, drinking establishments long since gone out of business, the United States army, and sundry other bodies and individuals. With his name writ large on panoramic magic lantern screens undreamed of even in the thousand-and-third tale of Scheherazade, he feels he has the attention of a general public who once gave him the shortest of shrifts—and wishes to plead for a redress of wrongs done long ago. I put these dreams down to the rich foods I'm able to afford thanks to "ass. prod." fees, and think hard about cutting down on lunches.

At the *Charles Dexter Ward* preview, we find out something mysterious and beyond imagining has happened during production. I settle into my seat with a big bucket of popcorn Sam has made me pay for, certain that the HPLSoP is going to trash the EAPSoB in the coming fiscal year. The lights go down, the curtains crank open, and the projector whirrs. The AIP logo fills the screen. The opening title is not *H.P. Lovecraft's The Curse of Charles Dexter Ward*... but *Edgar Allan Poe's The Haunted Palace*.

There's a rustling, creeping, sussurating, terror-filled sensation in the house. The wet cigar falls from Sam's open mouth. Roger puts on dark glasses and starts to cry. Jim gets up and checks with the projectionist that this is the right film. I know now we're all cursed, that we'll never be free of Eddy Poe Rex.

The velvet jackets are back. The fog swirls on those same tiny sets. There's a crypt in the basement, where the monster lives. It's out of focus. Vincent Price, grieving for lost chances on the Great White Way, plods through a part written for a much younger, scarier man, bidding a bittersweet farewell to life as the New Rex Harrison (or the White Sammy Davis Jr). Finally, as we sob in the screening room, the house burns down. It's another remake of *House of Usher*. After burning beams collapse for the ninth or tenth time, there's even a quote. "'While, like a rapid ghastly river, through the pale door, a hideous throng rush out forever, and laugh—but smile no more.' — Edgar Allan Poe."

We know how that pale throng feel...

In melancholy despair, Roger flees to Swinging England, vowing to make films about Oliver Cromwell and the Beatles. Unable to resist the fateful clutch of dread destiny, he shoots *The Masque of the Red Death* and *Tomb of Ligeia*—with Vinnie Price, buried girls, burning buildings, swirly credits, and end-quotes. "The boundaries which divide life from death are at best shadowy and vague. Who can say where the one ends and where the other begins?" "And Darkness and Decay and the Red Death held illimitable dominion over all." There's nothing Roger can do. He hires Richard Chamberlain, Christopher Lee, Shirley MacLaine, or Jerry Lewis, but visits the star's dressing room on the first day of the shoots to find ashen-faced, quivering-jowled, red-eyed Vinnie Price having his eyebrows powdered and being helped into another velvet jacket.

I wind up the HPLSoP and find myself shackled full-time to the interests of the EAPSoB, which has regional chapters in Boston, New York, Paris, and Antarctica. The Society brings a massive lawsuit against NASA, claiming that the Apollo program infringe the intellectual property rights of "The Balloon Hoax."

Boomba drowns in his swimming pool. At Hollywoodlawn, I march leaden-footed behind Cheetah, Bonzo, J. Fred Muggs, and Stanley (billed as "more fun than a barrel of teenagers" in Disney's *The Monkey's Uncle*) as they carry the child-sized coffin to the tiny grave. Judy, the simian slut who wormed her way into Boomba's affections then stole a plum continuing role on *Daktari!* from him, makes a show of honking bogus grief into her Kleenex. The wake is a gloomy, ill-tempered affair. I repress an urge to daub the sanctimonious surviving chimps with pitch, string 'em up from the beams at Ben Frank's and set light to them.

Poe goes on. Roger, running in vain from the Red Death, takes a trip around the world in eighty pictures. *City in the Sea*, *The Oblong Box*, *The Conqueror Worm*, *Murders in the Rue Morgue* (finally—but with a goddamn gorilla suit and made in Spain!), *X-ing the Paragrab*, *The System of Dr. Tarr and Professor Fether*. All the Tales and Poems are consumed, so AIP start in on the *essays*. In *Eureka!*, a velvet-jacketed philosopher is on the point of understanding how the universe functions when his buried alive niece claws at his eyes and the house catches fire.

My hair long and lank, my cheeks hollow, my eyes red-veined, my moustache floppy—I realize I *look* like Eddy Poe. Considering he was found near death in ill-fitting clothes borrowed from someone else, it seems I even dress like the unhappy poet whose still-beating heart of horror I discern beneath the floorboards of my office or bricked up in the basement of my bungalow (which doesn't even *have* a basement). Everywhere I go, every mirror I look into, I glimpse the specter of myself, silently accusing, "Thou art the man!"

I *am* that "unhappy master whom unmerciful disaster followed fast and follows faster till my songs one burden bore—till the dirges of his hope that melancholy burden bore—of 'Never–Nevermore!'"

But I'm not alone in being by horror haunted, by Eddy ensnared, by Allan alienated, by Poe persecuted…

By now, it's not just Roger films and Vinnie vehicles. It's *everything* Jim and Sam put into production. Alongside remakes of *The House of Usher*, AIP is doing annual reunions of *Beach Party*—itself a thinly-disguised remake of *Gidget*—with beach bums and bikini babes surfing and smooching to tunes from Frankie and Annette, plus comedy Hell's Angels led by Rocco Barbella from *Bilko*. Even in the first *Beach Party*, the first signs are there when "Big Daddy," who runs the hang-out shack on the beach, looks up and turns out to be… Vincent Price. AIP tries a James Bond skit and it comes out as *Dr. Goldfoot and the Bikini Machine*, with Vinnie Price using a razor-pendulum to part Frankie Avalon's hair. Soon, *all* beach pictures bear the mark of Poe—*Buried Alive Bikini*, *Beach Blanket Berenice*, *Muscle Beach Metzengerstein*. Annette spends more time in a shroud than a bathing suit, with a black cat entombed in her beehive hairdo. Rod Usher takes over the Hell's Angels, wearing a studded velvet jacket and a floppy-tasseled cap, and complains that the revving of bikes is torture to his over-sensitive ears.

We're all drinking heavily now, and choking on the poison. The *Hollywood Reporter* prints an item that Jim is on the point of marrying his thirteen-year-old cousin. *Variety* claims Roger is trying to raise funds for a Southern Literary Magazine when he ought to be shooting a motor-racing picture in Europe. At the Brown Derby, they say Sam is never seen without a raven flapping ominously after him, croaking whole stanzas. Vinnie lands a prime-time comedy special, but it comes out as *An Evening With Edgar Allan Poe*. My second-best client, a rare and radiant exotic dancer whom the angels name Lenore, flies from my agency door, and I spend much time agonizing about her lost and lovely tassels.

Still, it continues. AIP tries a war picture. It turns out to feature a brooding young commando who storms a Nazi castle in search of his missing girlfriend and finds Vinnie in a velvet SS uniform before inevitable torture, burial alive, and burning down. With his producer's hat on, Roger sends some film students and the Nicholson kid into the desert to make a Western, and they come back with Vinnie as an accursed cattle baron, doppelganger gunslingers, and a cattle stampede flattening the ranch house in place of the fire. *Rocket Voyage to the Planet of Prehistoric Women of Blood* eventually sells to television with the hammer and sickle insignia on the spacecraft blotted out. It is somehow re-edited. A brooding young astronaut lands on a haunted world where Mr. Touch-and-Go Bullet-Head

(Vincent Price) rules a telepathic tribe of ululating bikini girls who are interred living within the tomb as doom-haunted dinosaurs set fire to the whole planet.

Then, it's not just American International.

The plague shows up as little things in little films. Two Cavalry troopers called "William Wilson" in *The Great Sioux Massacre*. A "Pink Panther" cartoon called *Dial 'P' for Pendulum*. A premature burial in *John Goldfarb, Please Come Home*. Then, a descent into the maelstrom. The Red Death arrives during the revolutionary scenes of *Doctor Zhivago*, and the rest of the film finds Darkness and Despair descending illimitably over Omar Sharif and Julie Christie. *The Agony and the Ecstasy* features Charlton Heston laboring for decades over a small oval portrait of one of Roderick Usher's ancestors. *The Spy Who Came in From the Cold* winds up with Richard Burton clutching a purloined letter and ranting that the orangutan did it. Even a John Wayne-Howard Hawks Western turns on a Poe poem, *El Dorado*.

The curse is complete when movie theaters book *The Sound of Music* as a roadshow attraction and get *The Sound of Meowing*. In vast, empty, decaying haunted picture palaces across the land, Julie Andrews climbs ragged mountains and pokes around a basement only to find Captain von Trapp (Vincent Price) has walled up his wife along with her noisy cat. At the end, Austria burns down.

My senses are more painfully acute by the hour. I can not venture out by day unless the sun is completely obscured by the thickest, gloomiest cloud and after dark can tolerate only the tiniest, flickering flame of a candle. My ears are assaulted by the faintest sound. A housewife tearing open a cereal packet two blocks away reverberates within my skull like the discharge of a Gatling gun. I can bear only the most pallid of foods, and neglect my formerly-favored watering-holes to become a ghoul-like habitué of the new McDonald's chain, where fare that tastes of naught save cardboard may be found at the expense of a few trivial cents. The touch of my secretary becomes as sandpaper upon my appallingly sensitive skin, and raises sharp pains, sudden dizziness, and then profuse bleeding at my pores. Few in the industry return my telephone calls, which is all to the good since I can of course scarcely bear the torture of tintinnabulation… of the bells—of the bells, bells, bells, bells, bells, bells, bells—of the moaning and the groaning of the bells.

Movies are only the beginning. Soon, Poe is everywhere. The *house* is the monster, and the house is the United States of America. The break-out TV hits of the next seasons are *The Usher Family*, *The Man From U.L.A.L.U.M.E.* and *The Marie Tyler Roget Show*. Vincent Price takes over from Walter Cronkite, and intones the bad news in a velvet jacket, promising "much of madness, and more of sin, and horror the soul of the plot" in reports from Vietnam, Washington, and the Middle East. Sonny and Cher take "The Colloquy of Monos and Una" to Number One in the hit parade, followed by Procol Harum's "A Whiter Shade of Poe," Scott McKenzie's "San Francisco (Be Sure to Put some Flowers on Your Grave)," the Mamas and the Papas' "Dream a Little Dream Within a Dream of You," the Archies' "Bon-Bon" and Dean Martin's "Little Old Amontillado Drinker Me." Vinnie hosts *American Bandstand* too, warily scanning the dancers for a skull-faced figure in red robes.

A craze for floppy shirts, ink-stained fingers, and pale faces seizes the surfer kids, and everyone on the strip has a pet raven or a trained ape. Beauty contests for cataleptics are all the rage, and "Miss Universe" is crowned with a wreath in her coffin as she is solemnly bricked up by the judges. The Green Berets adopt a "conqueror worm" cap badge. Housing developments rise up tottering on shaky ground near stagnant ponds, with pre-stressed materials to provide Usher cracks and incendiaries built into the light-fittings for more spectacular conflagrations. The most popular names for girls in 1966-7 are "Lenore," "Annabel," "Ligeia," and "Madeline."

In a kingdom by the sea, we are haunted. In the El Dorado of Los Angeles, white fog lies thick on the boulevards. The mournful "nevermores" of ravens perched on statues is answered by the strangled mewling of black cats immured in basements. And the seagulls chime in with "tekeli-li, tekeli-li" as if that was any help.

During the whole of a dull, dark and soundless day in the autumn of the year, when the clouds hang oppressively low in the heavens, I pass alone in a Cadillac convertible through a singularly dreary tract of country; and at length find myself as the shades of evening draw on, within view of the melancholy House of Roger. I know not how it is—but, with the first glimpse of the building, a sense of insufferable gloom pervades my spirit. I try to shake off the fog, like the after-dream of a reveler upon maryjane, in my brain and rid my mind of the words of Poe. Yet he sits beside me, phantasmal, fiddling with the radio dial, breathing whisky and muttering in intricate rhyme schemes. I have taken the Pacific Coast Highway to Malibu, where AIP and Corman—flush with monies from the Poe pictures—have thrown up a studio in a bleak castle atop the jagged cliffs. From the road, it looks phony as a glass shot. The scrublands all around are withered and sere, and I'm not even sure what "sere" means.

The castle seems abandoned, but I gain access through a wide crack in the walls. In the gloom, I find the others. Roger, in dark glasses with side-panels. Sam, with raven chewing on his cigar. Jim, haunted by the doppelganger who no longer claims to be his son. Vinnie, worst of us all, liquid face dribbling over his frilly shirt, eyebrows and moustache shifted inches lower by the tide of loathsome, of detestable putrescence. A few others are with the crowd—the embalmed, toothless corpse of Lorre; an ancient withered ape just recognizable as Boris Karloff; barely-breathing girls and a teenage singer coughing blood into a handkerchief; an ignored brooding youth or two, hiding in the shadows and trying to avoid being upstaged.

All eyes are accusingly upon me. "Thou art the man," is written plainly on everyone's faces. I admit it to myself, and the plague-ravaged company. We have brought Poe back. Neglected and despised in life, to his mind cheated of the riches and recognition due his genius, he has been kept half-alive in the grave, plagiarized and paperbacked, bought and sold and made a joke of. No wonder we have raised an angry Eddy, a vindictive and a spiteful genius. This time, he has caught on and he will not let go, not of us and not of the world. This is the dawning of the Age of Edgar Allan, the era of Mystery and Imagination. We have *ushered*—ahem—it in, but we are to be its mummified, stuffed, walled-up victims, the sacrifices necessary for the foundations of even the shakiest edifice.

I have a new horror. It seizes my brain like a vulture's—no, a raven's—talons. I hear the faint whisper of nails against wood, the tapping of hairy knuckles against a coffin-lid, that first gibber of fear before the awful realization takes hold. I can hear Boomba, and know that—through my neglect—I have suffered him to be *buried alive*. The gibber becomes a snarling, hooting, raging, clawing shriek. The tapping, as of someone gently rapping, becomes a hammering, a clamoring, a gnawing, a pawing, a crashing, a smashing. Wood breaks, earth parts, and long-fingered, bloodied, torn-nailed, horribly semi-human hands grope for the bone handle of a straight razor.

Jim and Sam want to know what to do, how to escape. To them, every contract has a get-out clause. Roger and Vinnie know this isn't true.

Without, a storm rages. The heavens rage at the sorrows of the world.

A door opens with a creak. The attenuated shadow of a chimpanzee is cast upon the flagstones, gleaming cruel blade held high. We turn to look, our capacity for wonder and terror long since exceeded.

Brushfires burn all around, struggling against the torrents. The crack that runs through the castle—the crack that runs through *California*—widens, with great shouts as of the planet itself in pain and terror. A million tons of mud is on the march, and we stand between it and the sea. The walls bend and bow like painted canvas flats. A candle falls and flames spread. A maiden screams. A burning bird streaks comet-like through the air.

The ape's clutch is at my throat and the razor held high. In Boomba's glittering, baleful eye I discern cruel recognition.

Vinnie, before the burning beams come down, has to have the last quote…

"'… the screenplay is the tragedy Man, and its hero the Conqueror Worm!'—Edgar Allan…"

THE FIRST POE *story I can remember reading is "Metzengerstein," which was in an illustrated book of an educational nature; while writing "Illimitable Domain," I dug out a battered Everyman*

paperback of Tales of Mystery and Imagination *I've had since about 1971 to check quotes and details. I'm in the second generation of folks who were led to Eddy by the Roger Corman–Vincent Price–AIP pictures of the 1960s, starting with* The Fall of the House of Usher *in 1960 and—as mostly per this story—running on till* Tomb of Ligeia *in 1965. I think the first one I saw was* The Raven, *which is as atypical of the series as the gothic "Metzengerstein" (a terror which is of Germany, not the soul) is of Poe's stories. I missed the films on their original cinema releases, but saw them repeatedly on television (in black and white and panned and scanned) in the early 1970s, then sought them out in theatrical revivals which revealed sumptuous color and imaginative widescreen framing. I've owned all these films in successive formats—off-air VHS, retail VHS, laserdisc, and DVD—and will probably keep buying them, though no home cinema can quite replicate the experience of watching that pendulum swing from one end of a Panavision frame to the other in a darkened cinema. Though much that "Walter Paisley" says about the films in the story is true, I unreservedly love them all—despite repeated plots, sets and stock footage, variable supporting casts and problematic readings of the original stories. Without really meaning to, I've returned often to Edgar A. Poe in my work—he features as a character in my novels* Route 666 *(which I wrote as Jack Yeovil) and* The Bloody Red Baron *and the story "Just Like Eddy," which I wrote as part of my private campaign to combat the persistent misspelling of his adopted middle name as 'Allen'.*

MELANIE TEM has written ten solo novels including her Bram Stoker award-winning debut, *Prodigal*, *Slain in the Spirit*, and *The Deceiver*. She has also collaborated with Nancy Holder on the novels *Making Love* and *Witch-Light*, and with Steve Rasnic Tem on *Daughter* and *The Man on the Ceiling*. The earlier, novella version of *The Man on the Ceiling* won the 2001 Bram Stoker, International Horror Guild, and the World Fantasy Awards. The Tems also collaborated on the award-winning multi-media CD-ROM *Imagination Box*.

Her short stories have been published in the collection *The Ice Downstream* on E-Reads and in numerous magazines (including *Colorado State Review*, *Black Maria*, *Isaac Asimov's Science Fiction Magazine*, and *Cemetery Dance*) and anthologies (including *Snow White Blood Red*, *Little Deaths*, *Gathering the Bones*, *Hot Blood*, and *Acquainted with the Night*). She has also published non-fiction articles and poetry.

Recipient of a 2001–2002 associateship from the Rocky Mountain Women's Institute for script development, Tem is also a playwright. Her one-act play "The Society for Lost Positives" has been produced in Denver, Salida, and Chicago, and several of her full-length plays have received staged readings.

Tem lives in Denver with her husband, writer and editor Steve Rasnic Tem, where she works as a social worker. They have four children and four granddaughters.

THE PICKERS

by Melanie Tem

WIND BLOWING ICY snow against the patio door startled her from the *People* magazine she'd been nearly napping over. For a fierce instant she thought it might be Matt coming home, and the realization that it never again would be Matt, here or anywhere, burned through her as if she hadn't realized it a million times already.

It was midnight straight up, dreary as midday or dawn. The gas logs overheated the small living room and gave the impression of embers that would never die, until you turned the knob and they vanished and then instantly the room was cold. Toni was aware of a sensation that was probably hunger, and she didn't think she'd eaten for a while.

She'd rolled Ryan's crib in here, afraid tonight to let him out of her sight. He slept his usual peaceful sleep. His happy, easygoing nature hadn't changed. He hadn't seemed to notice what had happened to them. He wouldn't even remember the father who'd loved him so much. Toni wanted to shake him awake and make him understand, or to curl up next to him and let his obliviousness seep into her.

She stayed where she was on the couch. The silky purple curtains covering the patio doors looked sad and ridiculous in the fireplace light. She should have made Matt take them back to the thrift store. At least they kept her from seeing whatever was tapping. *It's just the wind.*

Under the rattle of the glass, she heard pickers in the alley going through the dumpster. Maybe one of them had come up to the building and was rapping on the door, wanting something, wanting in, a particularly scary thought since the patios faced an inside courtyard that was supposed to be private. She sat there wondering, doubting, half-dreaming about Matt.

After a while, feeling a little stronger, she threw down the magazine and got to her feet. When the dizziness passed, she turned off the lights, crossed the room, and tugged the curtains open. Blowing snow and darkness there, nothing more.

In the alley the pickers were laughing and singing, and Toni suddenly couldn't stand it another minute. Here she was, trying to make an honest living at a responsible job, taking care of Ryan and everything else by herself now, struggling to get through every day and to figure out life without Matt, trying to make herself believe really had to go on without him. The thought of human scavengers in her garbage, especially in the middle of the night in this kind of weather, making a mess for decent people to clean up, was just too much.

Shaking, she pulled on sweats under her nightshirt, threw on a jacket of Matt's from one of the boxes, shoved her feet into slippers, grabbed up the sack of trash waiting by the door to be taken out in the morning, and stormed out. Behind her, Ryan stirred in his sleep and made soft contented noises. Her relief at getting away from him, just for a few minutes, enraged her even more. In two steps her feet were wet, though Matt's jacket kept her warm. Snow and tears blurred her vision.

As she pushed through the gate into the parking lot behind the building, the commotion got louder. A truck engine idled roughly. Things banged and clattered. Their talk was no more than two or three sounds repeated over and over in some kind of primitive language, more cooing and squawking than words.

The first time she'd personally noticed pickers, or even really believed they existed, had been six and a half hours before Matt's accident. He'd come rushing back in while she was frantically cleaning up the baby's second poopy diaper of the morning while at the same time trying to finish what would turn out to be her last actual meal—wheat toast with jelly, she remembered, and grapefruit juice. "The pickers say they can use that old computer monitor!" he'd called to her, excited as always by anything out of the ordinary. Frazzled and resentful because she had to get to work, too, she'd yelled at him that he cared more about filthy scum like that than about his own family. He'd stopped short and stared at her for a long moment, then picked up the monitor and left without another word. Never another word.

Since then the pickers were everywhere. In broad daylight they'd be flocking around the dumpster at work. When she took Ryan to the park they'd be picking up litter and eyeing other people's picnic lunches. On garbage day she couldn't get to her car without practically having to push through them, and since she'd started forcing herself little by little to throw away Matt's stuff they'd been congregating here on other days, too.

The thought that she shared living space with these lowlifes gave her the creeps, and it was Matt's fault for encouraging them and then leaving her to deal with it. Whole families of them, whole clans, eating and wearing and selling and otherwise using what normal people had no more use for. Maybe it wasn't thievery, exactly, but there was something wrong about it, and if it wasn't illegal, it ought to be. She called the cops and Trash Removal and City Council, and they all told her there was nothing they could do. That wasn't right.

Matt had found them fascinating. They were an ancient people of several ethnic roots, he'd told her almost reverently, spread all over the world from pole to pole and in all kinds of terrain and climate. You had to admire people so adaptable, he'd said. They served an ecological purpose; they cleaned up after the rest of us; you had to be grateful, he'd said. No, she'd said, she didn't.

When Matt got interested in something he wouldn't shut up, and it had been hard not to let his useless information into your brain whether you wanted to or not. So now, in an annoying sort of haunting, she knew stuff about the Court of Louis XIV, the life of Edgar Allan Poe, the mating habits of crows, and urban legends about pickers.

Pickers could affect the weather. Some god had sent pickers named Thought and Memory—or maybe it was Darryl and Darryl, who knew?— out every night to bring back secrets from the ends of the earth so he could pretend to be wise and all-knowing, which sounded like something Matt would do. Pickers could divine the future. Pickers could foretell death. Pickers could bring death. Pickers were tricksters; they'd do things to make life difficult for normal people, just for the sport of it—set off car alarms, sell you stolen property to get you in trouble. Back when criminals used to be strung up at crossroads in the woods as an example to the rest of the population, travelers could tell there'd be a body hanging from a tree before they even got there because of the noise of pickers. Pickers associated with large predatory animals—polar bears, wolves, killer whales, humans. They hung around hospitals for the medical waste, and battlefields and slaughterhouses to clean up, around garbage dumps and landfills. Anywhere human beings lived, from caves to cliff dwellings to medieval villages to campsites to farms to mountain towns to this trendy downtown area of expensively converted warehouses and pricey new condos built to look like converted warehouses.

Matt had found all this disgusting nonsense colorful and cool. Toni suspected he'd made up some of his own legends to add to the lore, so he could be part of something that had gone on since the beginning of history. She hated it. Considering how much you paid to live down here, you'd think they could keep the riffraff out. When she'd said that to Matt he'd looked at her grim-faced and narrow-eyed and informed her self-righteously that they were just people like anybody else. Then he'd died.

As she came out into the alley now, they paid little attention to her, keeping at their repulsive work like the most natural thing in the world. Their kids dived and rolled and bounced in the dumpster the way other kids played in the ball pit at the McDonald's playground. Every one of them was eating something. Adults sorted and carried and arranged, making sounds that might have been exclamations of delight or dismissal. Snow kept falling.

"Hey!" she called and one of them deigned to look at her, a big ungainly woman about her own age. A spot the size of a saucer had been shaven at the crest of her head, and black hair hung below it to the middle of her back—oily, dirty, just like everybody said.

Toni didn't like noticing that the woman's hair was also beautiful, glimmering blue and green and purple in the alley lights with the snow on it. Her bare dark arms looked strong hoisting the sodden boxes of Matt's books onto the overloaded pick-up. Her long black-fringed shawl was elegant even though it had no doubt come out of somebody's trash. Her speech sounded intelligent and educated when she said, "Good morning to you, Ms. Barlow. May I take that off your hands?" and reached for the trash bag, which was slick from the snow and faintly stinking. Toni didn't let go and so they were both holding it, the woman's fingers intertwined with hers for an instant, no doubt passing along some contamination from neighbors' bubble wrap, coffee grounds, used condoms, shredded credit card slips, yesterday's newspapers, spoiled meat, mementoes of sorrow and passion and the excess packaging of everyday life, all secret filth until the pickers got to it.

"How do you know—" She stopped herself, supposing there'd be plenty of identification in garbage if you looked for it. But this was a dumpster for the whole building. How would the woman know which of its contents had belonged specifically to her? "Get out of here!" was the best she could do as she relinquished the sack.

When the picker laughed and tossed her head, the hair moved in a ghastly sort of way. Snow glowed in passing headlights. Cold now and wet, Toni moved under the narrow eave of the building for what little shelter it offered. In a reasonable, infuriating tone, the picker explained, "Of course the alley is public space."

The dumpster was crawling now with children and even babies. "This is personal stuff," Toni insisted. "Private property."

The woman had broken the trash bag and was peering into it. Toni thought furiously of the dirty diapers, baby food jars, unread *Newsweeks* and *New Yorkers,* and Matt's hardly-worn running shoes, the thing of his she'd made herself throw out today, after she'd made it through the books one box a day. She'd been thinking that tomorrow's one thing might be his watch, but wasn't about to give these people something that easy to sell. The woman pulled out the shoes and tried one on, leaving her own black loafer to catch snow. "When something is designated as no longer of use, personal and private claims have been forfeited. It becomes part of the common landscape we all have responsibility to maintain. One person's detritus is another person's sustenance. We do not create waste. We use it." Apparently satisfied with

Matt's shoes, she tossed her old ones, now powdered with snow, into the pick-up bed. Then she withdrew a small box from under her shawl and offered it to Toni. "Would you care for an herb-wheat cracker? Your neighbors at the other end of the block evidently had a gathering this week."

These days the mere thought of any sort of food made Toni nauseous. Now she thought she might actually vomit, though there wasn't much left in her stomach to get rid of. "No," she said, trying for sarcasm. "But thanks."

"We also have banana chips, mustard pretzels, honey almonds, and chocolate espresso beans. They seem to have had fewer guests than anticipated."

For some reason vaguely related to power, Toni demanded, "What's your name?"

After a slight but obvious hesitation, the woman said what Toni thought was "Dee."

"You're lying. Why would you lie about your name?" Well, duh. There were a lot of reasons.

"I was not lying. I was choosing. We have many different names."

"How very mysterious."

The woman shrugged, "It merely has to do with geographic locale."

"D-E-E?"

"Just the letter D."

"Okay, I'll bite. What does it stand for?"

"It stands for nothing. It is what it is."

"D what?"

"Rawnston."

"How do you spell that?"

The woman spelled it for her and added helpfully, "It is derived from an Old English place name meaning 'execution site.'"

"Lovely." Shivering and exhausted, Toni started through the snow toward the building, flinging back over her shoulder, "Get out of here or I'll call the cops. Now that I have your name." It sounded silly even to her.

The door was locked. She hadn't brought her keys. Inside, among his dead father's belongings boxed and bagged but not yet turned into trash, not quite yet, Ryan was quiet. You'd never have guessed there was a baby in there if you didn't already know. For a minute she just stood helplessly hoping somebody would come out of the building, dreading the prospect of slogging around to the front in nightshirt and slippers and buzzing the party-boy manager or a tenant she barely knew in the middle of the night.

A hand fell lightly on her shoulder. She gasped and twisted away. D slid something long and thin against the jamb, jiggled the knob, and opened the door. Faint with relief and unnerved by how easy it was to break in, Toni rushed past and then stopped, not wanting to lead the woman to her unit, then realized that door was also locked and the key on the same key ring.

D strode ahead. The place was a pit—Toni didn't do a lot of housecleaning anymore; Ryan wouldn't notice, Matt certainly wouldn't, and she didn't care. Matt's stuff scattered all over added to the general mess of everyday life with a baby. It was stupid to worry about housekeeping standards when your guest was uninvited and a garbage picker.

By the time she got there, her door stood open, the picker was inside, and Ryan was crying. Toni forced herself to go in.

They were already in the rocking chair with the blue quilt from Matt's grandmother wrapped around them. The woman's iridescent black hair feinted and fluttered over the baby like wings, shorn crest glistening as she bent her head to him. The song she crooned to him in her own simple language was obviously meant to be a lullaby, but Ryan was agitated.

"Are you hungry, sweet boy?" The picker looked up at Toni. "Do you have milk for him?"

She'd forgotten. "I—no, I have to go to the store."

"You are not nursing?"

"Not anymore. I can't."

The woman opened her shawl and the purple shirt under it and put Ryan to her breast. It took him a minute to latch on, but then he was sucking noisily. Toni felt faint. "Get out of those wet clothes," the picker crooned to her, making it part of the song. "You'll catch cold."

Toni's knees buckled and she sank onto the couch among Matt's clean socks and underwear and big cotton T-shirts she picked from to wear to bed. "I'm so tired."

"Get some sleep. I've got the baby."

"My husband—" She still couldn't say it aloud.

D nodded and kept on singing. Toni was starting to hear nuances in the words and phrases, complexities of inflection and pause. She thought Matt's name was scattered in there like bits of eggshell, and, though it broke her heart every time, she listened desperately for it in the sonorous chant. Outside, the noise of the other pickers had stopped, and Toni tried confusedly not to imagine what they might be finding in somebody else's garbage. Ryan was still nursing.

With effort she said, "I'm okay now. Thanks for your help."

"My pleasure." D smiled but didn't move.

Toni snapped wide awake, appalled by her own carelessness. She stood up shakily and took Ryan. D didn't resist but he did, holding on tight with tiny hands and mouth, wailing when his mother got him loose. "You've got more than enough kids of your own to take care of."

"One can never have enough children," D rebuked her placidly, fastening her clothes.

The nerve of the woman—barging into her home, sitting in her living room as if she owned the place, taking it upon herself to find and hold her baby, lecturing her about being a parent—made Toni stubborn. "You have to dig around in other people's garbage to support them. Haven't you people ever heard of birth control?"

Now D was chuckling. "Noah said something very like that."

"Noah who?" Playing guessing games with this person was seriously annoying.

"There was a ban on sexual activity, but of course we ignored it. After all, when the forecast is for floods and the end of civilization, one would think the goal would be more rather than fewer children, not to mention as much pleasure as possible."

Burning with sudden memories of Matt, Toni made herself sneer, "Noah like the Ark? What are you talking about?" The baby had quieted, but she could still feel him trembling against her.

"So we were evicted." D's laughter was hearty, too loud. "Then he called us back to search for land, which of course we found and of course we did not tell him about. Let the dove be his lackey."

"Whatever." Toni backed away from the musky smell of D's hair and clothes, the shape of her big hands. Ryan had settled down. "Please go now."

D didn't give her attitude. But as she swooped out into the hallway she said, "I would be honored to assist you in taking care of Matthew's belongings whenever you are ready. We can put them to good use, give them back into the world."

For Ryan's sake Toni kept herself to a ferocious whisper. "Get the hell out of my house!" D made a little clucking sound, nodded, and went away. On the back of the rocking chair was a black plume of hair, tangled in the rungs. She could hardly bring herself to touch it even through the newspaper she used to wrap it and throw it away. When she went indignantly to investigate another tap at the door, she found a case of formula in the hall, half a dozen cans missing and the cardboard stained, two used plastic baby bottles on top. Hand inside a sandwich bag, she threw away the bottles, but the cans of formula were unopened. She found a bottle in the cupboard, rinsed it under hot water, mixed up the formula, and gave it to Ryan in his crib. He wasn't interested.

When she got home from work the next day D was back, waiting politely by the dumpster with a big box in her arms. "Good evening, Antonia. How was your day? And how is my little buddy?" Ryan had been fussy from the minute his mother had picked him up at daycare. D came closer to peer at him. "Is he ill? His eyes look a bit rheumy."

Terror shot through Toni. "He's fine." Struggling to organize briefcase, purse, groceries, and baby, she steeled herself for the woman to try to take something out of her hands.

Instead, D held out the box. A microwave had come in it; now it was filled to overflowing with baby clothes and jars of baby food. "One of my nephews found these, brand new with the tags still affixed, behind an upscale downtown shop. Sizes six, nine, and twelve months. I thought perhaps you could use them for Ryan." She added with a sly smile, "The baby food comes from the supermarket. Please save the empties."

Toni locked the car, folded her keys into her fist, and carried her precarious load as fast as she could through the gate. Backing up into it to push it shut, she shouted, "Get out of here! Leave me alone!" On her way to the building she dropped her briefcase in the snow, and Ryan almost slipped out of her grasp so she held him too tightly and he was complaining loudly. The minute she got inside she left an irate and, with Ryan yelling, probably unintelligible complaint on the building manager's machine for all the good it would do. The next day she wasted time and money and sick leave taking the baby to the doctor, who said he was fine although a little underweight, prescribed a higher-calorie formula, and gave her a little speech about relaxing into motherhood and the importance of a support system. Toni didn't mention Matt.

She called the cops again but was told the pickers weren't doing anything against the law unless they were threatening her or panhandling or trespassing or stealing items not set out for the trash. She considered lying, or setting up those things to happen, but it wasn't worth the effort.

D was always in her face, opening the car door for her, foisting scavenged items like loaves of bread and bottles of orange juice off on her. She took them and set them on the floor or the counter. "You must eat," D said, "if you are to get through this hard time." Toni had no interest in eating or in getting through.

Having finally slept soundly since his first week home, now he was up and down all night wanting to eat. Nothing she did pleased him, and he wasn't pleasing her much anymore, either. She took him back to the doctor, who checked him again, again said there was nothing wrong and he'd even gained five ounces, and prescribed something for Toni's nerves that made her drowsy all the time but no calmer.

She kept trying to go through Matt's stuff, intending to get rid of most of it, maybe keeping just a few little things for Ryan for when he got older. Piles grew everywhere and she was helpless against them. Every now and then she'd try to eat, but her stomach cramped after a few bites and she had trouble swallowing. Dozing, fearing, wondering, dreaming, she took one personal day after another and began to lose track of time.

She also began to lose track of objects. Her car keys vanished for a day and a night and most of another day, and then were right there on their hook by the door. Early one morning, bleary from not enough food or sleep, she finally found the instant breakfast in the top of the coat closet, but couldn't make herself drink it.

Too tired and sad and scared to worry very much about the tricks her mind or the world was playing on her, she didn't even panic when Ryan wasn't in his crib where she was sure she'd left him, just looked for him in one room after another, upstairs and down, until she came upon him sound asleep in the cradle she hadn't used for months, tucked away in a corner of the ground floor room Matt had, for no good reason, called the study. She didn't remember putting the baby down here, or digging the cradle out of the closet. But she wasn't remembering much these days except Matt. She sat for a while and watched the baby. She ate three bites of baby food squash and gave up.

On another bleak midnight, she came upon the little wheeled stool with the violet velvet cushion that matched the curtains. Sinking onto it, she tried not to remember Matt's enthusiasm when he'd brought it home. The wheels were loose and the three legs uneven.

Having forgotten to close the curtains, she saw D before she heard the tapping on the glass. Close enough to reach the latch without getting up, she flipped it open. D stepped in like a fine lady, stately, grim, carrying a bulging trash bag. Cold snowless air swept in, shocking, and its disappearance when D slid the door shut was equally shocking. "Sure. Come right on in." She couldn't muster the sarcasm she'd intended.

D said, "Oh, my dear," dumped canned goods and cereal boxes and baby toys out of the bag among all the other clutter on the floor, and went straight to Ryan. Toni just sat there on the stool. Some of the toys looked like ones Ryan used to have that she hadn't seen for a while. Some of the food she used to like.

With the baby wrapped in a blanket Toni didn't think she'd ever seen before, D settled in the rocker and gave him a bottle, then held out a clamshell box of restaurant leftovers toward her. The steady glow of the gas logs cast long, feathery shadows on the floor. When Toni jerked back to protect herself from both the hand and the shadow of the hand, the stool teetered and tipped and she slid off into a mound of Matt's clothes. They smelled like him. She was so tired. She drifted in and out of jumbled half-sleep.

Some time later, Ryan was in her arms, small sturdy weight and baby smell, tiny fingernails pinching at her skin. Some time later, he was gone again, and Toni stirred, gave up and fell back into semi-consciousness. The air grew denser.

She became aware of things disappearing—Matt's clothes, the baby, the violet velvet curtains and stool, Matt's golf clubs, the rug they'd bought that time in Costa Rica, Matt's watch, candlesticks never used and the wedding photo from the mantel. Pickers came in, first a few cocky teenagers one-upping each other and arguing over cool stuff they found, then parents and grandparents and children and babies. Seeing that D had put Ryan down among them, Toni fumbled and retrieved him and bundled him close to her, where he squirmed and tried to nurse. D came at her with a spoonful of something, actually tapped it against her mouth, but Toni was long past any hunger that food could touch.

Clearly D was in charge, giving instructions in their intricate language. They clucked and cawed and chuckled and cooed as they gathered around and began to strip her of things she had no more use for—her wedding ring, her shoes, the locket with the tiny heart-shaped picture of Matt when they were dating. She struggled a bit when they removed her nightgown, but not much. "Evil!" she wailed when they took Ryan from her, "Devil!" but it was true that she was of no use to him anymore. Weak and weary, she couldn't even keep Matt in her mind.

Gathering around her, the pickers stroked and then clawed at her skin. They cut her hair and then pulled it out. They licked and bit her. The babies crawled over her like grubs, sucking. Still sitting, still sitting, D leaned and put her mouth on Toni's and never left her side.

I'VE ALWAYS LOVED *Poe's poetry, especially "Annabel Lee," "The Bells," and "The Raven." They're part of my creative subconscious, put there by my father who insisted I read aloud and memorize a poem a week for most of the weeks of my childhood.*

"Ah, distinctly I remember/It was in the bleak December/And each separate dying ember…"

"'Twas many and many a year ago…"

"… the tintinnabulation of the bells bells bells bells bells…"

Don't get me started.

At about the time I heard about this anthology, I was reading The Mind of the Raven *and* Ravens in Winter *by the naturalist Bernd Heinrich. Monographs and field reports at a level of detail only a scientist could love, these are nonetheless quite accessible to a (very) layperson like me, and I learned all sorts of fascinating things about ravens. They appear physically and in myth in a great many parts of the world, pretty much wherever there are humans and other large predators. They use what we have no more use for. Heinrich contends they're more intelligent than dolphins, with language second only to human languages in complexity and subtlety.*

So all this new information went into my subconscious where "The Raven" already was ("the silken sad uncertain rustling of each purple curtain"—sorry). As Poe's gaunt and ghastly bird rubbed feathers with Heinrich's beautiful and complicated ones, a sort of alchemy started.

Out of it, the character of D emerged, raven in human form. I worked with her to be both the witness of grief who won't go away and the scavenger who gets a bad rep for what might be thought of as recycling. Then Toni took shape, the character to be acted upon. And I had a story.

E. Catherine Tobler lives and writes in Colorado—strange how that works out. Among others, her fiction has appeared in SCI-FICTION, *Realms of Fantasy*, *Talebones*, and *Lady Churchill's Rosebud Wristlet*. For more visit www.ecatherine.com.

Beyond Porch and Portal

by E. Catherine Tobler

WHEN THEY FOUND my uncle wandering incoherent in the foggy morning streets he wasn't wearing his own clothes.

A man unknown to me brought word of my uncle's illness, presenting me with a small folded letter on fine ivory paper. The paper *shushed* between our bare fingers a moment before he turned away. He traced his way through the general store with its many occupants, back into the bustle of the street.

"Sir!"

Clutching the letter at which I'd only glanced, I followed him through the double doors, grabbing his jacket sleeve before he could be overcome by a claret and gold four-in-hand. The horses blew past us and onward down the cobblestones with the loud ring of their silver-shod feet overtaking my words.

The man glared down at me as if I had upset his day rather than he mine. There was something in his eyes, half familiar and frightening. He was not an older man; he seemed of a marrying age, but I knew he was not married. How I knew this, I could not say. He disliked my consideration of him and twisted his arm free from my hold.

"You'd best go *now*. He hasn't much time."

"Are you a friend to my uncle?"

He refused me even that much information and hurried down the street after the four-in-hand, October's breeze lifting the tails of his coat behind him. I blinked once and he was fully gone. If anyone else upon the street noticed something odd about that, they didn't look sideways. I expected someone to gasp and say, "But here, he walked here a moment ago, and now has vanished like a candle's flame under a breath!" No one said a word; the people were too wrapped in their own business.

Carefully I smoothed the letter I had crumpled. The ink had smudged upon the page, written in a hand I did not know. My uncle had been found this morning; he now rested at the college hospital and, as the mysterious man had, the letter urged me to hurry to his side before he passed into the next world.

There were things in that next world that my uncle would welcome, I thought as I left off shopping and followed the fingerboards to the hospital. I had never been there in my twenty years. My mother and father died there, so my uncle told me, leaving me in his capable care ever after.

He seemed capable no longer. Doctors led me to my uncle's side and he did not know me. He clutched at my skirts and muttered "Reynolds, *fonderous* Reynolds…"

I untangled his hand and saw that he indeed wore someone else's clothes. The trousers were butternut, the coat an earthy brown. My uncle always, even on Sundays, wore black. Even his boiled shirts would have been black, but this one was whiter than I'd ever seen, with a smudge of blood against the collar, were blood to be mostly ochre.

"Uncle?"

He startled and reached blindly out. I grabbed his clammy hand and lowered myself to his bedside, to breathe in the scent of him. There was no alcohol on his breath as I'd feared. He groaned and tried to roll away from me. This motion pulled his shirt cuff back, exposing the pink, abraded skin of his wrist.

"What happened to you?" I whispered. I couldn't fathom it.

Edgar Poe was my only kin; the man who taught me geography and history, the man who could scare a rational-minded young woman like me under my bed with his stories of vengeful madmen; the man who preferred spending rainy days writing poetry or walking Baltimore's streets in search of it.

"Fonderous R-Reynolds?" he asked. "The s-seam above the floor? Oh, vast sky." He closed his eyes and turned his head against the pillow, but held firm to my hand.

"Miss Franks?"

Dr. Griffin, an older man with soft hands and hard eyes, had been known to me for years. The first time my uncle was found publicly drunk, it was Dr. Griffin who brought him to the hospital to sober up. I saw pity on his face now, but I shook my head and stood to meet him.

"He's sober," I said.

The doctor scrubbed a hand over his unshaven cheeks. "Your assessment agrees with my own. Your uncle is suffering from a malady unknown to me. Did he recognize you?"

"No." I looked down at my uncle. "I saw him just yesterday and he was well. Have you seen his wrist?"

"Reynolds!" my uncle cried. "Endless lands! Vilest fire." He shoved the sheets off his body, scrambling backward in an attempt to get out of the bed. When he hit the headboard, he turned to his left, rolled onto the checkerboard floor, and crawled away.

Dr. Griffin called for his colleagues; I could not get near my uncle without him shrieking anew. I backed away, only realizing I was crying when Nurse Templeton shoved a handkerchief into my hand.

"Go home, Miss Franks," Dr. Griffin said over his struggles with my uncle.

"The seam!" My uncle screamed these words, over and over until I covered my ears to block it—but still, I heard it like a heartbeat. *The seam. The seam.*

Dr. Griffin and three other men carried my uncle back to the bed and firmly strapped him down. By hand and foot they bound him and when this made his screams worse, they also bound his mouth. He screamed even beyond the gag, muffled and strained.

"You can't!"

Nurse Templeton led me out of the room and closed the door behind us. I was shaking as she guided me to a chair and pushed me into it. I stared at her heavily lined mouth, unable to understand a word that came from it. She gave me a hard shake and then I heard, "…come again tomorrow; perhaps he will be well."

I knew, as I walked back to our townhouse in the mist, that one evening would not solve my uncle's problems. What had happened to haunt his eyes so? What part did the stranger from this morning play?

My uncle had employed a housekeeper these last two years, to tidy what he messed while I spent my days as a tailor's assistant. Though Mrs. Wine would have made me a warm dinner, I sent her home. I wanted only to be alone. I locked the door behind her, discarded my coat and bag, and went to my uncle's office.

It was the one room Mrs. Wine was asked not to touch, but nothing struck me as unusual as I entered. Papers and books were spread over the sofa and chairs, over desktop and floor. I lifted a pile from one chair and sat, bringing the sheets into my lap. He was working on a new poem.

I fell asleep reading of a city by the sea, where mortals bought fruit from angels carrying baskets. I didn't dream of this place; I didn't dream of anything. When I woke, I felt rested and wondered if morning had come, but the thought left my mind when I saw the man who gave me the note perched in a far corner, watching me.

Think of it. You believe yourself alone in your own home, are comfortable enough to sleep wherever you lay down; and when you wake, your mind still fuzzy from its rest, you discover yourself not alone, but watched.

Your mind races, but it can't catch your heart. How long has he watched you?

Was he there when I came in? Who is he and how did he gain entry? I pictured broken windows and doors, but felt it was worse than that; this man had come inside another way, a way unknown to me. That frightened me most of all.

"Please do not scream," he said.

I screamed. I flung my uncle's poetry and fled the office, feeling this man close on my heels. He yanked the door open when I meant to slam it; he snatched my skirts, slowing my escape. His fingers seemed to catch my hair and pull me backward. Through his fingertips I felt shackles around my uncle's wrists. Those hands had placed them there, but not in this world, in another.

"Reynolds?" I asked.

His touch vanished. I swung around in the darkness of the hallway and felt a presence, though I could not see him.

"He called me that." His crumpled velvet voice brushed against my cheek. "Go to your uncle."

The voice came from all around me now, disembodied. As I turned round, I would have sworn to the stroke of fingers against my skirts. *Shush. Shush.*

My heart pounded in my throat. "What did you do to my uncle?"

This man admitted nothing. Round and round he circled me. I felt his eyes upon me (half familiar and frightening!) but still I could see nothing of him. Maddening! His cold-kissed fingers brushed over my cheeks and then I was horribly alone.

I did not sleep that night. I checked the doors and windows, but decided it would not matter how securely they were locked. The stranger had come into our house another way. Taking no chance, I retrieved my uncle's small pistol from the locked box beneath his bed and sat with my back to the wall the entire night through. Rain drummed upon the roof; in its rhythm, I found words. *The seam. The seam.*

Come morning, I went to the hospital, the pistol concealed in my brocade reticule. I would not be caught unawares another time by Reynolds, whatever name he took.

My uncle was less coherent that morning, Dr. Griffin reluctant to allow me into his room.

"I have bled him twice to no effect," Griffin said to me outside my uncle's door. The doctor paced, slapping the back of one hand into the palm of the other. "I begin to fear, Miss Franks, that he has a blackness within him and if I cannot find and remove it, he shall perish."

Reynolds's first words echoed back at me. *"You'd best go now. He hasn't much time."* Would he perish at the doctor's hands or was my uncle already near death from whatever had befallen him?

I gripped my reticule, feeling through the fabric the line of the pistol. Was it the solidity of the gun that calmed me or the idea of pressing it against Reynolds's chin?

"I want to speak with my uncle," I said and made to move past the doctor, to open my uncle's door.

Griffin grabbed me by the arm to forestall me, then dropped it when a nurse passed us. He bowed his head to look at me through narrowed eyes.

"Absolutely not! I don't believe you grasp the seriousness of the situation, Miss Franks."

Being accosted by a strange man in one's own home was quite serious enough for me.

Griffin continued. His tone was low and calm, as though he were trying to calm a spooked horse. "When I remove his gag, he speaks of terrible things. I do not understand the blackness within him. I need to find it, cut it out. We loosened him for a bit this morning as a test and he nearly cut out his own eye—"

I grabbed Dr. Griffin by the arm as he had me in an effort to make him understand that on this matter I would not be budged. "I will speak with my uncle," I said. "No matter the terrible things he says, I will."

The doctor let me step into the room and did not follow. I closed the door to blot out his disapproving expression. However, now in the gray room with its scent of antiseptic and rapidly aging old man, I hesitated. I looked across the room at the figure in the bed and did not recognize it for my uncle. This man was gaunt and dark, lashed to a bed with a thin mattress. A hard rubber gag covered his mouth and now even his eyes were masked. Coarse hair covered his sunken cheeks.

"Uncle?"

He did not move and I wondered if he was sleeping. Or dead. I held my breath as I waited for the rise of his chest. Only when I saw that feeble movement did I step toward the bed.

I set my reticule on the bedside table and reached for the mask that covered Edgar's eyes. The tie was lost in the bird's nest of his hair; it took some time to find the end. When at last I loosened the ties, I found myself looking into unfamiliar eyes. Or let me say that upon longer examination, the eyes themselves were painfully familiar—it was the deep wrinkles around them, it was the pale white scar above the left eye, it was the freshly stitched wound below the right—these were the things I could not equate with my uncle.

With some difficulty I loosened and removed the gag from his mouth. Edgar closed his mouth, licked his lips, and swallowed.

"Do you know me?" I asked him.

His eyes rolled back into his head and he turned his cheek against the pillow. "Vilest fire." His voice cracked the words apart like they were nutshells in his throat. "Hunters stab never sleeping sky—the seam above the floor. The seam—"

He spoke of phenomena and contraptions I could not understand while his hands moved against his bonds, fingers straining to reach the unseen. His eyes seemed to watch an invisible dance in the air between the bed and ceiling: flit, flit, glide.

I had hoped to make some sense of the "terrible things" Dr. Griffin mentioned, but as my uncle spoke on and on until his voice dried to a whisper, I could find no reason in the words. There was only one word that made sense to me and when he said it at last, his eyes moved to the far corner of the room.

"Reynolds."

I turned in time to see the man called Reynolds slink out of the room. The tail of his brown coat (how like the coat my uncle had been found in) slithered out the door a second before it closed.

How long has he watched you?

How did he get in?

My heart stammered in my chest. I grabbed my bag and followed Reynolds from the hall, only in time to see his coattails once again slide around a distant corner. I fled past Dr. Griffin and into the blowing rain of the day. Reynolds was a tall man with a long stride and there was no keeping pace with him. By the time I reached the store where I had first met Reynolds, I could see no sign of him.

Then, coming down the cobblestones, appeared the same gold and claret four-in-hand I had seen the day before, Reynolds now perched beside the driver. The horses' hooves didn't seem to touch the ground, even though I heard them clearly ring against the street stone. I lunged into the street, for the driver would have to stop for fear that he might hit me, but he didn't. The hot breath of one horse curled over my cheek before the world went black.

I woke, if one can awaken when one does not remember sleeping, atop the auburn horse, harness and tack cutting into my left hand, while my right still clung to my bag with its pistol. The ground sped away beneath me at a dreadful haste and for a moment I buried my face in the horse's mane. My cheek lay against hot horsehide, silky red-gold mane blinding me, every part of my body jostled as the carriage continued onward.

I chanced a backwards glance at the driver and Reynolds and squeezed my eyes shut a second after. They were not men!

Another look proved this true. The driver sat tall in the seat, a black coat dripping from his narrow body. A tattered blue scarf gave the illusion of a neck, but I feared he truly had none. The octangular head was small and gray, with bulging black eyes that must have taken everything in at once. Surely he saw me staring at his four spindly legs and two arms, all of which seemed employed in driving the carriage. His arms bore spines and hooks, over which he had draped a couple of reins, but I felt certain this wasn't their main usage.

"Miss Franks!"

It was Reynolds who spoke, but a Reynolds I did not recognize. Reynolds possessed a squat body, colored brown with slim yellow stripes, and he now spoke through mandibles. His brown coat had pooled around him; why, his thin arms would never support the fabric!

"Hold fast!" he said. "We cannot stop in the endless lands."

I turned my head around so that I might see these endless lands for myself, lifted myself on elbows enough to see around the whipping horse mane.

Every bit of Baltimore had vanished and all around us spread a seemingly endless blur of gold shot through with ruby stars. Whirlpools twisted in the sky, churning nausea within me as I watched them. I watched until I felt I would be ill, then bowed and buried my head again. I prayed the ride would soon be over, but perhaps there was no one to answer that prayer, for the ride went on and on.

The motion of the horse beneath me soon became familiar, enjoyable. I had never known such a sensation.

Its warm hide was also a comfort as the air grew colder around us. There seemed to be no sun yet all around us were slanting shafts of light. Colored golden and ivory, they fell from above and the more I watched them, the more my eyes began to adjust and see what truly lay around us.

The land was no longer barren. Perhaps it never had been. My eyes became accustomed to the light and the way it changed the landscape around us. From one angle, the land was empty; from another, I could glimpse strange constructs in the distance. There seemed to be little near the horizon; everything I was able to see hovered in that sunless sky. If I saw other people, it was only briefly; I saw what seemed a woman, but the wind was tearing her apart. She shredded, arms and legs peeling apart like fabric, and then even her clothing lifted up and away. This didn't seem to bother her. She smiled and went on her way, into the vast sky.

Oh, that vast sky—my uncle's sky? Had he seen this place and breathed this air? This air, that smelled vaguely of apricots and roasting meat, washed over us in abrupt gusts, forcing my eyes shut. I savored the darkness.

I couldn't understand this place. What was it and how could it exist? The more I wondered, the more ill I felt. I remembered my Baltimore with its rain-washed streets, hints of sky caught between close buildings, people rushing to and from work. There seemed no such things here.

The carriage never slowed. My nausea deepened. I became aware of hands on my shoulders, an arm under my legs. Reynolds lifted me from the horse and carried me back into the carriage itself. I lay on the padded bench and stared at him sitting opposite me. In this light, he looked like a man and had a beautiful mouth.

The thought should have shocked me, but it didn't.

"You shouldn't be here," he said.

"That much is plain." I had to fight to say the words and my voice didn't sound right when I finally forced them out. I fought also to sit up, to focus my attention on Reynolds. Even though I knew he wasn't a man, he appeared as such and it gradually began to calm my mind.

"You've placed me in quite a predicament," he added.

I could hardly believe he was serious, but I recalled the look on his face the day we'd met, when I'd pulled him back from this very carriage. I now understood I had kept him from returning. What had drawn him out in the first place? What else tied us together? My uncle, I thought as my eyes settled on Reynolds's vest.

"You—You're wearing my uncle's vest," I said. "I sewed it for him—"

"A gift last Christmas," Reynolds said. His dark velvet voice was rough again.

"How can you know that?" My hands sought the bag at my side, but I no longer carried it; my pistol was lost.

"Edgar told me all about you." His mouth bent into a smile and I realized this man knew things about me he shouldn't know. He knew about my first pet (a kitten named Croak) and my first formal dance (how I'd stumbled down the last two stairs and fallen to reveal entirely too much to those gathered); he knew my uncle's stories could frighten me, and he knew that deep down, I loved the fear.

"I don't understand." I blinked back tears and looked out the carriage window. The angle of light allowed me to see to the horizon this time. Against its water-washed color, I saw a wrecked whalebone ship. Closer to the carriage wheels, I saw pallid bloated creatures upon the shifting ground. One of them held a golden key in its mouth.

"How long have you known my uncle?" I asked. I looked back at Reynolds, who watched me and not the world beyond the windows. "How long was he your prisoner?"

"I did not imprison your uncle, though others of my kind did."

"I felt you put those shackles on him."

Reynolds said nothing to that. Maybe it was an action he couldn't argue; maybe he had been forced. Whichever, he kept his silence, watching me with keen eyes that seemed to see all of me at once. He knew my parents were dead, and he knew—he knew Edgar was my only family.

"Stop watching me," I whispered.

"I will not," Reynolds said. "I spent far too many years dreaming of you to look away now."

I curled my hands into my skirts. "What the devil do you mean by that?" If I thought I could have survived it, I would have jumped from the carriage. I think Reynolds must have known this, for he grasped my hands and held me firm.

"Your uncle should never have come here. I tried to fix that and failed. The least I could do was see that he didn't die alone this time. He's gone now. All you've known is gone. You shouldn't be here, but I can't help but be happy you are."

I jumped from the carriage then. Reynolds's words scared me worse than the idea of death. I wrenched my hands out of his, pushed him backwards, and kicked the door open. I flung myself into the speeding landscape and landed in sandy, loose ground.

There was no sign of the carriage, nor any sound from it. Its wheels had left no tracks. Wherever I was, I needed to get out, but there was nothing to guide me. No sun, no landmarks, nothing on the horizon here. I wiped the grit from my eyes and strained to see through the beams of light.

Reynolds found me first. I caught him from the corner of my eye, running at me as fast as the carriage horses had flown. I turned to run, but the ground seemed to suck me down. Reynolds was on me before I could escape; he dragged me down and pinned my hands, slapping a shackle around one wrist.

"Beast!" I cried, unable to wrench myself free.

"Literally, that is true," Reynolds said. His nice mouth curled in a sneer. "Edgar called me fonderous."

I slapped him with my free hand. He felt of flesh and bone and his skin reddened as would any man's under a strike, but he only laughed and secured the other shackle to my other wrist.

"Come on."

Reynolds kept hold of the shackles, pulling me alongside him. The ground beneath our feet became increasingly more solid, less sandy, and I walked with a little more assurance. Even if I didn't have the first notion where we were going, we were certainly making a good pace.

"I want you to understand," Reynolds said as we crested a slight rise in the land. I could see beasts in the distance, moving high in the sky. Even so, they were still tethered to the ground by long, spindly legs.

"Then speak plainly. I am your captive audience."

A look of pain crossed Reynolds' face; I had seen the same thing in my uncle at the hospital just that morning.

"We must reach the city, Miss Franks," he said. "Will you come back into the carriage? We cannot reach it on foot."

I now saw the carriage awaiting us, a claret-colored shimmer in the strange air. There was no choice, was there? Go with Reynolds to his city, or stay here where I knew no direction and might wander forever. I lifted my hands.

"Unbind me and I will come with you," I said.

Reynolds did not argue. He unlocked my shackles with a key he kept in his sleeve. We climbed back into the carriage and, without word to the driver, were off. Reynolds watched me the entire ride and I told myself I didn't care. I didn't care.

I never witnessed stranger things than I did in the city itself. The light continued to play tricks upon my mind, and the buildings seemed half open to the sky. The people of the city were paper thin; on edge they could not be seen, though when they turned a certain way in the light their monstrous faces became dreadfully apparent. Some looked as our carriage driver did; others I could barely comprehend. I quickly learned how to look in order to see only the slimmest slice of them.

When I learned this manner of looking, I discovered something else. This city was not anchored to the ground. Indeed, the entire place was on the move, buildings and artworks balanced on the backs of immense creatures. A great distance below us, I could see their small feet moving; legs made of thin spire-wire upward to their fabulous bodies—bearing these incredible weights. So too I realized the carriage had come to rest upon its four horses; they carried us without effort through the buildings, the creatures, the people balanced upon a road of memory between.

"This place makes no sense," I said and Reynolds laughed darkly. He pressed behind me at the carriage window, his hand beneath my ribcage. Did he fear I would jump again? Or did he just find pleasure in touching me?

"Your uncle wanted to understand it. Do you remember his stories? His poems?"

I had forgotten them (and indeed Baltimore, my uncle, the rain, the everything) until Reynolds brought them back to me. I had trouble breathing when I remembered it all. All I had now lost.

"He wrote of this place," I said. Once the idea was voiced, I saw my uncle everywhere I looked. There, he had written of that strange creature with its shrieking hair; and there, he had written of that building, ever in flame. My uncle's mind sparked in every shadow of this place; as the creatures made their roads of memory, so too my uncle made the roads, circling ever on, one begetting the beginning of the other.

"He helped create this place," Reynolds said.

The horses carried us to an enormous throne, so large it took three of the creatures to support it. How they managed I'll never know. Reynolds bid me to hold his hand, for I'd never walked a street such as this; it was alive beneath my feet, guiding us from the carriage up to the throne where a woman awaited us.

Her boundless hyacinth hair spilled down her body like water, to her feet and beyond, where gardenias and sand dollars scattered. Silver stars gleamed around her head. She wore a comet for a bracelet; endlessly circling, sparking with vilest fire. Near her throne sat dark, hand-woven baskets filled with fruit. She reached down, plucked a green pear, and offered it to me.

I did not take it. I had read my uncle's stories and knew well enough what happened to young women who ate the fruit of strange lands. The queen, if she were such, took no offense. She smiled down at me, then looked at Reynolds.

"You failed," she said.

"I did." He bowed before her. "He has died alone yet again."

"Speak plain, the both of you." Granted, my uncle had also written stories of outspoken young women; their end was little better than that of those who ate the fruit. I didn't care; I was somewhere beyond care.

Neither spoke. Rather, they showed me.

The queen twisted the pear in half and within its gritty flesh I saw my uncle writing. He wrote of this place, of a city near a sea. He slept each night and thought he dreamed, but his dreams were not that at all. He came here, snatched away by these people. Fairy, he named them, but they were not; it was the only word he knew to apply.

They stole him away every night, him and more of his kind, artists all, for these creatures loved their minds. I felt this love equal to my own for Edgar Poe. But this love had a dark side for as they loved these artists, they consumed them.

When my uncle made to escape and leave this place behind, they chained him. They held him, naked and dirty in an unlit cell. How many cells stretched in the darkness? I could not count them all. This placed smelled of one's worst imaginings—darker, fouler. There was a seam of light that came through the door to hover above the floor. *The seam!* Within this light, dust sparked, dreams flicked.

In this place, my uncle wrote stories in his head. Despite their cruelty to him, some part of my uncle still loved the magic of these people, the impossibility. He loved that they made him create better stories, stories that helped create their fantastic reality.

Only one person visited my uncle; Edgar came to name him Reynolds. Reynolds came daily, to take stories for his people, to bring Edgar a measure of food and clean water. Eventually Edgar's stories turned from madmen to a sorrowful young woman who did not even know she was sorrowful. The thing that pleased her most were the stories, so my uncle kept on spinning them. Reynolds fell in love with this young woman. With me.

My uncle escaped them—I laughed through my tears at the sight of him slipping his bonds like a magician. He stole clothes—no, see there, it is a hand! A hand offering Edgar clothing that was not his own. Reynolds's hand.

"Death has little meaning here," the queen said as she squashed half of the pear and tossed it away. "Though it means much in your world."

"Please speak plain," I whispered, the scent of pear and despair sharp in the air between us. I glanced at Reynolds. "Please."

"I helped your uncle escape," Reynolds said. "The first time, he died alone, unknown. I undid that memory—"

As one undoes a knot, I thought. I had looked into his eyes before; I had kissed that mouth once. I remembered these things though through a wash of water; they were blurred and indistinct. Reynolds had tried once before; I had not listened.

E. Catherine Tobler

"—and tried again. I brought him to Baltimore, got you the note. You reached him, and yet now you've come here and he will die alone; *has* died alone. You—"

"Can only return to death," the queen said and threw away the rest of the now-rotted pear.

"Your uncle is dead," Reynolds said. "The moment he returned, the years he had been here caught up to him."

"But he wasn't gone years," I said. Surely there was a mistake. I felt desperate to make these creatures understand that. "Only overnight. I feared him drunk and sleeping it off."

"Overnight to you," Reynolds said and his voice skipped. "He was taken almost every night."

And every day returned to his world, to my world. To live years over the course of a night; to wake each morning in his bed, thinking it all a dream. How I had once laughed at my uncle and his small circle of friends, all of them old, bent men. How young might they have honestly been?

"Miss Franks—" He clasped my hands within his own. "Agnes. I never intended for you to come here. You are dead to your world; time has gone on without you and made what it will of Baltimore."

Though I wished to believe that all of this was some terrible dream, I knew within my heart that it was not. Edgar's stories of this place should have prepared me. He had seen this place; its people had loved him and in the end destroyed him.

"Only overnight," I said. "I can go back." I had to know, what had become of my world? Was my uncle truly gone? Had the thing I feared most come to pass? It could not be. What if he still lived?

"What are you not telling me?"

Reynolds grabbed my arm. "It isn't just overnight—not for you."

It was then that Reynolds's trespass became clear to me. I had misunderstood what the queen showed me. Every day my uncle woke in my world, it was Reynolds who brought him to that moment. Reynolds unstitched the decades that had passed within this strange world to bring my uncle back into my time, so that I might have a living relation at my side.

How many times should my uncle have died? It was no wonder he'd tried to cut out his own eyes when at last he seemed firmly rooted here.

"It remains her choice," the queen said to Reynolds. "You asked us to allow that, to never take another of her kind without their permission. This is no different because you love her."

I looked beyond the queen's star-wreathed head, to the vast sky where golden birds stretched their wings. No, not birds; angels. When I looked the right direction, I saw their slim bodies. But where was the sea my uncle wrote of, I wondered, and watched the slow ebb and flow of the entire city itself and realized *the city is the sea* and wanted to weep with the joy of it.

"You would live a full life here," Reynolds said.

My eyes met Reynolds's. When I looked at him a certain way, I saw the truth of him, his true body, and if I looked deeper, I saw to the heart of him. Darker, fouler; a seam of brightness. *He could take me back as he did my uncle,* I thought, *but he doesn't want to.* He wanted to keep me.

"I want to go back." I had to go. To look—to see whatever had become of whatever I loved.

The queen seized my chin in her pear-wet hand and my world went black.

When light returned, it fell in hazy curtains around me. The air was ashen, bits of burnt paper falling as snow would. Walls like skeletal fingers rose around me. Scattered bricks, the stench of burnt wood. I saw hunched figures in the street and ran for them, but as I neared they became only heaps of more debris. I saw no people.

Though my legs were tired and ached with each step, and my lungs burned, I walked on. I walked up streets once familiar to me; dead, burnt things crunched underfoot. I searched for anything I might recognize and while there were ruined shops aplenty, I knew none of them.

I walked through all the wreckage of this city, until the sun touched and began to fall below the horizon. Exhaustion dragged me to sit on a curb and I couldn't find the energy to mind the rubbish I settled in.

How many years had passed Baltimore by? How long had the city lain in ruin? Was it God who decided to destroy this place, or man? Did it matter at all?

In the remains at my feet, I found a scrap of poetry, about a woman with hyacinth hair. It could not be my uncle's handwriting—though perhaps it was, for as I stood to continue my journey, I could not remember his handwriting. I could barely remember his face.

It was his voice I remembered best of all, and the beat of those words in my head. *The seam.* It rested inside of me, unable to escape. He'd wept for it in the end, shouting for Reynolds to snatch him back to that world.

I folded the page into my hand and walked on. As far as I walked, the whole city through, there was only gray ruin. I yelled, but no one answered. Perhaps there was no one *to* answer.

"Anyone!" I cried as loud as I could from the middle of the street. I looked to the sky, the veiled sun now set in the gray west.

My world was dead. I had nothing. I looked at my filthy hands and saw them old and wrinkled. I was but twenty and felt the universe retreating from me.

"Reynolds! Fonderous Reynolds!"

The ring of hooves on cobblestones answered me. Sharp and distinct down the ruined street they came, pulling a claret and gold four-in-hand.

There was one thing left to me. Hope in the brightness in the seam above the floor. Hope that there existed in that place a life worth living, with beings I might one day love. My uncle was dead in both worlds, but I was only dead in one.

I stepped in the path of the carriage and my world went black—
But only for a moment.

WHILE MINDLESSLY BROWSING *the internet, I came across stories about the strange days leading up to Poe's death, how he was found wandering, in clothes that were not his own. I moved on to something else, but over the next week, my mind kept returning to that idea of him in a stranger's clothes. How would this come to be? Did he go mad at the end of his life? What could have caused it? I poked around a little more, and the idea of him having rabies came up. Far too tame... that couldn't possibly be it! I turned to Poe's own writing for an answer (the poems "Dreamland," "Spirits of the Dead," and "Fairyland"), and coupled with a few prompts from my writing group, this story is the result.*

GREGORY FROST is a writer of fantasy, horror and science fiction who has been publishing steadily for more than two decades.

His latest work is the fantasy duology, *Shadowbridge*, published by Del Rey Books. His earlier novels include *Fitcher's Brides*, a World Fantasy Award and International Horror Guild Award finalist for Best Novel; *Tain, Lyrec*, and Nebula-nominated SF work *The Pure Cold Light*. His short story collection, *Attack of the Jazz Giants & Other Stories*, was called by *Publishers Weekly* "one of the best fantasy collections of the year."

He is the one of two Fiction Writing Workshop Directors at Swarthmore College in Swarthmore, PA, and has thrice taught the Clarion Science Fiction & Fantasy Writers Workshop.

His web site is www.gregoryfrost.com; his blog, "Frostbites," lurks at http://frostokovich.livejournal.com

THE FINAL ACT

by Gregory Frost

MCGOWREN CAUGHT UP with him in the lobby amid the end-of-the-day exodus. One moment Leonard was heading through the gray granite lobby by himself, the next the person he least wanted to see was striding along beside him as if no bad blood lay between them.

Leonard pulled away as if from a foul odor, then set his jaw and kept walking at the same pace, refusing to be rattled or to acknowledge the intrusion beyond a sidewise glance.

McGowren's chinos were stained, his shirttail hung out on one side, he seemed to have lost his tie, and he had a heavy enough five o'clock shadow that he must have shaved the night before. Leonard, unconsciously smoothing down his own tie, wondered if the schmuck had met any clients like that. Had any of the partners on the fifth floor seen him in this shape? Maybe he'd been sacked already, he sure looked the part. But no, Len would have heard. Too many people knew he'd have liked nothing more than to hear that about McGowren, and someone would have called or even ridden up to tell him. Almost to himself he said, "You look like you slept under a bar."

"Nice to see you, too, Len."

"And unless you're here to beg forgiveness, you can fuck off." Then Leonard was in the revolving door, pushing his way to the sidewalk, ditching McGowren and merging into the departing throng. However, before he'd reached the corner, McGowren reappeared beside him. "Leonard, bro, I need to talk to you."

"Don't call me 'bro.' Or buddy or pal or anything else."

"Len—"

"I don't have time tonight. I have to pick up my car." At least he didn't have to fabricate an excuse.

"Geez, man, I was hoping you'd give me a ride."

"You take the train, asshole," he replied. He maneuvered around a light pole and then walked on the narrow strip outside the parking meters, passing most of the crowd and temporarily outstripping McGowren again. He heard behind him the words, "I don't have my pass on me. I lost it. I need a *ride*, man."

Leonard nodded his head. It might have meant he'd heard or it might have signaled that he would agree to help. He wasn't sure which, either.

It had been five months since he'd spoken to Gary McGowren—not since the Christmas party where he'd caught McGowren and Laurel in the coat closet, about two items of clothing away from a full-on fuck. The closet was the size of a meat locker and could have contained an orgy, but there were just the two of them, his wife and Gary. Idiots. At least Laurel looked horrified as she snatched up her clothes and ran past him. Leonard stood his ground. McGowren raised a hand in pathetic imitation of an apology, shambled forward and slurred, "Don' be mad, Len, 'm sorry, just too much punch at the watering hole is all, 'm sorry." He pawed, clutched Len's arm. "Listen, Laurel's just—" was all he got to say before Leonard shoved him sprawling into the coats, that clutching hand grabbing for purchase, catching hold of the rod as his forehead hit it and he fell, his weight snapping it out of the wall and dragging coats and furs down on top of him. With a displaced calm, Leonard collected his own and Laurel's coats from the other side of the closet. Why hadn't he done something? Why hadn't he stomped the bastard to death? But even there in that moment of fury he was afraid of violence, scared of acting out. He could stand in a courtroom and gloatingly reduce people to self-contradicting imbeciles, but he couldn't deck McGowren. Just couldn't touch him. He hated himself for it, and McGowren as the proof.

Laurel had cried all the way home except for the few moments she spent vomiting out the window. She hadn't meant—hadn't known—what she was doing. All the excuses failing to explain why, of all the people she could have drunkenly pursued, she'd picked McGowren. He was good looking, okay, but come on, the guy had the verbal skills of an ape. It was why he'd been passed over for promotions, never offered even a junior partnership, just maintained his position, handling work injury cases that he had next to no business pursuing, billing enough hours to get by but not much else. If they'd worked in the same department, crossed paths at all, Len would have had him fired. Instead, roiling in his own sense of inadequacy and failure, he'd just let him be, hoping McGowren would go away and die on his own. Laurel had seen a counselor and then she had insisted they see a counselor together, as if her indiscretion was somehow his fault as well, and he'd gone, he'd borne it. In five months they'd attained a kind of stability, forbearance moving toward acceptance, maybe some kind of forgiveness. Over and over she had told him how good he was, how kind, but he wasn't sure kindness wasn't just weakness. He doubted he would trust anything or anyone ever again.

At the corner of 12th and Locust, Leonard waited for the light and McGowren slid up beside him. The bastard did look pretty banged up. Maybe he *had* been sacked. Maybe he *was* sleeping under a bar. Good.

Leonard had told no one about the coat closet, but someone must have come upon McGowren, and it was only a few days before Debbie, his secretary, had stepped into his office and just said, "I'm really sorry." He'd looked in her eyes and known what she was saying, known that his co-workers all knew. McGowren had stayed away, the one smart thing he'd done. So what was this appeal all about? What did he want, sympathy? Forgiveness? Those ships had sailed.

They had known each other since high school, and McGowren been an ape then, too, a running back on the football team who was always playing pranks: convincing someone to climb out on the cafeteria roof and then locking the windows to keep them out there till some outraged faculty or staff member let them back in; turning a firehose on the cheerleaders just before they ran outside, where it was 45 degrees; filling a water bottle in chemistry class with mustard and spraying his chem partner with it. Mostly he started fights. The trouble was, for some perverse reason he wanted to hang around with Leonard's group. They weren't nerds exactly, but they weren't the popular kids, either, and they foolishly thought a football player in their midst could open a door into the world of girls. Instead, McGowren had only managed to get them in trouble by association so that they were drawn into every fracas, often in defense of the schmuck. Leonard had steered clear of him as much as possible. Even then he was petrified of confrontations, of violence, of being hit. So when McGowren had applied for a position at the law firm and given Leonard as a reference, it was an act of pure stupidity to have hoped he'd grown up.

Without looking at him, as if it was hard to express, McGowren said, "Listen, Len, we have history, okay? I just need a ride. I don't want your forgiveness. I don't expect it." The light changed. He finally glanced cautiously at Leonard. "So, can you?"

"Fine, I'll give you a ride, all right," he replied, amazed to hear the words, as if his mouth had answered without consulting him. He knew he didn't mean it, knew that he had reached the end with this jerk who'd followed him like a slug's smear from high school to the law firm. He didn't know what he was going to do yet, but it was time to get rid of Gary McGowren once and for all.

* * *

HE PAID THE bill for the lube job and oil change, and got in. Then he remembered his passenger and unlocked the doors. Where had McGowren got to while he'd looked over the bill and paid up? Restroom probably. For an instant he considered driving off without him. Then the door opened and McGowren folded into the seat. He sat in a forward hunch as if intrigued by the Infiniti's dashboard. "Put your seatbelt on, Gary."

"I hate 'em."

"Yeah? Well do it anyway. I'm not going to be liable when you go through the windshield."

As if with obvious reluctance and he clipped in, McGowren asked, "You remember that water balloon fight where I filled one with tempera paint and nailed you coming around the corner?"

Leonard pulled into traffic. "I caught hell for that prank. The red never came out of my shirt. My mom bleached it till the fabric disintegrated and it was still pink. So was one side of my face for like a week."

"It was pretty damned amazing. You dripped like some kind of swamp thing."

"Yeah, real fucking amazing. Thanks. What are you, still fifteen? You're an idiot, McGowren. You always were. You want a ride, then shut up."

In silence Leonard drove awhile, stuck in the jam to get onto the parkway. This was all a mistake. He wasn't going to do anything to McGowren—what *could* he do, push him out of the car at eighty mph? It would be just one more thing for him to stew over, one more imagined act that wasn't going to happen.

Then down the ramp and merging onto the faster parkway, he reached for the radio knob, and McGowren spoke up. "You never did get the dynamic, did you, Len?"

"What dynamic?"

"Us. You and me. Even in high school. You got this image of it being like we were buddies or something. Like I was the person you'd call if you wanted to do something."

"I don't think so." Where was *this* coming from?

"Oh, yes you do, and it was never like that. You didn't want me joining the firm, you don't want me in the car now—"

"Gee, I can't imagine why I don't feel much like doing you favors anymore."

"Anymore? When did you do me favors?"

"I could have shit-canned you when you put me down as a reference. I should have. But I thought, 'Hey, maybe he's grown up, maybe he turned into an adult.'"

"You're a snob, Len. You and your little pals, all you wanted from me was to score some girls, you didn't give a rat's ass about me otherwise."

Leonard looked out his side window. The driver passing stared back at him. "Jesus, it was high school, Gary." He turned to face him. "And you know, I'll tell you what I remember. I remember a dumbass jock who pissed off even the other jocks. Who managed to implicate everybody he was with so that they either had to fight on his behalf or else got hauled into the vice principal's office along with him. A guy who is so terminally fucked in the head he doesn't even know why maybe I'm less than enthused to be in his company right now, even though he's tried to screw my wife. Christ. Why am I trying to talk to you?"

"Maybe you want to know."

"What do I want to know?"

"Everything. Why you're the way you are. Why I'm talking to you, despite your rejecting—"

"We're not in high school, you asshole. What, you've been waiting for twelve *years* to get back at me for trying to convince the rest of our crew to get rid of you?"

McGowren glanced at him and smiled.

Leonard couldn't stop the laugh of disdain. "Are you serious? Never mind that this is all in your head, how long can you maintain a grudge? You put me down on your job application! And I let you pass when I could easily have told them not to hire you. *God.*"

McGowren said nothing.

"So, what, the thing in the coat closet was just you getting back at me through Laurel?"

"That was the first part of it."

"The first part? How many parts will we have? Two acts or three? I can stop at a bar so you can get tanked and recreate the night in the coats." He pushed his hand through his thinning hair. "Man, here I am, giving you a ride home because you lost your pass. And I'm the bad guy because I didn't like you in high school. You're really a piece of work."

Everything had changed now. Leonard could see that so long as McGowren was around, there would *always* be another prank, another act of eternal escalation. He had to get rid of him, there was no choice. The question was *how*? How to make him disappear for good and not pay for it? He flipped through scenarios: sledge-hammer McGowren's skull and then the floor in the basement and stick the body under that, except he didn't have the concrete; okay, in the back yard then, hit him with a shovel and then dig a hole in the garden and plant the bastard under the roses; or better still, drive twenty miles to the state park and dump his corpse in the woods. Let him rot outdoors where nobody would ever connect them.

"You know what, Gary. I should just bring you to my place. We'll have a drink or two and straighten this out between us once and for all. You can even talk to Laurel if she can stomach being in the same room with you."

"Fine. That's where I need to go, anyway."

The way he said it, Leonard knew even through the heat of his own anger that something had already happened. The second act of the revenge fantasy had already begun. The train pass, the ride home—he reached into his suit and drew out his cell phone, flipped it open. Before he could even thumb a number he saw that the battery was out of juice. The car charger was dangling out of the cigarette lighter but he couldn't plug the phone in on the parkway. He flipped it closed.

"Change your mind?" McGowren asked.

It seemed that maybe he didn't know the phone was dead. Leonard saw no reason to disabuse him of this idea. "Yeah. That's what you want me to do—call home."

He closed his eyes, still smiling carelessly. "Right." He brushed the hair down the back of his head, in the process pushing his collar down. Leonard saw scratch marks on the back of his neck. He forgot himself momentarily, and his foot backed off the gas pedal until the BMW behind him honked. He jerked up as if he'd fallen asleep, and accelerated. The next exit was his anyway, and he hit his blinker and edged off to the right. The BMW zoomed past, honking again to make sure he got the message. McGowren snorted.

"Anyway," he muttered, his eyes still closed, "you'd just get a busy signal."

"Really, how do you know that?"

"Because it's off the hook. The way I left it."

Leonard's desire to dispense with McGowren evaporated, replaced by sickening uncertainty. "*You* left it?"

"Yeah. Right after I killed Laurel."

He heard the words, so impossible they didn't make sense, like he'd heard them out of order and needed to rearrange them to make a sentence he understood. But McGowren wouldn't give him time.

"No, you know, we had quite a thing going. That night in the coats, that wasn't exactly the first, and, man, she wanted more than just a taste. I thought it was over the second you walked in, you know, but she called me—I mean, right at the office, right underneath you. Said you were none too spectacular in the sack and that she was gonna stay on the prowl and I could either get it on or get lost. How's your sex life been since Christmas, Len, hmm?"

Leonard's brain ran through images, memories, doubts: guilty red-eyed looks from Laurel, withheld responses in therapy—even the therapist had complained that she wasn't engaged—dinners shared in unbroken silences as she made eye-contact only with her plate. Silences were gaps and he could fill them with anything he chose. He sought and created hidden meanings everywhere. At the same time his body drove on auto-pilot, zooming past the speed limit, braking, turning, the car's air gone stale, dead. He needed to open a window. His mouth said, "No."

McGowren now looked straight at him and all but sneered. There was a bruise over McGowren's right eye now that hadn't been obvious before. It must have been recent, forming, hours old.

"You're bound to say no, Len. But it's yes. Yes, you've seen the signs. We've been meeting for months. Remember when they sent you to Boston? Oh, that was a night. Didn't know she liked that kinky shit. Did you?"

"We were... she was seeing a counselor because of you," he answered, but his mind had flown away back to a night last winter where she'd bound him with his ties and then teased him, tormented him, made him beg for her to sit on him. He'd loved it. *Kinky shit.*

"Counseling, yeah, right. She needed counseling." Laughing.

He swallowed the metallic thickness in his mouth. "Get out of my car."

"You kidding?"

"Get out—out of my car, out of my life, out of my *head*!"

"See what I mean, Len? Total prick. Here I am confessing to you, turning myself in to you and you're telling me to get lost. I'm filling in the blanks for you, dude. But if you want me out—" He started to open the door.

Leonard grabbed at him, but swung the wheel at the same time and the car veered. He screamed and slapped both hands on the wheel again, and narrowly failed to smack into the car in the right lane. Horns blared around him.

McGowren chuckled. He hadn't opened the door, hadn't gotten out. He was looking straight at the road. "You should have taken care of me at the Christmas party, Len. You should have kicked my head in through the coats. Shoulda woulda coulda. Now you won't ever know, will you? Am I lying or telling the truth about Laurel? You just won't ever be sure because a little worm's gone crawling right up inside your head. The night in the closet—oh, that's real. You can still feel the moment, it's so raw. You can box it off, put police tape around it. Isolate it. Sure, but the rest is going to run around and around the squeaky hamster wheel in your head, eeky-eeky." He laughed again.

Even as he made the final frenzied turn onto his street, Leonard saw the police cars—two on his front lawn—and the EMT wagon backed into the driveway. Neighbors outside, Monroe, the stockbroker across the street, standing idiotically beside his mailbox, envelopes in his hand.

McGowren leaned back and let go a deep sigh as if finally drained of all taunts.

Leonard slammed the car against the curb. The tire thumped, bounced. He fumbled, flung the door open before the car had stopped, snatching the keys, staring at his apparently dozing passenger one last time, then running, up the sidewalk, across the lawn. A cop at the front door put out a hand, but responded to the look of him and drew aside, saying, "Husband?"

He nodded as he pushed past, into his house, calling over his shoulder, "He's in the car, I left him in the car."

"Huh?" said the cop, but Leonard was already crossing the living room toward the hall. A flash went off in the kitchen, past the wall of live bodies. It seemed like a crowd, but it was no more than five: uniforms, plain clothes, medical, standing, gathered, starting to turn at his approach.

Between them as they parted, creating a sliver of an opening, he finally glimpsed his wife.

She was in the tall chair at the breakfast bar, her head hanging down. He thought again of the dinner plate. He should have made her talk, demanded to know why she wouldn't look at him. Below her now on the floor was a little card with a metallic strip across it. Her blouse was torn at the shoulder, the bra strap broken beneath it, her shoulder red, cut with parallel gashes—fingernails had done that. What had McGowren's fingertips looked like? Then, ever so slightly, she raised her bruised and swollen face, and saw him as he froze. She burst into tears. She sprang from the chair, reaching, reaching with red fingers. Everyone looked his way now, and he felt the impact of her against him, heard her wail, but he had come unmoored from the moment, from the world. The card on the floor, it was a train pass. And beside it... He stared into the half-lidded eyes watching him—the body on its back, scratched, battered, one arm flung out, fingers curled into a claw, the brown belt undone and chinos half down. The black handle of a German carving knife stuck out of the center of his chest like a flag planted on a hill. McGowren's head rested on its crown. His mouth was open as if in the middle of a word, a sentence, a laugh.

You won't ever know, will you?

Laurel had stepped back, sensing the wrongness of him, the immobility and hardness. He gazed from McGowren's dead eyes into hers. Was there guilt there? Something more than relief? Leonard could hear her story already—she would tell him McGowren had shown up drunk and attacked, wanting to finish what they'd started in the closet, would never let it go because there was so much more to destroy yet, the same as in high school, and even in the car. He wouldn't stop until he'd pulled everyone down along with him, that was McGowren. She was only act two. What was the last?

He pushed Laurel away, backed and then turned from the hall and ran out of the house, down the drive behind the EMT van. His car, parked askew with one wheel up over the curb. Empty. Empty. He'd told the cop, he'd said...

He shuffled his feet, unable to go in any direction, unable to get away to anywhere. He heard his name, and sure it was McGowren, he spun around. Two officers had pursued him, and the nearer one spoke his name again.

Up past the drive, Laurel stood at the front door, a million miles away across the lawn. She was calling to him, too, but her voice, his name, seemed to break apart beneath a crackling in his brain, the noise of something awful burrowing in for a long, long stay.

THE FIRST STORY *of mine that was published, in* The Twilight Zone Magazine *a long time ago, was about Edgar Allan Poe, and I feel as if I loop back upon him now and again.* When Attack of the Jazz Giants & Other Stories *was being put together for Golden Gryphon Press, the illustrator, Jason Van Hollander, made an illustration of Poe central to the design of that book. Poe, the self-destructive genius, will forever fascinate me.*

If anyone lived a life exemplary of "The Imp of the Perverse" it was Poe. His is the biography of a man who undermined himself at every opportunity, unleashing a demon of pettiness and jealousy. He would gratefully accept jobs and then, tiring of them, sabotage the position either via vituperative reviews upon writers who weren't measuring up to Poe's notions of literature—after which he had to be let go—or else by direct abuse heaped upon on the people who'd—more often than not, kindly—given him a job in the first place. It's remarkable that he could write such a story and then continue living it as if unaware of his part in it. Maybe we're all blind sailors to some degree, but Poe's imp sabotaged him even after his death. It would be hard to top that.

For "The Final Act" I began with Poe's man who couldn't keep his mouth shut about his crime. I'd been teaching a lot, and one of the exercises that I'd given my students that really seemed to catch fire is called "Two people come out of a building," an exercise by Alice Mattison from the book Now Write! *that I like a great deal. And so mostly as an experiment, I decided to take Poe's character and write my own "two people come out of a building" story. That's all I started with, and the story coalesced from there as it was written. I did not know, going in, who was alive and who was dead. That rather key element emerged as I wrote, surprising me as much as I hope it does the reader.*

LAIRD BARRON'S work has appeared in places such as *The Magazine of Fantasy & Science Fiction, SCIFICTION, Inferno: New Tales of Terror and the Supernatural*, and *The Del Rey Book of Science Fiction and Fantasy*. It has also been reprinted in numerous year's best anthologies. His debut collection, *The Imago Sequence*, was recently published by Night Shade. Mr. Barron is an expatriate Alaskan currently at large in Washington State.

Strappado

by Laird Barron

Kenshi Suzuki and Swayne Harris had a chance reunion at a bathhouse in an Indian tourist town. It had been five or six years since their previous Malta liaison, a cocktail party at the British consulate that segued into a branding iron hot affair. They'd spent a long weekend of day cruises to the cyclopean ruins on Gozo, nightclubbing at the elite hotels and casinos, and booze-drenched marathon sex before the dissolution of their respective junkets swept them back to New York and London in a storm of tears and bitter farewells. For Kenshi, the emotional hangover lasted through desolate summer and into a melancholy autumn. And even now, when elegant, thunderously handsome Swayne materialized from the crowd on the balcony like the Ghost of Christmas Past—!

Kenshi wore a black suit; sleek and polished as a seal or a banker. He swept his single lock of gelled black hair to the left, like a gothic teardrop. His skin was sallow and dewlapped at his neck, and soft at his belly and beneath his Italian leather belt. He'd been a swimmer once, earnestly meant to return to his collegiate form, but hadn't yet braced for the exhaustion of such an endeavor. He preferred to float in hotel pools while dreaming of his supple youth, once so exotic in the suburbs of white bread Connecticut. Everyone but his grandparents (who never fully acclimated to their transplantation to the West) called him Ken. A naturalized U.S. citizen, he spoke meager Japanese, knew next to zero about the history or the culture, and had visited Tokyo a grand total of three times. In short, he privately acknowledged his unworthiness to lay claim to his blood heritage and thus lived a life of minor, yet persistent, regret.

Swayne wore a cream colored suit of a cut most popular with the royalty of South American plantations. *It's in style anywhere I go*, he explained later as they undressed one another in Kenshi's suite at the Golden Scale. Swayne's complexion was dark, like fired clay. His slightly sinister brows and waxed imperial lent him the appearance of a Christian devil.

In the seam between the electric shock of their reunion and resultant delirium fugue of violent coupling, Kenshi had an instant to doubt the old magic before the question was utterly obliterated. And if he'd forgotten Swayne's sly, wry demeanor, his faith was restored when the dark man rolled to face the ceiling, dragged on their shared cigarette and said, "Of all the bathhouses in all the cities of the world..."

Kenshi cheerfully declared him a bastard and snatched back the cigarette. The room was strewn with their clothes. A vase of lilies lay capsized and water funneled from severed stems over the edge of the table. He caught droplets in his free hand and rubbed them and the semen into the slick flesh of his chest and belly. He breathed heavily.

"How'd you swing this place all to yourself?" Swayne said. "Big promotion?"

"A couple of my colleagues got pulled off the project and didn't make the trip. You?"

"Business, with unexpected pleasure, thank you. The museum sent me to look at a collection—estate sale. Paintings and whatnot. I fly back on Friday, unless I find something extraordinary, which is doubtful. Mostly rubbish, I'm afraid." Swayne rose and stretched. Rich, gold-red light dappled the curtains, banded and bronzed him with tiger stripes.

The suite's western exposure gave them a last look at the sun as it faded to black. Below their lofty vantage, slums and crooked dirt streets and the labyrinthine wharfs in the shallow, blood-warm harbor were mercifully obscured by thickening tropical darkness. Farther along the main avenue and atop the ancient terraced hillsides was a huge, baroque Seventeenth Century monastery, much photographed for feature films, and farther still, the scattered manors and villas of the lime nabobs, their walled estates demarcated by kliegs and floodlights. Tourism pumped the lifeblood of the settlement. They came for the monastery, of course, and only a few kilometers off was a wildlife preserve. Tour buses ran daily and guides entertained foreigners with local folklore and promises of tigers, a number of which roamed the high grass plains. Kenshi had gone on his first day, hated the ripe, florid smell of the jungle, the heat, and the sullen men with rifles who patrolled the electrified perimeter fence in halftracks. The locals wore knives in their belts, even the urbane guide with the Oxford accent, and it left Kenshi feeling shriveled and helpless, at the mercy of the hatefully smiling multitudes.

Here, in the dusty, grimy heart of town, some eighty kilometers down the coast from grand old Mumbai, when the oil lamps and electric lamps fizzed alight, link by link in a vast, convoluted chain, it was only bright enough to help the muggers and cutthroats see what they were doing.

"City of romance," Swayne said with eminent sarcasm. He opened the door to the terrace and stood naked at the rail. There were a few tourists on their verandas and at their windows. Laughter and pop music and the stench of the sea carried on the lethargic breeze as it snaked through the room. The hotel occupied the exact center of a semicircle of relatively modernized blocks—the chamber of commerce's concession to appeasing Westerners' paranoia of marauding gangs and vicious muggers. Still, three streets over was the Third World, as Kenshi's colleagues referred to it while they swilled whiskey and goggled at turbans and sarongs and at the Buddhists in their orange robes. It was enough to make him ashamed of his continent, to pine for his father's homeland, until he realized the Japanese were scarcely more civilized as guests.

"The only hotel with air conditioning and you go out there. You'll be arrested if you don't put something on!" Kenshi finally dragged himself upright and collected his pants. "Let's go to the discotheque."

"The American place? I'd rather not. Asshole tourists swarm there like bees to honey. I was in the cantina a bit earlier and got stuck near a bunch of Hollywood types whooping it up at the bar. Probably come to scout the area or shoot the monastery. All they could talk about is picking up on 'European broads.'"

Kenshi laughed. "Those are the guys I'm traveling with. Yeah, they're scouting locations. And they're all married, too."

"Wankers. Hell with the disco."

"No, there's another spot—a hole in the wall I heard about from a friend. A local.".

"Eh, probably a seedy little bucket of blood. I'm in, then!"

KENSHI RANG HIS contact, one Rashid Obi, an assistant to an executive producer at a local firm that cranked out several dozen Bollywood films every year. Rashid gave directions and promised to meet them at the club in forty-five minutes. Or, if they were nervous to travel the streets alone, he could escort them... Kenshi laughed, somewhat halfheartedly, and assured his acquaintance there was no need for such coddling. He would've preferred Rashid's company, but knew Swayne was belligerently fearless regarding forays into foreign environments. His lover was an adventurer and hard bitten in his own charming fashion. Certainly Swayne would mock him for his timidity and charge ahead regardless. So, Kenshi stifled his misgivings and led the way.

The discotheque was a quarter mile from the hotel and buried in a misshapen block of stone houses and empty shops. They found it mostly by accident after stumbling around several narrow alleys that reeked of urine and the powerful miasma of curry that seeped from open apartment windows. The entry arch was low and narrow and blackened from soot and antiquity. The name of the club had been painted into the worn plaster, illegible now from erosion and neglect. Kerosene lamps guttered in inset sconces and shadows gathered in droves. A speaker dangled from a cornice and projected scratchy sitar music. Two Indian men sat on a stone bench. They wore baggy, lemon shirts and disco slacks likely purchased from the black market outlets in a local bazaar. They shared the stem of the hookah at their sandaled feet. Neither appeared interested in the arrival of the Westerners.

"Oh my God! It's an opium den!" Swayne said and squeezed Kenshi's buttock. "Going native, are we, dear?"

Kenshi blushed and knocked his hand aside. He'd smoked half a joint with a dorm mate in college and that was the extent of his experimentation with recreational drugs. He favored a nice, dry white wine and the occasional imported beer, preferably Sapporo.

The darkness of the alley followed them inside. The interior lay in shadow, except for the bar, which glowed from a strip along its edge like the bioluminescent tentacle of a deep sea creature, and motes of gold and red and purple passing across the bottles from a rotating glitter ball above the tiny square of dance floor wedged in the corner. The sitar music issued from a beat box and was much louder than it had been outside. Patrons were jammed into the little rickety tables and along the bar. The air was sharp with sweat and exhaled liquor fumes.

Rashid emerged from the shadows and caught Kenshi's arm above the elbow in the overly familiar manner of his countrymen. He was shorter than Kenshi and slender to the point of well-heeled emaciation. He stood so close Kenshi breathed deeply of his cologne, the styling gel in his short, tightly coiled hair. He introduced the small man from Delhi to a mildly bemused Swayne. Soon Rashid vigorously shepherded them into an alcove where a group of Europeans crowded together around three circular tables laden with beer bottles and shot glasses and fuming ashtrays heaped with the butts of cigarettes.

Rashid presented Swayne and Kenshi to the evening's co-host, one Luis Guzman, an elderly Argentinean who'd lived abroad for nearly three decades in quasi–political exile. Guzman was the public relations guru for a profoundly large international advertising conglomerate, which in turn influenced, or owned outright, the companies represented by the various guests he'd assembled at the discotheque.

Kenshi's feet ached, so he wedged in next to a reedy blonde Netherlander, a weather reporter for some big market, he gathered as sporadic introductions were made. Her hands bled ink from a mosaic of nightclub stamps, the kind that didn't easily wash off, so like rings in a tree, it was possible to estimate she'd been partying hard for several nights. This impression was confirmed when she confided that she'd gone a bit wild during her group's whirlwind tour of Bangkok, Mumbai and this "village" in the space of days. She laughed at him from the side of her mouth, gaped fishily with her left eye, a Picasso girl, and pressed her bony thigh against him. She'd been drinking boleros, and lots of them, he noted. *What goes down must come up*, he thought and was sorry for whomever she eventually leeched onto tonight.

The Viking gentleman looming across from them certainly vied for her attention, what with his lascivious grimaces and bellowing jocularity, but she appeared content to ignore him while trading glances with the small, hirsute Slav to the Viking's left and occasionally brushing Kenshi's forearm as they shared an ashtray. He soon discovered Hendrika the weathergirl worked for the Viking, Andersen, chief comptroller and inveterate buffoon. The Slav was actually a native of Minsk named Fedor; Fedor managed distribution for a major vodka label and possessed some mysterious bit of history with Hendrika. Kenshi idly wondered if he'd been her pimp while she toiled through college. A job was a job was a job (until she found the job of her dreams) to a certain subset of European women, and men too, as he'd been pleased to discover during his many travels. In turn, Hendrika briefly introduced Kenshi to the French Contingent of software designers— Francoise, Jean Michelle, and Claude; the German photographer Victor and his assistant Nina; and Raul, a Spanish advertising consultant. They extended lukewarm handshakes and one of them bought him a glass of bourbon, which he didn't want but politely accepted. Then, everyone resumed roaring, disjointed conversations and ignored him completely.

Good old Swayne got along swimmingly, of course. He'd discarded his white suit for an orange blazer, black shirt, and slacks; Kenshi noted with equal measures of satisfaction and jealousy that all heads swiveled to follow the boisterous Englishman. Within moments he'd shaken hands with all and sundry and been inducted by the club of international debauchers as a member in good standing. That the man didn't even speak a second language was no impediment—he vaulted such barriers by shamelessly enlisting necessary translations from whoever happened to be within earshot. Kenshi glumly thought his friend would've made one hell of an American.

Presently Swayne returned from his confab with Rashid and Guzman and exclaimed, "We've been invited to the exhibition. A *Van Iblis!*" Swayne seemed genuinely enthused, his meticulously cultivated cynicism blasted to smithereens in an instant. Kenshi barely made him out over the crossfire between Andersen and Hendrika and the other American, Walther. Walther was fat and bellicose, a colonial barbarian dressed for civilized company. His shirt was untucked, his tie an open noose. Kenshi hadn't caught what the fellow did for a living, however Walther put whiskey after whiskey away with the vigor of a man accustomed to lavish expense accounts. He sneered at Kenshi on the occasions their eyes met.

Kenshi told Swayne he'd never heard of Van Iblis.

"It's a pseudonym," Swayne said. "Like Kilroy, or Alan Smithee. He, or she, is a guerilla. Not welcome in the U.K.; *persona non grata* in the free world you might say." When Kenshi asked why Van Iblis wasn't welcome in Britain, Swayne grinned. "Because the shit he pulls off violates a few laws here and there. Unauthorized installations, libelous materials, health code violations. Explosions!" Industry insiders suspected Van Iblis was actually comprised of a significant number of member artists and exceedingly wealthy patrons. Such an infrastructure seemed the only logical explanation for the success of these brazen exhibitions and their participants' elusiveness.

It developed that Guzman had brought his eclectic coterie to this part of the country after sniffing a rumor of an impending Van Iblis show and as luck would have it, tonight was the night. Guzman's contacts had provided him with a hand-scrawled map to the rendezvous, and a password. A password! It was all extraordinarily titillating.

Swayne dialed up a slideshow on his cell and handed it over. Kenshi remembered the news stories once he saw the image of the three homeless men who'd volunteered to be crucified on faux satellite dishes. Yes, that had caused a sensation, although the winos survived relatively intact. None of them knew enough to expose the identity of his temporary employers. Another series of slides displayed the infamous pigs' blood carpet bombing of the Vietnam War Memorial from a blimp that then exploded in midair like a Roman candle. Then the so called "corpse art" in Mexico, Amsterdam, and elsewhere. Similar to the other guerilla installations, these exhibits popped up in random venues in any of a dozen countries after the mildest and most surreptitious of advance rumors and retreated underground within hours. Of small comfort to scandalized authorities was the fact the corpse sculptures, while utterly macabre, were allegedly comprised of volunteers with terminal illnesses who'd donated their bodies to science, or rather, art. Nonetheless, at the sight of grimly posed seniors in antiquated bathing suits, a bloated, eyeless Santa in a coonskin cap, the tri-headed ice cream vendor and his chalk-faced Siamese children, Kenshi wrinkled his lip and pushed the phone at Swayne. "No, I think I'll skip this one, whatever it is, thank you very much."

"You are such a wet blanket," Swayne said. "Come on, love. I've been dying to witness a Van Iblis show since, well, forever. I'll be the envy of every art dilettante from Birmingham to Timbuktu!"

Kenshi made polite yet firm noises of denial. Swayne leaned very close; his hot breath tickled Kenshi's ear. He stroked Kenshi's cock through the tight fabric of his designer pants. Congruently, albeit obliviously, Hendrika continued to rub his thigh. Kenshi choked on his drink and finally consented to accompany Swayne on his stupid side trek, would've promised anything to spare himself this agonizing embarrassment. A lifetime in the suburbs had taught him to eschew public displays of affection, much less submit to a drunken mauling by another man in a foreign country not particularly noted for its tolerance.

He finished his drink in miserable silence and awaited the inevitable.

* * *

THEY CROWDED ABOARD Guzman's two Day-Glo rental vans and drove inland. There were no signs to point the way and the road was narrow and deserted. Kenshi's head grew thick and heavy on his neck and he closed his eyes and didn't open them until the tires made new sounds as they left paved road for a dirt track and his companions gently bumped their legs and arms against his own.

It wasn't much farther.

Daylight peeled back the layers of night and deposited them near a collection of prefabricated warehouse modules and storage sheds. The modules were relatively modern, yet already cloaked in moss and threaded with coils of vine. Each was enormous and had been adjoined to its siblings via additions and corrugated tin walkways. The property sat near the water, a dreary, fog-shrouded expanse surrounded by drainage ditches and marshes and a jungle of creepers and banyan trees.

Six or seven dilapidated panel trucks were parked on the outskirts; 1970s Fords imported from distant USA, their white frames scorched and shot with rust. Battered insignia on the door panels marked them as one-time property of the ministry of the interior. Alongside the trucks, an equally antiquated, although apparently functional, bulldozer squatted in the high grass; a dull red model one would expect to see abandoned in a rural American pasture. To the left of the bulldozer was a deep, freshly ploughed trench surmounted by plastic barrels, unsealed fifty-five gallon drums and various wooden boxes, much of this half concealed by canvas tarps. Guzman commented that the owners of the land were in the embryonic stage of prepping for large scale development—perhaps a hotel. Power lines and septic systems were in the offing.

Kenshi couldn't imagine who in the hell could possibly think building a hotel in a swamp represented a wise business investment.

Guzman and Rashid's groups climbed from the vans and congregated, faces slack and bruised by hangovers, jet lag, and burgeoning unease. What had seemed a lark in the cozy confines of the disco became a more ominous prospect as each took stock and realized he or she hadn't a bloody clue as to north or south, or up and down, for that matter. Gnats came at them in quick, sniping swarms, and several people cursed when they lost shoes to the soft, wet earth. Black and white chickens scratched in the weedy ruts.

A handful of Indians dressed in formal wear grimly waited under a pavilion to serve a buffet. None of them smiled or offered any greeting. They mumbled amongst themselves and loaded plates of honeydew slices and crepes and poured glasses of champagne with disconsolate expressions. A Victrola played an eerie Hindu-flavored melody. The scene reminded Kenshi of a funeral reception. Someone, perhaps Walther, muttered nervously, and the sentiment of general misgiving palpably intensified.

"Hey, this is kinda spooky," Hendrika stage-whispered to her friend Fedor. Oddly enough, that cracked everybody up and tensions loosened.

Guzman and Rashid approached a couple of young, drably attired Indian men who were scattering corn from gunny sacks to the chickens, and started a conversation. After they'd talked for a few minutes, Guzman announced the exhibition would open in about half an hour and all present were welcome to enjoy the buffet and stretch their legs. Andersen, Swayne, and the French software team headed for the pavilion and mosquito netting.

Meanwhile, Fedor fetched sampler bottles of vodka supplied by his company and passed them around. Kenshi surprised himself by accepting one. His throat had parched during the drive and he welcomed the excuse to slip away from Hendrika whose orbit had yet again swung her all too close to him.

He strolled off a bit from the others, swiping at the relentless bugs and wishing he'd thought to wear that rather dashing Panama hat he'd "borrowed" from a lover on location in the Everglades during a sweltering July shoot. His stroll carried him behind a metal shed overgrown with banyan vines. A rotting wooden addition abutted the sloppy edge of a pond or lagoon; it was impossible to know because of the cloying mist. He lit a cigarette. The porch was cluttered with disintegrating crates and rudimentary gardening tools. Gingerly lifting the edge of a tarp slimy with moss, he discovered a quantity of new plastic barrels. *Hydrochloric Acid, CORROSIVE!*, and a red skull and crossbones warned of hazardous contents. He quickly snatched back his hand and moved away lest his cigarette trigger a calamity worthy of a Darwin Award.

"Uh, yeah—good idea, Sulu. Splash that crap on you and your face will melt like glue." Walther had sneaked up behind him. The man drained his mini vodka bottle and tossed it into the bushes. He drew another bottle from the pocket of his sweat-stained dress shirt and had a pull. The humidity was awful here; it pressed down in a smothering blanket. His hair lay in sticky clumps and his face was shiny and red. He breathed heavily, laboring as if the brief walk from the van had led up several flights of stairs.

Kenshi stared at him, considering and discarding a series of snappy retorts. "Asshole," he finally said under his breath. He flicked his cigarette butt toward the scummy water, edged around Walther, and made for the vans.

Walther laughed. "Jap fag," he said. The fat man unzipped and began pissing off the end of the porch.

"I'm not even fucking Japanese, you idiot," Kenshi said over his shoulder. No good, he realized; the tremor in his voice, the quickening of his shuffle betrayed his cowardice in the face of adversity. This instinctive recoil from trouble, the resultant wave of self-loathing and bitter recriminations, was as it ever had been with Kenshi. Swayne would've smashed the jerk's face.

Plucking the thought from the air, Walther called, "Don't go tell your Limey boyfriend on me!"

Guzman gathered everyone into a huddle as Kenshi approached. He stood on the running board of a van and explained the three rules regarding their impending tour of the exhibition: no touching, no souvenirs, no pictures. "Mr. Vasilov will come around and secure all cell phones, cameras, and recorders. Don't worry, your personal effects will be returned as soon as the tour concludes. Thank you for your cooperation."

Fedor dumped the remaining limes and pears from a hotel gift basket and came around and confiscated the proscribed items. Beyond a few exaggerated sighs, no one really protested; the prohibition of cameras and recording devices at galleries and exclusive viewings was commonplace. Certainly, this being Van Iblis and the epitome of scofflaw art, there could be no surprise regarding such rules.

At the appointed time the warehouse doors rattled and slid aside and a blond man in a paper suit emerged and beckoned them to ascend the ramp. He was large, nearly the girth of Andersen the Viking, and wore elbow length rubber gloves and black galoshes. A black balaclava covered the lower half of his face. The party filed up the gangway in pairs, Guzman and Fedor at the fore. Kenshi and Swayne were the next to last. Kenshi watched the others become swiftly dissolving shadows backlit as they were by a bank of humming fluorescent lamps. He thought of cattle and slaughter pens and fingered his passport in its wallet on a string around his neck. Swayne squeezed his arm.

Once the group had entered, five more men, also clothed in paper suits and balaclavas, shut the heavy doors behind them with a clang that caused Kenshi's flesh to twitch. He sickly noted these five wore machetes on their belts. Blood rushed to his head in a breaker of dizziness and nausea. The reek of alcohol sweat and body odor tickled his gorge. The flickering light washed over his companions, reflected in their black eyes, made their faces pale and strange and curiously lifeless, as if he'd been suddenly trapped with brilliantly sculpted automatons. He understood then that they too had spotted the machetes. Mouths hung open in moist exclamations of apprehension and dread and the inevitable thrill derived from the alchemy of these emotions. Yet another man, similarly garbed as his compatriots, wheeled forth a tripod mounted Panaflex motion picture camera and began shooting the scene.

The floor creaked under their gathered weight. Insulating foam paneled the walls. Every window was covered in black plastic. There were two narrow openings at the far end of the entry area; red paint outlined the first opening, blue paint the second. The openings let into what appeared to be darkened spaces, their gloom reinforced by translucent curtains of thick plastic similar to the kind that compartmentalized meat lockers.

"You will strip," the blond man said in flat, accented English.

Kenshi's testicles retracted, although a calmness settled over his mind. He dimly acknowledged this as the animal recognition of its confinement in a trap and the inevitability of what must ultimately occur. Yet, one of this fractious group would argue, surely Walther the boor, or obstreperous

Andersen, definitely and assuredly Swayne. But none protested, none resisted the command, all were docile. One of the anonymous men near the entrance took out his machete and held it casually at his waist. Wordlessly, avoiding eye contact with each other, Kenshi's fellow travelers began to remove their clothes and arrange them neatly, or not so much, as the case might be, in piles on the floor. The blond instructed them to form columns and face the opposite wall. The entire affair possessed the quality of a lucid dream, a not-happening-in-the-real world sequence of events. Hendrika was crying, he noted before she turned away and presented him with her thin backside, a bony ridge of spine, spare haunches. She'd drained white.

Kenshi stood between an oddly subdued Swayne and one of the Frenchmen. He was acutely anxious regarding his sagging breasts, the immensity of his scarred and stretched belly, his general flaccidity, and almost chuckled at the absurdity of it all.

When the group had assembled with their backs to him, the blond man briskly explained the guests would be randomly approached and tapped on the shoulder. The designated guests would turn and proceed into the exhibit chambers by twos. Questions? None were forthcoming. After a lengthy pause it commenced. Beginning with Guzman and Fedor, each of them were gradually and steadily ushered out of sight with perhaps a minute between pairings. The plastic curtains swished and crackled with their passage. Kenshi waited his turn and stared at the curdled yellow foam on the walls.

The tap on the shoulder came and he had sunk so far into himself it was only then he registered everyone else had gone. The group comprised an uneven number, so he was odd man out. Abruptly, techno music blared and snarled from hidden speakers, and beneath the eardrum-shattering syncopation, a shrill, screeching like the keening of a beast or the howl of a circular saw chewing wood.

"Well, friend," said the blond, raising his voice to overcome the music, "you may choose."

Kenshi found it difficult to walk a straight line. He staggered and pushed through the curtain of the blue door into darkness. There was a long corridor and at its end another sheet of plastic that let in pale light. He shoved aside the curtain and had a moment of sick vertigo upon realizing there were no stairs. He cried out and toppled, arms waving, and flopped the eight or so feet into a pit of gravel. His leg broke on impact, but he didn't notice until later. The sun filled his vision with white. He thrashed in the gravel, dug furrows with elbows and heels and screamed soundlessly because the air had been driven from his lungs. A shadow leaned over him and brutally gripped his hair and clamped his face with what felt like a wet cloth. The cloth went into his nose, his mouth, choked him.

The cloth tasted of death.

* * *

THANKS TO A series of tips, authorities found him three weeks later in the closet of an abandoned house on the fringes of Bangalore. Recreating events, and comparing these to the experiences of those others who were discovered at different locations but in similar circumstances, it was determined he'd been pacified with drugs unto a stupor. His leg was infected and he'd lost a terrible amount of weight. The doctors predicted scars, physical and otherwise.

There'd been police interviews: FBI, CIA, NSA. Kenshi answered and answered and they eventually let him go, let him get to work blocking it, erasing it to the extent erasing it was possible. He avoided news reports, refused the sporadic interviews, made a concentrated effort to learn nothing of the aftermath, although he suspected scant evidence remained, anyway. He took a leave of absence and cocooned himself.

Kenshi remembered nothing after the blue door and he was thankful.

MONTHS AFTER THEIR second and last reunion, Swayne rang him at home and asked if he wanted to meet for cocktails. Swayne was in New York for an auction, would be around over the weekend, and wondered if Kenshi was doing all right, if he was surviving. This was before Kenshi began to lie awake in the dark of each new evening, disconnected from the cold pulse of the world outside the womb of his apartment, his hotel room, the cabs of his endless stream of rental cars. He dreamed the same dream; a recurring nightmare of acid-filled barrels knocked like dominoes into a trench, the grumbling exertions of a red bulldozer pushing in the dirt.

I've seen the tape, Swayne said through a blizzard of static.

Kenshi said nothing. He breathed, in and out. Starless, the black ceiling swung above him, it rushed to and fro, in and out like the heartbeat of the black Atlantic tapping and slapping at old crumbling seawalls, not far from his own four thin walls.

I've seen it, Swayne said. After another long pause, he said, *Say something, Ken.*

What?

It does exist. Van Iblis made sure copies were circulated to the press, but naturally the story was killed. Too awful, you know? I got one by post a few weeks ago. A reporter friend smuggled it out of a precinct in Canada. The goddamned obscenity is everywhere. And I didn't have the balls to look. Yesterday, finally.

That's why you called. Kenshi trembled. He suddenly wanted to know. Dread nearly overwhelmed him. He considered hanging up, chopping off Swayne's distorted voice. He thought he might vomit there, supine in bed, and drown.

Yeah. We were the show. The red door people were the real show, I guess. God help us, Ken. Ever heard of a Palestinian hanging? Dangled from your wrists, cinder blocks tied to your ankles? That's what the bastards started with. *When they were done, while the people were still alive...*" Swayne stopped there, or his next words were swallowed by the static surf.

Of course, Van Iblis made a film. No need for Swayne to illuminate him on that score, to open him up again. Kenshi thought about the empty barrels near the trench. He thought about what Walther said to him behind the shed that day.

I don't even know why I picked blue, mate, Swayne said.

He said to Swayne, *Don't ever fucking call me again.* He disconnected and dropped the phone on the floor and waited for it to ring again. When it didn't, he slipped into unconsciousness.

One day his copy arrived in a plain envelope via anonymous sender. He put the disk on the sidewalk outside of his building and methodically crushed it under the heel of his wingtip. The doorman watched the whole episode and smiled indulgently, exactly as one does to placate the insane.

Kenshi smiled in return and went into his apartment and ran a bath. He slashed his wrists with the broken edge of a credit card. Not deep enough; he bled everywhere and was forced to hire a service to steam the carpets. He never again wore short sleeve shirts.

Nonetheless, he'd tried. There was comfort in trying.

KENSHI RETURNED TO the Indian port town on company business a few years later. Models were being flown in from Mumbai and Kolkata for a photo shoot near the old monastery. The ladies wouldn't arrive for another day and he had time to burn. He hired a taxi and went looking for the Van Iblis site.

The field wasn't difficult to find. Developers had drained the swamp and built a hotel on the site, as advertised. They'd hacked away nearby wilderness and plopped down high-rise condos, two restaurants, and a casino. The driver dropped him at the Ivory Tiger, a glitzy, towering edifice. The lobby was marble and brass and the staff a pleasant chocolate mahogany, all of whom dressed smartly, smiled perfectly white smiles, and spoke flawless English.

He stayed in a tenth floor suite, kept the blinds drawn, the phone unplugged, the lights off. Lying naked across crisp, snow-cool sheets was to float disembodied through a great silent darkness. A handsome businessman, a fellow American, in fact, had bought him a white wine in the lounge; a sweet talker, that one, but Kenshi retired alone. He didn't get many erections these days and those that came ended in humiliating fashion. Drifting through insoluble night was safer.

In the morning, he ate breakfast and smoked a few cigarettes and had his first drink of the day. He was amazed how much he drank and how little effect it had on him anymore. After breakfast he walked around the hotel grounds, which were very much a garden, and stopped at the tennis courts. No one was playing; thunderclouds massed and the air smelled of rain. By his estimation, the tennis courts were near to, if not directly atop the old field. Drainage grates were embedded at regular intervals and he went to his knees and pressed the side of his head against one until the cold metal flattened his ear. He listened to water rushing through subterranean depths. Water fell through deep, hollow spaces and echoed, ever more faintly. And, perhaps, borne through yards of pipe and clay and gravel that hold, some say, fragments and frequencies of the past, drifted whispery strains of laughter, Victrola music.

He caught himself speculating about who else went through the blue door, the exit to the world of the living, and smothered this line of conjecture with the bribe of more drinks at the bar, more sex from this day on, more whatever it might take to stifle such thoughts forever. He was happier thinking Hendrika went back to her weather job once the emotional trauma subsided, that Andersen the Viking was ever in pursuit of her dubious virtue, that the Frenchmen and the German photographer had returned to their busy, busy lives. And Rashid... .Blue door. Red door. They might be anywhere.

The sky cracked and rain poured forth.

Kenshi curled into a tight ball, chin to chest and closed his eyes. Swayne kissed his mouth and they were crushingly intertwined. Acid sluiced over them in a wave, then the lid clanged home over the rim of the barrel and closed them in.

'STRAPPADO" WAS INSPIRED *by Edgar Allan Poe's oeuvre as a whole, but I credit the influence of that unholy duo "The Cask of Amontillado" and "The Masque of the Red Death" in particular. Revelry, privilege, decadence, and deceit are prevalent in both Poe tales and, as in my story, the revelers are participants in their own destruction.*

Favorite bits of symmetry between "The Cask of Amontillado" and my piece: Fortunato's inexorable descent into the catacombs (even as his animal brain protests) unto his eventual live burial, which corresponds with the seduction and betrayal of the thrill-seekers in "Strappado." The clues in "The Cask of Amontillado" are blatant; were it not for Fortunato's arrogance, his drunken stupor, it seems clear he would've escaped this most gruesome fate. He is paralyzed by disbelief and so perishes. I do not think any other piece of literature has ever so expertly provoked in me such a feeling of dread and revulsion; certainly, it remains a haunting tale.

The influence of "The Masque of the Red Death" is much different. Where "The Cask of Amontillado" has always struck me in a visceral, almost physical way, "The Masque of the Red Death" remains a much more visual proposition with its lush colors and descriptions and gothic symbolism. Prospero's seven chambers, and, of course, the Red Death Itself are powerfully compelling. Two rooms from the palace maze, the first, Blue, and the terminus, Red, are represented by the painted doors in "Strappado." Life and Death respectively. "The Masque of the Red Death" always impressed me with one lesson among others: there is no safety in numbers. That makes it a tremendously effective horror story.

SHARYN MCCRUMB is a Southern writer, whose novel *St. Dale*, considered the *Canterbury Tales* in a NASCAR setting, won a 2006 Library of Virginia Award as well as the AWA Book of the Year Award. Her most recent novel *Once Around the Track,* again set in NASCAR, was a nominee for the 2007 Weatherford Award. She has been selected by The Library of Virginia as one of their honorees for the 2008 Virginia Women in History.

McCrumb is best known for her Appalachian "Ballad" novels, set in the North Carolina/Tennessee mountains. Her novels include *New York Times* best-sellers *She Walks These Hills* and *The Rosewood Casket,* and *The Ballad of Frankie Silver, The Songcatcher,* and *Ghost Riders.* A film of *The Rosewood Casket* is currently in production, directed by British Academy Award nominee Roberto Schaefer.

McCrumb's honors include the Wilma Dykeman Award for Literature given by the East Tennessee Historical Society, AWA Outstanding Contribution to Appalachian Literature Award, the Chaffin Award for Achievement in Southern Literature, the Plattner Award for Short Story, and AWA's Best Appalachian Novel. She is a graduate of the University of North Carolina at Chapel Hill, and received her M.A. in English from Virginia Tech.

McCrumb's books have been translated into more than ten languages, and she was the first writer-in-residence at King College in

Tennessee. In 2001 she served as fiction writer-in-residence at the WICE Conference in Paris, and in 2005 she was honored as the writer of the year at the annual literary celebration at Emory and Henry College. Sharyn McCrumb has lectured on her work at Oxford University, the Smithsonian Institution, the University of Bonn, Germany, and at universities and libraries throughout the country.

The Mountain House

by Sharyn McCrumb

A PLAQUE, A *photo, a cardboard likeness*. Well, they will find none of those things here. Oh, they all exist, and I have them still, but they are packed away in the other house, buried with the life I have now escaped, as surely as Liam has escaped his.

I cannot honestly say that Liam loved this mountain house. Perhaps he did, for all I know, but he was never here very much. I was trying to please him when I chose it, but he may have let me buy it as much for the tax advantages as to spend time in this place. "But you grew up in these hills," I said once, as he looked down from our limestone terrace at the newly-landscaped ridges studded with what he called "stone and glass excrescences," built by the other summer people. He shuddered a little. "*I'm not from here*," he said. "*Not from this place*."

Well, naturally the area has changed since he was a raw-boned mountain boy. But at least it is close to heaven. One cannot argue with that.

He did come from these mountains, long ago before I knew him. Back when he was not Liam, the exalted racing champion, but plain old *Billy,* a north Georgia dirt track driver—before the fame and the money bronzed his life until the only mountains around him were barriers of handlers and managers, buffers between him and everything else. When I chose this stone and glass eyrie on a north Georgia cliff top, I thought I had found the best of both worlds for us: an elegant home in an exclusive enclave with other people from our social stratum, and all around us the enfolding hills he always said he missed so much. I don't know what else he could have wanted.

Sometimes I would stand outside under a blanket of stars and wonder if he might be up there, looking down on me in some form of heroic transfiguration. There must be scores of people out there who would believe that implicitly, but I was not one of them. Or else I fancied that he might be here beside me, if only I can turn around quickly enough. If there is a hereafter, he ought to spend it watching over me, instead of staying out there with *them*. Surely now that he's dead, it can be my turn at last.

The local people come by sometimes to deliver flowers (on *his* birthday, never on mine, or on the anniversary of some memorable race he'd won). Sometimes they bring me letters from strangers that were put by mistake into their mailboxes. As I stand on the threshold, I can see them peering past me, down the hall, into the glass-walled great room, looking for the contrails of Liam's fame: a model of the race car, a bronze plaque, a photo of him with a president or film star, a life-size cardboard effigy of Liam himself, taken a few weeks before his death—arms folded, staring into the camera with that bleak look I could never quite decipher. Now, though, I think I have worked out the meaning of that somber expression, so different from those first posed publicity pictures they took of him, back when he was just beginning the journey that has brought me here and him—nowhere.

In the earliest of the publicity photos—and ten years ago hardly seems a long time, looking back—Liam, with shaggy hair and dancing blue eyes, sports a royal blue firesuit, mugging at the camera with an aw-shucks grin, still marveling at his good fortune, happy to bask in the light of his new-found celebrity. He is a chosen one, ready to pay any price for that Cup ride. A decade later, the face in the frame is a solemn man in black and gold, with mournful eyes and a chiseled face infinitely more handsome through time and experience, but minus the joy he took with him when he started. I see nothing of the jubilant boy in the face of this somber successor. Now he is like a one-star general who has seen the war, not from a desk in the Pentagon, but from a blood-soaked battlefield. The youthful smile is gone; supplanted by the weary resignation of one who is forced to live with his wishes granted.

It isn't fun anymore. He knows it, but the rest of them don't. You can die out there. He knows that, too. He has a scar for every time that lesson was repeated. The younger ones drive dirt track in *podunk* on weeknights under playful *nommes de guerre*, too impatient for the clatter of their own heartbeats to wait for the real race on Sunday. But Liam only races professional. Through the week he goes to practices and crew conferences, meetings and banquets, publicity appearances and commercial shoots. He poses for pictures with rapturous fans and signs his name a few hundred more times, always with a weather eye on the inexorable approach of Sunday next.

At daybreak in the hours before the race, I pretend to be asleep as I listen to him throwing up in the bathroom. Later, when he steps out of the motor home into a field of microphones and camera lights, he makes bland remarks in a toneless voice, and they take his numbness for courage.

But he knew. *He knew.*

The people who come to the mountain house to pry probably know about that last trophy, too. It is not here, either. The one he did not win. The victor that day, that West Coast boy with the bland, perfect face of a plastic doll, won the race that Liam never finished, and afterward he brought the brass monstrosity to me as an offering, kindly meant, or perhaps subconsciously he intended it a sacrifice to some nemesis so that he should not be the next one... the next one. In racing there is always a next one.

I accepted the trophy, because to do so was easier than explaining why the thing meant nothing to me. It meant a great deal to the winner. That was the point. I took it, and, mindful of Biblical precedent, I kissed his cheek. I did not say, *Why don't you go back out there to the eternal sunshine, and lose yourself in the movies? Be famous for your face; it's good enough for that. What business have you out there, playing hole and corner with death every Sunday afternoon. The road is a circle, all right. Don't you know where it leads?*

I CAME HERE to the mountain house a few weeks after it happened. After the carefully choreographed public memorial service, after decorous press releases and days of business meetings that melded into one long ordeal of signing pieces of paper.

I work in the garden now in the cool of the evening. It gives me something to do with my hands while I think, turning over in my mind all the things I never actually said to Liam. *Why don't you quit then? Surely we have enough money for that. Why don't you walk away... while you can?* Unspoken. Useless, really. Because he couldn't walk away. Back to being nobody. Or perhaps he just loved it. Even when his hands shook so much he could barely put on his driving gloves, he would not have turned back.

The closest I ever heard him come to expressing regret came once when I walked him to the car at Darlington and he murmured, "I just wish it could be fun again."

The service was lovely. The governor said a few words. The president sent a telegram. Inside the church in a jungle of flowers were the same sleek people one might expect to find at a film premiere or aboard someone's yacht off St. Thomas. Drivers do not attend the funerals of their comrades in racing. I think it is a superstition, perhaps a shadow of guilt that some move of theirs in the race might have set in motion the fatal chain of events, or even a primitive fear that the taint of mortality will touch them, and that they will be next. It is too easy to die out there. But Liam had friends in many other areas of celebrity, and some of them came: the country singers whose music he loved, the movie stars he met when he did cameos in their films, and the football players and professional golfers who were his fans just as he was theirs.

Outside on the church lawn, standing vigil in the rain, were the others: the truck drivers, the store clerks, and all those pitiful women who loved whatever image of Liam they had conjured from that face on the key chain, the coffee mug. And somewhere, caught between the celebrities and the people in the rain, was Liam.

At the close of the service, a black pop star, blonder than I am, sang "Abide With Me" in a throaty gospel contralto. I think he would have liked that old hymn. As a child he had attended a mountain Baptist church, where they sang old-fashioned hymns and baptized the faithful in a cold mountain stream. Of course, most of the races are on Sunday, so the closest he came to church when I knew him was a little tent in the speedway infield, where a NASCAR pastor said a generic prayer that all the drivers should come back safely.

Abide With Me. I found the song in an old hymn book as I planned the service at the big church in Charlotte with the bishop, the rabbi, and the Air Force chaplain. Even in death, Liam must be all things to all people... One verse intrigued me.

Come not in terrors, as the King of Kings,
But kind and good, with healing in Thy wings...

"We don't usually sing that verse," the cathedral's music director told me, but I requested it anyhow. Its words comforted me in a way that nothing else had.

Afterward, I came away to this house in Liam's mountains, bent on solitude. I brought no one with me. The television stayed dark in the corner by the stone fireplace. When I ventured outside, it was only to instill perfection in the garden.

Once while I was pulling creeper vines out of a bed of pink impatiens, I found myself thinking, "I wonder where Liam has gone," and when I remembered that he had died, the question did not quite resolve itself.

THE FIRST TIME I saw the boy it was nearly dusk. I knew that he didn't belong to one of the families up here. He looked all right—they all wear shabby jeans and tee shirts nowadays—but there was an exotic look about his wiry frame, his black hair and dark almond eyes, that told me the boy was "local." I do not even think "hillbilly." Liam would not allow anyone to use that word. He said that political correctness had not made the public any kinder or wiser, only more careful about whom they bullied. He said he wouldn't have his people belittled by bigots too cowardly to pick on any of the more protected ethnic groups. *His people.* Even when he owned a jet, a yacht, and two beach houses, he still thought of himself as one of them. When I pointed out this discrepancy between his privileged life and the simple people of the mountains, he had laughed.

"Oh, there are plenty of rich people in these mountains. Doctors, lawyers, judges, millionaire furniture company owners whose families go back more than a century in these hills, but you'll never meet them. They wouldn't be caught dead associating with the likes of the summer people. The only folks you'll ever meet are the ones you hire. The gardener. The cleaning woman. The handyman."

"But you are from here originally," I protested. "Surely they'd associate with you,"

He shrugged. "Not up here," he said. So perhaps he passed the time of day with the local people when he went into town for a haircut or on some errand for me, but if he did have friends here, I never met them. He never brought them here to our home.

But now I had company—one of *them*. I judged this boy to be about fourteen. In another time he wouldn't have been out of place on this mountain in buckskin and moccasins, but now in faded Levis and battered sneakers, he simply looked like one of the cove dwellers scouting for odd jobs here among the summer people.

Squatting on his haunches beside the flower bed, he watched me work with clinical interest. I turned to ask him what he'd come about, and it was then that I noticed his tee shirt: *Davey Allison–Rising Star*. It was a crisp, unfaded black, the yellow star and the black and red-orange 28 car bright as new. *Davey Allison*.

"You shouldn't be wearing that shirt out and about," I told him. "It's probably worth something."

He raised his eyebrows. "Huh?"

"*Davey Allison. The Rising Star*? He died ten years ago at Talladega. The shirt is a collector's item. It ought to be kept in a box—not worn."

"You know about stock car racing?"

His tone of incredulity nettled me. "I should," I said, stabbing at the creeper vine with my trowel.

He watched me in silence for a few moments, and then without a word he bent forward and began to pull more vine tendrils from the bed of impatiens. If he had pressed sympathy on me, or asked about Liam; if he'd said anything at all, I might have snubbed him and sent him on his way, but the companionable silence was oddly comforting, as if a friendly collie had ambled up to keep me company.

"I was married to Liam Bethel," I said at last, still intent upon the encroaching weeds. "I suppose you knew that."

He shrugged. "Knew he lived somewhere up here."

"And *you* don't."

He smiled. "My people have been on this mountain a long time," he said.

I knew he was a local. NASCAR tee shirts are not worn up here on the hill. Summer people may watch the races on big-screen TVs, but they do not wear their hearts on their sleeves—or on their shirts. We are different from the local people. They are polite enough to us, but there is a wariness there that warns us not to try to get too close, in any sense.

"Do you mind how things have changed up here?" I had asked the boy after a few days' acquaintance. I nodded toward the cluster of stone mansions crowning the mountain top, barricaded away from his world in the valley by a gated guardhouse at the main road.

He shrugged. "I don't think these people really want to be here."

I was puzzled. Surely if you spend a million dollars on a home…

But he went on. "In the gift shops now they play Navajo flute music. They decorate their homes in desert colors as if they thought north Georgia bordered New Mexico. It's not that they're here that I mind. It's that they want to make *here* somewhere else."

"But we don't really live here," I reminded him. "We only come for a while to get away from real life."

In those dark Indian eyes I caught a flicker of Liam's bleak-eyed stare. "They come up here," he said softly, "they shouldn't change it and take it away from them that loved it like it was."

AFTER A FEW more evenings of weeding and comfortable silence, I learned that the boy's name was Eddie. I didn't quite catch his surname, but it sounded very like those peculiar place names one finds in Georgia and Alabama. Names like Ellijay and Hiwassee—oh, yes, and Talladega. I knew that last one well enough. The sight of the north Alabama speedway bearing that name gives me chills. Talladega is haunted, people said, built on an old Indian burial ground. Talladega is the fastest track in NASCAR, so fast that the race teams put restrictor plates on the carburetors to keep the cars from going airborne. Drivers often made the half-joking remark: *Be careful. Talladega will kill you.* Oh, yes.

Anyhow, Eddie's last name sounded like Cho-sto. I didn't like to ask again, for to misunderstand would be yet another way for me to be an outsider showing my ignorance of this place and its traditions. Once I tried to give him a handful of dollar bills for his help in the garden, but he only smiled and waved it away. By then I was glad of his company, and had only been looking for a way to cement the bargain. Liam would have known not to offer him money. He knew these people, but I can only guess at what motivates them to do anything.

I began to think that perhaps Eddie's people were better off than I had at first supposed. I had an idea that they might be silkscreen printers—these hills are full of jackleg craftsmen, making pottery in wood-fired kilns or fashioning oak furniture one piece at a time, making just enough money to get by on. We hire them to custom-make our kitchen cabinets or to build stone walls in our gardens.

I thought Eddie's people might be silkscreen printers, because every day he wore a different racing shirt of a racing legend—Dale Earnhardt, Neil Bonnett, Tim Richmond—all looking like new, even though all those drivers had been dead for years. *His family manufactures these reproductions of racing legends,* I thought, and I wondered if I ought to have a word with them about trademark infringement, but I was too tired to care, really. What does it matter if poor country people sell a few bootlegged tee shirts of dead drivers here in the back of beyond?

One day, though, when Eddie was decked out in *Fireball Roberts*, who had died at Charlotte in 1963, I felt an unaccountable spurt of irritation. "Don't you have a Liam Bethel shirt?" I said.

Eddie shrugged. "Wouldn't be right to wear one here. *You* being up here and all."

"I wouldn't mind," I said, although I didn't know that until I heard myself say it aloud. "Just don't wear some cheap reproduction. Come inside."

We kept caps and shirts and race trinkets in a drawer up here to give away in case, say, the TV repair man or the plumber should turn out to be a fan of racing. From the bureau in the guest room I dug out an old tee shirt commemorating Liam's first Cup win at Bristol. On the front of the shirt was the smiling boy that Liam had once been, grinning up at me with the radiant joy that had faded a long time ago. When it stopped being fun out there.

"Here," I said to that other mountain boy. "Have it. You were his neighbor."

Eddie thanked me solemnly, and soon afterward he went away, with the Liam Bethel tee shirt tucked reverently under his arm. It was only then that I remembered the curious sense of honor these mountain people had. If you ever did them the slightest good turn, they would be forever your vassal, and they would go to any length to repay a kindness. I hoped if the boy felt compelled to return a favor that it would come in the form of tomatoes from the family garden, and nothing more valuable or troublesome than that.

A DAY OR two later, in the gray evening when the deer venture out of the woods, Eddie returned, empty-handed, but still in my debt, it seemed.

"Come on. I want to show you something!" he said, fairly dancing with excitement.

Inwardly, I sighed. What had he to show me? A litter of pigs? A prize watermelon? A hundred newly-bootlegged copies of Liam's victory shirt? But I went with him anyhow, because I had grown tired of pulling up creeping vines from my flower bed. No matter how many times I ripped out the invader's new shoots, more would have taken their place by the next time I weeded. I had said as much to Liam once, and he had only smiled and said, "It is a fact of nature. That's probably why the folks around here don't burn down these McMansions."

In the gathering twilight I followed Eddie into the woods, away from the soaring glass houses on manicured lawns, over to the other side of the mountain top and into even deeper woods, following no path that I could discern, but Eddie's pace never slowed. The sun was nearly gone, and in the night air the chill deepened.

"Is it much farther?" I asked, but he simply gestured forward and quickened his pace, so I stumbled on after him, pushing aside the pine branches, as we went farther and farther from the bright, safe houses on the edge of the mountain. I knew that without him it would take hours to find my way back.

"Don't leave me!" I called out, but he only slowed down for a moment, before beckoning me forward again.

Long minutes passed, punctuated only by the sound of twigs snapping as I hurried to keep up with this boy, who neither stumbled nor slowed. I could see the stars again now, for the pines thinned as we reached the edge of the ridge.

We stood on the edge of a precipice, where an outcropping of rock formed a ledge overhanging the valley below. I was disoriented, and did not know in which direction we had come. Should this be the side of the mountain that overlooked the village crossroads far below, or was it the wilderness side that gave out onto trees and a rock-studded stream?

In any case, neither of those vistas spread out before me.

I saw the dark shape of a forest stretching to the mountains across the valley, but directly below us lay a circular field ablaze with lights. I could make out an oval of red Georgia mud, encircled by a rickety grandstand of the sort one saw at high school baseball fields forty years ago. Within the oval was an assortment of battered haulers, campers, old pick-up trucks, and here and there a garishly painted stock car.

A dirt track.

Well, they are common enough in north Georgia, but I had not known that one existed so close to our enclave. Surely some of the residents up here would have complained about it. Liam used to say that he attended the Residents' Meeting to make sure that they were not planning to hand out smallpox-infected blankets to the locals. Of course, they would do no such thing, but I did think that they would object to a dirt track in proximity of their luxury homes.

Eddie had knelt down on the ledge. He tapped my arm, pointing excitedly at the spectacle below. Mud flew and a phalanx of cars slid forward, spraying red mud in their wake. A race had begun. I watched the rainbow of cars circle the track for a moment, and the one that pulled ahead as it took the corner at full speed caught my eye. Red and silver. Liam's number. The paint scheme identical, even down to the sponsors' logos.

Rage struggled with amazement. Was this what he had come to show me? This cheap imitation, this flagrant image theft, a greater sacrilege than a few knock-off tee shirts?

"You can't do this!" I said, shouting into the silence, for the sounds of the track did not carry all the way to the mountain top. They had copied my husband's race car in every detail. I kept staring down at the track below, while I screamed the words into the wind. *Copyright infringement... lawyers... fraud...* "I won't allow it!"

I shook with fury, the grieving widow now suddenly transformed into the keeper of the flame. Of the business, at least. I was ready to call lawyers to this solitary mountaintop, as one might summon dragons.

I paused, gasping for breath, and I would have said more, but all the while I had been staring down at those cars weaving and cornering around the track in a pavane on wheels. The way they took the corners at full speed, but never got loose. The way they passed on the track, a tap on the bumper here and there, but no driver spun out. No one hit the wall.

How many races had I seen over the years? Five hundred? A thousand? Watching at first only to see if Liam would walk away, but finally understanding the rhythms of the dance. At last able to judge the skill of the dancers themselves. I had seen them all, and without consciously trying to train my eye, I became able to tell good from great. I could discern style. I cannot explain it. A horse show judge will tell you that before a rider is halfway across a ring he will know the novice from the expert, even at a walk. After a while you just *know*.

As I knew now.

The pink 51. The red 25. The black and red-orange 28. The black number three. Oh, yes. I knew them all. And right out there among them, where he belonged, was Liam in his red and silver Chevy. All of them driving like no backwoods dirt track driver ever could, in perfect control, with surgical precision at breathless speeds—reaction time a blink, a heartbeat. A hundred things to watch all at once, swoop and glide, cut and corner, but never, never slowing down in the river of air.

It was them.

Neil Bonnett, killed at Daytona in 1994. The late Tim Richmond. Davey Allison, who had crashed his helicopter on the speedway grounds at Talladega in 1993. *Talladega will kill you.* Dale Earnhardt, the Intimidator, the man in black, who wouldn't take no for an answer, even from Death, apparently.

And my lost love, Liam.

Impossible, but just slightly less impossible than the notion that anyone but they could drive with such perfection... *And I looked and a whirlwind came out of the north...* Like angels in chariots. NASCAR's legends, but without crowds or cameras or a licensed speedway... Just *them...* Out here in the middle of nowhere.

And Liam. I had found him.

"But he shook his head, and held up his hands, imploring me not to follow as he turned back toward the dark woods. I stumbled after him, crying out for him to stop, not to leave me alone on the mountain. But in an instant he was gone, and when I could no longer hear the sound of his footfalls in the bracken, I turned back to the ledge, thinking that I would find my own way down to the valley. I would follow the lights.

But they, too, were gone.

I knelt down and crawled to the very edge of the precipice, leaning as far over as I dared, straining for a glimpse of what had been so clear before. All I saw from the rock outcrop was a dark and silent plain, black with an unbroken sea of trees. Cold and silent under the distant stars.

I HAVE WALKED this mountain every day since then, at dawn, at twilight, even sometimes at midnight when the dew soaks my shoes and the night mist turns my hair to sodden strings. But Eddie never came back, and the local people swear they have never heard of him. Or perhaps they had. At the general store one old man smiled at my question. "Choestoe, he said his name was? Why, ma'am, he must have been joshing you. I reckon there could be folks still around named that, but Choestoe means rabbit in Cherokee. The rabbit was the trickster god in Cherokee lore. He could help you or hurt you, depending on his mood—and,"—he looked at me appraisingly—"on how you treated him, I reckon."

I thanked the old man and left the store, knowing it was no use searching for the boy any more. But I could not help trying to find the place.

Abide with Me. Though I have walked those woods a hundred times, with that old hymn circling in my head, keeping time with my heartbeat, I have never found the rock ledge or that place in the valley where *heaven's morning breaks and earth's vain shadows flee.*

A plaque, a photo, a cardboard likeness. I have all these things still. And a stone and glass house on a mountain, close to heaven.

"THE MOUNTAIN HOUSE" *was quilted together from several sources of inspiration, beginning with "The Haunted Palace." That poem reminded me of the time I was giving a speech in a North Carolina mountain resort community on a Sunday afternoon, which meant that I was missing the NASCAR race. (In the course of researching my novel* St. Dale, *the* Canterbury Tales *set in NASCAR, I had become a fan of stock car racing, a sport which began in these mountains where the story is set.) When I finished my speech that afternoon, the race was still going on, so a kind stranger invited me up to watch it on TV at the mountain top mansion, where he was the caretaker. That house became the setting for the story, and both Eddie and Liam voice the sentiments of the native mountain people about this yuppie invasion. The rock ledge in the story exists atop Fort Mountain. I saw it a few months earlier while I was hiking with Georgia fantasy author Tom Deitz.*

The heart of the story is Liam, the dead race car driver. To create the character I propped two photos on my keyboard: the rookie year photo of a NASCAR driver friend of mine and a shot of him taken ten years later. I wrote what I saw in his face, and what I felt when I watched him race. In the 2001 Daytona 500, fourteen cars slammed into him broadside at 200 mph, and 25 laps later in that same race, Dale Earnhardt did die. That's where the story's grief and the terror came from—watching a good friend race week after week, and never being sure that he would come back safe.

The emotions in this story are genuine: the feelings about the danger and the beauty of stock car racing, and the resentment of the human kudzu who are invading the mountains.

BOTH OF GLEN HIRSHBERG'S first two collections, *American Morons* and *The Two Sams* won the International Horror Guild Award and were selected by *Locus* as one of the best books of the year. He is also the author of a novel, *The Snowman's Children*, and a five-time World Fantasy Award finalist. With Dennis Etchison and Peter Atkins, he co-founded the Rolling Darkness Revue, a traveling ghost story performance troupe that tours the west coast of the United States each October. His fiction has appeared in numerous magazines and anthologies, including multiple appearances in *The Year's Best Fantasy and Horror*, *The Mammoth Book of Best New Horror*, *Inferno*, *The Dark*, *Dark Terrors 6*, *Trampoline*, and *Cemetery Dance*. He lives in the Los Angeles area with his wife and children.

THE PIKESVILLE BUFFALO

by Glen Hirshberg

LATE THAT NOVEMBER, a few months after his twenty-four year-old wife was diagnosed with breast cancer, Daniel felt a sudden urge to see the Great Aunts. He tried Ethel first, calling five times over a two-hour period, but kept getting the busy signal which meant either that she was talking to one of her children or stepchildren or—more likely—that she'd taken her phone off the hook to avoid talking to them. Finally, he called Zippo and got her on the first try.

"Of course, dear," she told him, sounding muffled as ever, as though she were speaking through the orange wool shawl she always kept about her shoulders.

"Could you beam the news over to Aunt Ethel?"

"What? Oh, Daniel." It was an old joke, his father's, about the telepathic link that seemed to connect the sisters.

"How's your lovely Lisa, honey?" Zippo asked.

"Okay, I think. Still not sleeping very well. The doctors think they got it all."

"Poo-poo," said Zippo, and Daniel hung up.

The next morning, he awoke before five, kissed Lisa where she lay twisting in the blankets, and, for the first time in over a year, drove the hour and a half from his dumpy beach-neighborhood shack on the Delaware coast into Baltimore and out Reiserstown Road toward Pikesville. The early morning gray never lifted, and the grass everywhere had already died. Something about the old neighborhoods near the Great Aunts had always unsettled Daniel, even during his childhood when he'd visited them every weekend. The low, red-brick houses seemed to have too few windows, too many chimneys, and they were always tucked back in the shadows of the tallest trees on their lots like little warrens. Rotting, unraked leaves littered the lawns. The oaks and elms and black locusts stood midwinter-bare.

Pulling up outside Ethel's house—which was small, stone, and too long at either end for its slanted roof, as though emerging from the maples with its hands on its hips—Daniel shut off the car and was surprised to see his own hands shaking. He sat a few seconds, staring through the windshield at the gray, thinking not of Lisa but of cancer. It was true, what Zippo had told him not long after his father had died. Cancer didn't just kill people; it blurred them, left a hazy, pointillist blotch where memories of the lives they'd lived before the disease should have been.

Abruptly, he slammed his fist down on the horn. For all they knew, Lisa really was finished with cancer. Forever. They'd caught it early, taken it out. He really needed to get the hell over it.

Which was exactly why he'd come. Popping open the door, he stepped onto the pavement, expecting Pikesville silence, winter wind. Instead, he got Xavier Cugat.

Before he even reached his Aunt Ethel's front steps, Daniel was smiling. It wasn't just the incongruity—all those congas and horns sashaying down this street of old homes and older Jews—but the volume. Daniel swore he could see the surrounding houses shuddering on their foundations, the drawn curtains in nearby windows twitching their skirts. He half-expected the police to arrive any second.

Daniel tried the front doorbell first, but of course, that was useless. Hunching against the cold, he slipped around the side. He was already past the screened-in porch when his Aunt opened the side door.

"Oy-yoy-yoy," she said, nodding at his coat, one hand fluttering off the hips she could no longer shake and making mambo motions. "Is it really that cold out?"

Daniel stared. The rooster-crest springing from his aunt's scalp glowed a luminous, freshly dyed red. She was wearing blue-jean shorts, a yellow t-shirt with a Queen of Hearts playing card and the legend *Aunty Up, Baby* imprinted on it, and yellow vinyl slipper-sandals that displayed her virtually nail-less hammer toes in all their glory.

"Can't you feel it?" Daniel half-shouted, moving forward to give her a kiss.

"Skin of a crocodile." Aunt Ethel pulled demonstratively at the folds on her forearms.

"Toes of a troll."

She smacked him playfully on the cheek before kissing him in the same place, then smeared the lipstick she'd imprinted there. "You find a troll who looks this good at eighty-two, give him my number, okay?" With an arthritic lurch Daniel realized afterward was a butt-bump, Aunt Ethel shuffled off inside, beckoning him with more of her rhythmic, slinky hand movements.

"Aren't you worried about the neighbors?" Daniel called, shutting the door.

"What?"

"The racket. What if they call the cops?"

"The music? Honey, everyone within four blocks is stone deaf."

She disappeared into her tiny kitchen to bring him the bagel, lox, and purple onion tray he knew she'd have prepared and refrigerated for him last night. The stereo shut down, and for one delicious moment, Daniel found himself alone, submerged in the familiar dimness of his Aunt Ethel's house.

The memories that assailed him centered mostly around shivas, but were no less sweet for that: there was the midnight flag football game in the sleet fourteen years ago, two days after Uncle Harry's death, when Daniel's father—frail already, and with a hacksaw cough, but still slippery as a snowflake—solved the absence-of-spare-socks problem by suggesting they use yarmulkes for the flags instead; there was the morning he'd crept upstairs with Ethel's perpetually wan, humorless thirty-four year-old son Herm after the early Mourner's Kaddish at the shiva for Zippo's second husband Ivan. He and Herm had used an entire roll of electrical tape, some torn-up egg cartons, and a box of discarded nine-volt batteries to try to get Herm's homemade, childhood train set to run just one more time. It hadn't, but the light-towers at the miniature baseball stadium flicked on a few times, and one of the crossing gates lowered and its bells rang. There was the three-hour jokefest after Rabbi Goldberg went home on the last night of Mack's funeral two years ago. It began with Daniel's recitation of Mack's favorite about the rabbi, the leather worker, and the circumcised foreskins, and ended when Daniel's father—barely able to speak, and confined to a wheelchair he couldn't even sit up in—somehow gasped his way through the Fuck One Goat joke, while all the cousins and step-cousins alternately giggled and snuck glances at Aunt Ethel's half-horrified mouth, quivering as it fought the laughter welling behind it. Daniel had been laughing, too, until he saw Zippo leaning into the shadows against the hallway wall, her eyes riveted on his father, her mouth pursed and her shoulders drawn back as though she could do his breathing for him.

Or had that been at the shiva for Zippo's third husband, Uncle Joe, whom Daniel had only met twice, but who had the gorgeous lesbian granddaughter? Or for Uncle Bob, Mitchell's shyer, gentler oldest friend?

No. Mack's, because of the jokes. Just the way Mack would have wanted it. If he'd had his way, he'd probably have had Aunt Ethel blasting Xavier Cugat during the graveside service, too.

Standing now in Aunt Ethel's tan-carpeted living room with the tea mugs on glass shelves and the library-sale Dick Francis hardbacks lining the walls, Daniel thought of what his mother had called Aunt Zip, years and years ago:

the Angel of Mercy, or else the Worst Luck in the World. Tears teased the corners of his eyes, which had adjusted to the gloom, now. He glanced toward the wall of photos, blinked and moved closer.

"Uh… Aunt Ethel? Where'd everybody go?"

In she came, balancing not just the bagel tray but a chipped, porcelain jug of orange juice and a set of thirty year-old novelty glasses featuring stencils of Jim Palmer in his Jockey underwear on the sides.

"Eat; you look thin," she said, somehow maneuvering the tray and glasses onto the tiny coffee table. "I got your favorite. Onion, sesame, pumpernickel." She gestured toward the pile of toasted bagels.

"Just one of my favorites would have done."

"Well, I have to eat, too, don't I?"

Without waiting for him to choose, Aunt Ethel bent forward, drew half an onion bagel from the stack, and began slathering it with cream cheese and onion bits. Daniel gestured at the wall.

"Aunt Ethel, we really have to talk about you letting the buffalo herd play with the photographs."

She lifted an old, open hardback off the table out of the way of the food and held it to her chest. The phone rang.

"Ugh," she said. "I don't feel like talking."

Daniel grinned. "Okay, I'll leave."

She tsked and smacked his leg with the book, then studied him a while.

"Too thin," she said.

She reoffered the bagel, and Daniel took it, though he wasn't hungry. Almost casually, he glanced at his aunt's hands, looking for signs of shaking. There were none.

"Seriously," he said. "What happened to the boys?" He nodded toward the wall, most of which was blanketed with the same collage of framed snapshots of children and stepchildren and grandchildren Daniel had practically memorized during all those childhood visits, or more likely during the shivas, when there was so little to do but eat and stare at faces. But sometime in the past year, Aunt Ethel had apparently replaced the photos of herself and Aunt Zippo and the six husbands they'd buried between them.

"They're right there." She began pointing down the row of new photos, each of a different shaggy, horned, decrepit-looking buffalo standing atop a grassless little hill in front of a cyclone fence. Unless it was the same buffalo.

Laughing through a mouthful of bagel, Daniel said, "I meant your boys. Joe, Mack, Har—"

"There's Harry." Aunt Ethel directed his gaze toward the farthest-right buffalo. "Sleepy-eyed and slow as ever. Here's Joe. And see Mitchell, could he be any more of a cliché, do you think?"

Baffled, Daniel followed his Aunt's finger. This buffalo had one of its legs off the ground and its head lifted, gazing not at the grassless ground but through the fence.

"Look at him," Aunt Ethel said. "Still busy. Somewhere in that yard, some overwhelmed, mesmerized sheep dog just agreed to purchase the complete long-term care plus annuities package."

Daniel started to laugh again, but the expression on his aunt's face stopped him. She wore the same loving smile she'd always leveled at him. But she was looking at the photographs.

"Aunt Ethel. You're naming your buffalo pictures?"

"The buffalo, not the pictures." Folding the book against her chest, Aunt Ethel gave a satisfied sigh. "And we didn't name them, what are you talking about? Did you name Lisa?"

"What?"

"How is she, by the way? Oy vay, she's been through so much. You both have. So young."

Laying the book on the couch and pinching his cheek, Aunt Ethel toddled out of the room with the empty orange juice jug. Daniel stared after her. It should have been funny. Just the latest of the thousand ways his aunt had found to flood her days with happier thoughts than her days seemed to merit. He wondered if she'd told Zippo. Somehow, he didn't think Zippo would be amused.

Daniel looked down at the hardback on the couch, and bent to pick it up. It had no cover. But a number of its pages had been dog-eared, and when Daniel flipped to the first, he found a passage highlighted in bright pink marker. "*The Holy Spark that fell when God built and destroyed the worlds, man shall raise and purify, from stone to plant, from plant to animal... purify and raise the Holy Sparks that are imprisoned in the world of shells.*" Next to the word "shells," in the mock-parchment margins of the page, his aunt had drawn a smiley face.

Not Dick Francis, then. He flipped the book on its spine and raised an eyebrow. He'd never known his Aunt to crack a Sidur in synagogue, let alone the Kabbalah in her home.

"You're going to have to come to the graves, okay?" Aunt Ethel said from the other room, and Daniel started.

"I'm sorry?"

"Thursday's cemetery day, remember? I'd be okay skipping, I mean, they're not *there* anymore, but you know your other aunt. 'A grave needs stones.' So come with us, and afterwards we'll go get coddies."

"Ugh," Daniel murmured. "Is that even real fish in those things?"

"What do you think the mustard's for?"

Daniel started to smile, but stopped halfway. He was looking at the buffalo. Remembering Mitchell coming home from work, which is pretty much all anyone remembered of Mitchell. Harry with the trains. Most of all, Mack, spooling jokes through endless dinners, teaching his Aunt to rumba on two replaced hips.

For the first time in his life, he wondered if it had been a good idea coming here. He leaned forward to lay the book back on the couch, came face to face with the photograph of the buffalo with its leg in the air—Mitchell—and saw the cheetah for the first time.

Had that been there a second ago? Had he really not noticed that?

There it was, anyway, its nose to the gate of the fence in the background, one paw through the chicken wire. The blotchy, irregular spots on its fur looked more like mange than coloration, and there was an ugly pink patch above its back right haunch and another at the base of its neck.

"Aunt Ethel?" he called. "About this cheetah…"

"Mack?"

"*Mack?*"

The front door burst open, and Daniel swiveled toward it. From the tiny entranceway, he heard the scuffle of heavy boot heels, started to call a hello, but stopped when he heard the tremor in Zippo's voice.

"They're out. Ethel, my God, they're loose. All of them."

Daniel arrived just in time to see Aunt Ethel stumbling for the front closet, grabbing at the long, yellow overcoat she'd worn all of his life, and starting out the front door before Aunt Zip put a crooked, age-stained hand on her wrist.

"Honey, you're going to freeze."

With an annoyed glance at her shorts and t-shirt, Ethel hurried off down the back hallway toward her bedroom. That hallway, too, had always been lined floor to ceiling with family photographs, including a random series of Daniel at various ages, some of them with his parents. From where he was standing, Daniel could only see that there were still pictures. Had the one of his father been replaced, also? With orangutans, maybe?

Was there even one of Lisa? Had he ever given Aunt Ethel one?

Then Zippo's hand was on his cheek, pulling his gaze around. Where Ethel was essentially a fire hydrant with hammer toes, Zippo loomed like a tall, bent oak. Whatever dye she used either never took or she kept washing it out, because her gauzy hair was mostly white tinged with blue.

"Hello, Aunt Zip." He leaned in to kiss her, but halted midway. "Aunt Zip? What is it?"

Both of his aunts could produce tissues from mid-air the way magicians did coins. Almost always, the tissues were for others, but now Zippo dabbed at her own eyes. The orange eye-shadow on her lids looked caked and layered and permanent, like veins in sedimentary rock.

"Nothing, sweetie," she said. "It's your silly old aunts. You look thin."

Even more unsettled, Daniel kissed her anyway. "It's great to see you."

"Oh, Daniel. I'm so sorry you're having to deal with all this again. So soon after your dad, I mean. It's not fair."

"It's never fair," Daniel said quietly. "Isn't that what you taught my mom?"

"Yes." Aunt Zippo's face had long since begun to cave in, the nose sinking into its cavity and the mouth losing shape, and there were red, spidery blotches everywhere. She looked like a cherry pie. With whip cream hair. She dabbed once more with the tissue. The tissue vanished. "But I meant for me." With that singular smile that always looked half-melted, almost all mouth-turned-down, Zippo touched his cheek. Daniel felt simultaneously near tears and buoyed.

The Angel of Mercy. The Worst Luck in the World.

Ethel rumbled back into the entryway, and Aunt Zippo clucked.

"What?" Ethel snapped. "Let's go. Daniel, you're driving."

Ethel hadn't changed her top or her shorts. But she'd somehow yanked on yellow winter tights and a long-sleeved thermal undershirt beneath them. Feeling a surprising grin creep onto his lips, Daniel followed his aunts out the front door into the icy morning.

He actually had to hurry to get to the car before them and flip the locks. Before he could do it for her, Ethel had somehow bent low enough on her creaking hips to pull the passenger seat-lever and climb into the back.

"Ethel, I'll sit there," Zippo said.

"Oh, be quiet, you're too tall." Ethel yanked the seat into position in front of her. "Come on, Daniel."

"Ladies. Would either one of you like to tell me where we're going?"

For an astonishing moment, even Zippo looked exasperated with him. "The farm, honey. Where do you think?"

"The farm. Right. Either of you want to tell me which…" But he realized that he knew. At the same moment, he also realized what had seemed so strange about the buffalo on their hill. Other than the fact that there were photographs of them on his aunt's wall.

He'd seen those buffalo. Knew that hill.

"Buddy's Farm," he said.

"Of course, Buddy's Farm," Ethel snapped, "let's—"

"Oh," said Zippo, and moved off toward the white Le Sabre parked a good five yards behind Daniel's car and another five from the curb.

"Zippo!" Ethel called.

Ignoring her sister, Zippo leaned into her front seat and returned with a white baker's box wrapped in bowed white twine. She handed Daniel the box before circling the car and lowering herself into the passenger seat.

"That couldn't have waited until we got back?" Ethel asked as Daniel keyed the ignition.

"Daniel's here." Zippo smiled that upside down, half-melted smile and patted his leg. "Daniel gets chocolate tops."

The shudder that rippled across his shoulders startled him. At least it passed quickly. "Thank you, Aunt Zip," he said. He started to wrestle with the twine, and Zippo clucked and took the box from him and neatly unpicked the knot.

"Let's go," Ethel barked.

Mostly, Daniel knew the way, though he couldn't remember driving to Buddy's Farm himself before. In fact, he didn't even think he'd been there in at least ten years. The sun had slipped through the cloud cover, though its light served only to turn the dead grass and the bare trees whiter. He started to turn right, Ethel corrected him with a clipped, "No," and Zippo began pushing random buttons trying to tune his radio.

"What do you want to hear?" Daniel asked through a mouthful of thick, fudgy frosting from the cookie Aunt Zip had practically stuffed between his lips. "Don't know if I've got any big Xave, but—"

"The news, honey. The update. Hurry."

The hurt in Zippo's voice—and even more, that low trill of panic—alarmed Daniel all over again. He punched the Band button and got a talk station, expecting weather, traffic, the usual babble. Instead, there it was.

"*The National Guard has been activated,*" the reporter's voice was panting. "*Once again, residents of Pikesville, Sudbrook Park, and Woodholme are asked to stay indoors and off the roads. And if you're driving on the beltway, until these animals are located and secured please use extreme caution, and be aware that there may be substantial delays.*"

"*Even more substantial than usual,*" laughed the throaty, in-the-studio host, and Daniel stared at the dial.

"What the hell?" he said, and the first sirens screamed behind him.

He barely had time to pull to the gravel shoulder before a train of police cars rocketed past. In the window of the last, Daniel glimpsed a deputy loading a long, black rifle.

"Oh my God," he murmured, turning toward his aunts. "Did you see…"

But they had seen. He could tell by the looks on their faces. Ethel's eyes had gone steely, her mouth firm and flat. Even more disconcerting was the way Zippo dropped her head into the folds of her shawl and hugged her arms around herself.

"Maybe we should go home," he said. Neither aunt answered.

Checking the rearview mirror multiple times, Daniel edged back onto the street. A helicopter whirred past overhead. Cautiously, Daniel turned the radio lower. When neither of the aunts objected, he turned it off. They drove in silence for a while.

"Hurry up," Ethel murmured, though her tone lacked its usual barking cheerfulness.

On both sides of them, the houses vanished. The road cut through crop-less farm fields now, divided only by stands of oak and elm, a few half-hearted wooden fences.

"So," Daniel finally said, if only to break the strangely pregnant silence. "I guess Buddy still lives there?"

"He still does," Zippo said.

"And he still keeps random animals, just for fun? Buffalo? Cheetahs? Remember when he had that elephant? How is he even allowed to have animals like that? Ooh, remember those hairless alpaca or whatever they were, and—"

"They're *our* animals," Ethel said, and smacked the backseat. "Goddamn him."

"Yours?"

"We're sponsoring them," Zippo said. "Ethel and I. Buddy's their caretaker."

"Some care," Ethel snapped, and Zippo shushed her.

Then, abruptly, they'd arrived. Daniel recognized the hillside with its sagging cyclone fence, and the prickly ash tree with the forked trunk and the bare branches curling in on each other like clawed fingers on an arthritic hand. The parked police cruiser with its rooftop light-bars flashing was another clue. By the time he'd brought the car to a stop on the gravel, Aunt Zippo had her door open, and Ethel was practically pushing her from the car.

"Hold on," Daniel said. "They're not just going to let you…"

But both of them were out, now, and Aunt Ethel had already lumbered to the top of the long drive that dropped through the field of dead grass to the farmhouse. A burly police kid with shoulders roughly the width of the tire axle on his cruiser had stood to block her. He wasn't really a kid, Daniel realized as he hurried forward. Just a whole lot younger than Ethel or Zippo. His black night stick and the holster of his gun bumped against his leg.

"You're going to escort me?" Aunt Ethel was saying. "They really are teaching better manners at the academy these days."

The cop—blond, probably not even thirty, cheeks flushed with the cold—just stared at the bobbing, flame-haired bird-woman in front of him. Ethel was several steps past before he recovered himself and stepped into her path again.

"Are you telling me you didn't notice the police cars?" the cop said, folding his arms. "The helicopters everywhere? Lady, you really ought to turn on your radio." He reached out, intending to steer her firmly back up the hill.

"What? Son, I don't hear so well."

Somehow, she'd got by him again. Beside Daniel, Zippo sighed and moved to follow her sister. A nervous tremor twitched in Daniel's throat, and he hurried after them.

The cop had moved to grab Aunt Ethel's arm again. Only when she glared at his hand did he think better of it. From across the fields, somewhere on the other side of the hickory forest that bordered Buddy's farm, a siren wailed. Answering wails and their echoes flooded the air, as though a wolf pack had materialized in those trees.

Which, all things considered, didn't seem so improbable.

"Look. Ma'am," said the cop. "You can't go down there."

"Why, did Buddy warn you about us?"

The cop stared again. Ethel waddled off with Zippo right behind her. By the time Daniel reached the policeman, he was staring down at his own hands. There was a chocolate top cookie in them. The policemen looked up and Daniel shrugged, started to smile.

"They're going to get hurt. Laugh about that," said the policeman, and returned to his car.

Daniel had just reached the bottom of the drive when Buddy himself came around the side of the farmhouse with a hose and a slop-bucket. His glasses really were as outsized as Daniel remembered them, ballooning from his sockets as though his eyes were blowing bubbles. His paunch had swelled and sagged, and his still-thick hair had finished draining of color. He took one goggle-eyed look at Ethel and dropped the bucket.

"Aw, Christ, now my morning really is complete. I thought it was complete before, but now it's perfect."

"You let them out," Ethel snarled, and Daniel all but ran to reach her side. Never in his life had he heard Aunt Ethel snarl. At anyone.

They're going to get hurt.

Ethel was still snarling. "You let them go."

Flinching, Buddy lifted the hose. Daniel really thought he might blast them, started to lunge into the path of the spray. "Let them?" Buddy shouted back. "Let them?"

"How does this happen? What do you pay your fence guy for? With our money."

"It was that goddamn cat." Buddy was looking at Daniel now. Pleading, Daniel realized. He fell back a step. "That fucking cheetah."

"There's no need for that sort of talk," Zippo said quietly.

"He got the lock off, don't ask me how. Pushed open the gate. I saw him do it. But by the time I got out here..." Waving his free hand in front of his bubble eyes, Buddy the Exotic Animal Farmer seemed to sag into his skin. "Look, I'm the one in trouble. Big trouble. So just..."

But Ethel was shaking her head, staring at her feet. And smiling now. "Oh, Mack," she said.

"Where did they go?" Aunt Zippo asked.

Buddy shrugged, seeming to sag more but also puff out, like a pillow being smacked and fluffed. He gestured with the hose toward the woods. "Mostly that way."

"Mostly?"

"That's where the cops are. They're worried about that elementary school over there. One of them broke straight off that direction, though." Buddy waved behind the house. "Toward the beltway."

"Which one?" Ethel asked.

Buddy's head rolled up out of his neck wrinkles. Behind his glasses, the magnified frog-eyes blinked.

"What?"

"Which one? Who headed for the beltway?"

"Which one? Lady. They're buffalo."

"You're thinking Mitchell," Aunt Zippo said, and Ethel nodded.

"Be just like him, wouldn't it? First chance he gets, straight for the office."

Without another word, his aunts set off side by side, not back up the path but around the side of the house toward the woods. Buddy just stared after them. But when Daniel moved to follow, the farmer grabbed his wrist.

"Watch them, okay? They're going to get shot."

For a second, Daniel thought he meant the buffalo. But those eyes were trained on his aunts. And Buddy's other hand kept banging the bucket nervously against his own leg. Daniel nodded, and the farmer let go.

In the woods, sirens screamed again. His aunts had already gotten a surprising distance down the slope toward the forest, and they'd linked arms. Ethel had her head on Zippo's shoulder, so that her red hair and the wool shawl blended into a sort of mane. They moved in lurches through the winter light, the birdless, silent morning, and Daniel felt his breath catch, hard, and shook his head to fight back the black thoughts.

"Aunt Ethel," he called. "Aunt Zip. Stop."

But they didn't stop. Indeed, they seemed to gain speed, like fallen leaves the wind had caught. He started to call again, but didn't want to draw the attention of the ghost-wolves in the woods. Or the very real policemen with the shotguns. He started to run.

He caught his aunts just as they drifted through the tree line, and they looked surprised to see him.

"Daniel, what is it, honey?" Aunt Zip said, but he couldn't answer. Aunt Ethel patted his arm.

They stepped together into a hollow, empty silence. No ground animals rustled the dead leaves here. The trees stood farther apart than they'd looked from the farmhouse—this was more an orchard than a wood—and daylight lay between the trunks like white paper where something had been erased. Daniel watched the steam of his breath coalesce momentarily and then evaporate, leaving more blank places.

"Listen," Aunt Ethel hissed.

Sirens shattered the quiet, and Daniel ducked and threw his gloves over his ears as his aunts clinched together. This time, the answering echoes seemed much closer.

"That way," said Aunt Zippo, the moment the wailing stopped.

"Both of you, wait," Daniel said. "This isn't a joke. They've got guns."

"Joke?" said Aunt Ethel. "Got any good ones? No one's told me a good one since Mack died."

"Except my father," Daniel murmured.

"You mean the goat? Oy." She shuffled away through the leaves. Zippo followed, and again their speed surprised Daniel. He had to hurry to keep up.

"Aunt Zip," he said. "We're going to get shot."

"Honey, why would they shoot us?"

"See the hair?" Aunt Ethel was gesturing at her own head but only half-turning. "If I could grow enough of this, I could sell it as a hunting jacket. Hurry up."

"We're coming, dear," Aunt Zip said, and they both moved ahead of him again.

Through the trees a considerable way ahead, Daniel thought he could see chain-link fence, and he also heard voices.

Aunt Ethel somehow moved faster still. In the path, they came across a steaming pile of shit. The smell burrowed straight up Daniel's nostrils, and he gagged.

"What?" said Aunt Zippo,

He pointed at the ground. "Can't you smell that?"

"I can't smell anything anymore. I miss smells."

"Trust me. You don't miss this one."

"You wouldn't think so."

"Is it buffalo?"

Aunt Ethel should have been too far ahead to hear. But she slapped a hand to her forehead and said, "Oh, brother." In her tights, on her stick-legs, she looked like a little girl dressed as a crone. Or a clown. She couldn't really get shot, Daniel thought. Anyone who got her in his rifle sights would be too busy laughing.

"I'm worried about her," he whispered.

Beside him, Zippo sighed. Her shallow breath barely made an imprint on the air. "She's just old, honey. The way we all get. If we're lucky."

"Yeah, but she's different. Acting different."

Without slowing, Zippo looked her sister up and down. "She looks pretty much like Ethel to me."

"Yeah, well, she's changed her reading habits."

"Her reading habits?"

"All my life, she's read Dick Francis. Pretty much only Dick Francis."

"Have a cookie, Daniel," Aunt Zippo said.

He had no idea from where she produced the chocolate top, or how she'd managed to keep the dollop of frosting from getting smashed.

"Aunt Zippo, she's naming the buffalo."

"She didn't name them." It was her voice, not her words, that prickled in Daniel's chest. She sounded dreamy, or maybe just distant, as though settling into that detachment that supposedly comes for the old at the end and makes dying easier. Except that his mother had always said that was bull-shit. A bedtime story people told their children as they watched the life leave their parents. Daniel felt tickling in his tear ducts again. He thought of his father, his lost uncles, and was overcome by an urge to grab his aunts' crooked, cold hands and hug them to his chest. He took one of Zippo's, tugged her forward to where Ethel had stopped, and came out of the trees into sight of the schoolyard.

Then he dropped Zippo's hand and stared straight ahead.

It was like being at a Natural History Museum. Like looking through glass at a diorama full of stuffed dead things.

There was the section of fence, first of all, trampled into the ground. Half a dozen police knelt in a ring around the perimeter of the schoolyard with their rifles aimed through the links in the remaining chicken wire. The lights from their cruisers flung splashes of red, like paint ball blotches, across their otherwise colorless faces and the dead grass and the hunkered, gray brick of the school building thirty yards away and the whimpering, teary-eyed children clutching each other by the swing sets. Between the children and the school, their shaggy flanks heaving as they panted and chuffed and lowered their horny heads, four full-grown buffalo bumped around and against each other and expelled geysers of breath into the freezing air.

"Oh, no," Ethel said. "Oh, boys."

How long, Daniel wondered, had this scene been frozen like this? He could see what had happened. The recess bell ringing. The sound startling the buffalo, who'd rumbled right through the fence, smack in between this last group of straggling kids and the safety of their classroom.

On the blacktop, Daniel saw two teachers and a towering African American man in pinstripes gesturing furiously at each other, the kids, the cops. All along the fence, walkie-talkies spit static and snatches of hard, unintelligible instruction.

"Harry?" the African American man called abruptly, and both Ethel's and Zippo's heads jerked toward the buffalo. The same buffalo, Daniel noticed, the one farthest to the right with his nose in the grass and the broken tip of his horn jutting toward them like a shiv.

But the man was talking to one of the kids. And the kid was lifting his red hood off his ears. He was maybe eight, blond-haired, with chipmunk cheeks that would have amused either of Daniel's aunts for weeks on end if they could have gotten their pinching fingers on them. He wiped a hand across his tear-streaked face and waited.

"Just walk this way, son," the pinstripe man was saying. "Around the fence there. Come to us. Harry, lead them this way. All of you, now. Come on."

None of the children moved. In the center of the yard, the buffalo stamped. One of them knocked horns with its closest neighbor, though the gesture looked accidental to Daniel. More like two old men bumping into one another with walkers than rutting.

Then the kid in the hood moved. The moment he did, the buffalo with the broken horn looked up, snorted loudly, and raked its foot along the grass.

Instantly, rifles leapt to shoulders as the cops locked in, and the buffalo froze, sweeping its gaze once across the whole assembled mass before him. It chuffed again, pawed more frantically, and tore a huge hunk of dirt out of the lawn.

"Damn it," spat a nearby radio.

Harry—the kid, not the animal—burst into fresh tears. Half a dozen safety catches popped free on half a dozen guns. Daniel was so busy watching the police that he didn't notice Aunt Zippo moving until she was halfway across the yard.

"Jesus," a policeman yelled. "Someone grab her!"

But Aunt Zippo had already reached the herd, and as Daniel's mouth dropped open, she disappeared amongst them.

Even the children went silent. Around the old woman, the buffalo began to pant and paw nervously. One of them bumped her with its flank, and Daniel saw her stagger and get bumped by another and almost go down amidst their stamping feet. The one with the pointed half-horn had moved into the circle, now, and it was poking at Aunt Zippo with its head lowered and its front foot working furiously at the grass.

For one more moment, the unreality held. Daniel stared at the animals snorting around his aunt, alternately ignoring her and then brandishing horns and banging themselves against her. The eeriest thing wasn't their presence. It was their *physicality*. Their breath and their scraped, hairy sides and their deep-set, black-brown eyes and the way their skin seemed draped over their skulls rather than attached to it, as though they were already skeleton and hide, and there was something else, something not-buffalo, underneath there.

His aunts' faces, Daniel realized, looked the same way. Everyone's did. His father's. His wife's. Hell, even his own face. Our features little more than cloaks life shrugs on while it camps inside us.

Somewhere to his right, a walkie-talkie crackled. Rifles shifted, held. Ethel was just staring, her hands over her mouth. Daniel threw his arm around her shoulder, squeezed once.

"I'll get her," he said.

"Oh, God," said his aunt.

Then he was through the fence, flinging up his hand, screaming, "Wait! Don't shoot!"

"*Hold fire*!" someone shouted.

Two guns exploded. Daniel ducked, whirled, waved a frantic hand, and broke into a run as the kids screeched and bolted for the blacktop. Over the tops of the nearest buffalo, Daniel could see his Aunt's orange shawl, the back of her head with its thinning, blue-white hair like a cloud coming apart. The head disappeared as his aunt went down.

"No!" Daniel screamed, and the buffalo broke as one into a plunging, sideways dash toward the far end of the schoolyard, away from the children and the blacktop and the mass of muzzles and threatening faces.

All of them, that is, except the one with the horn. Harry. He had slid, with surprising grace, onto his front knees. Aunt Zippo was kneeling beside him. The buffalo seemed to hover there a moment, and then slipped the rest of the way to the grass.

Aunt Zippo laid both her hands on the animal's throat, under its mane. Its great black hooves had splayed to either side of her, and blood bubbled from the holes in its gut and over Zippo's gloves.

"Ssh," she was saying, in that hypnotic, even cadence she seemed to have been born with, or maybe just learned through too much practice. So many years of practice. "Ssh, Harry." She never looked up, not once. She just kept whispering, over and over, until the buffalo died.

IT TOOK HOURS, after that, for the truck to come, and for the animal wranglers to wrestle the surviving bison into it. By the time Daniel and his aunts got back to Ethel's, it was too late to drive home, and he was too shaken, anyway. Ethel ordered pineapple pizza, which Daniel barely touched but which his aunts devoured. Ethel burst into tears once, and Zippo sat beside her and said, "I know. I know."

"How many times?" Ethel sobbed, swiping at her cheeks and smearing pizza grease there.

Producing yet another of her magic tissues, Zippo wiped the grease away. "There doesn't seem to be a limit."

"You know, I still miss him the most. Harry."

"I know."

"I didn't love him the most. He pretty much slept and worked and built Herm's trains with him and wouldn't let us eat donuts enough. But I miss him the most."

"He was the first," Zippo said.

"Don't eat that last pineapple," Ethel said, and snatched the final pizza slice from the box. Abruptly, she looked up at Daniel, held the slice toward him. "Unless you want it, honey."

Daniel shook his head, closed his eyes, saw skeleton-flashes of white light, like the projected shadows of a CAT-scan. When he opened his eyes, his aunts were holding hands.

Zippo went home, and Ethel set him up in her son Herm's old room with the train bedspread still draped over the bed. Daniel read a Dick Francis novel until well after midnight because he didn't think he could sleep, nodded off with the book on his chest, and woke up weeping.

He didn't think he'd called out, but his Aunt was at the door within seconds anyway, in a pink nightgown that had to have been at least thirty years old, and with what looked like a matching bonnet on her head. She didn't *ssh* him—that was Zippo's purview—but she asked several times if he wanted a bagel, and she clucked a lot, and in the end she sat on the edge of the bed and patted his hand, over and over.

"How do you do it, Aunt Ethel?" Daniel asked, through tears he couldn't seem to stop. "How do you survive the love you outlive?"

Aunt Ethel just patted his hand, glanced around the room, out toward the hallway, still lined with photos of the families she'd created or joined, the children she'd borne and the families they'd formed. The hallway was also where she'd moved the pictures of the men she and her sister had buried, after replacing them in the living room with the buffalo.

"I know what Mack would have said," she told him.

"What?"

"'Did you hear the one about the rabbi and the stripper?'"

That just made Daniel sob harder. When he'd gotten control of himself again, he looked at his aunt. "What about you, Aunt Ethel?"

"Me?" She shrugged. "Mostly, hon, I think I just keep deciding I want to."

It was a long while before the tears stopped completely and Daniel felt ready to lie back on his pillow. Ethel brought him warm milk, and he actually drank it. And it was after two when he awoke the second time, to the sound of the porch door swinging open.

Instantly, he was bolt upright. "Aunt Ethel?" he called. Grabbing his pants off the chair, he hurried down the darkened hallway, through the living room onto the screened-in porch. The side-yard lights were on, flooding the tiny yard.

Ethel was by the screen. Fifteen yards away, right where the grass disappeared into the stand of pines that marked the edge of her property, the cheetah crouched on its haunches, its tail whapping at the dirt. In life, even more than in its photo, the thing looked ancient, its yellow eyes rheumy, its fur discolored or missing entirely. It also had its disconcertingly tiny head cocked, its mouth open, and one front paw crossed over the other. There was something almost cocky in the pose. Composed, at the very least. Like a gentleman caller.

"Oh my God," Daniel mumbled. "How on earth did it..."

"Mack's home," his aunt said, and glanced just once over her shoulder at Daniel.

"What?" But he was thinking of the buffalo on the wall. The ones Ethel and Zippo both insisted they hadn't named, just called by name. "Aunt Ethel, that isn't..."

Smiling, she stepped out the door.

It was those next, fleeting moments Daniel would remember, years later, at Lisa's three-years-clean checkup, and again at her five years, when the doctors told her she didn't need to come back every six months anymore, she just had to stay vigilant, always. Or at least, it was those moments he would focus on. Not what came afterward. From then on, when he let himself think about this night, he would picture his aunt's bare, gnarled feet in the grass. Her lumbering gait as she approached the cheetah, which hunched, coiled, its purr—or growl—audible even from the house. The pink bonnet on her head, the yellow overcoat on her shoulders, and the swing of her hand off her hip that told him she was dancing.

THIS SHOULDN'T HAVE *been hard. I mean, a strange tale inspired by Poe should be like breathing encouraged by air, right?*

Maybe that was the problem. Great and terrible and awe-inspiring as he can be, Poe has become the Pachelbel of horror, so ubiquitous and familiar as to be drained, if not of his own impact, at least of his power to spark.

At least, that's how it was for me. When first contacted for this anthology, I went straight to "A Descent into the Maelstrom," "The Fall of the House of Usher," "The Black Cat." They are all as grand as I remembered, and also over-familiar. So I started to read around in some of the stories I remembered less well.

Finally, in desperation, I turned to pieces I'd never before encountered and discovered "Morning on the Wissahicon." There, I found first that universal writer's longing to get off the well-traveled path, to discover—primarily by walking, and getting lost—hidden places where adventures are possible and stories flourish. Near the end, I came across the following anecdote:

> "I saw, or dreamed that I saw, standing upon the extreme verge of the precipice, with neck out-stretched, with ears erect, and the whole attitude indicative of profound and melancholy inquisitiveness, one of the oldest and boldest of those identical elks which had been coupled with the red men of my vision...
>
> A negro emerged from the thicket, putting aside the bushes with care, and treading stealthily. He bore in one hand a quantity of salt, and holding it towards the elk, gently yet steadily approached... The negro advanced; offered the salt; and spoke a few words of encouragement or conciliation. Presently, the elk bowed and stamped, and then lay quietly down and was secured with a halter.
>
> Thus ended my romance of the elk. It was a pet of great age and very domestic habits, and belonged to an English family occupying a villa in the vicinity."

Immediately, a memory surfaced, and a Baltimore memory, to boot: visiting a farm in the suburbs populated with exotic animals. Llamas, I think. Snakes. Definitely buffalo. There may have been an elephant. I visited this farm in the company of two aunts I dearly loved, one of whom is dead now. I asked the surviving aunt whether I was misremembering, and where that farm was. And she told me a story about the day the buffalo got out. And suddenly— finally—I had myself a Poe-derived tale to tell...

BARBARA RODEN was born in Vancouver, British Columbia, in 1963, and has been an enthusiast of the writings of Edgar Allan Poe since she was nine, when her mother first read her "A Cask of Amontillado." She also has a long-standing interest in Arctic exploration, and was delighted to be able to combine both enthusiasms in one tale. With her husband, Christopher, she runs the World Fantasy Award-winning Ash-Tree Press, and co-edits *All Hallows*, the journal of the Ghost Story Society. Her short fiction has appeared in a number of publications, and her 2005 story "Northwest Passage" was nominated for a World Fantasy Award and included in *Year's Best Fantasy and Horror 19.*

The Brink of Eternity

by Barbara Roden

The knife is long and lethal yet light, both in weight and appearance; a thing precise and definite, which he admires for those reasons. It has not been designed for the task at hand, but it will suffice.

The sound of a heart beating fills his ears, and he wonders if it is his heart or the other's. He will soon know.

The knife is raised, and then brought down in a swift movement. A moment of resistance, and then the flesh yields and vivid spatters spread, staining the carpet of white, bright and beautiful.

He brings the knife down again, and again. He can still hear the beating, and knows it for his own heart, for the other's has stopped. He fumbles for a moment, dropping the knife, pulling off his gloves, then falls to his knees and plunges his bare hand into the bruised and bloody chest, pulling out the heart, warm and red and raw.

He eats.

WALLACE, William Henry (1799–?1839) was born in Richmond, Virginia. His family was well-to-do, and William was almost certainly expected to follow his father, grandfather, and two uncles into the legal profession. However, for reasons which remain unknown, he abandoned his legal studies, and instead began work as a printer and occasional contributor of letters, articles, and reviews to various publications. In this respect there are interesting parallels between Wallace and Charles Francis HALL (q.v.), although where Hall's Arctic explorations were inspired by the fate of the Franklin Expedition,

Wallace appears to have been motivated by the writings of John Cleve Symmes, Jr. (1779–1829), particularly Symmes's "hollow earth" theory—popular through the 1820s—which postulated gateways in the Polar regions which led to an underground world capable of sustaining life.

From *We Did Not All Come Back: Polar Explorers, 1818–1909*
by Kenneth Turnbull
(HarperCollins Canada, 2005)

HE COULD NOT remember a time when he did not long for something he could not name, but which he knew he would not find in the course laid out for him. The best tutors and schools, a career in the law that would be eased by his family's name and wealth, marriage to one of the eligible young ladies whose mamas were so very assiduous in calling on his own mother. Their eyes missed nothing, noting his manners, his well-made figure, strong and broad-shouldered, his prospects and future, of which they were as sure as he; surer, for his was an old story that they had read before.

But he chafed under his tutors, a steady stream of whom were dismissed by his father, certain that the next one would master the boy. School was no better; he was intelligent, even gifted, yet perpetually restless, dissatisfied, the despair of his teachers, who prophesied great things for him if he would only apply himself fully. He was polite to the mamas and their daughters, but no sparkling eyes enchanted him, no witty discourse ensnared him; his heart was not touched. He studied law because it was expected of him and he saw no other choice.

And then… and then came the miracle that snapped the shackles, removed the blinders, showed him the path he was to follow. It came in the unprepossessing form of a pamphlet, which he was later to discover had been distributed solely to institutes of higher learning throughout America, and which he almost certainly would never have seen had he not, however reluctantly, wearily, resignedly, followed the dictates of his family, if not his head and heart. Proof, if it were needed, that the Fate which guides each man was indeed watching over him.

The pamphlet had no title, and was addressed, with a forthright simplicity and earnestness Wallace could only admire, "To All The World." The author wrote:

> I declare the earth is hollow, and habitable within; containing a number of solid concentrick spheres, one within the other, and that it is open at the poles 12 or 16 degrees; I pledge my life in support of this truth, and am ready to explore the hollow, if the world will support and aid me in the undertaking.
> JOHN CLEVES SYMMES
> Of Ohio, Late Captain of Infantry.

* * *

HE OPENED THE pamphlet, his hands trembling. A passage caught his eye:

> I ask one hundred brave companions, well equipped, to start from
> Siberia in the fall season, with Reindeer and slays, on the ice of the
> frozen sea: I engage we find warm and rich land, stocked with thrifty
> vegetables and animals if not men, on reaching one degree northward
> of latitude 62. We will return in the succeeding spring.

THE WORDS SEEMED to inscribe themselves on his heart. "One hundred
brave companions," "start from Siberia," "find warm and rich land,"
"return in the succeeding spring."

In an instant he knew what it was that he had to do. After long years of
wandering and searching, his restless feet were halted and pointed in the
only true direction.

*It is his first food in—how long? He has lost count of the days and weeks;
all is the same here in this wasteland of white. He remembers Symmes's
"warm and rich land" and a laugh escapes his throat. It is a rough, harsh,
scratched sound, not because its maker is unamused, but because it has been
so long since he has uttered a sound that it is as if he has forgotten how.*

*The remains of the seal lie scattered at his feet; food enough to last for sev-
eral days if carefully husbanded. There will be more seals now, further
south, the way he has come, the way he should go. Salvation lies to the
south; reason tells him this. But that would be salvation of the body only. If
he does not continue he will never* know. *He fears this more than he fears
the dissolution of his body.*

*He grasps the knife firmly in his hand—he can at least be firm about
this—and begins to cut up the seal, while all around the ice cracks and cries.*

ONE OF THE earliest pieces of writing identified as being by Wallace is a
review of James McBride's *Symmes' Theory of Concentric Spheres* (1826),
in which Wallace praises the ingenuity and breadth of Symmes's theory, and
encourages the American government to fund a North Polar expedition
"with all due speed, to investigate those claims which have been advanced
so persuasively, by Mr. Symmes and Mr. Reynolds, regarding the Polar
Regions, which endeavor can only result in the advancement of knowledge
and refute the cant, prejudice, ignorance, and unbelief of those whose long-
cherished, and wholly unfounded, theories would seek to deny what they
themselves can barely comprehend."

From *We Did Not All Come Back*

HIS PATH WAS SET. He threw over his legal studies, to the anger of his father
and the dismay of his mother, and waited anxiously for further word of
Symmes's glorious expedition. How could anyone fail to be moved by such

passion, such selfless determination, such a quest for knowledge that would surely be to the betterment of Mankind?

Yet no expedition was forthcoming. Symmes's words had, it seemed, fallen on the ears of people too deaf to hear, too selfish to abandon their petty lives and transient pleasures. Wallace had fully expected to be a part of the glorious expedition; now, faced with its failure, he cast round for something that would enable him to dedicate his life—or a large part of it—to those Polar realms which now haunted him, in preparation for the day when Symmes's vision would prevail and he could fulfill the destiny that awaited him.

He became a printer, for it seemed that his only connection with that region which so fascinated him was through words, so words would become his trade. He found work with a printer willing—for a consideration—to employ him as an apprentice, and learned the trade quickly and readily. When he was not working he was reading, anything and everything he could to prepare himself. He read Scoresby's two volume *Account of the Arctic Regions* and found, for the first time, pictures of that region of snow and ice, and of the strange creatures living there, seals and whales and the fearsome Polar Bear and, strangest of all, the Esquimaux who, in their furs, resembled not so much men as another type of animal. It was true that Scoresby scorned the idea of a "hollow earth;" yet he was only a whaling captain, and could not be expected to appreciate, embrace the ideas of someone like Symmes, a man of vision, of thought. Wallace expected more from Parry, that great explorer, and was heartened to find that the captain believed firmly in the idea of an Open Polar Sea, although he, like Scoresby, declined to accept a hollow earth.

Wallace knew that it existed, knew with his whole heart and soul that such a thing must be; those who denied it, even those who had been to the North, were either willfully blind, or jealous that they had not yet managed to discover it, and thereby accrue to themselves the glory which belonged to Symmes. When Symmes came to Richmond on a speaking tour Wallace obtained a ticket to the lecture and sat, enthralled, while Symmes and his friend Joshua Reynolds preached their doctrine. He hung on to every word, eyes greedily devouring the wooden globe which was used by way of illustration, and displayed the hollows in the earth at the Polar extremities which led to a fantastic world of pale beings and weak sunlight.

In 1823 he heard that Symmes's friend, the businessman James McBride, had submitted a proposal to Congress asking for funding to explore the North Polar region expressly to investigate Symmes's theory. Here at last was his opportunity. He waited in a fever of excitement for the passing of the proposal, the call to arms, the expedition, the discovery, the triumphant return, the vindication.

The proposal was voted down.

* * *

He has been living thus for so long that his body now works like a thing independent of his mind, an automaton. The seal meat is still red, but no longer warm; the strips are hardening, freezing. He must... what must he do? Build a snow house for the night; yes. And then he must load the seal meat on to his sledge, in preparation for the next day's travel. In which direction that will be he cannot say. He does not know what lies ahead, what awaits, and it frightens him as much as it elates him; he does know what lies behind, what awaits there, and that frightens him even more, with no trace of elation whatever.

FOLLOWING SYMMES'S DEATH in 1829 his theory largely fell out of favor, as a wave of Polar exploration failed to find any evidence of a "hollow earth." Symmes's adherents gradually deserted him, or turned their attentions elsewhere; Joshua Reynolds successfully lobbied Congress for funding for a South Seas expedition which would also, as an aside, search for any traces of a "Symmes hole", as it came to be known, in the Antarctic. Although no sign of such a hole was found, the voyage did have far-reaching literary consequences, inspiring both Edgar Allan Poe's *The Narrative of Arthur Gordon Pym* and Herman Melville's *Moby-Dick*.

Poe published an article in praise of Reynolds, and the South Sea expedition, in the *Southern Literary Messenger* in January 1837; a reply to this article, penned by Wallace, appeared in the March 1837 issue. Wallace commends Poe on his "far-sighted and clear-headed praise of what will surely be a great endeavor, and one which promises to answer many of the questions which, at present, remain beyond our understanding," but laments the abandonment of American exploration in the North. "A golden opportunity is slipping through our fingers; for while the British Navy must needs sail across an ocean and attack from the east, through a maze of channels and islands which has defied all attempts and presents one of the most formidable barriers on Earth, the United States need only reach out along our western coast and sail through Bering's Strait to determine, once and all, the geography of the Northern Polar regions."

Elsewhere in the article Wallace writes of the Arctic as "this Fearsome place, designed by Nature to hold and keep her secrets" and of "the noble Esquimaux, who have made their peace with a land so seemingly unable to support human existence, and who have much to teach us." These references make it clear that Wallace had, by 1837, already spent time in the Eastern Arctic, a fact borne out by the logbook of the whaling ship *Christina*, covering the period 1833-5. On board when the ship left New London in May 1833 was one "Wm. H. Wallace, gent., late of Richmond," listed as "passenger." In late August the log notes starkly that "Mr. Wallace disembarked at Southampton Island."

Where he lived, and what he did, between August 1833 and March 1837 remains a mystery; Wallace left behind few letters, no journals or diaries that have been discovered, and did not publish any accounts of his travels. It has been assumed that he, like later explorers such as Hall and John RAE (q.v.), spent time living among the Inuit people and learning their way of life; if so, it is unfortunate that Wallace left no account of this time, as his adoption of the traditional Inuit way of life, in the 1830s, would mark him as one of the first white men to do so.

From *We Did Not All Come Back*

EVEN WHEN SYMMES died, and his theory looked set to die with him, Wallace kept faith. There would, he now knew, be no government-backed venture in search of the hollow earth; it would be up to one man of vision, daring, resolve to make his own way north. That man, he swore, would be William Henry Wallace, whose name would ever after ring down the annals of history.

Yet it was not fame, or the thought of fame, that spurred him on; rather, it was the rightness of the cause, the opportunity to prove the naysayers wrong, and a chance to break truly free from the shackles of his life and upbringing and venture, alone, to a place shrouded in mystery, to see for himself the wonders that were, as yet, no more than etchings in books, tales told by travelers. He had lived frugally, not touching the allowance still provided by his father, who hoped that the Prodigal Son would one day return to the family home. With this he set out, early in 1833, for New England, where he persuaded a reluctant—until he saw the banknotes in the stranger's pocketbook—whaling captain to let him take passage on board his ship. Only when the *Christina* had set sail for the north did William Henry Wallace, for the first time in many years, know a kind of peace.

But it was a restless peace, short-lived. He spent the days pacing the deck with anxious feet, eyes ever northward, scanning the horizon for any signs of that frozen land for which he longed. When the first icebergs came in sight he was overcome with their terrible beauty, so imperfectly captured in the drawings he had pored over until he knew their every detail as well as if he himself had been the artist. Soon the ice was all around, and while captain and crew kept a fearful eye on it always, Wallace drank in its solemn majesty, and rejoiced that each day brought him closer to his goal.

When the *Christina* left him at Southampton Island he was oblivious to the crew's concern for a man whom they obviously thought mad. Yet they did not try to dissuade him; they had business to attend to, and only a short time before the ice closed in and either forced them home or sealed them in place for long, dreary months. The captain did try, on one occasion, to stop Wallace; but after a few moments he ceased his efforts, for the look in the other's eyes showed that no words the captain could muster would mean anything. At least the man was well provisioned; whatever qualms the captain might have about his mental state, his physical well-being was assured for a time. And once off the ship he was no longer the captain's concern.

Wallace had studied well the texts with which he had provided himself. In addition to clothing and food and tools, he had purchased numerous small trinkets—mirrors, knives, sewing needles, nails—and they paid handsome dividends amongst the Esquimaux, who were at first inclined to laugh at the *kabloona* come to live among them, but soon learned that he was in earnest about learning their ways. Before long Wallace had shed the outward garb of the white man and adopted the clothing of the Esquimaux, their furs and skins so much better suited to the land than his own cotton and wool garments. Their food he found more difficult, at first, to tolerate; it took many attempts before his stomach could accept the raw blubber and meat without convulsing, but little by little he came to relish it. His first clumsy attempts at building a snow house, or igloo, were met with good-natured laughter, but before long he was adept at wielding the snow knife, a seemingly delicate instrument carved from a single piece of bone which ended in a triangular blade of surprising sharpness. He learned to judge the snow needed for blocks, neither too heavy nor too light, and fashion the bricks so they were tapered where necessary. He learned to make windows of clear ice, and of the importance not only of a ventilation hole at the top of the structure, but of ensuring that it was kept free of the ice that formed from the condensation caused by breath and body warmth, lest it become a tomb for those inside.

The casual way in which the Esquimaux men and women shared their bodies with each other shocked him, at first; after a time he came to see the practicality of sleeping, unclothed under furs, in a group, but he remained aloof from the women who plainly showed that they would welcome him as a partner. In all other ways he admired the natives of that cold land: what other travelers remarked on as their cruelty he saw as a necessity. Illness or frailty in one could mean death for all; there was no room in that place for pity, or sentiment, and he abandoned without regret the last traces of those feelings within his own soul.

He became skilled at traversing the fields of ice and snow, and would often set out alone. The Esquimaux, who only ventured across the ice when necessity compelled them in search of food, were puzzled by his expeditions, which seemed to serve no purpose. In reality he was searching, always searching, for any indication that he was drawing closer to the proof he sought, the proof that would vindicate Symmes, and his own life. He did not mark, in that realm of endless snow, how long he searched; but eventually he realized that he would not find the answers he was seeking in this place of maze-like channels. Symmes had been correct when he said that the answer lay from the west, not the east; and if he had been correct in this, why should he not be correct in much else?

When the *Christina* put in at Southampton Island in 1836 he had been cut off from his own kind for three years. The captain—the same man who had left him there—was astounded when he recognized, among the natives who crowded to the ship to trade for goods, the figure whom he had long thought dead. He was even more astounded when Wallace indicated—in the halting tones of one mastering a foreign tongue—that he sought passage back to New London. He spoke vaguely of business, but further than that he would not be drawn, except to say, of his time in the north, that he did not know whether he had found heaven on earth or an earthly heaven.

His igloo is finished. Small as it is, he has had difficulty lifting the last few blocks into place. He is vaguely surprised that the seal meat, coming as it did to revive him after his body's stores had been depleted, has not given him more energy. Instead, it seems almost as if his body, having achieved surfeit in one respect, is now demanding payment in another regard. After days, weeks, months of driving his body ever onward, all he can think of now is sleep; of the beauty of lying down under his fur robes and drifting into slumber even as the ice bearing him drifts closer to those unknown regions about which he has dreamed for so long.

WALLACE'S REFERENCE, IN his article, to the west coast of America and "Bering's Strait" suggests that he felt an attempt on the Arctic should be made from that side of the continent, and this would have been in keeping with Symmes's own beliefs. No such formal expedition along the west coast was to be made until 1848, when the first of the expeditions in search of the Franklin party set out, but it is clear that Wallace undertook an informal— and ultimately fatal—journey of his own more than a decade earlier. An open letter from Wallace, published in the Richmond *Enquirer* in April 1837, states his intention of traveling via Honolulu to Hong Kong and thence to Siberia, "which location is ideally placed as a base for the enterprising Polar traveler, and has inexplicably been ignored as such by successive governments, which have declined to take the sound advice of men such as Mr. Symmes, whose work I humbly continue, and whose theories I shall strive to prove to the satisfaction of all save those who are immune to reason, and who refuse to acknowledge any thing with which they do not have personal acquaintance."

Wallace's letter continues, "I shall be traveling without companions, and with a minimum of provisions and the accoutrements of our modern existence, for I have no doubt that I shall be able to obtain sustenance and shelter from the land, as the hardy Esquimaux do, until such time as I reach my journey's end, where I shall doubtless be shown the hospitality of those people who are as yet a mystery to us, but from whom we shall undoubtedly learn much which is presently hidden."

It is not known when Wallace left Virginia, but the diary of the Rev. Francis Kilmartin—now in the possession of the Mission Houses Museum in Honolulu—confirms that he had arrived in the Sandwich Islands, as they were then known, by March 1838, when he is mentioned in Kilmartin's diary. "Mr. Wallace is a curious mixture of the refined gentleman and the mystic, at one moment entertaining us all with his vivid and stirring tales of life among the Esquimaux, at another displaying an almost painful interest in any news from the ships' Captains arriving in port from eastern realms. His theories about the Polar region seem scarcely credible, and yet he appears to believe in them with every fiber of his being." In an entry from April 1838 Kilmartin writes, "We have said our farewells and God speeds to Mr. Wallace, who departed this day on board the *Helena* bound for Hong Kong. While I am, I confess, loath to see him go—for I do not foresee a happy outcome to his voyage—it is also a relief that he has found passage for the next stage of his journey, which he has been anticipating for so long, and which consumes his mind to the exclusion of all else."

From *We Did Not All Come Back*

HE HAD NOT wanted to return to Virginia, but there was that which needed to be done, preparations he needed to make, before setting out once more. He was uncomfortable with his parents, although not as uncomfortable as they with him. His father declared, publicly, that he would wash his hands of the boy, as if Wallace were still the feckless lad who had abandoned his studies so long ago; his mother thought, privately, that she would give much to have that feckless lad back once more if only for a moment, for she found herself frightened of the man who had returned from a place she could barely imagine.

He left Richmond—which he had long since ceased to think of it as home—in early summer of 1837, and made his way to the Sandwich Islands, thence to Hong Kong, and thence—but later he could hardly remember the route by which he had attained the frozen shore of that far country about which he had dreamed for so long. He seemed to pass through his journey as one travels through a dream world, the people and places he saw like little more than ghosts, pale and inconsequent shadows. It was not until he stood on that northern coast, saw once more the ice stretching out before him, that he seemed to awaken. All that he had passed through was forgotten; all that existed now was the journey ahead, through the ice which stretched as far as his eyes could see.

The ice moves, obeying laws which have existed since the beginning of time. Currents swirl in the dark depths below, carrying the ice floe upon which he has erected his igloo, carrying it—where? He does not know. It is carrying him onward; that is all he knows.

KILMARTIN'S FEARS WERE well founded, for it is at this point that William Henry Wallace disappears from history. What befell him after he left Honolulu is one of the minor mysteries of Arctic exploration, for no further word is heard of him; we do not even know if he successfully reached Hong

Kong, and from there north his passage would have been difficult. His most likely course would have been to travel the sea trading route north to the Kamtschatka Peninsula and then across the Gulf of Anadyr to Siberia's easternmost tip and the shore of the Chukchi Sea, from whence he would have been able to start out across the treacherous pack ice toward the North Pole.

Whether or not he made it this far is, of course, unknown, and likely to remain so at this remove, although one tantalizing clue exists. When the crew of the *Plover* was forced to spend the winter of 1848—9 in Chukotka, on the northeast tip of the Gulf of Anadyr, they heard many tales of the rugged coastline to the west, and met many of the inhabitants of the villages, who came to Chukotka to trade. One of the party—Lieutenant William Hulme Hooper—later wrote *Ten Months Among the Tents of the Tuski* about the *Plover*'s experience, and in one chapter touches on the character of these hardy coastal people. "They are superstitious almost to a fault," he wrote, "and signs and events that would be dismissed by most are seized on by them as omens and portents of the most awful type... One native told of a man who appeared like a ghost from the south, who had no dogs and pulled his own sledge, and whose wild eyes, strange clothes, and terrible demeanor so frightened the villagers that they—who are among the most hospitable people on Earth, even if they have but little to offer—would not allow him a space in their huts for the night. When day came they were much relieved to find that he had departed, across the ice in the direction of Wrangel Land to the north, where the natives do not venture. They were convinced that he had come from—and gone to—another world."

Historians have debated the meaning behind Hooper's "a man who appeared like a ghost from the south." The author would, of course, have been hearing the native's words through an interpreter, who might himself have been imprecise in his translation. Hooper's phraseology, if it is a faithful transcription of what he was told, could mean that the stranger appeared in ghost-like fashion; that is, unexpectedly. However, another interpretation is that the man appeared pale, like a ghost, to the dark-skinned Chukchi people; this, when taken with the direction from which the man appeared (the course Wallace would almost certainly have taken) and his decision to head northeast toward Wrangel, means that Hooper's description of "the man like a ghost" might be our last glimpse of William Henry Wallace, who would have gone to certain death in the treacherous ice field; although whether before, or after, finding that Symmes's theory was just that—a theory only—will never be known.

From *We Did Not All Come Back*

THE LAND ICE—the shelf of ice permanently attached to the shore—was easy enough to traverse. He towed a light sledge of his own devising behind him; he had no need of dogs, and now laughed at Symmes's idea that reindeer would have been a practical means of transport. Here there was one thing, and one thing only, on which he could depend, and that was himself.

An open lead of water separated the land ice from the pack ice, and it was with difficulty that he traversed it. From that moment his journey became a landscape of towering ice rafters and almost impenetrable pressure ridges, formed by the colliding sheets of ice. On some days he spent more time hacking a trail through the pressure ridges, or drying himself and his clothes after falling through young ice or misjudging his way across a lead, than he did traveling, and would advance less than a mile; on other days, when his progress seemed steady, he would find that the currents carrying the ice had taken him further forward than he anticipated.

He headed ever northward. He passed Wrangel Land on his left, and could have confirmed that it was an island, not a land bridge across the Pole connecting with Greenland; but by now such distinctions were beyond him. All was one here, the ice and snow and he himself, a tiny dot in the landscape of white. Did he believe, still, in Symmes? Would he have recalled the name, had there been anyone to mention it? But there was no one, and with every step forward he left the world, and his part in it, further behind.

Each night he built his house of snow. The Esquimaux had built their igloos large enough to accommodate several people; his own houses were small, large enough to accommodate only one, and consequently he had had to train himself to wake every hour or so, to clear the ventilation hole of ice so that he could breathe. It was not difficult to wake at regular intervals; the ice cracked and groaned and spoke almost as a living person, and more than once he sat in the Arctic night, listening to the voices, trying to discern what they were saying. One day, perhaps; one day.

His provisions, despite careful husbanding, gave out eventually, and for several days he subsisted on melted snow, and by chewing on the leather traces of the harness which connected him to his sledge, his only remaining link with his past. In reality, he was almost beyond bodily needs; he only remembered that it was time to eat when the increasing darkness reminded him that another day was drawing to a close. The seal was the first living thing that he had seen in— how long? He did not remember; yet instinct took over, and he killed it and ate it, and when he had sated his hunger he had a moment of clarity, almost, when his course seemed laid out, stark and level. Either he hoarded the seal meat, turned, and set back for the coast, or he continued, onward through the ice, toward what? An Open Polar Sea? Symmes's hollow earth?

It did not matter.

Nothing mattered.

His destiny was here, in the north, in the ice. It was all he had wanted, since—he could not remember when. Time meant nothing. The life he had left behind was less than dust. This was the place that he was meant to be.

He would go on.

* * *

He crawls into the igloo and fastens the covering over the opening, making a tight seal. His fur-covered bed beckons, and he pulls the robes over himself. Around and below him the ice cracks and cries, a litany lilting as a lullaby which slowly, gradually, lulls him to sleep.

The ventilation hole at the top of the igloo becomes crusted with ice, condensed from his own breath.

He does not wake to clear it.

And the ice carries him, ever onward.

"THE BRINK OF Eternity" was inspired by Poe's "MS Found in a Bottle" (from which my story takes its title) and "A Descent into the Maelström," as well as his non-fiction piece "Eureka." It incorporates Poe's belief that at one time mankind was united with the Godhead, and that there was a subsequent division, with man getting further away; at some point man will start to return towards the Godhead, and at the moment of collision there will be ultimate knowledge, as well as annihilation. We see this in the protagonists of the two stories I mention above, who fear their ultimate destiny, but also embrace it, realizing that they will gain knowledge they desire, even at the cost of their own death.

The story itself is a mix of some fact and much fiction. Poe was a proponent of Symmes's "Hollow Earth" theory, and a supporter of Joshua Reynolds, and Poe did write an article in support of Reynolds, which appeared in the Southern Literary Messenger *of January 1837; the Poe quote I use is taken from this article. The two quotes from Symmes's pamphlet near the beginning of the story are also real; all other quotes are fictitious, as is William Henry Wallace and the book* We Did Not All Come Back. *The Mission Houses Museum does exist in Honolulu; the Rev. Mr. Kilmartin and his diary are my own invention. Scoresby and Parry were real, while the* Christina *and her captain were not. The* Plover *did over-winter in Chukotka in 1848-9, and Lt. Hooper did write a book about the experience, called* Ten Months Among the Tents of the Tuski, *but I've put words in his mouth (or rather, in his book).*

DELIA SHERMAN is the author of numerous short stories, many of which are to be found in anthologies edited by Ellen Datlow and Terri Windling. Her adult novels are *Through a Brazen Mirror* and *The Porcelain Dove* (which won the Mythopoeic Award), and, with fellow-fantasist and partner Ellen Kushner, *The Fall of the Kings*. Her first novel for younger readers, *Changeling*, was published in 2006. She is an active member of the Endicott Studio of Mythic Arts and a founding member of the Interstitial Arts Foundation board. She lives in New York City and writes in cafes wherever she finds herself.

THE RED PIANO

by Delia Sherman

AMONG MY UNIVERSITY colleagues, I have a reputation for calm. Whatever the emotional upheaval around me, I can be counted on to keep my head, to make plans, to calculate the cost and consequences, and then to act. If they also say that I live too much in my head, that I lack passion and perhaps, compassion, that is the price I must pay for being one of those still waters that run much deeper than they appear.

It is perhaps no surprise that I remained single all through my younger years. No male who shared a classroom with me ever asked me on a date, although some were glad to debate with me over endless cups of coffee and too-sweet muffins in smoky little cafés near the University. My discipline was archaeology, my area of concentration the burial customs of long-dead societies, my obsession the notion of a corporeal afterlife, rich with exotic foods and elaborate furniture, jewels and art and books and servants to wait upon the deceased as they had in life. Wherever they began, all conversations circled back to the same ever-fascinating questions: whether such preparations reflected some post-mortem reality, or whether all the elaborated pomp of preservation and entombment were nothing but a glorified whistling in the dark of eternity.

In the course of these debates, I gained a reputation for an intensity of focus that discouraged my café companions from seeking more intimate bonds of friendship or romance. I did not mind; my own silent communion with dead worlds and languages gave me intimacy enough.

Thanks to my attention to study, I throve in my field, finally rising in my thirties to the position of a Full Professor of Archeology at a prominent University situated in a great city. Armed with the income this position offered me and a comfortable sum left to me by a great-aunt, I set out to look for a house to buy.

It was not an easy quest. In a city of apartment buildings and bland new construction, a detached dwelling of historical interest and aesthetic character is not easy to come by. At last, my realtor showed me an old stable, renovated as a townhouse late in the last century by an eccentric developer. It sat on the market for some time before going to an equally eccentric ballerina, recently retired from the stage. After she had suffered a crippling accident on the circular iron staircase, the stable had come back on the market, where it had remained ever since.

The realtor showed me this property with some reluctance, evincing considerable surprise when I told him that I would take it. Like a man in the grip of leprosy checking each limb in fear of discovering an unsuspected infection, he pointed out the inconvenient kitchen, the Pompeian masterbath, the unfinished roof deck with its unpromising view of a back alley and the sheer brick sides of the adjoining houses, and, worst of all, the grand piano that was attached to the sale and could not, by deed, be destroyed or removed from its position in the darkly paneled living room. Enchanted with the very eccentricities that had scuttled all previous negotiations, I made my offer, arranged for a mortgage, and hired a lawyer to draw up the papers.

I well remember the day I took possession. I'd thought my realtor the kind of small, dark, narrow man who shivers on even the hottest day. But as he handed me the key to the front door, he stopped shivering and smiled the first genuine smile I'd seen on his face.

"Here you are, Dr. Waters," he said. "It's all yours. I sure hope you know what you're getting into."

I thought this an odd thing to say, but I was too dazed with legal complexities to comment on his choice of words. Not that it would have changed anything. Once the papers were signed, so was my fate.

I have said my new house was flanked by larger houses—two mansions of ancient aspect and noble proportions that had shared, in their vanished youth, the stable I now called home. One of these had been refurbished, renovated, and repurposed to a glossy fare-thee-well, losing much of its character in the process. The other was infinitely more charming. There was a vagueness about its soot-streaked brownstone and clouded windows, an aura of fogs and mists that spoke of gaslight and the clop of horses' hooves on cobblestones, as if it somehow occupied an ancient lacuna in the roar and clatter of the modern city.

Accustomed as I am to keeping to myself and mindful of the ancient city habit of never acknowledging that one has neighbors at all, I did not knock on either door. I moved into my stable, arranged my books and my great-aunt's antique furniture, my Egyptian canopic jars and Roman armbands, my Columbian breastplates and Hellenic funerary steles in the wide wooden spaces where the horses of my neighbors' predecessors had drowsed and fed.

I also had the piano tuned. It was an unusual instrument, made of close-grained wood stained a deep, ox-blood red, its keys fashioned of a uniform polished ebony. Its tone was resonant and full, more akin to an organ than the tinkling parlor uprights I had played as a girl. It was intricately carved with a myriad of identical faces clustered around its legs and above its pedals and around the music stand. I had lost all interest in practicing the piano when I discovered archeology. But I could not feel settled in my new home until I had not only dusted and waxed all the many whorls and complexities of its ornamentation, but also restored its inner workings to their original state.

After a lengthy and expensive tuning, this was accomplished. To my surprise, the piano continued to unsettle me. Waking in the small hours of the night, grading papers or reading or laboring on my comprehensive analysis of the Egyptian Book of the Dead, I sometimes fancied that I heard it playing a melancholy and meditative concerto. More than once, I crept downstairs, my heart in my throat and a sturdy brass candlestick in my hand, intent on surprising the midnight musician. But on each occasion, I found the living room empty and dark, the piano silent. After a month or more of increasingly disturbed and sleepless nights, I formed the idea that the sounds haunting me must come from the house next door, the house whose antique air had so enchanted me. I decided to break the habit of years and introduce myself to my neighbor with the intention of asking him to remove his piano from the wall it must share with my study, or failing that, to confine his playing to daylight hours.

Accordingly, on my return next day from a seminar in reading papyri, I mounted the six steps of the ancient brownstone and tugged the rusted bell-pull hanging beside the banded oaken door. Deep within the house, a bell tolled, followed by a listening silence. Again I rang, determined to rouse the inhabitants, from sleep if need be, as they had so often roused me. The echoes of the third and last ring had not yet died away when the door opened.

My first impression of Roderick Hawthorne was that he was very beautiful. He was tall, over six feet, and slender as a reed, with long, prominent bones. His forehead was broad and domed under an unruly mass of bronze-dark curls like chrysanthemum petals that rioted over his head and down his long and hollow jaw in an equally unruly beard. His nose was Egyptian in the spring of its nostrils, pure Greek in its high-arched bridge; his eyes were large and dark and liquid behind round gold-rimmed spectacles. His gaze, mildly startled at first, sharpened when it fell upon me, rendering me sufficiently self-conscious that I hardly knew how to begin my complaint.

"Your piano," I said at last, and was startled when he laughed. He had a laugh as beautiful as his person, deep and musical as an organ's *Vox Humana*. Then he said, "At its old tricks again, is it?" and I was lost. His voice was oboe and recorder, warm milk and honey. I could have listened to that voice reading the phone book with undiminished pleasure and attention. He spoke again: "Do come in, Miss... ?"

I realized that I was staring at him with my mouth ajar, more like a cinema fan in the presence of a celluloid celebrity than an Associate Professor of Archeology at a major American university. "It's Doctor, actually. Dr. Arantxa Waters."

"Dr. Waters." He held out a long hand, the fingers pale and smooth as marble, delicately veined with blue. Cold as marble, too, when I laid my own within it. "I am Roderick Hawthorne," he said. "Welcome to Hawthorne House."

The interior of Hawthorne House was as untouched by the modern world as its exterior. The walls were hung with richly figured papers and the windows with draperies of velvet and brocade in crimson, ultramarine, and the mossy green of a forest floor. The furniture was massive, dark, ornamented with every kind of bird and fruit and animal known to the carver's art. Precious carpets covered the floors, and precious objects crowded every surface not claimed by piles of books. Everything was illuminated by the soft yellow glow of gaslights hissing behind etched glass shades. It would have been perfect, if it hadn't been for the dust and neglect that lay over it all like a pall. Still, I complimented him on the beauty of his home with complete sincerity.

"Do you like it?" he asked, a touch anxiously. "It's gone woefully to seed, I'm afraid, since my wife's death. I suppose I could hire a housekeeper, but the truth is, I hardly notice the mess. And I do value my privacy."

I felt an unaccustomed color climb my cheeks, shame and irritation combined. "I shall conclude my business quickly," I said, and explained that his piano playing at night was disturbing my studies. As I spoke, it seemed to me that the intensity of his gaze grew ever more concentrated, so that I could almost imagine my blush rather ignited by the fire of his eye than my own self-consciousness.

"I understand," he said when I fell silent. "Although I am somewhat at a loss as to the remedy. Come, see for yourself."

He led me from the parlor, where we had been talking, up a wide and sweeping staircase to the floor above, where he turned *away* from the direction in which my own house and its study lay, into a room across the landing, illuminated, like the parlor, by gas and oil lamps. The soft golden light showed me a formal music room, furnished with a gilded floor-harp and a cello as well as a brocade sofa, a gallery of shadowy pictures in filthy glass—and a piano, the precise twin of mine, down to the carved heads and the unusual deep crimson stain.

"As you can see," he said as I stared at the piano, "the sound of my playing is unlikely to carry across the landing and through two brick walls to disturb you in your study. But I do believe that you have been so disturbed." Observing my look of bewilderment, he gestured towards the sofa. "Sit down, please, and I shall tell you the story.

"You have noticed, of course, that our pianos are a matched pair. Your piano was, in fact, made for the wife of the Hawthorne who built Hawthorne House, not long after she entered it as a bride. In this very room they played duets until her untimely death caused him, in the extremity of his grief, to banish her piano to the stable."

Feeling I should make some observation, I said, "A very natural response, under the circumstances."

"Oh no," Hawthorne said seriously, "he was quite mad. And went madder with time. A sane man might have given the piano to charity or sold it or even caused it to be destroyed. The founder of Hawthorne House had his lawyers draw up a rider to the deed preventing the piano from being moved from the stable or destroyed, in perpetuity, no matter who might come to own the stable or what might be done to it."

"Your ancestor does seem to have been a trifle eccentric," I said. "But it was a romantic and morbid age."

His large, bright eyes dwelt on my face. "You are very understanding," he murmured, his voice thrilling in my ear.

"Not at all," I said briskly. "Is there more to the story?"

He seemed to collect himself. "Very little of substance. Yet, a piano with such a history is as likely to attract rumors as a corpse attracts worms. Most pertinent of these is that, under certain circumstances, it plays in sympathy with its mate."

"And do you believe in such rumors?

"I believe in everything," Roderick Hawthorne said. Shrugging away his melancholy, he turned a hospitable smile on me. "As long as you are here, will you take a glass of sherry and hear me play?"

Although I myself place little credence in ghosts and hauntings, it was clear from his nervous hands, his febrile eye, the urgent note in his plangent voice, that Roderick Hawthorne was utterly convinced that the music I was hearing was the result of a species of supernatural possession. Nevertheless, the charms of his person and his voice were such that I accepted both sherry and invitation and sat upon the sofa while he laid his beautiful long hands upon the red piano's ebony keys and began to play.

How shall I describe Roderick Hawthorne's playing? I am, as I have said, a woman whose passions are primarily intellectual, whose reason is better developed than her emotions. My host's music delved into the unplumbed depths of my psyche and brought up strange jewels. The nut-sweet sherry blended with salt tears as I wept unashamedly, drunk on music and the deep rumble of my host, humming as he played.

Afterwards, we sat in the parlor with lamplight playing on Chinese urns and Renaissance bronzes and talked of the subject precious to us both: the wide range of humanity's response to the ineluctable fact of death. By the time I left him, long after midnight, I was well on my way to a state I had never before experienced and was hardly able to identify. I was infatuated.

In taking leave of me, Roderick proposed that I call upon him soon. "I have no telephone," he said. "Nor do I often leave my house. I would not like to think that my eccentricity might prevent the deepening of a promising friendship."

Even in the face of such clear encouragement, I waited almost a week before calling on him again. Out of his presence, I found myself as disquieted by his oddities as charmed by his beauty. I was reasonably sure that the use of gas for household lighting was against all current city building codes. And his superstitious belief in the haunted bonds between our twin pianos and the supernatural origin of the sounds I heard, combined with the fact that he himself was (I presumed) recently widowed and not yet recovered from his loss, made me reluctant to further the acquaintance. Still, there was his playing, and the intoxication of conversation with one whose obsessions so perfectly complemented my own. And there was my own piano, singing softly at the edge of my hearing in the deep of the night, reminding me of the emotions I had experienced hearing him play its mate, and could experience again, if only I should take the trouble to go next door.

Unable to resist longer, I put aside my reservations, rang the rusty bell, and saw again his large, mild eyes, his sweet mouth nested like a baby bird in the riot of his beard, felt his cold, smooth hand press my own, heard his voice like an oboe welcoming me, questioning me, talking, talking, talking with delight of all the things that were closest to my heart.

On this second visit, it seemed to me that the house was cleaner than it had been when I'd first seen it—the hangings brighter, the air clearer. The change was most apparent in the music room, where the piano gleamed a deep crimson and candlelight sparkled off the new-polished glass of the gallery of pictures. When Roderick began to play, I rose from the sofa to examine them.

They were sketches, in pencil or charcoal, of a female figure surrounded by shadowed and threatening shapes. Sometimes she fled across a gothic landscape; more often she sat in intricately rendered interiors that I recognized at once as my host's parlor and music room, alone save for demonic shapes that menaced her from the shadows. The figure bore only the faintest resemblance to an actual woman, being slender to the point of emaciation, burdened with dark curly hair inclined to dishevelment, and possessed of eyes stretched in an extremity of terror. It was not until I came upon a head and shoulders portrait that I realized, with a feeling of considerable shock, that the face gazing out so anxiously from the gilded frame was, when seen in relative repose, very like mine. Had I allowed my hair to grow out of the neat crop I had adopted to tame its natural wildness, lost twenty pounds or so, and assumed clothing over a century out of fashion, there would have been no difference between us.

Behind me, the music modulated into a melancholy mode. "The first Mrs. Hawthorne," Roderick said. "Drawn not long before her death, by her husband. The others were drawn later. He became obsessed by the idea that demons had sucked the life from her. There are boxes full of such sketches in the attic."

"They seem a very gloomy subject for a music room," I commented.

"They have always been here," he said simply. "I do not choose to move them."

"And your own wife," I asked diffidently. "Have you any pictures of her?"

Under Roderick's long, pale fingers, the ebony keys of the red piano danced and flickered in an unquiet mazurka. "My wife," he said precisely, "died some while ago. She, too, was pale, with dark eyes and dark hair. Isabella Lorenzo, who last owned your stable, was of similar coloring. So are you."

For a moment, I was both frightened and repelled by the intensity of his gaze over the crimson-stained music stand, the throb and tremor of his beautiful voice. I felt that I had intruded unpardonably upon a grief too terrible and private for my eyes. Embarrassed almost beyond bearing, I was on the point of quitting his music room and his house, never to return. But then he smiled, and the tune beneath his fingers grew bright and gay and light. "But all that is past now, lovely Arantxa," he said softly, "and has nothing to do with you and me."

Foolishly, I believed him.

The subject of Roderick's lost wife did not arise again between us, as fearful to me as it must have been painful to him. Nor did I learn anything more of the history of the first Mrs. Hawthorne, my long dead doppelganger. These shadows on his past did nothing to decrease my fascination with him, which only grew more intense as the year faded towards winter.

Over the next weeks, I came by insensible degrees to spend almost every evening in his company. I always went to him; he would not venture even so far from his house as my adjacent stable. No stranger to the terrors that agoraphobia can visit on a sensitive spirit, I did not press him, but returned his hospitality by providing our nightly dinners. An unenthusiastic cook, I provided take-out from one of the local restaurants, but I will never forget the first time I descended to his kitchen in search of a teapot and hot water, only to discover that the stove was wood-fed, the water pumped by hand into the sink, and the milk kept in an icebox chilled by an actual block of ice.

"It has always been that way," he said when I came up again, defeated by the primitive technology. "I donot choose to change it."

On subsequent visits, I found the stove had been lit and water pumped ready in the kettle for our nightly cup of tea. Indeed, Roderick showed himself unfailingly solicitous of my comfort. When I complained that I was too tired, on returning home late each night, to keep up with my work, he gave me the room across the hall from the music room as a study. There I would sit, lapped in antique fur and velvet against the chill, grading papers by gaslight while the glorious waves of Roderick's music washed over my senses. Often, emotion so overcame me that I would have granted him whatever he might ask, even to those intimacies I could hardly bring myself to contemplate. But every night, when the great clock at the foot of the steps chimed midnight, he would lower the cover over the keys, wish me goodnight, and escort me to the door.

I soon became aware of an inconvenient lack of energy. At first I blamed my growing enervation on too little sleep and the extreme stimulation of Roderick's conversation and music. I confided my state to Roderick, who insisted that I leave at eleven, so that I might retire earlier. "For now that I've found you, Arantxa, I cannot do without you. I might have sunk into melancholy altogether, and my house with me, had it not been for you."

Indeed, both Roderick and his house had improved since I'd first seen them. Someone had cleaned and dusted, washed and polished everything to the well-cared-for glow that bespeaks a truly dedicated housekeeper. When I asked where he'd unearthed such a jewel, he smiled and turned the subject. I began to sleep longer and for a time, felt a little better. But my classes were a struggle to prepare and my students a constant irritation.

Early in the spring semester, my department chair called me into his office. He was concerned about my health, he said. I seemed languid, forgetful of meetings and deadlines. There had been complaints. It was all very troubling. To silence him, I made an appointment with a doctor at the University Health Services. He subjected me to a series of annoying and expensive tests, and in the end confessed himself no wiser than when he started. He diagnosed me with non-typical chronic fatigue, and prescribed a stimulant.

Roderick laughed when he heard this diagnosis. "Chronic fatigue? Nonsense. You possess more vitality than any woman I have known." He took my hand and raised it to his lips. "Dear Arantxa," he murmured, his breath warm on my knuckles. "So strong, so utterly alive. You must know that I adore you. Will you marry me?"

My heart stuttered in my breast with fear or passion—I hardly knew which. His bright and fixed gaze filled my mind and my senses, leaving room for nothing else. Words of acceptance trembled on my lips, but were checked at the last moment by inborn caution.

"You overwhelm me, Roderick," I said shakily. "I have never thought of marriage. You must give me time to consider your proposal."

Releasing my hand, Roderick shrank back into his chair. "You do not love me as I love you," he said, his oboe-like voice clouded with disappointment.

I leaned forward, and for the first time, touched his softly curling beard. "I might," I said truthfully. "I don't know. I need to think what to do."

He nodded, his beard sliding under my fingers. "Then you shall think. But please—think quickly."

That night, he played the red piano with unsurpassed passion. I lay on the music-room sofa overwhelmed with sound, my arm flung over my eyes to hide my slow, helpless tears. Of course I loved him. I had never found anyone who listened to me as he did, looked at me with such hunger. Why then did I hesitate? In my extreme perturbation, I could hardly find the energy to rise from the sofa, and was forced to accept his arm to support me to the door. "Are you well?" he asked anxiously. "Shall I help you home?"

Knowing what the offer must have cost him, I was deeply moved. "My goodness," I said, forcing a light tone through my deadly fatigue. "Do I look that bad? No, I'll be fine by myself."

"I will see you tomorrow, then," he said, and for the first time, laid his lips against mine. His kiss, both passionate and cold, excited my nerves, lending me the strength to traverse the short distance to my own door.

I slept fitfully that night. Whenever I fell asleep, I was haunted by a groaning, as of pain unbearable, echoing up the spiral stairs. I would wake with a start and lie quivering in the darkness, ears straining to hear past the beating of my heart. The next day passed in a kind of stupor. I could barely totter down to the kitchen to boil water for tea and recruit faltering nature with soup and toast. By evening, I was simultaneously exhausted and restless beyond bearing. Which was, perhaps, why I found myself sitting on the piano bench.

I had not come near the piano in some time. As I sat before it, I noticed that the little carved faces were familiar. I knew that domed brow, that coolly sensual mouth in its nest of hyacinthine curls. My exhaustion was such that I saw nothing odd in finding Roderick's visage carved upon his ancestor's piano. It only inspired in me a desire to touch him, speak to him, draw comfort from him. Impulsively, I raised the cover, lifted my hands to the ebony keys and ran my fingers from treble to bass. If I was too weak to drag myself to him, perhaps I could touch him through our linked instruments.

Tentatively, I embarked upon a simple song I had learned as a girl. I stumbled at first, and then sense memory took over. My fingers began to move as of their own accord, progressing from the song into a nocturne, and then into improvisation. As I played, I forgot my fatigue, my undone work, even Roderick and his proposal. The music I made lifted me into a realm of beautiful abstraction, spirit without substance, clean and pure and bright. When at last I stopped playing, it was a little after midnight. Strangely, I felt better—tired certainly, but not exhausted. My mind was clearer than it had been for months.

I slept soundly that night, never stirring until early afternoon, when I rose well-rested and able to eat a proper meal and do some real work. When I looked up from my papers, it was far too late to go to Roderick's. Wanting to recapture that feeling of perfect communion, I sat down once again at the red piano, and rose some hours later, strong, refreshed, and as sure as I could be that I loved Roderick Hawthorne and wanted to be his wife.

The next afternoon, I dressed myself with more than usual care. I brushed out my hair, which had grown during my illness, into a dark cloud that made my face more delicate and white in contrast. I put on a dress I had not worn since college—black velvet cut tight to my hips, the skirt full and sweeping below. I clasped my mother's pearls around my neck, and thus bedecked, once again rang the bell of Hawthorne House.

No sooner had my hand fallen from the pull than the door opened on a haggard figure I hardly recognized. Roderick Hawthorne's hair was uncombed, his collar unbuttoned, his cheeks gaunt and his eyes reddened. "Arantxa!" he exclaimed. "I have not slept or eaten in two days, waiting for your answer, fearing what it must be when you did not return."

My heart contracted with pity. "Oh, my dear." He smiled at the endearment, the first I'd ever used. "I could not come. I was so tired. And I did need to think."

"My poor angel. Of course. I'm glad you're better. And you are here now. It is yes, isn't it? Your answer?"

Something in his voice—satisfaction? triumph?—stifled my agreement on my lips. I smiled, but said nothing.

Dinner was a depressing meal. The dining room was cold, the fire sullen and low, the food indifferent. Both of us avoided the subject most pressingly on our minds, every other topic of conversation an unexpected minefield of references to love or matrimony. At length, we rose from an unaccustomed silence.

"I will not plead for myself," he said. "Perhaps you will let my music plead for me." He took my hand; his was colder than ice. As we walked from the dining room to the music room, I noticed that the whole house was cold, neglected, dusty, as though none had swept or polished or built a fire there for weeks rather than the two days I'd been absent. Roderick hurried me up the stairs, and fear grew in me. On the threshold of the music room, I hesitated, searching for some way to excuse myself from a situation grown suddenly intolerable. Roderick's cold hand grasped mine more tightly, drawing me inexorably towards the red piano and down onto the bench beside him

The carved faces peered at me from the music stand. It was the first time I had seen them close up, but I was not astonished to discover that they were as like the first Mrs. Hawthorne, like me, as the faces on my piano were like Roderick. In a flash, I understood everything. It utterly defied rational belief, but I could not afford the luxury of disbelief. My very life depended on acting quickly.

I took a deep, calming breath and smiled deliberately into his face. Roderick Hawthorne smiled back, predatory as a wolf, then released me, rubbed his long hands together, and flexed his fingers. He disposed them gently on the ebony keys, and prepared to play me to utter dissolution.

Before he could sound a single note, I seized the heavy wooden cover and slammed it shut on his fingers with all my force.

He screamed like a wild animal, a scream with a snarl in it, rage and pain mingled. Springing to my feet, I ran from the music room, snatching up my cumbersome skirts. Weak and in pain, he was still stronger than I, infinitely older and wise in the terrible sorcery that had animated him so far beyond his natural life. If I fell into his hands, I knew I could not escape him a second time. I ran headlong down the stairs, resisting the impulse to look behind me, knowing he must follow me, clumsy with pain, utterly determined to catch me and drain me of my strength and my life.

Tearing open the door, I stumbled into the open air a step ahead of him, and down the stoop into the alley. I knew that his life must be intimately intertwined with the house he had inhabited for so long. He might not be able to step over the threshold; then again, he might. I could not afford to take the chance.

In the light of a single lamp, my living room seemed calm and homelike. Then I clicked on the overhead, and there was the red piano, squatting beside the stair, oversized, over-decorated, garish, out of place among the beautiful simplicities of my collections.

A scream of rage at the end of the alley sent me flying to the box I kept under the stairs. Screwdriver, hammer, pliers, wire cutter—inadequate tools for the task ahead, but all I had at my disposal. Terror made me strong. I splintered the ebony keys and the music stand with the hammer. An inhuman howling came from the alley. I attacked the carved faces on the legs and case. Something heavy began to slam against my front door, causing it to quiver in the frame. Furiously I hammered at the carved wood, squinting against the splinters stinging my cheeks and chest.

With a great crack, the door burst inwards. I looked up, and there was Roderick Hawthorne, framed in darkness, his face stark in the electric glare. If I had harbored any lingering doubts as to the uncanny nature of the night's events, I did so no longer. His face was scored and bleeding, his beard ragged and clotted with gore, his eye a bloody ruin, his mouth swollen and misshapen. I glanced down at my hammer, half-expecting to see it smeared with blood. In that moment of inattention, he sprang towards me, gabbling wildly, his beautiful voice raw and ruined, his beautiful hands bruised, swollen, bleeding, reaching for me, for the broken piano keys.

Snatching up the wire cutters, I thrust open the piano lid and applied myself to the strings. One by one I clipped them, in spite of Roderick's howling and wailing, in spite of his hands clawing at my shoulders as he tried in vain to prevent me from severing his heart strings. As I worked my way down to the bass register, the howling stopped, and I felt only a weak pawing at my ankles. And then there was nothing.

When I completed my task, I turned and saw what I had done. For a moment, a horror lay on my rug, the red and white and black ruin of the man I had loved. And then his flesh deliquesced in an accelerated process of decay as unnatural as his protracted life. A deep groan sounded, as of crumbling masonry and walls, and then my world was rocked with the slow collapse of Hawthorne House, falling in on itself like a house of cards, dissolving, like its master, into featureless dust and rubble.

I was rescued from the wreckage by my neighbor on the other side. He gave me strong coffee laced with rum and chocolate chip cookies for shock and called the police and the fire department. He is neither beautiful nor mysterious, and he made his fortune writing code for a computer game I had never even heard of. He prefers klezmer music to opera and *South Park* to the Romantics. He reads science fiction and plays video games. We were married in the spring, right after final exams, and moved uptown to an apartment in a modern tower with square white rooms and views across the river. We have no piano, no harp, not even a guitar. But sometimes in the deep of winter, when the dark comes early and the wind shrills at the bedroom window, I think I can hear the red piano playing, deep and wild and passionate.

WHEN I WAS *in seventh grade, I discovered a book on my parents' bookshelves. It was large, black, and impressive-looking, and had an oddly creepy illustration on the cover of a lady in a huge skirt, her breasts bare, and a man in a truly splendid black robe kneeling at her feet. The interior was creepier still, both words and pictures. The words were Edgar Allan Poe's, the illustrations were Harry Clarke's, and really, I don't know which entranced and repelled me more. I was particularly drawn to their deathly ladies: pale, learned, sickly, beautiful, and doomed, doomed, doomed to die horribly so that their pale, learned, beautiful, and tortured lovers could enjoy—and lovingly, lingeringly describe—torments of grief and/or guilt. "The Red Piano" is a kind of homage to those women, to Morella and Berenice, to Ligeia and the Marchesa Aphrodite and the unfortunate Lady Madeline Usher. I only wish I could see what Harry Clarke would do with Arantxa and Roderick.*

M. RICKERT'S short story collection, *Map of Dreams*, won the William Crawford and World Fantasy awards. Her next collection, *Holiday*, will be published by Golden Gryphon Press in 2009. She lives in Cedarburg, Wisconsin.

SLEEPING WITH THE ANGELS

By M. Rickert

WE SHARED THE secret until she said we had to stop or we would burn. I told her to close her eyes and think about heaven. I was immediately filled with regret and waited in the dark for the devil to come but instead morning arrived with its golden wings. I placed the pillow under her head, crawled out of her bed into mine, and determined that I would never do something like that again. I wondered if I would meet something terrible in the days to come and then I met a girl made by fire. She threw stones at me while I stood outside the funeral parlor where everyone was weeping for Mazie. Poor Mazie, only nine and the family's blessing, they whispered, their eyes sliding towards me and back again to her. Even dead, Mazie was preferred. Later, after Mazie was in the ground, my father was in the tavern, and my mother was in the cleaning mood that never left her I saw the fire girl again. She was standing near the graveyard, her braided hair ratty as a nest. "Hey Laurel, come here," she said, "I wanna show you somethin'."

I followed her through the spit bugs and itchy grass into the woods behind the dish factory where butter flowers blossomed beside black water and the sky was green. "Hurry up slowpoke," she said. "I ain't got all day." We climbed rocks and grassy hills, swatting at mosquitoes.

"You are going to be so surprised," she promised. I looked at the wine colored stains on her neck and arms. "Whatcha staring at?" she asked.

"Nothin'," I said. "That's right, nothin'." Her messed up braids were tied at the end with rubber bands, the kind that hurt.

"Wait till you see this," she said and waved her arm like a magician over a pile of torn flowers, grass and a dead dog.

I bent down to get a close look. It was the Egler's dog, Sally.

"You know what happened to that dog?" she said, stepping towards me.

I pretended not to be scared. "What? You think I ain't ever seen a dead dog before?"

She was standing there with a rock in her hand. She let it drop like it was suddenly struck by gravity. "Come on," I said, pretending to be in charge. I turned and walked back the way we came. When we got to the end of the woods, the street littered with tricycles and the torn noise of the Fellmore kids, I bolted. She shouted, but I pretended not to hear and ran all the way home, slamming the screen door. My mom hollered. She was in the kitchen washing the windows. She had on an apron with giant cabbages. Some of the cabbages had faces.

I opened the icebox and leaned into the cool air.

"Don't stand there like you're stupid; pick something and close the door."

I took the milk and poured myself a glass.

"You feeling all right?"

I acted like *Brady Bunch* Cindy. "I feel great," I cheered.

She started scrubbing the window again to let in all the bright.

I set the empty glass in the sink. "I think I'll just get a head start on my seventh grade reading. Didn't Mrs. Mallory send home a list? Yep, I'm going to go get started on my reading."

My mother's yellow hand kept polishing the glass. I thought she might stop but she didn't. When I walked out of the kitchen each room got warmer and warmer until when I got upstairs I thought maybe I had a fever.

Almost right away my mom came into the room. She didn't knock; she just came in and put her hand on my forehead. It was clammy from the plastic gloves she'd been wearing.

"Your stomach hurt?"

I shook my head.

"Your throat all right?"

I nodded.

"You need to talk?"

I thought of telling her about the burned girl and I thought of telling her about what I did but I wasn't sure she'd understand.

"You ever need to talk, we can talk, all right?"

Then she started talking about Mazie. When it seemed like she was winding down I said, "Gram says Mazie's a flower now."

Her eyes got small, her mouth got hard, even the cabbages squinted at me in disgust. "Mazie ain't no flower," her words chopped the air.

"Okay, Mom."

* * *

THE GIRL MADE of fire never asked what my name was, right from the start she knew. "Hey, Kid," she said, and when I didn't answer, "Hey, Laurel, I'm talking to you. What are you, some kind of freak?"

I was standing outside the funeral home. It was a gray day. Water was hanging in the sky. Everyone came in all wet like it was raining but it wasn't. I was on the porch not thinking about Mazie when all of a sudden this girl showed up on the cracked sidewalk, with her ratty hair and fire scars, talking to me all rude.

"Ain't you supposed to be somewhere?" I asked. "Ain't you got folks looking for you?"

Her mouth dropped open. She pointed at her dirty t-shirt and said, "What? You seen someone looking for me?" She shook her head, rolled her eyes, and smirked. "I don't think so." Then she started throwing stones, aiming for my heart. I picked up one and threw it back. She ducked, but I missed by a lot.

A car parked across the street. Mr. and Mrs. Swenson and all three of the Swenson kids got out: Mickey, Mikey, and Mary dressed to match. When Mrs. Swenson saw me, her face crumpled up like a wad of tissue. I wondered if the burned girl would throw stones at the Swensons but I didn't wait to find out. I escaped into the funeral parlor where it was warm and sweet and strange. Someone patted me on the head. My mom was sitting with her hands in her lap. Church ladies stood touching her to keep her from floating away.

MY MOM WAS sitting on Mazie's bed, saying my name.

"You have to stop this," she said in a straight voice.

"What?"

"You are a healthy child. You don't got whatever Mazie had, all right? That was just a freak accident. Doctor Brunner said. So quit acting like you are on death's door. You gotta cry, cry, but no more sleeping all day."

"But, Mom—"

"From now on I want you playing outside 'less it's raining. Even then you can get a little wet once in a while, long as it's not lightning. This house is off limits between nine and five, you hear?"

I opened my mouth but she continued. "I know you got your reasons, but I am telling you this for your own good. Now, git." She nodded. "You heard me," she said, rubbing her hand on Mazie's bedspread.

The girl was sitting on my back step like she was expecting me. She draped her bony arm over my shoulder. Close, she smelled bad. "Come on," she said.

I tried to pull away.

She smiled cinnamon freckles and crooked teeth as she led me past the dry bird bath and our weed garden. Cicadas screamed from dark pine branches. They sounded like metal. Her bony arm on my shoulder got heavier and heavier. She was talking but I wasn't listening. We walked past the plumbing store, the post office, and the foundry. Greasy men sat on the lawn smoking. They watched us with stone eyes. We walked past the Catholic Church where blackbirds pecked at the cross. Mrs. Wydinki was working in her garden and didn't answer when I said hi. She was wearing a giant hat that made her face a shadow. She was cutting flowers from their stems with a large shears.

"Don't talk to her, else she'll cut your head off."

I glanced back at Mrs. Wydinki slicing roses like an assassin.

"Where we going, anyway?"

"Kingdom by the Sea." Her breath was sour.

"There's no sea around here," I said.

"You ever seen a mermaid?"

I shook my head.

"Before we moved we lived right on the beach. We used to make sand castles and we had picnics. After they got married everything was supposed to be nice." She shrugged. I used the opportunity to release myself from her arm. We stood in front of a tavern. It had a sign with a picture of a mermaid on it. She had big round breasts and long blonde hair. She was holding a book just above her green tail. The title of the book was *Kingdom by the Sea.*

"That's my mom. From before."

She was pointing at the sign but I looked at the burns on her arms.

"Come on," she opened the tavern door. "Hurry up. They don't like the light."

The dark smelled of alcohol and smoke. She stuck her fingers in a bowl on the bar. "Here," she said, and dropped peanuts into my hand. The music pounded in my ears. My dad sat at the bar. Next to him sat a lady with black lines around her eyes and bright red lips like one of Mrs. Wydinki's blood roses. She was smoking a cigarette. There were some people sitting in a booth, and some men with loud voices playing pool in the back. The bartender said something low to the woman with rose lips and she cackled.

"You checked on my mom?"

The bartender shook his head.

She took me all the way to the back. I followed her up the crooked steps. She bent down and reached under the dirty mat for a key. An old couch squatted over a gold rug made out of yarn shaped like fat worms. The windows were small, closed and gray. A wheelchair was folded up against the wall, like a giant squashed bug.

"Mom! Hey, Mom!"

She walked to a closed door and opened it. I could see the edge of a bed. From the bed came murmuring.

"My friend," I heard her say.

The murmuring mumbled. I leaned over to get a better look but I couldn't see much. I heard her say, "I told you I made a friend." Again there was that strange murmuring. She came out and shut the door behind her. Firm. "Well. Now you know," she said. "You gonna eat those nuts?"

I opened my fingers. She grabbed the peanuts and tossed them back. There was a refrigerator next to the sink, behind the couch. She opened it and shut it fast. A sour smell hung in the air.

"Where's your room?" I asked.

The voice in the bedroom hollered. It made no sense. It sounded like cicadas. We left fast. Down the wooden stairs, past the cackling woman and my dad who stared into his empty glass. When we walked out into the sunshine it felt like we made a great escape. We ran until my side hurt. I think she could have kept on running. I think she ran a lot. She took my hand. Smiled her crooked teeth. She wasn't even breathing fast. Her breath smelled like peanuts. We walked together. I tried not to step on the cracks but she didn't seem to notice. She stepped on several. We were too old for that baby game, anyway.

SUMMER DAYS MADE of dandelions, sky, scent of green, pesty flies, mosquitoes, hoses, sprinklers, bubbles, screaming, laughing, running, holding hands—not caring when the teenage boys drove by in their souped-up cars and called us homos. At first I didn't like the smell of her breath. Or the way her bones felt, heavy and sharp when she draped an arm over my shoulder. Or the way she laughed, her mouth wide open, her eyes always watching. But I got used to her. Sometimes we'd sit on the porch and she'd tell me stories about when it was just the two of them and they lived by the sea with mermaids, flying fish, and shooting stars. ("Did you ever eat seaweed? I have.") I liked the way her name felt on my tongue. Annabel. Like rolling marbles in my mouth. Only sweet.

"Annabel, can you come?" I'd stand outside the door at the top of the stairs. Below me the bar would hum with juke music and the drift of voices.

"Who is it?" she'd say. Like there was a line of visitors at the door.

"It's me. Can I come in?"

She had instructed me, one knock, then wait. "If I'm home, I'll hear you. Otherwise you don't gotta talk to no one. Just see if I answer. Give me a minute. If I don't answer, come back later."

I'd go to the playground. Swing in the rusty air. Sometimes I'd think about Mazie and what I did to her. There was no taking it back. Nothing to be done about it. I would never do anything like it again, I promised, and kept that promise for a long time. Sometimes I'd just sit there, dragging my shoes in the dirt while the sun hated me with its big hot eye.

"What took you so long?" she'd say. We'd run down the stairs like we were being chased by monsters. Grab a handful of nuts. The bartender ignored us. Sometimes my dad was there. "Hey, pops," I'd say. I didn't say boo to the cackling woman even when she spoke to me. I hated her big red lips like she'd eaten someone alive. We'd walk into the bright sunshine, Annabel draping her heavy arm over my shoulder. After a while I liked the weight of her. It made me feel like I mattered.

"Come on, I wanna show you somethin'."

She showed me the tree shaped like a skeleton ("You should see it in the dark," she said. "It will terrify you."), the ghost trapped in the church window ("Can you see her? Can you?"), the rock shaped like an angel. ("At night she comes alive. She flies all over. Grants wishes and shit.")

"Angels don't grant wishes. You're confusing them with fairies."

"Come on."

We slid down the hill and made scraped knees and bloodied palms. The highway whipped past on the other side. She whispered into the rock. Then she waited for me. I didn't wanna do it. "Just try," she said. "When did you get to be so godless?" I leaned against the rock and whispered. A car honked. I looked at Annabel. "What you wish for?" she asked.

I shrugged.

"Come on, you can tell me." Her voice flat. Mean. "We're best friends."

"Shut up. You know how it works."

She smiled. Her heavy arm draped over my shoulder. She leaned close.

"Come on," I said. "Race you up the hill."

She won. Of course. When I got to the top, I had a stitch. She walked ahead. Like she didn't care. I looked back at the stone angel. Hunched there. A creature ready for the kill.

HERE WE ARE in summer. Here we are behind glass. I have only this one photograph of us. Me and Annabel framed in my backyard. Behind us stands the dry bird bath, the scraggled weeds, but what I see is my mother, standing there in her cabbage frowning apron, pretending she loves me. "Let me take your picture," she said. Annabel holds me close. I like the shape of her at my side. My mother lowers the camera. She stares at us. I am the happiest I have ever been. It is summer and the sun is good. Mazie is still dead, but I forget about her sometimes.

"Laurel," my mother says, her voice sudden.

"What?" we both say. As if we are one.

My mother looks at our two heads. "Laurel can't play any more today." Annabel and I look at each other. Shocked. My mother hasn't wanted me all summer. She holds her hand out. "Come along," she says, pulling me away. I trot beside her like I am six. I look back at Annabel who stands next to the dry bird bath.

"See you tomorrow," I call. She nods. Slowly.

"Not tomorrow," my mother says, pulling me along. Squeezing my hand. My mother opens the door to the forbidden house. Smiles at me like a television commercial, but the words are sharp. "Look at you." She bites her lip. Changes her voice. "You need a bra." The sun shines bright through the clean kitchen windows. The house smells like soap and bread. "I know! You can help with the ironing!" She says it like it's a wonderful, wonderful thing.

The house is hot. The iron steam reminds me of dreams. I make sharp neat corners. Annabel, I think. I like the round shape of her name. I like the shape of her next to me. Annabel, Annabel, Annabel. Like the angel trapped in the rock, I am trapped in this house. If someone saw me from a distance, would they know what I am?

What is Annabel doing now? She is standing at the kitchen window staring at me. I blow her a kiss. Her smile opens her face.

"What's that smell? I smell burning." My mother comes into the room. Annabel runs. My mother's head turns toward the window and then to me. "What are you doing?" she says.

My brain gets stuck on Annabel. Annabel, Annabel, Annabel.

My mother lifts up the iron to reveal the brown stain on her blouse. She fires me on the spot.

"Can I go back outside? 'Cause Annabel—"

"No. Go to your room."

I walk through the fever rooms to my bedroom. I lay down on my bed and close my eyes. Imagine Annabel beside me. It isn't long before Mazie comes. "You won't get away with what you done," she whispers, her cold lips close.

"I didn't do nothing," I say.

"I'm going to set you on fire."

I sit up straight. My heart beating. My skin hot. Alone, of course. There's Mazie's empty bed. There's the window and summer. I shiver in the heat. I imagine Annabel beside me. Hot as a match, her gold eyes burning.

When I see her again, almost a week later, she wraps her skinny muscled arms around me. Squeezes tight. "Oh, I missed you, baby," she says. Not mean at all. "Come on, I wanna show you something."

It is hot. So hot that steam rises from the road like snakes from hell. So hot our hands are sticky. The souped-up car passes us. Boys lean out the window, "Homos," they shout. Honking the horn. We walk past the electric poles with pictures of Sally tacked up. Lost Dog. Reward! I wonder what it would be like to make a sign like that for Mazie. A little kid idea.

Blue-bottle flies buzz at us. "Like we are either flowers or full of shit," Annabel says, and laughs.

She takes me to a small hill covered in dirt, fresh turned where we lay down. "Hey," I say, "What happened to you?"

"What do you mean?" I touch a burn spot and then another. Each place I touch is cold. Her blonde hair blazes in the sun.

"I'm going to tell you something vital," she says. "Remember how my mom is a mermaid? Well my dad was too but he couldn't take it no more and went back to the ocean. Then my mom married the bartender." (That guy? I say. She nods solemnly. Guess what? My dad is the one I call pops. I figured, she says. He wasn't always like that, I say. Here's the thing, she says. None of us are.) "My mom couldn't change back into a mermaid no more after the fire. That's why we moved here, far from the ocean, 'cause it disturbed her to be near it. She ain't never forgived me, and she ain't never will. That's why they do things to me." (What things? I ask but she just keeps talking.) "There ain't nothing I can do about it. You gotta promise me, all right? Promise you'll tell someone. Not your dad. Someone more like your mother. She knows something ain't right about me, you gotta tell her what it is. You gotta tell her what they done to me."

What did they do? I mean to ask but my mind is stuck on Mazie rotting underground and I stare into Annabel's yellow eyes, which, I only just realize, remind me of Mazie. Maybe, I think, just maybe you are the devil after all. Sometimes my mind thinks things I have no control over. Sometimes my body does things all on its own.

"Come on," I say. Annabel sits up, blinking like she's surprised. Her hair is knotted with sticks and weeds. I start untangling them. "It's ok, baby," I whisper. We tiptoe through the forest.

Annabel takes me by the wrist and holds tight. "Ask if I can sleep over, all right?"

But when I bring Annabel into the house, my mother stares at us like we are demons. "What have you girls been doing?"

"Playing."

Annabel nods. "We rolled down the hill, but landed on some rocks."

"Can Annabel sleep over?"

"No. You go home now, Annabel."

"But, Mom—"

"You go to your room," she says like she knows everything.

Annabel wraps me in her arms and screams like a screech owl. My mother stands there stunned. I am impressed. When it seems like Annabel is winding down she turns to my mother, stares at her with slit eyes and says, "I bet you killed your daughter."

My mother's hand comes down hard, printing Annabel's face with pink fingers near the snake burn. Annabel turns to me, her arms outstretched.

"Get out," my mother says. "Don't you dare come back here, you nasty child."

A dead leaf falls from Annabel's hair. She is very scary looking. Why didn't I ever notice that before? Besides, what she said to my mother feels too close. What if she ever said something like that about me? I turn away from her, walking through the fever rooms and up the stairs. I crawl into bed, and wait for forgiveness.

When I wake up, the bedspread is streaked with dirt and broken grass. My body aches. My mother calls me down for dinner but I don't go. Later, when the whole house is dark, I press against the window screen.

The night smells heavy with scent of green. I take a deep breath. Stand there for a long while. Wishing on the distant angel. Then I go back to bed.

By morning I have kissed her a thousand times, felt her bony flesh sear into mine. "Annabel."

"No," my mother says. "She's not a nice girl."

"Annabel," I say again using her name like a stone.

"No."

"Annabel."

"Anyone else."

"Annabel."

"No."

"Annabel," I say with my burned lips.

"Go to your room."

"No."

My mother assesses me, measuring my size and will against her own. We stare at each other. For a moment, equal. Then, she looks away.

I am victorious. I walk out of the house, into the bright and frightening sun. Mrs. Wydinki is in her garden again, digging in the dirt, a furious expression on her face, thrusting small plants into the black soil. I step on all the cracks. Open the door to the tavern. The juke music is rough and sharp as a paper cut. The red lip woman sits there, grinning. My father rests, his face mashed against the bar.

I walk up the rickety stairs, knock on the door.

A voice calls from inside. "Who is it?"

"Is Annabel home?"

The voice comes out just as I am about to turn away. "Let yourself in."

I lift the mat and pick up the key. After all, what could happen? My own dad is right downstairs. I open the door. The stench is like the rotting fruit that sat too long on the kitchen table after Mazie died.

She sits in a wheelchair on the wormy rug, her legs covered with a blanket.

"Shut it, I can't stand the noise."

I close the door. Annabel's mother's hair is long, dry as old corn stalk, and her face is as squashed as a November Jack O' Lantern.

"Is Annabel—"

"Laurel? Right?"

I nod. What is that sound? I glance at the closed bedroom door.

She smiles a crack in her broken face. Pulls the blanket tight across her lap. "I wanted to get a good look at you."

A noise comes from the bedroom. Could be a mouse, I suppose. Or something terrible.

"You've been spending a lot of time with our little arsonist. Her and her stories."

The rattling sound coming from the bedroom continues, slightly louder. Annabel's mother eyes me. Though I just tamed my own mother, I decide that my best defense with this one is to act innocent. I smile, "Oh, yeah, Annabel tells great stories."

The mermaid presses her thin lips together. "She's told stories about you as well."

It hits me in the heart like a threat but I pretend not to notice. "Is she here, 'cause—"

"Annabel is staying with her cousin now."

"She didn't tell me that."

The mermaid sighs. "Well, you see, that's how she is. Rude. And here I am stuck without any help. See this fucking carpet? I can't move anywhere without getting stuck. Would you do me a favor and—"

"I gotta go."

"But—"

"Sorry," I mumble as I turn to the door.

"I just need—"

"Sorry," I say again, this time louder, for the sound in the bedroom, whoever, whatever it might be. I slam the door behind. Tumble down the stairs. Right to my dad. I pull him by the elbow, "Come on Pops."

"You go," he slurs.

"No." The bartender stares at me with hooded eyes. The red lipped woman leers. "Come on," I whisper, leaning close to my father's ear and the stubbled hair of his smoky cheek. "You can't stay here. These people are murderers."

My father pulls his shoulders back. Frowns.

"Come."

He slides off the stool.

"Hurry."

"Don't go," Red Lips says with her bloody mouth.

"I'm sorry," my father says, "I am needed at home."

When we walk into the sun he holds his hands in front of his face against the light.

"Hurry," I say.

"Who's dead?" he says.

"You know. Mazie."

He stumbles over dandelions thrust through the cracked sidewalk. He shouts nonsense at Mrs. Wydinki who stops her violent gardening to stare at us. Even the blackbirds pecking the cross outside the church stop when we pass. He has trouble walking up the steps to our house. My mom stands in the kitchen wearing the cabbage apron. "So you decided to come back," she says.

My father bows his drunken head.

I go to my hot room, and lay on my bed. "Annabel," I whisper. "Annabel?"

Later, when night beats like a purple heart she comes. "Remember?" she says but I don't tell anyone her secret for fear that somehow, they will find out mine. By the time school starts, Annabel's mom and stepdad are gone, and "Kingdom by the Sea" is shut down, the door nailed shut, windows boarded up. The sign swings on squeaky hinges and I am afraid to look at the mermaid's eyes. Recently a city reporter came to town investigating a rumor of murder but hardly anyone remembered much about the skinny child with burns who only lived here for one summer. I thought of leaving an anonymous note under the hotel room door, but the reporter was gone before I could do anything about it. Just as well, for there is danger in the unearthing of ghosts.

The years are like sea kelp. No one has guessed my secret, the dark hours of joy in which I burn. Night after night Annabel comes, begging. She never comments on the strangeness of my body, now turned into woman shape. All she asks, over and over again, is that I tell someone what was done to her. But the dead are as ignorant about life as the living are about death. I know it doesn't seem like it would be that way, but it is. The night beats its purple heart when she rests her hot head against my breast and I know I should apologize, and I know I should make amends, but instead I find comfort in death, the way it keeps all my secrets and holds all my lies. Night after night I promise. They won't get away with it, Annabel. You will be saved. Annabel. You will rest in peace. Annabel. I promise. I tell her, tomorrow. I tell her not to worry. I tell her to come closer, and she does.

MY BEST FRIEND *moved to Racine, Wisconsin after eighth grade. There, she made friends with a group of young people whose idea of entertainment was very different from the hard drinking notions of Fredonia's small town and farm-raised youth. During one particularly memorable visit, my friend and I were chauffeured by her older brother in their father's car. (I have no particular knowledge of cars so insert your own model here, but be sure to make it one that is appropriately middle class and fatherly.)*

My friend's brother removed a long, cloth, snaky-looking leopard skin device which turned out to be a steering wheel cover. Once that was placed securely over the steering wheel, he hung some beads from the rearview mirror. This, we believed, transformed the car from a dadmobile to ours... the young, free, unfettered mobile.

We drove around Racine, picking up various friends until finally we ended our version of Kerouac's journey in someone's basement rec room, furnished with old couches and the parents' bar. There, we turned off the lights, lit some candles and read Poe out loud to each other. My friend said that it wasn't as fun as the other times they did it, that it had lost its spontaneity and a good deal of its charm, but I thought it was wonderful.

As I navigated my high school years, watching one friend sink into schizophrenia, my brother fall into the despair of addiction, my mother and siblings navigate the tenuous reality of my father's mental illness, that simple night of reading Poe by candlelight with a group of kids my age helped me hold onto the belief in a world where literature exists as a source for renewal, no matter how odd its shape. I often describe how much of my work is about dealing with monsters, what I don't say often enough is that sometimes it's the monsters that will save you from those that will eat you alive.

Given the opportunity to write an homage to Poe's work, I knew right away I wanted to use one of his poems as the source of inspiration, and quickly narrowed it down to "Annabel Lee." While working on the story a ghost appeared from my youth, so long ago now; swimming in a hot lake, at a crowded beach, I remembered making friends with her, this skinny girl who couldn't get her cast wet. "How'd you break your arm?" I asked. "My dad did it," she said.

STEVE RASNIC TEM'S three–hundred–plus stories have garnered him numerous nominations and awards. Some recent work has appeared, or will appear, in *Cemetery Dance*, *Dark Discoveries*, *Albedo One*, *Blurred Vision*, *Matter*, *Exotic Gothic*, and in *That Mysterious Door* (Noreen Doyle, editor), an anthology of stories set in Maine. His latest novel, written in collaboration with wife Melanie Tem, is *The Man on the Ceiling* (Wizards' Discoveries), built around their award-winning novella of the same name. In the fall of 2009 Wizards' Discoveries will be bringing out his novel *Deadfall Hotel*, with a full complement of ghosts, vampires, were-wolves, zombies, and things which cannot be named.

SHADOW

by Steve Rasnic Tem

"I JUST WASN'T prepared for them, to have so much shadow enter my life."

The man in the video is your Uncle Mark, but you hardly recognize him. His face is puffy, unshaven, dirty. You recognize his weary voice only because of the resemblance to other male voices in your family. The poor sound quality emphasizes the weariness in his voice, in the world from which he speaks. This equipment is old—you haven't watched television in years. At a certain point you found it too irritating to bear—the sounds it made actually hurt your brain. But you can't remember exactly when that was. If the video player hadn't already been hooked up to the television you would have been helpless to make it work. You are surrounded, in fact, by numerous appliances you never use and have forgotten how.

You wonder how old he was when he made this recording. You're not good with ages, especially where men are concerned, but you think he might have been ten years older than you are now, which would place him in his early fifties. You think you must have been eight or nine years old, just a little girl, when he died. Which means, what? You must try to keep yourself from being annoyed by all these numbers because you will no longer be able to sit here and watch this man and find out some things. What, exactly, those things will be and what use you will make of them you have no idea. You do not want to be annoyed—bad things happen when you are annoyed.

Thirty years. It's been more than thirty years since he made this recording. You wonder if he would be surprised by how different the world is now. From the look of his face you think not.

His lighting is harsh, inexpert, overpowering. Why so much light? Then you notice how it is concentrated in the area immediately around him, as if he were enveloped in some brilliant bubble. The rest of the room is gloomy, hung with curtains, sheets, bedspreads. You think of sailing ships, although you have never actually seen one outside old magazines. Sheets and curtains shroud the furniture, smother the windows.

He says nothing more for a while. He rearranges the lamps, moving them forward, in and out of the frame, burning your eyes so that you have to look away.

"I won't be seeing you again," he says, finally. "And you won't much care, if this is my niece and nephew watching this. But I do wish you well."

You are so disturbed by his mention of a "nephew" that you slap the Stop button on the player. His image is suddenly swallowed up by dark gray murk. You press the Rewind button, press Play again. "... my niece and nephew watching this." You press Stop. You hope your uncle will not use Tommy's name—it wouldn't seem right. You yourself have not spoken Tommy's name aloud in years. How long ago was it? You start counting on your fingers, but you don't have enough. Fifteen years, perhaps sixteen, since Tommy's suicide. You punch the Play button so hard the player slides back several inches on its shelf. The screen jitters to life.

"Life is hard for all but a few of us—I think it is our business to wish each other well. It's quite possible you are years away from me now. I'm sure those of your generation still have your dark nights of the soul, do you not? 'Yea, though I walk,' and all that? Do you still read the Bible? I hadn't in years, before these last few days. Not that I'm a believer, I just felt a need to connect to the tormented.

"My hope is that you have someone to hold onto when things go very badly. I suspect you'll find much to doubt in my account, or it is possible things will have devolved even further than I imagined, and you'll know what I'm speaking of all too well. You may be watching this from some terrible future.

"And do you remember who I was? Does anyone?"

You're not sure if you will watch much more of this. You think you feel a vague sort of embarrassment for the man. You can't remember the last time you felt embarrassment. If your uncle starts to weep, you know you will rip the tape out of the machine and throw it in the trash. So much for being remembered, Uncle Mark.

You have never had any use for the sentimental. Watching this tape is a strange and disturbing exercise for you. Even that word—"nostalgia" is it?—sounds like some illness. You hate the touch of old things; you despise the smell. This house, the one in your uncle's video, has passed to you, and you accepted only because you needed the roof over your head.

When you first moved in it just seemed easier to pretend these old things weren't here. You managed to throw everything out of your bedroom, sleeping on a pallet on the floor. Every few months since then you have steeled yourself in order to take boxes of these old things into the alley for disposal.

That is how you found this video, at the bottom of a box in the living room closet, with your name and Tommy's name and that date scrawled in shaky blue ballpoint pen on the label. You were curious, you have always been cursed with an annoying curiosity, and then when you saw that it was your Uncle Mark on the tape and realized that was the date of his death and your father's death, or disappearance, you had this immediate and annoying curiosity. You wanted to hear what your Uncle Mark had to say.

You were almost nine, you remember now. You were almost nine and you found out your Uncle Mark was dead, and your father had disappeared, presumed dead. You had a lousy ninth birthday—your mother couldn't get you to even come out of your room.

"So what news have you brought, Uncle Mark?" you whisper to his sad, flickering face. "What news?"

Shadows drift over his pale skin as he moves across the screen: at first so subtle they might be a veil of dust on the lens, then stark, black bands suggestive of bars or limbs. You have the impulse to get up and turn more of your own lights on, but you make yourself stay in your chair, because you're nothing like your uncle, or any of those crazy old men in your family. You have been able to protect yourself. You have stayed alive.

"It's been…" he makes a sound that might have been intended as a laugh, but it fills his throat like a sob. "A *hellish* year. You remember your Aunt Trish, I hope. I just want you to know, for one thing, that she liked everybody, pretty much. And when they treated her less than honorably she either didn't notice or she didn't care. She was a generous woman, maybe too generous. I thought she was my life before she died. And now, I *know*. I haven't been able to figure out if her mugger was from the neighborhood or not, but he very well could have been. I don't know if he was black or brown or white. I'm no racist, understand, it doesn't matter. But I would like to know. The police say he was probably young. They say he jumped a fence getting away. Like an animal, is the way that sounds to me. A throw-back. A walking piece of garbage. How do you handle garbage in your day? Do you keep it around until it starts to stink, or do you get rid of it?

"They said he evidently didn't mean to kill her. God knows she didn't mean to die. Her heart was good, but it was weak. She had a heart attack, and even though there were a dozen people less than twenty yards away, she died. I can't tell you the number of times she'd get so scared on some ride at the amusement park, unable to breathe. Still, she wanted me to take her, said it was fun. Well, I stopped taking her; I was scared of what might happen. I didn't deserve her, but I knew the treasure I had in her. That made me angry and cold sometimes, which I guess frightened her even more. Isn't that a big joke? Being scared of what might happen; that's what I'd call living a life. Maybe it's different in your time and place."

He is making you uncomfortable. You resist the impulse to strike the screen. He is making you think of your father. He is making you think of

Tommy, and you can barely control your annoyance. Only the living care about such things. The shadows don't care.

Your uncle is up on his feet, prowling like a bear trapped in a small space. You know the feeling. Some people do not belong inside walls. But sometimes they have no choice if they want to protect themselves. Every time his pacing brings him near the camera the image shudders. "I don't pretend I will be able to explain myself," he begins, his voice deeply hoarse, threaded with brittleness. "So many things happen in a life that you cannot understand, but I wouldn't want you to think I've always disliked people." Your uncle stops himself, staring at you, then looks around the room with a vague, stupid expression, as if he's not sure where or when he is. "We're just a bad fit, I think, people and me."

He stares into the lens, so close he's distorted into a thin version of himself, looking a great deal, in fact, like your father. You remember your father reaching down to stroke your face, how gentle he could be for such a tall man, for someone with such large, rough hands, and even though you do not value gentleness, you do not mind this memory. You try to remember what he smelled like, and you remember him crying, and you also remember him angry and out of control.

"I'm sure there are good people out there, trapped by their circumstances." He leans closer, his eye so large that you imagine you can see yourself reflected in his iris. "But I want you to know that predators watch these streets. They hang out near the back alleys and the parks and the unlit intersections of our cities. They wait there for the weak or the old or the foolish, the ones straggling behind the herd. Then when they see the opportunity they pick them off one by one. For them it isn't an issue of morality—they have a need and they fill that need as best they know how. You almost have to admire that quality in them."

He reaches forward then, his rough, stained palms framing each side of the picture, and you draw back, surprised by the feeling that he is trying to strangle you, not you personally, but any of the children that came after. You think this is the kind of person who could kill his own family.

Then your view of him swings, a sudden blur of color as he has apparently detached the camera from its stand, and now it is airborne, shaky and handheld, and he is moving about the house at random, speaking to you, hardly aware of the camera now so it records great jittery expanses of water-stained ceiling, a garbage-strewn floor, rotting leftovers on tables and chairs, scattered across the rug like vomit, smearing the already filthy walls. Then as he continues his speech you can detect the slight deterioration in the image, the corruption of color, which gives a certain hysterical quality to his confession.

"I have sensed this shift in the world for a long time now, even before your aunt's death. The signs are there; you just have to know what you're looking for. Often when I would go out I would watch people, when they did not know I was looking. I would stand at the corners of buildings, at the edges of things. Sometimes I would just stand under a window, very still, and bear witness. It was quite subtle at first, but I began to detect a certain aggressiveness in the way people held themselves. There was an aura of *illness*, for lack of a better term, in the way they interacted. A fevered look in the eyes, a gray cast to the face, an agitation in the fingers, a stumble in the gait. They watched one another, apparently without recognition. I became convinced that a kind of isolation of the soul had occurred in vast numbers of the population. A cataclysmic psychic event, I think. It affected everything. Even the architecture, the nature of the sky, the stars spinning overhead changed.

"If I'm overreacting, then so is the world. Because shadow has come into it, you see. The knowledge of it. That no-man's land between living and dying, when you are neither, you just *are*. And you have no hope for better. You look into the mirror, and all you can see is that corpse you will one day be, and there is no fix for it. Your obsessive consciousness of the past and fear of the future have let shadow in, and there is little you can do once that tide has turned.

"That shadow has always been here, but there seemed to be a balance, don't you think? We had become complacent with the conviction that we could protect ourselves. But a gradual, subtle change has taken place. The tide has reversed itself, the meat has turned, the hourglass has tumbled over."

Your Uncle Mark is crazy, of course. *Was* crazy. You know the signs. Tommy was that way, near the end. *You* could be that way. Locked up in this house, seeing no one. The only person he allowed in that last year was your father. Your missing father, all those years ago. At least that was the story you heard. People lie, of course, but you think that story was probably true.

This is still his house. Crazy Uncle Mark. His crazy house. So much of his stuff is still here. You can hardly bear to touch it.

He is leaning over, the camera dizzy with shuffling walls, rug, that ugly ceiling, remounting the camera so it is now aimed like a gun at the front door. "Your father helped me secure this house. No, let me be completely truthful. Your father secured this house from the threats closing in around us—I have little skill in matters mechanical, electrical, in plumbing, in carpentry. At first he saw no need, but toward the end, I think he was beginning to see things my way. If only he had come around sooner."

Now he has your undivided attention. *Your father* and *toward the end* and *if only*. Magical words, the doors to the secrets unlocking. You push your chair up closer to the television, your eyes aching from the shifting lights and darks. Your uncle comes up over you, making further adjustments to the camera. The zoom level changes; he blurs out to white and then walking away from you he is back in focus. Standing at the large wooden front door now, he gestures at its detail brought so close to you by the zoom.

"Your father did *exquisite* work. I asked him to make the strongest door he could make, one that a tank would have a problem getting through, and he made me this work of art."

You glance at the heavy but rather plain door there currently. You'd like to believe that your father's door was so wonderfully made, so universally admired, that he sold it, that it could even be hanging in a museum somewhere. Yours is a family of dreamers.

"He put a contented face on one side, counterpoint to the threatening face on the other side. It's a wonderful door, but he hung it with the wrong side facing out. He was always so careful, I have no idea how he could have made a mistake like this. I would have had him correct it, but we ran out of time."

Out of time. You are waiting for him to tell you more, but he has stopped talking, and now the camera is jerking forward, so that you imagine he must have gone back and around and is now moving the tripod closer so that you can see your father's work in greater detail. Your Uncle Mark really wants you to see this door.

The face covers the entire center, probably five feet from top of head to tip of chin. Approximately two feet wide. Long and narrow. The eyes are squeezed to slits, but still you can see the deep, shadowed holes gouged out for the pupils hiding under the lids. The mouth is a sneer, exposing teeth carved so aggressively they look like giant, jagged splinters wedged just behind the wrinkled lips. The ears are narrow and pulled back close to the head like those of an angry animal. At first you think the mottled background of the door is just its natural roughness, but when your uncle drags a floor lamp closer you can see that the remainder of the door around the face is completely carved with shallow reliefs of faces just beginning to emerge from the wood, showing an eye, or a mouth, the top of a nose, the side of a chin. The impression is of people floating up from the depths of dark, liquid wood, the moment of their initial emergence painstakingly recorded.

You cannot believe your uncle doesn't see it. That is *his* face on the door! The likeness is unmistakable! Distorted, certainly, mutated, but obvious. It doesn't surprise you at all. You don't have to see the face on the other side to know how it must have looked: your Uncle Mark on one of his better days, hair combed, smiling, the image he'd want the outside world to see.

"This door wasn't the only fortification he made for me. The windows all around are double-barred, deep anchored in hard-cured concrete. He even extended the foundation out another foot, in case anyone tries to dig their way in."

He looks at you as if he wants to send an apology across the years. "I miss him tremendously—he had been good company since your Aunt Trish's death. I really wish he had stayed.

"Six months ago I locked myself up inside this house. Windows shut, curtains closed. They deliver my food, but I never see them, I just know when they're gone, and when everything looks clear I go out and drag it all inside. You can do this so easily nowadays.

"Your father worked on this house for months. Certainly he thought I was over-reacting at first. Then for a long time he said nothing, just showed up, worked, and left here before dark. He never liked being here after dark. The last few months, however, there was a change. We talked about many things. We talked about the world, history, politics. We talked about the family, how we had always been with each other. He talked about you, his children, and your future. We talked until after dark, until long after dark, until he felt compelled to sleep here, because he was uncomfortable going out to his truck after dark, winding his way down that long walk to the bottom of the hill where he had to park, finding his way through all those layers of shadow. Those times we often talked most of the night, both of us reluctant to go to bed. We talked and talked, and still I think I got very little sense of how he really felt about things.

"He has not been back for over a month. I don't believe that has been intentional. I burn the lights all night long. I drink. Sometimes I drink too much. I imagine what it is like outside. And I try to imagine solutions for myself, to fix myself, without much luck.

"Maybe in the future you will understand better. You will know what I'm talking about. Maybe in the future you won't think me crazy. It is almost dark now, I don't know how much we'll be able to see, but I think you will have a better understanding if we look outside. I don't know what I can show you, but I can show you something."

He walks unsteadily up to you, above you, and out of focus, blurred fingers shaking into some kind of gauzy representation of a spirit abandoning its body, and with a great deal of fiddling and wildly swinging views of the ceiling, his hands, his pale, sweating face, the floor, he removes the camera from its mount and suddenly it's as if you are stumbling drunken down the hall, dizzy with the multiplying views of skewed ceilings, tilting walls, the crashes as objects fall, glass breaking, furniture exploding out of nowhere and just as suddenly disappearing. You are hugged tightly to his chest, enveloped by his filthy clothes, in darkness and then glimmers of light, food stains on cloth, and you imagine you can smell his stench. Suddenly you are staring at his feet, and you can hear keys going into multiple locks, the clang and snap of metal. This requires some time, allowing you to examine his feet at your leisure: the mismatched, filthy socks, one bloody toe emerging from a tear. Then you are outside, some kind of porch roof below you, a vertiginous display of aerial views of the ground, trees, sidewalk. It all stops and you are looking into the gleam of his sweaty face, surrounded by the dark silhouette of trees appearing like some massive hair-do above his shining forehead, or his over-stimulated nerves that have pushed their way out of his skull and into the sky. The camera waves unsteadily across the streetlights and traffic below, as if this is what he wanted you to see, as if it were evidence of anything, and you are staring up into his dark, wet nostrils, his eyes like pale tumors mounted high up on his face, and from the sharp angle of limb you see that he is holding the camera at arm's-length to speak to you.

You are disoriented as he shakes the camera, pans it too rapidly. You're not sure if he's even trying to show you anything. Street lights smear across the surfaces of the gray buildings. Passing cars ripple, then melt into the pavement. Here and there angry faces run together, burning like frantic candles. Your eyes weep from the strain of watching.

"I don't know how much you can see, but I have this telephoto lens," he says, and then his image falls sideways. You're covered in darkness, the muffled noise of his hand working metal against metal. You catch a glimpse of his face as if at the end of a long tunnel, then a distant view of figures moving, crossing in front of each other, fires in oil drums, blurred. Everything is closer, in focus so sharply it's as if you'd taken something to clear your head and it just kicked in.

You see not exactly a gathering, more a random passing in close proximity, of shabby figures, male and female, although the two are difficult to distinguish, hunched and leaning, weary, dumb.

Your uncle's voice begins to narrate, like in one of those nature films you saw as a girl, a hint of desperation, as if from a teacher who knows his student is too stupid to understand. "I see more of them every day. Some are homeless; most I think live somewhere else, but have nothing to do. Nothing satisfies them, nothing speaks to their hearts. Maybe they had a job and one day they forgot why they were journeying every day to this place. Or they were returning to their homes after a long day at work and lost their way. No matter how much they thought about it, they could not remember the place where they had lived."

The camera slowly pans. Here and there you can see a face more clearly: blank, rough-hewn, the lips moving silently but the eyes disengaged, painted on. You do not see what your uncle is seeing. To you they're all pretty much the same. Human debris. The "no one special." You assume they have been here since humanity began. And they will be here at the end, the last human beings alive before the rats and the roaches take over. People who have been eaten by their own shadows.

The camera swings back to his face for just an instant—softly blurred, his image losing form as his voice builds. "You can see it, can't you? What I've been hiding from? This disease? They all look so normal, really, from a certain angle, or at least, harmless." Then the camera is back on the crowd, the bustling figures, the hot, uncomfortable faces. "Sometimes I think they can smell my fear."

You realize these people are closer to the house than you had thought. You see them milling like insects seeking safe haven but having forgotten what a safe haven would even look like.

"And there are others out there, I think. You read about them in the papers, or in those terrible supermarket paperbacks. They could be young or old, but they don't think like normal people. They don't have the same loyalties. Other people to them are no better than vermin. They are shadow. They act, vaguely, like you. But they are not you. They want to care, but caring is beyond them. They are not you—and there is no cure for that.

"What do you say to someone like that? Do you say 'please don't hurt me?' They see someone like my wife having a heart attack, and they do nothing. It begins in childhood, I think—you can't always tell, but these children are not like the others. I suspect it develops at different rates. For some it never reaches its final stages. Maybe it's like cancer, you know? For others, they reach a certain age, a critical point occurs, and they become exceedingly dangerous—mad dogs who need to be put out of their misery. There are more and more of them every year. Before you know it they will fill the cities, then the towns. Before you know it they will be wandering the countryside, like in one of those terrible horror films.

"I saw on the news the other day, they were talking about the economic situation, the job situation, the credit situation. They were talking about how close so many of us are to homelessness. Only a paycheck or two away. Your father was concerned about this. He loved you; he wanted you to have everything. But what if he lost everything?

"For myself, I wondered, if we are all that close to homelessness, to living on the streets, maybe we are close to this new illness as well, this plague of malaise."

The camera moves quickly, your view becoming a rapid smear of faces as if he was attempting to show you everything he could in the failing light.

"There! Do you see him? It's your father! Bob! Bob! What are you doing out there? Come inside! Bob, it's *dangerous* out there! Stay away from those *things*!"

The camera flies across warped faces, and one of them might be your father's, but you can't really be sure. You wish your uncle would just stop talking. You wish he would just focus a little more and point his camera where it needs to be pointed. You think no wonder he's dead. You think that's what happens to people who talk too much.

"Bob, what are you *doing*? Bob, *please* come inside! Come to the door! I'll be right there!"

The trip down from the rooftop is heedless of the camera's safety. You're banged against walls, pulled into his shirt, jostled sickeningly with rapid steps. Again you see glimpses of his feet: that toe continuing to bleed, the dark stain spreading through the cloth. His voice is tired now, raw, struggling against silence.

"When you lose someone you love, someone you're devoted to, a child, a wife, everything looks wrong. The colors, the weather, the everyday actions of everyday people. Even food tastes differently. You can't put your finger on what's different—it just happens. Everything starts going wrong, bad luck begets bad. It all seems like some terrible... conspiracy.

"I have never been able to throw away any of her clothes. I have thought about it many times, convinced that I must do some cleaning, some winnowing to rid myself of all this debris, but still, I have kept all of her things. Her toiletries still fill the bathroom and most of the bedroom we shared. Usually I sleep out on the couch. In the living room there is very little to remind me of her. We all drag around with us this enormous shadow. But now I have her shadow as well. I can't seem to get rid of it.

"One of them out there slashed my tires, went right into my driveway and cut them. Can you imagine?"

His voice sounds increasingly frayed. Sometimes he stops in the middle of a sentence, his throat worn down to silence.

He is at the front door now. More than before, you have the sensation of being a spirit hiding inside his camera, watching. His nervous hand shakes you up and down, bringing the door in and out of focus, as if it were breathing. "I can't do it," he says, beginning to cry. "I can't open the door with those things outside!"

You become aware of the scratching, the scraping. You think it has been going on for a very long time now, but it had become a background to his voice, an odd musical backdrop softly played. A faint pattern of beats, a subtle, insistent drumming. Now, inside his silence, and within the locked-in quiet of the house, you can hear it so clearly.

"You should understand that I didn't *ask* your father to help me secure this house, or to spend so much time here away from you. He just came, and he stayed with me for hours, listening to my theories and concerns—it was completely his own idea. When he came over we drank together. We sang together until we lost our voices."

When he remounts the camera onto its stand you have the strangest impression. As if he has been carrying your head around the house, and has now reattached it to your body, which has been sitting by itself in his living room during the tour. Now, your head safely back in place, he seems calmer. He seems to be trying to talk to you more sanely. But sanity seems incongruous now, what with that loud scratching, that distant tearing, that irregular beating from the other side of the door.

"Your father is a brave man, a rational man. He'll stay away from them. He'll find a way to get back inside." Uncle Mark leans forward and whispers, "Just so you know, I don't lie to myself. I know that no matter how well I hide myself here, shadow will still find me."

That, you think, is the wisest thing he has said so far. Shadow always finds you. People think they can protect themselves. They can build enough, they can arm themselves enough, they can pay enough. They are fools.

Your uncle has left the camera running, simply filming this beautiful, ornate door your father created for him. It seems foolish now that your father would go to all that trouble to make this for your crazy uncle. But you are fascinated by this huge, distorted face, and how much it resembles your uncle, how its features mirror the characteristic features you have seen in other members of your family. How it also resembles your father. How it resembles Tommy. How it resembles you. This is your family; this is how your father saw the future of your family. This is how your father saw the future of himself. This is what he was trying to tell them. This is what he was trying to tell his children. But now it's down to only you to hear. What would happen. How none of you were protected. How the insanity had gotten into the wood, into the grain.

When you first notice the splintering of that grand door behind your uncle, you think it's just some deterioration, some bubbling, some flaw in the film.

"Our obsession with the past and our fear of the future murder the now. Today arrives each morning as a steaming corpse in the chill air. We are so afraid of shadow, and yet we invite him into our homes without realizing it!" Your uncle is shouting now, because it's the only way he can be heard over the thunder at the door.

Then those dark floating faces in the door and that one huge, monstrous head come forward and out; as the door comes apart the room is filled by a multitude of shadows, dismantling, dismantling, with a cry that is one voice, yet many.

And the last face in view, before the film runs out, is so familiar. You think it's your father, but can you be sure? And that screaming? Who is that screaming? Then you know it is your uncle dying.

You sit there in your living room, which used to be your uncle's living room, watching as the images burn away to gray. The dusty old player stops. Static explodes into the room and you pound at the Power button until it dies. Then you sit there and stare at the empty screen, your curiosity sated.

What stares back at you is a gray-toned image of your own face, a shadow which is also a portrait, the old TV screen turned into a mirror by the lights behind you and to each side. Out of curiosity you get up and move the floor lamps to the left and right, then check your image, then adjust the lamps again, until you achieve the clearest mirror image possible. You crouch in front of the screen examining yourself. You haven't owned a mirror in years.

Even within the gray cast of the image you can see your fevered look, the darkness under your flesh, darkest beneath the eyes like a woman laid out at her funeral, the embalmer's makeup unable to hide the basic tones of death. You remember that these were among the symptoms your uncle mentioned, the characteristics of this cataclysmic disease, this "isolation of the soul." But your uncle was crazy. There is an agitation in your fingers as you pull your hair back for a better look at your face. You were a pretty girl at one time, you believe, until your own shadow ate you.

You have just seen, or at least heard, your uncle die. So who could have left this tape for you? You realize now that it must have been your own father who left the tape behind. It had been his shaky ball point pen writing that final message, before he became whatever it was he became. But what did your father expect you to do with this knowledge? If he thought you would be unhappy with the person you have become he was sadly mistaken.

Would your father have been happier if you had been more like Tommy, and taken your own life rather than be this way? You loved Tommy—he was the last person you have ever loved, and yet Tommy was a fool. Survival is the only lesson here, the only knowledge worth having.

But you are hungry now, and all this speculation has annoyed you, and annoyance is an unpredictable thing. It can make you careless and put you at risk, or it can make you a dangerous woman indeed. You stand and retrieve your sharpened pole from its place in the corner. It is not the most sophisticated weapon in the world, but it is quiet, and keeps you at a safe distance from the hand weapons carried by others of your inclination, and you use it well.

You slip on your thick leather coat, light enough in weight while still offering some protection. You would like to have a front door like your uncle's, but you have no idea how you might obtain one. You undo the series of locks on your own plain but sturdy door. Knowing that you are your family's terrible future, before you step outside you slip one hand beneath your shirt and adjust the straps binding down your breasts. You don't know if it actually helps when you have to move quickly, but you think it does, and besides, you like the way it feels.

Poe's "Shadow—A Fable" (published in 1835, revised and re-titled to "Shadow—A Parable" in 1845), for all its impressionistic brevity, has numerous images and themes familiar to lovers of his work: a small group of well-to-dos isolated indoors as a plague rages outside (à la "Masque of the Red Death"), an obsession with mirrors and doubles, the presence of a corpse, a worry over clocks and times, and a setting wrapped in shadow where spirits are physically manifest, where the boundary between life and death is drawn. It also employs a not uncommon device of that age: the story is addressed to a future reader, a "you" of another time.

It was that last element, that mysterious audience member, that inspired me to base my own "Shadow" off Poe's fable (or parable). I wondered who that person might be, and if they were at all receptive to this message from the past. It was also an opportunity to play with second person. You will find other elements from the original as well: a kind of mirror is employed, there certainly is a plague, time is running out, and shadow appears to have taken over the audience.

PAT CADIGAN has won the Arthur C. Clarke Award twice for her novels *Synners* and *Fools*. She lives in North London with her husband the Original Chris Fowler, her son Rob Fenner, and her minder, Miss Kitty Calgary, Queen of the Cats.

TRUTH AND BONE

by Pat Cadigan

IN MY FAMILY, we all have exceptionally long memories.

Mine starts under my Aunt Donna's blond Heywood Wakefield dining room table after one of her traditional pre-Christmas Sunday dinners for the familial horde. My cousins had escaped into the living room to watch TV or play computer games while the adults gossiped over coffee and dessert. I wasn't quite two and a half and neither group was as interesting to me as the space under the table. The way the wooden legs came up made arches that looked to my toddler eyes like the inside of a castle. It was my secret kingdom, which I imagined was under the sea.

That afternoon I was deep in thought as to whether I should take off my green, red, and white striped Christmas socks and put them on my stuffed dog Bluebelle. I was so preoccupied—there were only two and they didn't go with her electric blue fur—that I had forgotten everything and everyone around me, until something my mother said caught my ear:

"The minute that boy turned sixteen, he left home and nobody begged him to stay."

All the adults went silent. I knew my mother had been referring to my cousin Loomis. Every time his name came up in conversation, people tended to shut up or at least lower their voices. I didn't know why. I didn't even know what he looked like. The picture in my mind was of a teenaged boy seen from behind, shoving open a screen door as he left without looking back.

The silence stretched while I studied this mental image. Then someone asked if there was more coffee and someone else wanted more fruitcake and

I almost got brained with people crossing and uncrossing their legs as the conversation resumed.

One of the relatives had seen Loomis recently in some distant city and it had not been a happy meeting. Loomis still resented the family for the way they had treated him just because (he said) of what he was, as if he'd had any choice about it. The relative had tried to argue that nobody blamed him for an accident of birth. What he did about it was another matter, though, and Loomis had made a lot of his own problems.

Easy to say, Loomis had replied, when you didn't have to walk the walk.

The relative told him he wasn't the first one in the family and he certainly wouldn't be the last.

Loomis said that whether he was the first or the thousand-and-first, he was the only one right now.

And just like that it came to me:

Not any more, Loomis.

IN MY FAMILY, we all have exceptionally long memories and we all... know... something. Only those of us born into the family, of course—marrying in won't do it, we're not contagious.

That's not easy, marrying in. By necessity, we're a clannish bunch and it takes a special kind of person to handle that. Our success rate for marriages is much lower than average. Some of us don't even bother to get married. My parents, for instance. And neither of them was an outsider. My father was from one of the branches that fell off the family tree, as my Aunt Donna put it. There were a few of those, people who had the same traits but who were so far removed that there was no consanguinity to speak of.

It only took one parent to pass the traits on; the other parent never figured it out—not everything, anyway. That might sound unbelievable but plenty of people live secret lives that even those closest to them never suspect.

IN MY FAMILY, we all know something, usually around twelve or thirteen. We call it 'coming into our own.'

Only a few of us knew ahead of time what it would be. I was glad I did. I could think about how I was going to tell my mother and how we'd break it to everyone else. And what I would do if I had to leave home because no one was begging me to stay.

In the words of an older, wiser head who also may have known something: Forewarned is forearmed.

MY MOTHER KNOWS machines: engines, mechanical devices, computer hardware—if it doesn't work, she knows why. My grandfather had the same trait; he ran a repair service and my mother worked in the family business from the time she was twelve. Later she paid her way through college as a freelance car mechanic. She still runs the business from a workshop in our basement. My Aunt Donna keeps the books and even in a time when people tend to buy new things rather than get the old ones fixed, they do pretty well.

Donna told me once that my mother said all repair work bored her rigid. That gave me pause. How could she possibly be bored when her trait was so useful? But when I thought about it a little more, I understood: there's just not a whole lot of variety to broken things.

MY FATHER KNOWS where anyone has been during the previous twenty-four hours. This is kind of weird, specific, and esoteric, not as handy-dandy as my mother's trait but still useful. If you were a detective you'd know whether a suspect's alibi was real—well, as long as you questioned them within twenty-four hours of the crime. You'd know if your kids were skipping school or sneaking out at night, or if your spouse was cheating on you.

My father said those were things you might be better off *not* knowing. I wasn't sure I agreed with him but it was all moot anyway. My parents split up shortly after Tim was born, when I was six and Benny was three, for reasons that had more to do with where they wanted to be in the future than where either of them had been the day before.

In any case, my father wasn't a detective.

He was a chef on a cruise ship.

This was as specific and esoteric as his trait so I suppose it fit his personality. But I couldn't help thinking that it was also kind of a waste. I mean, on a cruise ship, *everyone* knows where everyone else has been during the previous twenty-four hours: i.e., on the boat. Right?

MY AUNT DONNA knows when you're lying.

Most people in the family assume that's why she never married. It might be true but there are other people in the family with the same trait and it never stopped them. Donna was the oldest of the seven children in my mother's family and I think she just fell into the assistant mother role so deeply that she never got around to having a family of her own. She was the family matriarch when I was growing up and I guess being a human lie detector is kind of appropriate for someone in that position.

The thing was, unless someone's life was literally in danger, she refused to use her trait for anyone else, family or not.

"Because knowing that someone is lying is not the same as knowing the truth," she explained to Benny on one of several occasions when he tried to talk her into detecting my lies. I was ten at the time and I'd been teasing him with outrageous stories about getting email from movie stars. "Things get tricky if you interfere. When you interfere with the world, the world interferes with you. Besides," she added, giving me a sly, sideways glance, "sometimes the truth is vastly overrated."

* * *

A FEW WEEKS after that I was out with her and my mother on the annual back-to-school safari—hours of intense shopping in deepest, darkest shopping-mall hell—and she suddenly asked me if I felt like my body was changing. We were having food-court fish and chips and the question surprised me so much I almost passed a hunk of breaded cod through my nose.

"Hannah's entirely too young," my mother said, bemused. "I wouldn't expect anything to happen for at least another three years."

My aunt had a cagey look, the same one she had worn when she had made the comment about truth being overrated. "That's what you think. Puberty seems to come earlier all the time."

They turned to me expectantly. I just shrugged. A shrug was just a shrug and nothing more, least of all a lie.

"Well, it's true," Donna went on after a moment. "Ma didn't get her period till she was almost fifteen. I was thirteen, you were twelve. The girl who delivers my paper? She was *ten.*"

"And you know this how?" my mother asked. "Was there a little note with the bill—*Dear valued customer, I have entered my childbearing years, please pay promptly?* Or do they print announcements on the society page with the weddings and engagements now?"

Donna made a face at her. "Last week when she was collecting, she asked if she could come in and sit down for a few minutes because she had cramps. I gave her half a Midol."

My mother sobered at once. "Better be careful about that. You could find yourself on the wrong end of a lawsuit."

"For half a Midol?"

"You can never be too careful about giving medicine—*drugs*—to other people's children. She could have been allergic."

I was hoping they'd start trading horror stories about well-intentioned adults accidentally poisoning kids with over-the-counter medicine and forget all about me. No such luck. My mother turned to me with a concerned look. "So *have* you been feeling any changes, Hannah? Of any kind?"

"Do we have to talk about that *here?*" I glanced around unhappily.

"Sorry, honey, I didn't mean to embarrass you." She touched my arm gently and the expression on her face was so kind and, well, motherly that I almost spilled my guts right there. It would have been such a relief to tell her everything, especially how I didn't want to end up like Loomis.

Then I said, "That's okay," and stuffed my mouth with fries.

"I don't care if your papergirl already needs Midol," my mother told Donna, "Hannah's still too young. We shouldn't be trying to hurry her, we ought to let her enjoy being a kid while she can. Kids grow up too fast these days."

The conversation turned to safe, boring things like where we should go next and what, if anything, I should try on again. But Donna kept sneaking little glances at me and I knew the subject wasn't really closed, just as I knew it hadn't really been about menstruation.

No matter when I came into my own, I decided as I bent over my lunch, I was going to hide it for as long as possible. It might be hard but I had already managed to hide the fact that I knew about my trait.

Besides, hiding things was a way of life with us. It was something we were all raised to do.

WE ALL KNOW something and no matter what it is, we virtually never tell anyone outside the family.

"It's like being in the Mafia," my cousin Ambrose said once at a barbecue in Donna's back yard. "We could even start calling it 'this thing of ours' like on TV."

"Nah, we're not ethnic enough," said his father, my Uncle Scott.

"Speak for yourself," my cousin Sunny piped up and everyone laughed. Sunny was Korean.

"You know what I mean," Scott said, also laughing. "You're the wrong ethnic group anyway."

"Maybe we should marry into the Mafia," Sunny suggested. "Between what we know and what they can do, we could take over the world."

"Never happen," said my mother. "They'd rub us out for knowing too much." More laughter.

"Ridiculous," said someone else—I don't remember who. "Knowledge is power."

Knowledge is power. I've heard it so often I think if you cracked my head open, you'd find it spray-painted like graffiti on the inside of my skull. But it's not the whole story.

Sometimes what power it has is over you.

And it's always incomplete. *Always.*

MY COUSIN AMBROSE knows what you've forgotten—the capital of Venezuela, the name of the Beatles' original drummer, or the complete lyrics to Billy Joel's "We Didn't Start The Fire" (Caracas, Pete Best, and don't go there, he can't sing worth a damn). When he came into his own at fourteen, Donna threw him a party and he told everyone where they'd left their keys or when they were supposed to go to the dentist. Apparently reminding people to buy milk or answer their email wasn't interfering with the world, at least not in the way that got tricky.

We all knew the real reason for the party, Ambrose included: he was Loomis's younger brother. Just about all the local relatives showed up and they all behaved themselves, probably under threat of death or worse from Donna. Even so, I overheard whispers about what a chance she had taken, what with Loomis being the elephant in the room. It was hard to have a good time after that, watching my own younger brothers giggling as they asked Ambrose to remember things they'd done as babies.

There were other mutterings suggesting that Ambrose had come into his own earlier than he had let on. He was a straight-A student and who wouldn't be with a trait like his? Just jealousy, I knew; Ambrose had always been brainy, especially in math. He was three years older than I was and I had been going to him for help with my homework since third grade.

Still, I was tempted to ask. If he really had hidden his trait, maybe I could pick up some pointers.

I CAME INTO my own in the school library on a Thursday afternoon in early April, when I was thirteen.

After knowing for so long in advance, I had expected to feel different on the day it finally happened, something physical or emotional or even just a thought popping into my head, like all those years ago under my aunt's table. But I didn't. As I sat at a table in the nearly-empty library after the last class of the day, the only thing on my mind was the make-up assignment my math teacher Ms. Chang had given me. I had just been out a week with strep throat so I was behind with everything anyway but this was the worst. X's and y's and a's and b's, pluses and minuses, parentheses with tiny twos floating up high—my eyes were crossing.

I looked up and saw Mr. Bodette, the head librarian, standing at the front desk. Our eyes met and I knew, as matter-of-factly as anything else I knew just by looking at him—there was a spot on his tie, he wore his wedding ring on his right hand, his hair was starting to thin—that in a little over twenty-eight years, he was going to fracture his skull and die.

Mr. Bodette gave me a little smile. I looked down quickly, waiting to get a splitting headache or have to run to the bathroom or just feel like crying. But nothing happened.

I must be an awful person. I stared at the equations without seeing them. A nice man was going to die of a fractured skull and I didn't feel sick about it.

I curled my index finger around the mechanical pencil I was holding and squeezed until my hand cramped. Was it because twenty-eight years was such a long, long time away? For me, anyway. It was twice as long as I had been alive—

"Takes a little extra thought."

I jumped, startled; Mr. Bodette was standing over me, smiling.

"Algebra was a killer for me, too." He took the pencil out of my hand and wrote busily on a sheet of scrap paper. "See? Here, I'll do another one."

I sat like a lump; he might have been writing hieroglyphics.

"There." He drew a circle around something that equaled something else. "See? Never do anything to one side of the equation without doing the exact same thing to the other. That's good algebra. Got it?"

I didn't but I nodded and took my pencil back from him anyway.

"If you need more help, just ask," he said. "I needed plenty myself. Fortunately my mother was a statistician."

I stared after him as he went back to the front desk. Twenty-eight years; if I hadn't been so hopeless in math, I'd have known if that was equal to x in his equation.

A student volunteer came in and went to work re-shelving books. She had red hair and freckles and she was going to live for another seventy-nine years until a blood vessel broke in her brain. I had to force myself not to keep staring at her. I didn't know her name or what grade she was in or anything about her as a person. Only how and when she was going to die.

PERVERSELY, THE EQUATIONS began to make sense. I worked slowly, hoping the building would be empty by the time I finished. Then I could slip out and hope that I didn't meet anyone I knew on my way home—

—where my mother and Benny and Tim would be waiting for me.

A cold hard lump formed in my stomach. OK, then I'd go hide somewhere and try to figure out how I was supposed to look at my mother and my brothers every day knowing what I knew.

Is that really worse than knowing the same thing about yourself? asked a small voice in my mind.

That was an easy one: Yes. Absolutely.

KNOWING ABOUT MYSELF wasn't a horrific blaze of realization, more like remembering something commonplace. In ninety years, two months, seven weeks, and three days, my body would quit and my life would go out like a candle. If twenty-eight years seemed like a long time, ninety was unimaginable.

I slipped out of the library unnoticed and got all the way up to Ms. Chang's classroom on the third floor without meeting anyone. I left the worksheet on her desk, started to leave and then froze, struck by the sight of the rows of empty seats staring at me. Today they had been filled with kids. Tomorrow they'd be filled with heart attacks, cancers, strokes... what else?

More fractured skulls? Drownings? Accidents?

Murders?

My skin tried to crawl off my body. Would I be able to tell if people were going to be murdered by the way they were going to die? Was Mr. Bodette's fractured skull going to be an accident or—

What if someone close to me was going to be murdered?

What if it was going to happen the next day?

I would have to try to stop it. Wouldn't I? Wasn't that why I knew?

It had to be. My mother knew what was wrong with a machine so she could fix it; I knew about someone's death so I could prevent it. Right?

No. Close, but not quite. Even *I* could see that was bad algebra.

Just as I went back out into the shadowy hallway, I heard a metallic squeak and rattle. Down at the far end of the corridor, one of the janitors was pushing a wheeled bucket with a mop handle. I braced myself, waiting as he ran the mop-head through the rollers on the side of the bucket to squeeze out excess water.

Nothing.

He started washing the floor; still I felt nothing. Because, I realized, he was too far away.

I dashed down the nearest staircase before he got any closer and ran out the front door.

Now that was very interesting, I thought as I stood outside on Prince Street looking back at the school: people had to be within a certain distance before I picked anything up from them. So the news wasn't all bad. I could have a career as a forest ranger or a lighthouse keeper. Did they still have lighthouse keepers?

Should've walked toward *the janitor, you wuss,* said a little voice in my mind; *then you'd know how close you had to be to pick up something.* No, only a very general idea; I wasn't good with distances—math strikes again. Too bad Ambrose's sister Rita hadn't been there. She knew space. All she had to do was look at something: a building, a room, a box, and she could give you the dimensions. Rita had capitalized on this and become an interior decorator. Sadly, she didn't have very good taste so she worked in partnership with a designer who, Ambrose said, probably had to tell her several times a week that knotty pine paneling wasn't the Next Big Thing.

I crossed the mercifully empty street but just as I reached the other side, I knew that eleven years and two months from now, a woman was going to die of cancer.

There was no one near me, not on the sidewalk nor in any of the cars parked at the curb. Up at the corner where Prince met Summer there was plenty of traffic but that was farther away from me than the janitor had been.

I didn't get it until the curtains in the front window of the nearest house parted and a woman's face looked out at me. She glanced left and right, and disappeared again. Another useful thing to know, I thought, walking quickly—people had to be within a certain distance but they didn't have to be visible to me.

In the house next door, there was a head injury, forty years; a stroke, thirty-eight years in the one after that. Nothing in the next two—no one home. Internal bleeding, twenty-six years in the next one. A car passed me going the other way: AIDS, ten years behind the wheel and heart failure, twenty-two years in the passenger seat. More AIDS, six years in the house on the corner.

Waiting for a break in the traffic so I could cross, I learned another useful fact—most of the cars on Summer Street passed too quickly for me to pick up on anything about the people in them. Only if one had to slow down or stop to make a turn would something come to me.

Eventually the traffic thinned out enough to let me cross. But by the time I reached the middle of the road, cars had accumulated on every side. My head filled with cancers, heart attacks, infections, organ failures, bleeding brains, diseases, conditions I didn't know the names of. I hefted my backpack, put my head down and watched my feet until I reached the other side.

Baron's Food and Drug was just ahead. I spotted an old payphone at the edge of the parking lot and hurried toward it, digging in my pockets for change (I was the last thirteen-year-old on the planet without a cell phone). It was stupid to hide that I'd come into my own. I would call my mother right now and come clean about everything, how I'd known for years and how I was afraid to tell anyone because I didn't want to end up like Loomis, leaving home with nobody begging me to stay.

I was in the middle of dialing when a great big football-player type materialized next to the phone.

"Hey, girlie," he said with all the authority of a bully who'd been running his part of the world since kindergarten. "Who said you could use this phone?"

I glanced at the coin slot. "New England Bell?"

"'Zat so? Funny, nobody told *me*. Hey, you guys!" he called over his shoulder to his friends who were just coming out of Baron's with cans of soda. "Any a you remember anything saying little girlie here could use our phone?"

My mouth went dry. I had to get the hell out of there, go home, and tell my mother why I now needed a cell. Instead, I heard myself say, "Should've checked your email."

He threw back his head and laughed as three of his pals came over and surrounded me. They were big guys, too, but he was the biggest—wide, fleshy face, neck like a bull, shoulders so massive he probably could have played without pads.

"Sorry, little girlie. You got no phone privileges here."

His friends agreed, sniggering. I tried to see them as bad back-up singers or clowns, anything to keep from thinking about what I knew.

"Come on, what are you, deaf?" The mean playfulness in his face took on a lot more mean than playful. "Step away from the phone and there won't be any trouble."

More sniggering from the back-up chorus; someone yanked hard on my backpack, trying to pull me off-balance. "I need to call home—"

"No, you need to *go* home." He pushed his face closer to mine. "Hear me? Go. The fuck. *Home*."

I should have been a block away already, running as fast as I could. But the devil had gotten into me, along with the knowledge that three days from now on Sunday night, the steering column of a car was going to go through his chest.

"If you'd let me alone," I said, "I'd be done already. Nobody's using this phone—"

"I'm waitin' on an important call," he said loudly. "Right, guys?"

The guys all agreed he sure was, fuckin' A.

"From who?" said the devil in me. "Your parole officer or your mommy?"

Now his pals were all going *Woo woo!* and *She gotcha!* He grabbed the receiver out of my hand and slammed it into the cradle. My change rattled into the coin return; I reached for it and he slapped my hand away, hard enough to leave a mark.

"Smart-ass tax, paid by bad little girlies who don't do as they're told," he said, fishing the coins out with his big fingers. "Now get the fuck outta here before something *really* bad happens to you."

The devil in me still hadn't had enough. "Like what?"

He pushed his face up close to mine again. "You don't want to find out."

The guys around me moved away slightly as I took a step back. "Yeah? Well, it couldn't be anywhere near as bad as what's coming up for you," the devil went on. "Yuk it up while you can, because this Sunday you're gonna d—" I stumbled slightly on a bit of uneven pavement and finally managed to shut myself up.

He tilted his head to one side, eyes bright with curiosity. "Don't stop now, it's just getting' good. I'm gonna what?"

Now I had no voice at all.

"Come on, girlie." He gave a nasty laugh. "I'm gonna *what?*"

I swallowed hard and took another step back and then another. He moved toward me.

"Come *on*, I'm gonna *what?*"

"You—you're—" I all but choked. "You're gonna have a really bad night!"

I turned and ran until I couldn't hear them jeering any more.

You're not just a bad person, you're the worst person in the world. *No, you're the worst person who* ever lived.

Sitting at the back of the bus, I said it over and over, trying to fill my brain with it so I couldn't think about anything else. I actually managed to distract myself enough so that I didn't notice as many deaths as I might have otherwise.

Or maybe I was just full of my thug's imminent death. That and what I had told him.

Except he couldn't have understood. When that steering column went through his chest, he wasn't going to think, *OMGWTFBBQ, she knew!* in the last second before he died.

Was he?

THE PUBLIC LIBRARY was my usual hideout when I felt overwhelmed or needed somewhere quiet to get my head together. Today, however, I was out of luck—the place was closed due to some problem with the plumbing. Figured, I thought. No hiding place for the worst person in the world.

By this time, my mother would be teetering on the threshold between annoyed and genuinely worried. I called her from the payphone by the front door of the library.

"This had better be good," she said, a cheery edge in her voice.

I gave her a rambling story about having to finish a math assignment and then going to the library to get a head start on a project only to find it was closed.

"Just get your butt home," she said when I paused for breath. To my relief, she sounded more affectionate than mad now. I told her I'd be there as soon as I could and hung up.

If I were going to live a long time, I thought as I walked two and a half blocks to a bus stop, then wouldn't the chances be really good that my mother and brothers would, too?

And if any of them were going to die in an accident, then I *had* to tell them so we could stop it from happening. I shouldn't have been afraid to go home. I should have *rushed* home.

I had to tell my mother everything, especially what I had said. She would know what to do.

Was this the kind of problem Loomis had made for himself, I wondered? Was this why no one had begged him to stay?

At least being home wasn't an ordeal. My mother would fade away in her sleep at ninety-two, Benny would suffer a massive stroke at eighty-nine, and Tim would achieve a hundred-and-five before his heart failed, making him the grand old man of the house. We were quite the long-lived bunch. I wondered what Mr. Bodette's mother the statistician would have made of that. Maybe nothing.

And it *was* nothing next to the fact that I didn't tell my mother anything after all.

But I had a good reason. It was Benny's night; he'd gotten a perfect score on a history test at school and my mother had decided to celebrate by taking us all to Wiggins, which had the best ice cream in the county, if not the world. We didn't get Wiggins very often and never on a school night. I just couldn't bring myself to spoil the evening with the curse of Loomis.

MY THUG'S NAME, I discovered, was Phil Lattimore. He was sixteen, a linebacker on the varsity football team. There were lots of team photos in the school trophy case, which was the first thing you saw when you came up the stairs from the front door. I had never paid much attention to it. Sports didn't interest me much, especially sports I couldn't play.

When I went to school on Friday, however, the trophy case that had once barely existed for me seemed to draw me like a magnet—any time I had to go from one place to another, I'd find myself walking past it and I couldn't pass without looking at my thug's grinning face.

Worse, I was suddenly noticing photos of the team everywhere, adorned with small pennants in the school colors reading !PRIDE!, !STRENGTH!, and !!!CHAMPIONS!!!, and it wasn't even football season any more. You'd have thought they'd cured cancer or something.

Unbidden, it came to me: this could be a sign. Maybe if I saved my thug's life, he *would* cure cancer—or AIDS, or Ebola. Or maybe he'd stop global warming or world hunger. Plenty of people turned their lives around after a close brush with death. It was extremely hard to imagine my thug doing anything like that, but what did I know?

Unless I really was supposed to leave him to his fate.

That was like a whack upside my head. Was I supposed to fix this the way my mother fixed broken machines? Or just live with what I knew, like my Aunt Donna?

I couldn't do anything about what I didn't know, I decided. I had to do something about what I *did* know.

I was thirteen.

AMBROSE MADE A pained face and shoved my math book back at me. "Liar."

"What do you mean?" I said, uneasily. "This stuff's driving me crazy."

"You're a liar. You make me come all the way over here when you don't need any help. Not with that, anyway. You just need your head examined." He started to get up from my desk and I caught his arm.

"Gimme a break—"

"Give *me* a break." My cousin gave me a sour, sarcastic smile. "Let me remind you of something you've forgotten: I know what you've forgotten." He tapped my math book with two fingers. "You haven't forgotten this. Ergo, you actually understand it. Congratulations, you're not a moron, just crazy. It's Saturday, it's spring, and there are a gazillion other things I'd rather do."

"Do you know Phil Lattimore?" I blurted just as he reached the doorway of my room.

He turned, the expression on his face a mix of surprise and revulsion. "Are you kidding? Everybody knows Phil the Fuckhead. According to him, anyway. What about him and why should I care?"

I took a deep, uncomfortable breath and let it out slowly. "I, uh..."

Ambrose stuck his fists on his narrow hips and tilted his head to one side. "You what?"

I swallowed and tried again. "There's something..." I cleared my throat. "Close the door."

He frowned as if this were something no one had ever asked him to do before.

"And come back over here and sit down," I added, "so I can tell you what I know."

He did so, looking wary. "You mean... *Know?*"

"Yeah," I said. "Tomorrow night, Phil Lattimore—" I floundered, trying to think of the right words. "Okay, look—if you knew you could save some-one's life, wouldn't you do it? Even a fuckhead?"

Ambrose's face turned serious. "What are you saying?"

"It's a car accident. Phil Lattimore—he—he'll be hurt."

He stared at me for I don't know how long. "You really, like... *know* this?" he said finally.

I nodded.

"Anyone else going to get hurt with him?"

"Not that I... uh... *know* of."

"Damn." Ambrose shook his head and gave a short, amazed laugh. "You *really* haven't told anyone else?"

"No one. Just you."

"I don't know why not." He ran a hand through his thick, brown hair. "If *I* could warn people when they were going to have an accident instead of just telling them where they left their keys—man, that would be fuckin' awesome." He gave me a significant look. "A hell of a lot better than telling people when they were going to die."

THERE ARE SO many ways you can go wrong without meaning to.

You can make a mistake, an error, or a faux pas. You can screw things up, you can screw things up royally, or just screw the pooch. Or you can fuck up beyond all hope, like I did. Deliberately.

I knew it was wrong but I was afraid he wouldn't help me. But a life was at stake and that was more important than anything, I told myself. As soon as Phil Lattimore was safe, I'd tell Ambrose the truth. He might be angry with me at first but then he would understand, I told myself. So would the rest of the family. They couldn't possibly *not* understand. I told myself. I was thirteen.

"BUT WHY DON'T you want to tell anyone?" Ambrose asked as he worked on a Wiggins butterscotch shake.

"It's complicated. And keep your voice down." We were sitting outside at one of the bright yellow plastic tables near the entrance to the parking lot.

Ambrose made a business of looking around. The only other people there were a young couple with a baby three tables away. "Right. Because they might hear us *over the traffic noise!*" He bellowed the last words as a truck went by on the street. The couple with the baby never looked in our direction.

"Fine, you made your point," I said. Normally two scoops of coffee ice cream topped with hot fudge was enough to put the world right but not today. The people with the baby had arrived after we had and they were directly in my line of sight.

"You know, it's rare but there are a few other people in the family with your trait," Ambrose was saying.

"There are?"

"Yeah, one of our cousins, she lives in California, I think. My dad mentioned her once. Also one of his aunts, which I guess makes her our great-aunt. Dad said she so was high-strung that sometimes she was afraid to go out."

"Because of what she knew?" I said.

Ambrose frowned. "Not exactly. Something real bad happened—I don't know what—that everyone thought was an accident. Only it wasn't, because she didn't know about it in advance. Since she had no connection to anyone involved and no evidence; there was nothing she could do. Dad said she freaked out and never really recovered."

"She couldn't have made an anonymous call to the police? Or sent a letter or something?"

Ambrose shrugged. "I don't know the whole story. Maybe she tried that and it didn't work." His expression became slightly concerned. "I hope nothing like that ever happens to you."

"I can't worry about that right now," I said. "Are you sure Phil the Fuckhead's gonna be here?"

"I told you, my friend Jerry works weekends here and Phil always shows. After the fill-in manager goes home, he comes in to hassle the girls on the counter. Is there something about those people that bothers you?"

The sudden change in subject caught me by surprise. "What people? Why?"

"You keep putting up your hand to your head like you want to block out the sight of them but at the same time you're sneaking little peeks. Something wrong with them?"

Not really. Other than the fact that in nine years, seven months, and one week, the kid is going to drown, it's all good. I had to bite my lip.

Ambrose's eyes widened as he leaned forward. "Are *they* going to have an accident?"

The dad and mom would go on for another forty-five and sixty-eight years respectively before they died of two different cancers. I hoped they'd have other children.

"Nothing in the immediate future," I said.

"What about you and me?" His face was very serious now. "Are we gonna be OK?"

Ambrose had another fifty-two years ahead of him. Not as long as anyone at my house but not what I'd have called being cut off in his prime. "We're fine," I said. "We seem to be pretty l—ah, lucky." I'd been about to say *long-lived.*

"For the *immediate* future," he said, still serious. "How far ahead do you know about—two months? Six months? Longer?"

I took an uncomfortable breath. "I—I don't know. I haven't picked up on anyone else yet. What about the cousin and that great-aunt? How far ahead did they see?"

"My dad said the great-aunt wouldn't tell. He thinks maybe six months for the cousin but he couldn't remember."

"Six months would be pretty helpful," I said lamely.

Ambrose wasn't listening. He was looking at a car pulling into the parking lot.

"Fuckhead alert," he said. "Driving his land yacht. The only thing big enough for his fuckhead posse."

Land yacht was right; the metallic brown convertible was enormous, old, but obviously cared for. The top was down, either to show off the tan and plaid upholstery or just to let the guys enjoy the wind blowing through their crew cuts. Phil parked down at the far end of the lot by the exit, taking up two spaces. Not just typical but predictable, like he was following a program laid out for him. The Fuckhead Lifeplan. Maybe I really *was* supposed to leave him to his fate.

As if catching the flavor of my thoughts, Ambrose said, "You *sure* you want to help this asshole? He's got plenty of friends. Let *them* rush him to the hospital."

"Shut up." I slipped over to Ambrose's side of the table. "And turn around; don't let them see we're looking at them."

"Whatever." Pause. "Hey, we're not doing this because you have some kinda masochistic crush on him, are we?"

"*No, I hate* him."

"Oh, look—it's my little girlie friend!" bellowed that stupid, awful voice. "And who's that with her? Hey, you're not cheating on me, are you? Better not or I'll have to teach you both a lesson—"

I wiped both hands over my face, begging the earth to open up and swallow me but as usual it didn't. Phil Lattimore loomed over me like the Thug of Doom, his chuckling goon squad backing him up. I glanced at Ambrose. He sat with his arms crossed, staring straight ahead.

"Oh, hey, you got a pet fag!" my thug said with loud delight. "I got no problem with fags as long as they're housetrained and don't try to hump my leg or nothing. You wouldn't do something like that, would you, pet fag? Hey, you got a name? You look like a Fifi. Right, guys?"

Fuckin' A, said the guys, high-fiving each other.

Phil Lattimore bent down so we were eye to eye. "Who said you could eat ice cream here?"

Would his buddies be in the car with him when it happened, would they be hurt? If so, they'd recover. The soonest any of them would pass away was thirty years from now; the goon on Phil's immediate left would die of blood poisoning. Another avoidable death. Should I make a note to phone him in three decades, two months, and six days: *Hey, if you get a splinter today, you'd better go to the hospital immediately because you'll die if you don't.*

All this went through my head in a fraction of a second, before Phil straightened up and went on. "Any a you guys get a memo saying girlie and Fifi could eat here?"

The goon squad chorus didn't answer; instead, they all turned and went into Wiggins.

I turned to Ambrose, stunned. "What just happened?"

"A minor miracle." He pointed; a police car had just pulled into the lot. "Maybe they've been following him." We watched as the cops got out of the car and went inside. "Bunch of guys riding around on Saturday night. Could be trouble."

"It's not night yet," I pointed out.

"But it will be soon. Let's get out of here before Phil and the posse come back out. They're not gonna feel like hassling the waitresses with a couple of cops watching."

We threw our empty dishes away and got into the VW. Technically the car was his mother's but she had left it behind after moving out. His parents, like mine, both carried traits but, unlike mine, they had gotten married. Despite splitting up, however, they still weren't divorced.

"You sure this isn't a pervy crush?" Ambrose grumbled as he backed out of the parking space. "Wanting to help that asshole—"

"I don't *want* to," I said. "I *have* to."

"Because?" Ambrose prompted as we approached the exit; it was right near where Phil Lattimore had parked his land yacht. "Or is that a deep, dark, pervy secret?"

"Because I said something to him about what I know."

Ambrose slammed on the brakes so sharply I flopped in my shoulder harness.

"You *told* Phil the Fuckhead that you know he's gonna have an accident tomorrow night?" My cousin's voice was half an octave higher than I'd thought it could go. "You really *are* fucking crazy!"

"I didn't mean to—"

"Don't you realize that he might think you threatened him?"

The idea of Phil Lattimore thinking I could threaten him was so funny I laughed out loud.

"You idiot," Ambrose said. "He could say you did something to his car! For all you know, he told his father or his mother—or maybe he's telling the cops in Wiggins right now."

"I don't think so," I said unhappily, looking at the side view mirror.

"OK, maybe not, but—"

"*Definitely* not. He—"

Phil Lattimore slammed up against the driver's side door and stuck his head through the window. "Hey, why're you sittin' here starin' at my car? What's goin' on, Fifi?"

Ambrose stamped on the accelerator and we shot out of the parking lot, barely missing an oncoming SUV.

"DON'T TALK," AMBROSE said for the fifth or sixth time.

"I wasn't," I said, glaring at him.

"I thought I heard you take a breath like you were gonna say something."

"You were mistaken."

"Okay. Don't talk any more now."

"Fine. I won't." I stared out the passenger side window. We were out in the countryside now, taking the long way back to my house. The really long, long way, all the way around town, outside the city limits; a nice drive under other circumstances. "Phil Lattimore would never in a million years believe me," I added under my breath and waited for Ambrose to tell me to shut up. He didn't so I went on muttering. "He wouldn't believe it if *you'd* said it. That's why we don't tell anyone outside the family anything—"

"*Shut* the fuck *up*," Ambrose growled. "You think I spent my life in a coma? I know all that. Now I'm gonna drive you home and you're gonna tell your mom everything, what you know and what you said to Phil—hey, just what *did* you say? No, don't tell me," he added before I could answer. "I'm probably better off not knowing. If I don't know, I'm not an accessory."

"A *what?*" I said, baffled.

"An accessory to your threatening Phil."

"*He* threatened *me,* just because I wanted to use a payphone," I protested. "I only told him he was going to have a bad night."

"I told you not to tell me!" Ambrose gave me a quick, pained glance. "Okay, never mind, just don't tell me any more."

"There isn't any more to tell," I said, sulking now.

Ambrose eased off the accelerator and only then did I realize how fast we'd been going. "Are you shitting me?" He looked at me again and I nodded. "Oh, for cryin' out—*that's* not a threat. We're gonna go home and forget the whole thing. And don't worry, I won't remind you."

"We can't," I said.

Ambrose shook his head in a sharp, final way. "We can and we will."

"I thought you said you hadn't spent most of your life in a coma. Don't you get it? I can't just turn my back. If Phil the Fuckhead is in the hospital for months and months, that's on me for not doing anything. If he ends up in a wheelchair for the rest of his life, that's on me."

"He could also just walk away from the wreckage with nothing more than a scratch on his empty fuckin' head," Ambrose said. "Guys like him usually do."

"What about any other people in the accident? If they're crippled or—or worse? That's on me, too. And you. For not doing anything."

Ambrose didn't say anything for a long moment. "It could happen no matter what we do."

"Yeah, but we'd have tried. It wouldn't be like we just stood by."

"Shit." Ambrose turned on the radio and then immediately turned it off again. "But you don't know anything about any other people, do you?"

"I only know about Phil Lattimore getting badly hurt in an accident. If I don't try to do something about it, I might as well stand next to the wreckage and watch him d—suffer."

"And that's why you need to tell your m—"

"*No!* If I tell my mother, then I have to tell her what I said to him."

"But it's not that bad," said Ambrose. "It really isn't. If you're that scared, I'll tell her for you. You can hide in your room."

"Please, Ambrose, I'm begging you—do this my way. I swear I'll confess everything to everyone after it's all over, even if the worst happens. I just—I need to do this as a test. I'm testing myself."

Ambrose gave me a startled glance and I realized I was crying. "But it's not just you," he said. "You dragged me into it."

"And that's on me, too, making you share this," I said. "I know that."

"You *better* know it." His voice was grim. "If I had any sense, I'd take you straight home and tell your mom the whole thing. But I'm not a rat, because—" he took a deep breath. "Just between you and me, okay?"

I looked at him warily. "Okay. What?"

"I came into my own a year and a half before Aunt Donna gave me that party."

"You did?" I was stunned. "Why did you hide it?"

"Because I felt weird about it. Some of the things that people had forgotten—my father would have realized I knew some things that—well, it wouldn't have been good. But Aunt Donna found out."

"How?"

"She just asked me. I tried to lie by being evasive but I was too young and stupid to do it right. We had a talk and she promised not to tell on me. And she didn't."

I was flabbergasted.

"I know, everyone was suspicious anyway because of how well I always did in school," he said, chuckling a little. "You, too, maybe. But I hadn't come into my own when I started school and after I did, it didn't matter. I was already in the smart-kid classes and smart kids don't forget much. I get straight A's because I'm smart, too, and I study my ass off. Anyway, you can trust me. I won't say anything. But promise me that tomorrow night, when this is all over, you'll tell your mom."

"Okay," I said.

"Good." He looked at me sternly. "Because it's not ratting you out if I make you keep that promise."

I GOT HOME and went straight upstairs to run a bath for myself. When I took off my clothes, I discovered I had gotten my first period and burst into tears.

My mother waited until I had quieted down before coming to check on me. To my relief, she didn't rhapsodize about becoming a woman or ask me any questions. She just put a new box of sanitary pads on the counter by the sink, gathered up my clothes, and let me have a good cry in peace, up to my neck in Mr. Bubble.

* * *

THE NEXT MORNING, I came down to breakfast to discover that she had sent Benny and Tim off to Donna's for the day.

"Estrogen-only household, no boys allowed," she said cheerfully as she sat at the kitchen table with the Sunday paper. "We've got plenty of chocolate in a variety of forms and an ample supply of Midol. There's also a heating pad if you need it."

"Thanks, but I'm fine," I said. She started to say something else and I talked over her. "I'm going over to Ambrose's. Algebra."

She looked surprised and then covered it with a smile. "All right. It's your day, after all." And she wished I were spending it with her. So did I.

I started back upstairs to get dressed.

"Hannah," she called after me suddenly. I stopped. "No later than five. You've got school tomorrow. Okay?"

Phil Lattimore would die at six-fifty-two unless I saved him. "Okay."

"I mean it," she added sharply.

"I know," I said. "No later than five; it's a school night."

Her expression softened. "And if you decide to knock off the studying early, the chocolate and everything else will still be here."

"Thanks, Mom." I got two steps farther when she called after me again.

"Are you really having *that* much trouble with algebra that you have to spend all weekend working on it with your cousin?"

"You have no idea," I replied.

I'd gone another two steps when she said, "Just one more thing."

I waited.

"Is there anything else you want to tell me about?"

"Not yet."

"LEAVE IT OPEN," Ambrose told me as I started to close the door to his room. "New rule. All the time we're spending together is making my father nervous."

I blinked at him. "You kidding?"

Ambrose shook his head gravely. "I wish I were. He thinks it's more than algebra."

"But we're *cousins*," I said, appalled and repelled.

"No shit. Just remember to keep your voice down and your algebra book handy for those moments when he just 'happens' to pass by on his way to the linen closet." He gave a short laugh. "You know, I thought that when I finally told him what we're doing, he'd be mad at me for hiding stuff from him. Now I think he'll just be relieved."

THE DAY CRAWLED by. Ambrose sat at his desk, tapping away on his computer while I stretched out on the bed, trying to ignore the mild discomfort in my lower belly. But after Uncle Scott went past a couple of times, he called Ambrose out of the room for a quick word. Ambrose returned with a request for me to sit up, preferably in one of the two straight-back chairs. I compromised by stretching out on the floor. "If your dad has a problem with this," I said, "I'll give him a complete description of how my first period is going."

Ambrose blanched. "I didn't need to hear that."

"Neither will he."

We finally went out for lunch at two, driving out past the city limits into the country again.

"Won't your dad worry about what we could do in a car?" I asked.

Ambrose shook his head. "Not in a Volkswagen."

I gave an incredulous laugh. "We could get *out* of the Volkswagen."

"And then what? I don't have enough money for a motel and he thinks I'm too hung-up to do it outside." He glanced at me. "Forget it. Grown-ups are fuckin' weird, is all. Every last one of them, fuckin' weird. Especially in our family."

Anxiety did a half-twist in my stomach, or maybe it was just cramps.

"And we're giving them a run for their money right now ourselves," he added. "Skulking around so you can play hero single-handed for an asshole who wouldn't appreciate it even if he *did* know what you were doing. Fuckin' weird? Fuckin' A."

The moment hung there between us, a silence that I could have stepped into and confessed everything—the truth about my trait and what I was really trying to do. Then he went on.

"Anyway, I didn't want to talk about this before in case my dad overheard." He glanced at me; anxiety did another twist, high up in my chest where it couldn't have been cramps. "When you come into your own, you don't just get one of the family traits. They let you in on other things. Family things."

"Like what? Skeletons in the closet or something?"

Ambrose gave a small, nervous laugh. "Not just that. There are skills to learn, that go along with the traits."

"Skills?"

"Coping skills. There are ways to compartmentalize your mind so you don't get caught up in something you know when you're supposed to be doing something else. Some traits, you have to learn how to distance yourself. Mind your own business."

I bristled. "If this is a sneaky way of trying to talk me out of—"

"Relax. I should but I'm not."

"You never mentioned any of this before."

"I didn't think you'd want to hear it."

"I still don't."

"I know. But shut up and let me talk, OK? I promised you I'd help you and I will. I am. But I had to talk to somebody. So after my dad went to bed last night, I called my sister Rita and talked to her."

"You *what?*" My voice was so high that even *I* winced.

"*Relax.* I didn't tell her about you. I talked to her about Loomis."

I felt my stomach drop, as if there were thousands of miles for it to fall inside me. "Why..." My voice failed and I had to start again. "Why Loomis?"

"I would have asked Dad about his aunt or the cousin but I was afraid he might start wondering why I wanted to know. Then he'd put two and two together about you and I'd have to explain why you won't tell anyone and it'd be a big mess. Asking about Loomis would've been worse—he'd have gotten the wrong idea about your trait." I winced, wondering if Ambrose would ever speak to me again when the truth did come out. "So after he went to bed, I called Rita."

"But why Loomis?" I asked again.

"Because your trait is similar in a lot of ways. I know, you said Phil Lattimore *could* die, not that he *would,* but there are parallels. You and Loomis know a specific thing about one particular person. So I thought anything Rita told me about him would apply to you, too."

"Good algebra," I said, mostly to myself.

"What?" Ambrose gave me a funny look.

"Nothing. What did she tell you?"

He flexed his fingers on the steering wheel. "The closer it gets to *that* time, the more likely we are to run into Phil Lattimore."

"Why?"

"Because you know what's going to happen and you talked to him. It's a synchronicity thing. Your separate courses affect each other."

"Our 'separate courses?'"

"It's a mathematical thing, really advanced. I kind of understand it but I'd never be able to explain it to you."

"And Rita told you this?" I gave a small, incredulous laugh. "Since when is knotty pine's biggest fan such a brainbox?"

"My sister may be tacky but she's not stupid." Ambrose sounded so serious I was ashamed of laughing even a little. "She knows *space.* Every so often, she picks up on something weird, like two points that are actually far apart registering as being in the same spot."

"What does that mean?" I asked.

"It means she has to use her tape measure."

"Very funny," I said sourly.

Ambrose shrugged. "You're nowhere near ready for quantum mechanics or entanglement." He flexed his fingers on the steering wheel again. "You know, something like this happened with Loomis. When he told somebody something he shouldn't have."

All of a sudden I felt weightless, the way you do in the split second before you start to fall. "Who?" I asked, or tried to. What voice I had was too faint for Ambrose to hear.

"Rita said as soon as he did that, it was like they couldn't keep out of each other's way," my cousin went on. "Not so strange in a small town like this. The strange part was every time Rita read the distance between them, it came up zero."

"You believe her?" I asked before I could stop myself.

"Of course I believe her!" Ambrose glanced at me, his face red with anger. "What kind of fuckin' question is that? I wish to God she were here now, you'd *eat* those words."

"I'm sorry, I wasn't trying to insult anybody."

"My sister and I sit up half the night just for your benefit and that's the thanks we get?"

"You *did* tell her!" I shouted. "You said you wouldn't—"

"I had to tell her *something*," Ambrose shouted back at me. He slowed down and pulled onto the dirt shoulder of the country road we were on. "She knew I'd never call in the middle of the night just to chat about Loomis and I couldn't get away with lying to her—"

"So you lied to me about lying to her."

"Shut up and let me finish!" He turned off the ignition. "I figured it wouldn't matter if she knew the truth; she's in Chicago."

"What else did you tell her?" I asked, managing not to scream in his face.

"Just that you'd come into your own and you didn't want to tell anyone yet. Nothing about Phil or what we're doing."

I gave him a poisonous look. "Can I really believe you?"

He blew out a short breath that might have been a humorless laugh. "Don't you think she'd have hung up on me and called your mom if I *had* told her everything?"

"Okay," I said after a bit. My heartbeat had finally slowed from machine gun to a gallop. "Why did we stop here?"

"I don't drive when there's yelling in the car," Ambrose said, sounding almost prim. "That's practically guaranteeing a wreck." He raised an eyebrow at me and I had a sudden vision of him at his father's age, paternal but firm: *You kids behave yourselves* right now *or I'm turning this car around*.

"Fine," I said. "No yelling."

He started the VW again.

"Wake up," Ambrose said.

"I'm not asleep," I said thickly, blinking and sitting up straight in my seat. Most of the daylight was gone and we were no longer out in the country but pulling into the parking lot at Wiggins. "What time is it?"

"Fifteen minutes to Operation Save the Fuckhead." Ambrose cruised slowly through the crowded lot. It was a Sunday night in spring; everyone wanted to end the weekend with one last treat. "Uh-oh."

"What 'uh-oh?'"

"I don't see his car."

My stomach seemed to twist, then drop; at the same time, my cramps woke up with a vengeance. I leaned forward with my arms across my middle. "Maybe he was here already and left. Or maybe *he's* out in the country now."

"I'll drive down the road to Westgate Mall, turn around, and come back again," Ambrose said. "There's no place to park here anyway."

Just as we pulled out of the exit, a car roared up from behind and swerved sharply around us, horn honking, headlights flashing from low to high. Ambrose jerked the wheel to the right and we veered off the road into the dirt. The tires crunched on something as he slowly steered the car back onto the pavement.

"Who do you suppose *that* was?" he said wearily.

"Let's go," I said, hoping I wasn't yelling. "We've got to catch him!"

But as we sped up, the VW began to shudder hard from side to side.

"What the hell is that?" I yelled as Ambrose brought the car to a stop.

"Flat tire."

"Can't we change it?" But even as I asked, I knew. "The spare's flat," we said in unison.

High beams swept across the road and shone through the windshield and lit up the inside of the VW. The driver had crossed from the opposite lane to stop in front of us, facing the wrong direction. "Uh-oh," Ambrose said softly as we watched Phil Lattimore get out of his land yacht and lumber toward us. We rolled up the windows and locked the doors.

"Car trouble?" Phil asked, pressing his nose against my window.

"Can't reach my mom or my dad," Ambrose said unhappily, snapping his cell phone shut.

Lying across the front of the VW, Phil Lattimore waved cheerfully. "Hey, I told you we're *happy* to give you a ride!" He gestured at his friends waiting in the convertible; I could barely hear the *Fucking A's* with the windows rolled up.

"Call a tow truck," I said.

"I'll call the cops."

"You can't! As soon as Phil sees a cop car, he'll take off and it'll happen. We'll have *caused* the accident. Just call a tow-truck. What time is it? How long have we got?"

Ambrose tilted his watch toward the light, trying to read it. "Shit. My watch stopped." He turned the key in the ignition so the dashboard lit up. The digital clock read 88:88.

"What about your phone?" I asked. He showed it to me. The screen said: —/—, *Set Time?*

"What the hell does *that* mean?" I asked.

"Just guessing, I'd say it means you won," Ambrose said. "Now if we can just lose the ugly hood ornament."

Phil was squinting at his own watch in a puzzled way. He tapped the face hard with a fingernail, then held his wrist up to the light again. Ambrose leaned hard on the horn, startling Phil so much that he fell off.

"What'd you do *that* for?" I yelled.

"It worked. Now we can call your mother instead of a tow truck. I don't have enough money for a tow truck and you promised you'd tell her. She can take us to a service station and I'll pump up the spare while you tell her everything. It's killing two birds with one stone."

Phil Lattimore was back on his feet, brushing himself off as he went back to his land yacht. I unlocked my door and started to get out.

"Hey, don't!" Ambrose caught my arm. "Are you crazy?"

"I've got to keep him out of his car for just a little longer." I twisted out of his grip and ran toward Phil Lattimore. His buddies gestured, hooting and cheering wildly; the surprise on his face when he turned and saw me was utterly genuine, which surprised me just as much.

"What do you want?" he asked and for a moment he actually seemed concerned. *Hey, girlie, you're doing it wrong—I scare you and you run away, that's how the game goes.*

I stopped in front of him. The smell of beer was like a cloud around him. "Just… wait a minute."

He gazed down at me as if from a great height. "Sorry, girlie, no can do. Watch died. Your ugly face break it, or Fifi's?" He turned away and kept going.

"I said, *wait!*" I yelled, going after him.

He spread his arms as his buddies hooted some more. "She loves me, what can I—"

I made a two-handed fist and walloped his right butt cheek.

He stumbled, more from surprise than from the blow itself. I barely saw him whirl on me before he grabbed my upper arms, lifted me off my feet and threw me into the back seat of the land yacht.

It wasn't a soft landing and his buddies were no more ready for it than I was. I was struggling in a tangle of arms and legs. There was laughing and someone yelling *Jesus are you crazy toss her out she's jailbait* and another voice saying *she wants a beer.* I kicked out, hoping to hit something tender but connected with nothing but air. Beer cans crumpled against my face, dug into my skin as the car jerked forward.

"Stop!" I screamed. *"Stop! Don't let him! Don't let him, make him stop!"*

"What the fuck?" somebody said. No more laughing. One guy in the front seat was insisting that we'd better stop, another guy agreed, and then a third guy yelled *Look out!*

For a fraction of a second, I thought it was pure noise, an impact from sound waves. The car skidded at an odd angle and I managed to pull my head up just in time for the second impact. The air went out of my lungs in one hard blow. When my vision cleared I was trapped on the floor; someone seemed to be kneeling on my ribs. Fighting to breathe, I tried to drag myself up toward air.

I don't remember hearing the third impact.

I CAME TO inside something moving fast.

"Do you know your name?" said a woman's voice, all brisk concern. A hand squeezed mine. "Do you know your name?"

The light was blinding me; high beams?

"Do you know your name? If you can't talk, squeeze my hand."

I tried to pull my hand away and sit up but I couldn't move at all.

"Do you—"

"Hannah," I croaked. My mouth tasted funny. "Tell me he's okay."

"You don't worry, everyone's in good hands."

"No, tell me." The light in my eyes grew more painful as I became more alert. "Tell me he's okay. Tell me I saved him."

"Don't worry, honey, everything's gonna be fine."

I had a glimpse of a woman's face, dark brown, with short black dreadlocks. In thirty-five years, degeneration in her brain would finally reach its end-stage.

Abruptly pain erupted everywhere in my body. I would have howled but all that came out was a long croaky moan. The woman turned away quickly and did something; the pain began to ebb, along with my awareness.

"Midol," I whispered. Or maybe not.

AFTER THAT, I was in and out, almost like channel surfing. Doctors and nurses appeared and disappeared and I never knew which was which. Sometimes I saw my mother, sometimes my brothers; once in a while Donna was there as well. Although I was never sure if I was dreaming, even when it hurt.

At one point, I was trapped in the back seat of Phil Lattimore's land yacht again, feeling it spin around, tires screeching, glass breaking, metal smashing. I think I heard the third impact that time but afterwards, there was no one asking if I knew what my name was while we traveled. But it was much easier to breathe.

PHIL LATTIMORE CAME to see me. He peered over a nurse's shoulder and made stupid faces, mouthing *Who said you could have a car accident here?* That was no way to treat the person who had saved his stupid thug ass and I'd tell him that as soon as I was well enough.

MY MOTHER WAS sitting next to my bed, gazing at me with an anxious, searching look.

"Yeah, it's me." It hurt to talk. My voice sounded faint and hoarse.

"No kidding." She tried to smile. "I'd know you anywhere."

I swallowed hard on my dry throat and winced. She poured me a glass of ice water from a sweating metal pitcher and held the straw between my lips for me. "Did Ambrose tell you?"

It was like a shadow passed over her. "Ambrose? No."

"He made me promise—" I sucked greedily at the straw; suddenly ice water was the most wonderful thing in the world. "Said if I didn't tell you, he would. After it was all over. Which it is. Isn't it?"

She made a small, non-committal movement with her head. "Yes, honey. It's all over." She poured some more ice water for me. "Rita got here as soon as she could."

"Rita?" It took me a few moments to remember. "Did she come because Ambrose told her?"

She made that little movement with her head again.

It was easier to talk now; I turned my face away from the straw to show I'd had enough. "I feel bad about that. Because now I have to admit I lied to Ambrose."

My mother closed her eyes briefly as if she had had a sudden pain, then she put the ice water down on the table beside the bed. "Yes, I know. We know."

We? Pain nibbled at the edges of my awareness, as if it had just woken up and wanted to join the conversation without drawing too much attention to itself. "How? Who told you?"

"You did." My mother sighed, looking at me sadly. "You don't remember talking to me, do you?"

"Not exactly," I said.

"The doctors said you'd have a spotty memory thanks to the combination of the head injury and the medication." She put her hand over mine on the bed and I realized I had a cast on my arm up to my knuckles.

"Everything's all dreamlike." The pain was getting more assertive. "Did he make it? Is he alive?"

Now she hesitated. "Your uncle Scott's been sitting with him. He hasn't left the hospital since—"

"Uncle Scott?" Pain definitely wanted more attention now; I tried to ignore it. "Why is Uncle Scott sitting with Phil Lattimore?"

"Phil who?" My mother looked as mystified as I felt. "He's with *Ambrose.*"

Uh-oh, said a small voice in my mind, under the pain. It sounded exactly like Ambrose. "Phil Lattimore is the guy I was trying to save," I said. "I knew Ambrose would be all right."

"'All right?'" My mother looked mildly stunned now, as if she had bumped her head.

"Ambrose isn't going to die for f—for a very long time," I said. "I knew I didn't have to worry about him."

My mother took a deep breath and let it out. "Is that so?" She gazed at me for a long moment, her expression a mixture of hurt, frustration, pity, and something else I couldn't read. I started to say something else and she suddenly rushed out of the room.

Caught completely by surprise, I tried to call after her but the pain stole my voice. Before it got really bad, however, a nurse came in with some medication.

WHEN I WOKE up again, there was a man sitting in the chair next to the bed. I had never seen him before but even without the strong family resemblance I'd have known who he was.

"Hello, Loomis," I croaked.

"Hello, yourself." He got up and gave me some ice water the way my mother had, holding the straw between my lips. I drank slowly, studying his face. He was a little taller than Ambrose, wiry and lean, as if he spent most of his waking hours running. His hair was curly but darker than Ambrose's and he had a full dark beard with a few white hairs here and there. I found it really interesting that although his eyes were same shape as Ambrose's, they weren't the same clear green color but dark muddy brown, like mine.

I finished the water and told him I'd had enough. He put the glass aside and continued to stand there looking me over.

"Guess you know," I said after a bit.

He didn't bother nodding. "You weren't surprised, were you. Knew it almost your whole life and never told anyone."

"That how it was for you?" I asked.

He pressed his lips together. "So, was this premeditated or spontaneous?"

I frowned. "What?"

Loomis took a breath and let it out; not quite a sigh. "Were you always planning to save someone's life or was it a spur-of-the-moment thing?"

I hesitated. "I was gonna say spur of the moment but now I'm not so sure. Maybe I was always gonna do something like this and never knew it."

Loomis's eyebrows went up. "Good answer. Insightful. More than I was at your age. Otherwise—" he shrugged.

"Otherwise what?"

"Otherwise you're just as much a dumb-ass as any of us."

I was offended and it must have showed. He laughed and patted my hand. "Hackles down, kid. Till the body cast comes off, anyway." He looked me over again. "Damn. Even I never took a beat-down this bad."

"Was it for nothing?" I asked.

Now it was his turn to be confused. "Say again?"

"Phil Lattimore. Did I save him?"

"Fuck, no." He grimaced and poured another glass of water. Before I could tell him I didn't want any more, he drank it himself. "There are two rules, cuz. Number one: Never tell anyone. And that's *anyone,* even family. Never. Tell. Anyone. *Never.* And rule number two: *Never* try to save them.

You can't do it. All you can do is make things worse." He gestured along the length of my body. "Exhibit A."

Alarm bells went off in my mind; I shut them out, made myself ignore the cold lump of apprehension in the middle of my chest. I'd be getting more pain medication soon; that always made all the bad feelings go away, physical and emotional. "Yeah, but I knew I was gonna be all right."

Loomis stuck one fist on his hip; the move was pure Ambrose. "You call *this* 'all right'? Hate to tell you, cuz, but after the casts come off, you've got a whole lot of physical therapy ahead of you and you'll probably lose a year of school. At *least* a year."

"You know what I mean," I said defensively. "I knew I wasn't gonna get killed. It was just Phil Lattimore. No one else."

"Yeah, that was all you needed to know, wasn't it? Only this Phil Lattimore would die so that meant everybody else would be *all right*." He looked at me through half-closed eyes. "Like you and Ambrose."

The lump in my chest was suddenly so large it was hard to breathe around it and my heart seemed to be laboring. "Ambrose wasn't driving, we had a flat—"

"He ran into the road after the car you were in," Loomis said. "One of those things you do without thinking. The car that swerved to keep from hitting him hit another car, which in turn hit the car you were in. Which hit him before skidding into yet another car." I started to say something but he put up a hand. "There were two fatalities—this Phil Lattimore person who was apparently too cheap to install airbags in his old land yacht and got spindled on the steering column, and someone else who you apparently hadn't met."

"But Ambrose is ali—"

"Alive, yes, and will be for another fifty-odd years," Loomis said, talking over me. "Exactly how odd nobody really knows yet. The doctors told my parents it's a miracle he survived that kind of head injury. They won't know how extensive the impairment is until he wakes up. My mother believes he's going to wake up any minute because he's breathing on his own."

It was like I was back on the floor of the car with some thug kneeling on my ribs, but harder, as if he were trying to force all the air out of my lungs.

"Hey, stay with me." I felt Loomis tapping me lightly first on one cheek and then the other. "I wasn't trying to be cruel." He ran a small ice cube back and forth across my forehead. "But you had to be told."

I started to cry, my tears mixing with the cold water running down from my forehead.

"Shouldn't have happened," Loomis went on. "Wouldn't have, but they just won't talk about it in front of the kids. They tell you everything else— why we keep the traits secret, how to be careful around those poor souls who have the misfortune and/or bad judgment to marry one of us, how to cover if you say something you shouldn't to an outsider. But not how I 'accidentally' broke a kid's wrist playing football so he couldn't go to the municipal swimming pool afterwards like he planned and drown. And he didn't. He went straight home because he didn't know his wrist was broken and he drowned in the bathtub. His parents were investigated for child abuse and his sister spent eight months in foster care."

"Stop," I said. "Please."

"They were all so mad at me, the family was." Loomis shook his head at the memory. "They claimed they weren't, they told me it wasn't really my fault because I didn't know any better. Everyone kept telling me they weren't upset with me even after the authorities found out *I* had broken the kid's wrist and called me in for questioning. Along with Mom and Dad and Rita. Ambrose was a baby; they examined him for bruises."

"Stop," I pleaded. "I mean it."

Loomis was talking over me again. "It all came out all right; there was no reason to be upset with me. They said and they said and they said. But after my mother searched my room and found my journal with everybody's dates in it—*then* they got upset. Oh, they got *furious* with me. I said it was my mother's fault for snooping and then telling the rest of the family about it but they weren't having any of that. Writing down *those dates*—how could I have done such a thing? I stuck it out till I was sixteen and then I booked."

The silence hung in the air. I closed my eyes hoping that I'd pass out or something.

"When you're well enough to travel," he said after a while, "you'll come with me."

My eyes flew open.

"Death is the one thing you never, ever even *try* to mess with. Everything in the world—everything in the *universe* changes. But not that. Death *is*. If you went down to the deepest circle of hell and offered resurrection to everyone there, they'd all say no and mean it."

"That's not where you live, is it?" I asked.

Loomis chuckled. "Not even close."

"They won't beg me to stay, will they? They all hate me now."

"They don't hate you," Loomis said, patting my hand again. "They love you as much as they ever did. They just don't like you very much any more."

The nurse came in with my pain medication and I closed my eyes again. "Let me know when we leave."

WHEN ELLEN DATLOW *asked me to contribute to this anthology, I was honored but apprehensive. Pick a horror, any horror, and it's very likely that Poe did it first. The fears of his time—rampant disease, maddening guilt, torture, being walled up or interred with no*

escape—may come in different wrappers now but they are still with us. And because Poe's gift was his ability to keep the human-ity of his characters foremost, he is still with us, too.

He was also a poet, which makes him especially accomplished— very few writers are capable of both prose and poetry. The first of his poems to come to mind for most people is "The Raven" with its thumping meter and punctuation of "Nevermore." There are others: "To Helen," "The Conqueror Worm," "The Haunted Palace," and "Oh, Tempora! Oh, Mores!," to name a few.

But the one that captured my imagination many years ago was "The City in the Sea." The first few lines sucked me in:

> *"Lo! Death has reared himself a throne*
> *In a strange city lying alone*
> *Far down within the dim West..."*

It has haunted me since I first read it and, although I seriously considered working from one of Poe's stories, my thoughts kept wandering back to the place where

> *"... from a proud tower in the town,*
> *Death looks gigantically down..."*

You may have noticed there is no actual tower in this story, nor is there any sea as such. But you don't have to be in a real sea to be in over your head; you don't even have to be near water to drown.

In the end, we must all die. Death is not only the Great Equaliz-er but the Great Truth—true for all of us, no exceptions. Which is why

> *"... Hell, rising from a thousand thrones*
> *Shall do it reverence."*

NICHOLAS ROYLE, born in Manchester in 1963, is the author of five novels—*Counterparts*, *Saxophone Dreams*, *The Matter of the Heart*, *The Director's Cut*, and *Antwerp*—and two novellas—*The Appetite* and *The Enigma of Departure*. He has published over one hundred short stories and to date has one collection to his name: *Mortality*. Widely published as a journalist with regular appearances in *Time Out* and the *Independent*, he has also edited thirteen original anthologies. Since 2006 he has been teaching creative writing at Manchester Metropolitan University. He has won three British Fantasy Awards and the Bad Sex Prize once. His short story collection was shortlisted for the inaugural Edge Hill Prize.

THE REUNION

by Nicholas Royle

On arrival, we'd had to wait behind a man in jumbo cords and a pastel polo shirt who was giving the receptionist a hard time about some problem in his room, a missing towel or a faulty light, and we formed an immediate impression of him that was somewhat negative. It wasn't long, however, before we realized he had a point.

They didn't have any record of our booking, despite having sent us an email of confirmation, which happily Maggie had printed out and brought along. So we had to fill in a form, holding up those who had arrived after us, and finally the girl behind the desk gave us a key card and a map. Yes, a map. It was a big hotel. A huge hotel. One of those places you get apparently in the middle of nowhere but actually no more than twenty miles from one or other dreary Midlands town. A former RAF training camp or stately home or converted mental asylum. This appeared to be all three, with not only west wings and east wings, but whole houses and vast halls tacked on to the main building. The room belatedly assigned to us was in one of the modern blocks. We walked along one edge of a grand, colonnaded reception hall, past a tuxedoed piano player, through a little anteroom dominated by two stags' heads mounted on adjacent walls. We passed a bar with its shutter down, turned right into a wide corridor.

The further we got from the main part of the hotel with its marble columns and wide, red-carpeted staircases, the shoddier and tattier everything became. There was an armchair in a corner that was missing a castor, a cabinet of drawers covered in scuff marks. I said to Maggie that it was like that scene in

Jacob's Ladder where Tim Robbins is wheeled down into the bowels of a hospital that turns into a vision of hell with crazy people banging their heads against the wall and gobbets of bloody flesh lying around on the floor.

Maggie gave me her standard nod of impartial assent, the one kept for observations beyond her frame of reference. I realized, though, that if I was overly critical of the hotel, and therefore, by extension, of the evening itself, it could provoke a reaction. This was Maggie's evening—a medical school reunion—and the fact that I had readily agreed to come along meant that if at any point I regretted my decision, it would not be fair to allow it to show. As we trailed past a rather tired series of framed prints of the hotel in its heyday, I felt the swollen glands in my neck. The prints on the wall were undated and there were no outward signs that would enable you to assign them to a particular period. They were like idealizations or artist's impressions. One hung askew and I wanted to straighten it, but I sensed Maggie's impatience to get to the room and so left it.

We pushed through a set of glass doors and found ourselves in a lobby area. There was a lift to our right, a corridor behind wood-paneled doors beyond that, and another corridor heading off from the far side of the lobby. An old-fashioned three-piece suite occupied the middle of the space. Facing the lift doors was a walnut table that had seen better days. On it was a folded copy of the *Independent*.

It appeared that we had to go up two floors; I'm not very good at waiting around for lifts. Or buses. Or anything that you suspect might never come.

"I'll take the stairs," I said, "and I'll still get there before you."

I took Maggie's bag in my spare hand and shouldered open the door to the stairs. I ran up one flight, barged through the equivalent door on the next floor and found myself in an identical lobby space. I pressed the call button and while wondering if the lift would ever arrive tried on a number of expressions. It was certainly taking its time, the lift. On a walnut table that was indistinguishable from the one on the floor below was another copy of the *Independent* folded in the same manner. I thought to myself it had been a waste of money my buying one that morning. When the lift arrived, the doors trundled open to reveal Maggie and a middle-aged couple, who looked as though they wanted to get out. She introduced them to me as Henrik and Caroline. I thought I could see a slightly guarded look in Henrik's eyes as we swapped places; Caroline looked as if, like Maggie, she just wanted to get to their room. Henrik had been a contemporary, Maggie told me as the lift doors closed behind me and I turned to press the button. He'd seemed a lot older than me, but then Maggie is four years my senior and some men age worse than others.

The interior of the lift was mirrored on three sides, which created a theoretically endless series of reflections in both side walls. I checked myself out. I wasn't ageing too badly. My problems were *inside* my head. I knew that. Maybe physiologically; certainly mentally.

"You look beautiful," Maggie said in a way that managed to be affectionate and mocking at the same time.

When we finally got to our room, the third on the left beyond the wood-paneled doors, and managed to get the key card to flash green rather than red on the fifth attempt, we found we had one small towel between the two of us, no complimentary toiletries, and the shower produced either a trickle of boiling water or an icy torrent. I thought about helping Maggie out of her traveling clothes and suggesting we test out the mattress, but I sensed she wanted to get back downstairs for pre-dinner drinks as soon as possible. So while Maggie plugged in her hair-straighteners I stood to one side of the hot trickle in the shower cubicle pressing at my neck and trying to work out if the gland was bigger or smaller than the day before. I had mentioned it to Maggie and she had dismissed it. Ideally, this would have sufficed. Whereas the average person might think they had a cold coming on and the raised gland was their body's natural way of fighting it, my thoughts turn to leukemia, lymphoma, Hodgkin's disease.

I leaned over the washbasin and wiped a swathe of condensation from the mirror so that I could see my reflection. I fancied that it was studying me rather than I it. If so, perhaps it felt sorry for me with my imaginary ailments and constant nagging anxiety. Or perhaps it just thought I was ridiculous. It wasn't bothered by anything like that. It was free.

Toweling myself dry, I returned to the bedroom, where Maggie was just stepping into her specially bought ball gown with its flatteringly high waist and gratifyingly plunging neckline. I slipped into my oversize dead man's dinner jacket and a pair of highly polished shoes that were coming away from their soles. We left the room and headed back to the lifts. I suggested we walk down and Maggie acquiesced. She looked good in the ball gown and I thought she would prefer to watch the movement of the dress over her long legs than stand around waiting for the lift that might never arrive. I knew that was my preference. I pushed open the door to the stairwell and ushered Maggie through. As we walked down, a small party in tuxedos and ball gowns was coming up. They passed us and turned left. They were going in the right direction, but they were on the wrong level.

"They're going the wrong way," I whispered to Maggie.

But as I made the remark, I lost confidence in its content.

"Are you going to the reunion?" I asked the disappearing party while they were still within earshot.

"Yes," they said.

"It's this way," I said. "Down two flights. Unless you can get down at the other end?"

"No, this is the way," said a tall man with thinning hair and a perfectly fitting suit.

"How *can* it be?" I said to Maggie.

I pictured the two identical lobbies with their walnut tables and copies of the *Independent*. How had we gone wrong?

Maggie had stopped. We exchanged puzzled looks. The people who knew where they were going headed off while we dithered on the stairs. Eventually, I thought we might as well follow them. When we got as far as we could go and hadn't reached the main part of the hotel, and couldn't find another stairwell, *then* we could come back. So Maggie and I walked down the corridor, which was as similar to the one down which we had walked to get to our room as it is possible to be without actually being the same corridor. There would be no way out at the far end, and even if there was it would only be a stairway and we'd have to descend two flights to get to where we wanted to be.

Even the series of prints on the wall looked the same, one hanging askew. We passed a facsimile of the scuffed cabinet. I looked at the armchair in the corner. It sat unevenly due to a missing castor.

We entered a wide corridor and turned left at the end of it, past a bar that still had its shutters down. Next there was the room with the stags' heads, the piano player on the edge of the main reception hall (which was now heaving with well-dressed bodies) and we were back where we'd started, without having had to go down two floors. Maggie and I looked at each other in puzzlement and I just had time to start asking, "What the fuck—" when a tall woman in a taffeta ball gown swept past and dragged Maggie off to meet someone else she hadn't seen for twenty years.

They were giving out drinks. The choice was champagne or orange juice. I wandered off to a bar in an adjoining room where I waited behind a fat man who was ordering two turkey sandwiches. Back on the fringes of the main room where the welcome drinks were still being served, I stood with a pint of Guinness—the nearest I could get to something drinkable—and looked on. At the far side of the room I could see Maggie laughing generously at somebody's joke, her head dropping forward so that her straightened hair fell in front of her face. I became aware of a tall, slim man with silver hair standing near to me. A picture of understated elegance in his own tailored suit and carefully polished shoes, he sipped at a glass of champagne.

"It's strange being an outsider at one of these events," he said with an almost imperceptible turn of the head.

"Very strange," I agreed. "Will," I added, offering him my hand.

"Gordon," he said with a warm smile.

We raised our glasses to our lips and watched the increasingly animated crowd in the centre of the room.

"Do you know?" he began, "I was reading in the paper today—just now, upstairs, in fact—that during the Cold War the East Germans used to pay Bulgarian border guards for every East German they shot trying to cross the frontier into the West. It's almost unbelievable, isn't it?" He tipped the last of his champagne into his mouth and swallowed. "I don't know what made me think of that."

"Extraordinary," I agreed.

"I'm not sure I could kill anybody, even if ordered to do so."

"Not even for money?" I joked.

"Especially not for money," he said, turning to me. "Nice to meet you, Will. Excuse me."

As he walked away to look for his wife, I ticked myself off for my banal and unfunny joke.

I became aware of my fingers probing inside the collar of my dress shirt. I wondered if this latest fixation on head and neck cancers would end up with another referral to a specialist. I remembered with a jolt the not-so-smooth progress of the endoscope up my nose and down past my ear.

One of the organizers appeared up in the gallery with a photographer. Cupping her hands, the organizer announced a complicated sequence of group photographs. I took this as my cue to wander back to the bar and secure a second pint of Guinness. When I returned to the reception hall the photographer had finished. I looked for Maggie and saw her talking to a man with a paisley-patterned bowtie but when she lifted her head up to the light I saw it wasn't Maggie at all. The direct light revealed deeper lines, a less youthful skin texture. I felt a hand on my shoulder and turned around. *This* was Maggie, looking several years younger than the woman I'd thought was her. She introduced me to a well-meaning gastroenterologist from Peterborough and we had a conversation about five-a-side football. Despite both being regular players of the game, neither one of us was at all interested in what the other had to say.

Fortunately dinner was announced, so I was able to escape and find Maggie again and together we joined the throng heading towards the ballroom.

"I can't remember," I said to her, "is Jonathan coming to this?"

Maggie and Jonathan had met in their first year and started going out. They'd stayed together for a number of years, until a mutual acquaintance had lured Jonathan away from Maggie for a one-night stand that had turned into marriage, kids, the lot.

"No," Maggie answered, looking all around as she spoke, "this is not Jonathan's scene at all."

I wanted to say that it wasn't mine. It wasn't mine possibly even more than it wasn't Jonathan's. But I kept quiet. My hand crept up to my neck as we shuffled towards the seating plan resting on an easel by the entrance to the ballroom.

"No doubt we'll be on a table at the back," Maggie said, "with all the other people who booked at the last minute."

As we duly made our way towards the back of the ballroom, I had a look around. Two large video projection screens were each showing a series of stills, mugshots taken on enrollment. They were monochrome and the images had either become degraded or had been drenched with a sepia hue. There were probably two hundred, maybe three hundred people at the event; less than half of those would be partners, and possibly a not insignificant proportion of the partners would have been fellow students. I was trying to work out how long I might have to watch the parade of faces before Maggie's might appear. I had seen photographs of Maggie—and Jonathan—from back then. I was confident I'd recognize her. It's not as if the passage of twenty-five years actually makes you a different person. You just look a little older. Or a lot older.

I saw a picture of the organizer, the woman who had appeared on the balcony to orchestrate group photographs. She'd been slimmer, but you could already see the confidence in her eyes. For her it seemed a short step from enrolling to sending out invitations for a twenty-five-year reunion. She already knew she was going to do it. Maybe not explicitly, but she knew herself very well, she knew what she was capable of.

On the other screen I saw an early mugshot of the guy from the lift, Henrik, and he did indeed look a lot younger, but, again, the eyes were the same. That reticence, suspicion even.

I looked away from the mugshots in order to be introduced to the people at our table. Through a combination of first impressions, whispered intel from Maggie, and the fruits of my own efforts at conversation, I gathered that they were a mixture of old friends of Maggie's and former fellow students: a likeable psychologist whose husband had left her for another man; a guy in his early fifties who had given up medicine for web design, but whose ideas seemed mired in the 1990s; a woman who had trained as a GP, before taking time out to have kids and finally going back to do a day a week; another part-time GP and editor of medical journals and his wife, a teacher who called herself a freelance journalist on the strength of writing a column for her husband's magazine about being married to a doctor.

When I next looked towards the front of the ballroom, there was Maggie's mugshot just fading from the screen on the left. I'd gathered now that the two screens were showing the same photographs, but out of synch. I saw the psychologist from our table. She was smiling at the camera, her eyes full of hope and expectation.

I turned back to the table, where three Polish waitresses in black and white costumes had converged. Drinks were being ordered, but the choice appeared to be limited to red or white, as far as I could tell from my attempts at dialogue with the three Poles, who, in terms of their mental and practical preparedness, were still on the plane from Warsaw.

"I'm going to the bar," I told Maggie.

I watched the faces fade in and fade out on the screens as I crossed the room. The last face I saw before the angle became too narrow to see anything at all made me come to an abrupt halt with a silly expression on my face.

Because it was mine.

I backtracked. The face that had looked a lot like mine twenty years earlier had gone and been replaced by that of Gordon, the man I had met in the reception hall. I looked at the other screen, but it would be a while before the shot came around again and I'd be able to see it and realize that the guy who looked like me didn't look that much like me after all.

I stood waiting for the bartender to pour me a pint of Guinness. He tried to make conversation. He was Greek, very friendly, and he didn't have many customers, but I wasn't up for it. I felt strange, dissociated from my surroundings. I palpated my neck.

"Hello, Will," said a voice.

I turned around to see Henrik leaning on the bar. He asked the bartender for a Scotch. From the glassy look in his eyes I guessed he'd already had a couple.

"It's weird, isn't it?" he said.

"What?"

"This. This place. This whole evening. The mugshots. I didn't know they were going to do that. With that picture constantly flashing up on screen, it's like there's two of you. You now and you then. Do you know what I mean?"

"I saw yours," I said. "You've not changed a bit."

He gave a little laugh and knocked back his Scotch.

"I'm going to head back," I said.

"Cheers."

Seated at the table with the starters arriving, I waited for a gap in the conversation and turned to Maggie.

"What was going on with that whole lift thing?" I asked her.

"I can't explain it," she said, her eyes shining. "We went up but then didn't need to come down again. It's this place. The rules are different here."

I could tell Maggie was having a good time; she wouldn't normally come out with something like that. She's a very rational person. Either being a doctor made her like that or she became a doctor because that was the kind of person she was. Bit of both probably.

"Do you think it's possible," I said, "that we actually went down when we thought we were going up? After I got in?"

"But then we'd have just got back where we started and that wasn't the right floor. It's just—" She stopped and her eyes widened and she sang the theme tune to *The Twilight Zone*. I couldn't remember the last time she'd done that—perhaps ten years ago. I smiled and she leaned forward and I kissed her, then immediately she turned away and put her hand on the psychologist's arm to impart some fascinating piece of gossip she'd just remembered.

Thinking that it would be a while before the main course arrived, I got up from the table. On one of the big screens I recognized the sequence of mugshots that had preceded that of the guy who looked a bit like the younger me. When the face came up again, I studied it. Was he here, in the room? He would be four years older than me if he was Maggie's contemporary. Would he have aged better?

I thought of him as a version of me four years on, just as the second lobby I'd visited with the identical walnut table was a version of the one on the floor below. It was simply a floor higher. Separated in space rather than time.

I wondered if I should get another pint, but remembered I hadn't finished the last one.

On a table next to the easel just outside the ballroom was a laptop. It was playing a slideshow of the pictures taken in the hotel's reception hall. I picked out Maggie, smiling broadly and looking up at the camera just like everybody else. I saw the web designer and the boring gastroenterologist and even, standing on the edge of the group, Gordon, the man I had talked to briefly. I spotted Henrik and his wife, Caroline. There was the divorced psychologist, the tall man with the thinning hair who had known where he was going, there was the woman in taffeta and the man from the reception desk who had changed out of his jumbo cords and pastel polo shirt. And there, just to the left of centre, was I, my neck tendons straining with the effort of holding my head up to smile for the camera. Maybe I looked a little tired around the eyes, perhaps I appeared a tad heavier in the jowls, even slightly paunchier.

I turned around and headed back into the ballroom. I checked out the nearest tables, but there was no sign of anyone who looked a bit like me. I reached our table, but remained standing, scanning the room, running my eyes over every table in there. He wasn't to be seen. I sat down, thanked the waitress for my main course and smiled at Maggie, who still looked like she was having a good time.

"This is *so* weird," she said quietly but emphatically.

She didn't know how weird.

I pushed back my chair.

"Where are you going?" she asked.

"I won't be long."

"How's your neck?"

I looked at her.

"Are your glands still up?"

"I've just got to…"

My legs took me away from the table. I didn't like it when she didn't show concern, and I didn't like it when she did. She couldn't win, and neither could I. I prodded my neck as I crossed to the exit. I glanced at the group photo on the laptop, wondering, as I sometimes did, what was the point of a life like this, a life lived in constant fear of its ending. Wouldn't it just be easier to cut short the wait?

I fingered the keycard in my pocket with one hand and the raised gland in my neck with the other as I walked slowly and softly past the wonky chair and the scuffed cabinet. I stopped to straighten the print that was hanging askew. The glass doors gave on to the lift lobby. The walnut table looked bare. Sitting on the shiny velveteen sofa reading the *Independent* was Gordon.

"Hello, Will," he said, turning the page.

I had no doubt that if I were to go up a floor, there he would be again sitting on the sofa reading the same newspaper. And whichever floor I was on, our room would be three doors down on the left beyond the wood-paneled doors.

I reached the door and slid the keycard into the slot. It flashed red. I tried again. Still red. I tried sliding it in very slowly and extracting it just as slowly. Still the red light flashed. I stood for a moment and listened to my breathing, which was fast and shallow. And then I heard a man's voice. It was very close. I looked behind me to see if someone had left their door open. They'd left the ballroom to make a phone call and decided to do it in the privacy of their room. But the doors on the other side of the corridor were all shut and the corridor was empty. Sometimes, when I play five-a-side football and we're warming up while waiting to begin, I count the players to see if we're all there. I count four and wonder who's missing, and it takes me a few moments to realize I've failed to count myself. The frightening thing was that the corridor did genuinely feel empty, as if even I wasn't there. I would try the card in the door one more time before going to report the fault. I shoved it into the slot, which pushed the door open half an inch with an audible click of the mechanism. I wondered if we'd left the door unlocked and what valuables might have been at risk. Then I heard the voice again, louder this time. It was coming from inside the room.

IN FREUD'S ESSAY *on the Uncanny he spends twelve pages discussing the meaning of the word (in German,* das Unheimliche, *providing the adjective* unheimlich) *and its derivation. Key, as I understand it, is the sense of strangeness, unfamiliarity; yet at the same time something that is familiar can also be uncanny. So what could be more uncanny—familiar and unfamiliar at the same time—than the double or* Doppelgänger? *It is a theme to which I have been attracted since I started writing (indeed before). So when invited to pick a Poe story, I didn't have to think for very long. "William Wilson" is not my favorite Poe story and I didn't get to read it until some years after my first encounter with the author, which was prompted by finding a lovely old Pan paperback edition of* Tales of Mystery *and* Imagination, *that of course does not*

include "William Wilson." But of all Poe's work, this is the story closest to my heart for its treatment of the Doppelgänger theme.

I myself have a Doppelgänger. Nicholas Royle does not resemble me physically, but like me he is a writer and a teacher of creative writing. His many books include The Uncanny (Manchester University Press). If you look us up on Amazon, which makes no distinction between us (why should it, although the British Library notes that Nick was born in 1957), his are the non-fiction titles, while mine are all fiction. I published a short story of Nick's in one of my anthologies, while he writes about me in a chapter of The Uncanny called "The Double." We have survived several meetings, even given readings together, and at some point hope to publish a jointly authored book.

KAARON WARREN's short story collection *The Glass Woman*, published by Prime Books, won the ACT Writing and Publishing Awards Fiction Prize in its Australian edition. She had a story reprinted in *The Year's Best Fantasy and Horror 2007: Twentieth Annual Collection*, and has had stories in the anthologies *The Worker's Paradise* and *Paper Cities*. She also has stories forthcoming in *Futuristic Motherhood, 2012*, and *New Ceres*. You can read *Seeing Eye Dog* on Amazon Shorts. Warren is an Australian who wrote this story while living in Fiji. You can reach her on her blog at: kaaronwarren.livejournal.com.

THE TELL

by Kaaron Warren

THROUGH HER HOTEL window, the men seemed to be crying. It was the rain, Siri thought, an illusion. But the image stayed with her as she prepared for her day of meetings. Three men, arm in arm, painted onto a car-park wall. Color lost to pollution; all three were gray. Siri squinted, squeezed her eyes. She felt a deep ache across her shoulders; she hadn't been that tense, had she?

THE RAIN EASED by the time of her final meeting, so Siri walked the two blocks to the Mütter Museum. She looked forward to this one, although she knew it wouldn't have a positive outcome. The application itself interested her: it sought funding for a "Causes of Death" exhibit. Bullets removed from brains or hearts, knife tips from livers, poisoned kidneys and other damaged organs. The Mayor wouldn't like it; he preferred the institutions to demonstrate Brotherly Love, not Murder Capital of America.

Siri was led to a small room by the receptionist—two old armchairs pushed close together, flickering light—and told nothing.

Not a good start, she thought.

An old man came into the room, stared at her, then hunched into the other chair. Siri smiled at him, nodded a greeting. He shook his head in return. He jittered. Leg bouncing, knee jiggling, hand holding mug shaking so much he splashed coffee over the sides to burn his hands but he didn't seem to notice. Liver spots on his hands, arms covered with white, wiry hair. His throat was wattled but his face was smooth, pink. It looked to Siri as if the top layer of his skin had peeled off, leaving an earlier self underneath. He was partially bald; his hair the same wiry white stuff on his arms.

He looked worried; at his feet, a large brown paper bag. On his wrist: a hospital ID strip. Siri wondered: *Why is it still there? Was he not released? Has he released himself against doctor's orders? Why didn't he cut it off? What sort of hospital was it and what sort of disorder does he have? What's in the paper bag?*

Her mouth was dry because she had been staring at him, loose-jawed. She felt safe doing it; he seemed blind, incapable of focus.

She saw such anxiety in him, such terror, her heart started to beat more quickly.

He held his palm up to her: *wait.* It was crisscrossed with deep, clean lines and he held it up while he scrabbled in his bag.

She didn't want to see what he had but at the same time she did: a knife? A bomb? Some human tissue sample or souvenir of his last kill?

A book placed on his knee then he delved again.

He pulled out something the size of her outstretched hand, then stood and stepped forward to her. He held it out, nodding at her. She shook her head.

"Take it," he said. "It's good."

"No. I'm okay."

He shook his head. She noticed he had no socks.

"Here." He shoved something into her hand. A heart.

It was delicately woven, horsehair, she thought, each strand made up of ten or so individual hairs. It was old, she could tell that by the gentle discoloration along the outside.

It was the width of a paperback book and felt solid. When she tilted it to look at the base, she felt something heavy thump inside.

"What is it?"

He nodded, and it seemed to her that the anxiety lifted from him.

"Will you sit with me on the train? I'll tell you a story." Her brother-in-law always warned her not to leave her Amtrak ticket in the clear pocket of her case.

"You're catching the same train?" she said, surprised.

He winked at her. "A train is a good place to talk."

He was too old to be hitting on her. He didn't seem the type to ever have hit on anybody; he seemed shy, nervous, and lonely. Did she want to spend three hours listening to the ramblings of an old man? She had a book to read, but it was dull, and the thud of the horsehair heart intrigued her.

"All right," she said, and that is how she came to hear of the disappearance of Edgar Allan Poe, and what happened to his heart.

The curator, a young man with bright, clear blue eyes set in a very large face and a morbidly obese body, came into the room and shook her hand.

"Sorry, Siri," Tony said, blinking at the alliteration. "Didn't mean to keep you waiting."

"Was the gentleman first?" she said.

Tony turned a shoulder, physically blocking the old man from his view. "He's some Poe nut. We get them."

Siri offered the horsehair heart to the old man; he held his hand up, shook his head.

"I'll tell you on the train," he said.

Tony held the door open for her and she followed him into the hallway. "You've brought the rain with you," he said, grinning widely. Siri had dealt with him via phone before and knew that, once you got beyond the jovial "aren't we fun, even though we're scientists" surface, he was an intelligent, informed man who could be relied upon not to gloss over details such as cost and potential audience of an exhibit. He was vocal in his defense of truth in presentation. He liked current thinking and the latest research to inform the way the exhibits were presented, whereas others thought that old descriptive passages were part of an exhibit's nature.

THEY WALKED THROUGH the hallways and down stairs to his office. Siri liked the environment: boxes in the hallway labeled "beaks," posters for past exhibits, notices to "wash hands after handling human remains." All so interesting compared to her plain office with its matte pastel walls and sensible carpet.

His room was dark, the window covered by stacks of paper sitting on a table near the window sill. The lightglobe was so dim she wondered why he bothered. The spare chair was covered with small boxes (knuckle bones, he told her, shifting them off.)

Siri took her papers out. "Your application is a good one. I've seen the figures, run through them, and looked at your proposal. It is good; I wouldn't be here otherwise. Most institutions can't write a report. Something to do with their idea of their importance, I think."

"The head curator's daughter did it. She's studying business. She thinks we're all crazy. Playing with bones and bodies. She doesn't see where the money making happens."

He poured coffee into mugs. Siri wished she'd thought to walk in with one to avoid this. The mug was crusty around the lip, looking like it could be in an exhibit itself. She took it, all sticky and dusty, and found room on a stack of papers on the desk.

"Tell me what your inspiration is. For the exhibit. Why you want to do it."

"I think it's a good local exhibit as well as an international one. People will love it. It's interesting. They'll come to see the Poe knife at the very least."

"No!"

The old man had crept into the room. He said again, "No!"

"Sir, you'll need to wait for a junior curator," Tony said.

"This is not the knife that killed Poe."

"I thought he died of alcoholism," Siri said.

"This is not the knife!"

Tony stood and gently ushered the man out. "We can discuss this when the exhibit goes ahead, okay? We'll need your expert opinion."

Siri waited until Tony was seated again.

"Nice local touch. Poe stayed nearby here?"

"He did, for six months or so. Disappeared on his way to New York. Turned up in Baltimore."

Siri nodded. "So the thing is, Tony, for all the worth of your application, the committee has voted to say no. You will be invited to submit again. If I were you I'd do it. You'll need to add your passion, though. This, while excellent financially, has no passion. You'll need both, to win funding. I'll give you an example. I saw a mural of three men, linked arms. They're meant to symbolize brotherly love, but the mural is out of shape. They look angry and sad. Something like that on the front cover of your report might help."

SHE CAUGHT HER train easily; the old man was there ahead of her. He'd saved her a seat, which he patted. Even before she'd sat down, he said, "So many of our geniuses end badly." She fussed with her papers but he wanted her full attention, leaning in to her. "Impoverished, murdered, unappreciated, starving, unhappy, hated. Afterwards we feel badly for this, guilty, but then it is too late.

"Edgar Allan Poe was on his way from Richmond, Virginia to New York City, a simple journey he looked forward to. Peace and quiet on the steamer because often he wasn't recognized. He could ride without talking about why, why the horror, the nightmares, why do you inflict those images on your readers?

"'You think it's any easier for me? I am the one dreaming,' he told one inquirer. That was reported, repeated and it was good in the long run; with the reputation of a bad-tempered, nightmare-driven man, people were less likely to bother him.

"This trip, however, was not destined to be peaceful. Poe was recognized by a struggling writer, a very poor writer in both quality and funds. He convinced Poe (so perhaps he did have a way with words after all) to get off the steamer midway through the journey."

The conductor came their way. The old man physically shrank back and his jitters returned.

"Tickets, please." The old man's hand shook so much he could barely hold his ticket. Siri took it and handed both to the conductor.

"We're together," she said.

"Good girl," the conductor said, approving a daughter out with her father, or grandfather, approving of a girl looking after her old relative.

"Three days later, a man thought to be Poe was found in Baltimore, beaten beyond recognition and close to death. Three days. Long enough for readers to gather in great and terrible lamentation. His family gathered but he was to have no last words. His tongue was split down the middle and every finger was broken. He could not even wriggle a toe with both ankles shattered.

"Such thoughts must have been in his head. Such frustrations and fury, such sadness and loss.

"His eyelids fluttered four times. Maybe five. And twice flicked open to reveal blood-filled eyes. His mother-in-law couldn't recognize her own dear son-in-law. Try as she might to read his thoughts she couldn't, to her everlasting regret. He was buried as Poe and that is how it remains."

"But you said he was only thought to be Poe?"

"That man was not Poe, but an indigent sailor found dead drunk in the street. Poe was dead, but his body was never found. His heart? Removed. Preserved. His body? Cut up, I would say. Fed to the rats."

Siri lifted the horsehair heart. "Preserved? In here?"

He nodded. "Oh, yes. They wanted to keep it safe. Protected."

"But why? Why did that writer kill him?"

"The writer believed in tales of the macabre. He was certain that if he owned Poe's heart, he would own Poe's nightmares and his genius as well. He was half right."

Siri tilted the heart again.

"The writer was never caught. He never became famous, either; never put another word to paper. He was already quite a skillful silversmith, so he built this box to keep the heart in. His sister, a lace maker of high reputation and dry existence, wove the horsehair over it."

The old man's throat was dry. Siri bought him a soda from the café carriage and he drank it in three deep swallows.

"I like sugar," he said. "It's sweet." The corners of his mouth twitched up and she was glad to have made him happy.

Siri ran her fingers over the smooth, sharp horsehair lines of the heart. He watched her for a moment.

"The killer earned a living as a silversmith, as time went on. He made magnificent, intricate necklaces that fitted tightly around the throat, accentuating length and grace. It is said that his creations tightened on contact with perspiration, though. If a woman stayed perfectly cool, silent, motionless, she could breathe. Once she sweated, the necklace would constrict, and if there was no one there to help her remove her jewelry, she would choke."

"Did that ever happen?" Siri could feel her own breath thickening in her throat.

"They say so. They say he made watch chains for the gentlemen, also. These chains had a magnetism about them which sucked time. The men aged more quickly than their counterparts, without the subsequent maturity." He tapped his fingernail to the horsehair heart.

"The killer's nightmare?"

He nodded. "I knew you were the person I needed to tell. This heart gives you an understanding, an appreciation, of your nightmares. The power to harness them."

"I never have nightmares."

"What you think is a nightmare may not be the true nightmare. It is what lies beneath, in your heart. That's where the true nightmare is. I was told the story of the heart the way I am telling you, by an old woman, close to death."

The heart smelled of mothballs and Siri imagined it resting on a woman's bedside table for sixty years. Or sitting in a kitchen drawer, the third drawer, full of oddities and mysteries. A spoon with a twisted handle, Rupert James Military Hospital. An unusual corkscrew, a penknife set in a miniature Dutch clog, clumps of costume jewelry.

Siri wished she had the whole imaginary drawer. Unsorted, straight from the dead woman's kitchen. Siri wanted clues; she wanted the story of the woman's life.

The old man watched her. "I was told the story and the heart became mine. My dreams were of damaged people and I did the damage." He looked out the window, his jitters still for a moment. "So you see why this must go to a good person? A deserving one?"

Me! Siri thought. *I'm always good.*

The conductor headed their way again and the old man shrank back, his shoulders up to his ears, his eyelids squeezed shut, like an ostrich hiding away. Siri tried to read the hospital bracelet, at least to see where he'd come from. His name was Carney, she could see that, and the hospital Saint something.

The old man excused himself to go to the bathroom. Siri hoped he'd be careful; she didn't fancy sitting next to him smelling of piss and shit.

She placed her hands over the horsehair heart. It felt warm, as if the metal inside had heated gently in the sun, though no sun had reached it. She closed her eyes. She could smell a dream coming from around the corner. Strawberry syrup. Fresh paint. Singed hair.

The train pulled into a station but Siri thought nothing of it; her stop was fully ninety minutes away. She looked out though, as you do. Looking for differences, some indication of place.

The train began to pull out. She worried about Carney; he had been in the toilet for a while and she hoped he hadn't fallen and hit his head.

But no. There he was on the platform. Had he said he was getting off? She'd thought he was on board for longer than she was; yes, his ticket had him three stations further than hers did.

He waved at her, joyful, two-handed, full-armed waving. He leapt up and down, span around like an excited dog. Smiled. Yellow-toothed pure joy.

His bag was at her feet; she held it up to him as the train pulled away. He shrugged, *I don't care!* And he waved at her, more gently, as the train left the station.

Siri sat in shock for a few minutes. That was too fast; he hadn't finished the story. And he had left his bag of belongings and... the horsehair heart.

She looked in his bag and found some chips, opened and stale. Three books, airport thrillers, airport pickups. A shirt with St Gerard's on it, and his name. Nothing more. St Gerard's was a hospital for the dispossessed. Some called it the hospital for the possessed; most people who ended up there had more than one voice to listen to.

Siri shook the heart gently. She found the thud comforting, like something fitting into place neatly. Once home she'd read into Poe's life, see if there was any hint that it was not Poe buried in Poe's grave.

She felt the horsehair; sharp and slightly slimy, her finger slid easily along its strands.

She would call Tony at the Museum, tell him she'd send the heart to him. If the old man didn't reclaim it, the Museum could have it. Poe's Heart, on display? People would line up for that.

One stop from home she felt her eyelids drooping, so she stood up, stretched her legs, got her bag ready. Siri lived as close to New York as she could without it being New York. She liked it that way; could take New York when it suited her.

In the seat behind, a thin, tall woman with a felt hat squashed on her head. She was asleep; glancing at her travel card in the luggage rack, Siri saw she was one stop from home, also.

Siri leaned over and tapped the woman gently on the knee. She used the horsehair heart; her free hand kept her steady, holding the seatback.

The woman's face screwed up and her mouth opened. She sucked in a lungful of air; the ferocity of the breath choked her, and she woke up.

She saw Siri watching her. "I had the worst nightmare. These children, like a swimming pool of children..." She stopped. "Sorry. You don't need to know that." The woman was shaking so hard she couldn't stand up.

"I think yours is the next stop. Can I get your bag for you?" Siri said, and, shoving the horsehair heart into her pocket, pulled down the woman's hot–pink overnight bag.

The woman recovered, and thanked Siri on the railway track. "You're a kind person. I'll help someone else like you helped me, okay? Pass it on."

Siri nodded. She felt as if she had spent her life being kind; listening, helping, advising.

ON THE WAY out for drinks with her fiancé that night, he had the news playing on his tiny car TV. "You can't live ten minutes without news?"

"You gotta be informed."

"This isn't information. It's mostly opinion."

Siri wondered how he concentrated. The picture was gritty, the colors mixed, with blue close to red, and red very yellow. So when footage of a swimming pool came on, she at first couldn't tell what it was.

"Can you see what that is?" she asked her fiancé, curious, because it looked like an indoor swimming pool, and that woman's nightmare...

"It's a bunch of children," he said off-hand. So off-hand she wanted to hit him. "They pumped something into the pool by mistake or something."

She could see now; children in the pool.

He parked out the front of one of his favorite bars. Siri could see the drinkers inside, pressed up against the steamy windows.

"Here?" she said.

"Come on."

As she stepped out of the car, something flashed red and like a crow she swooped for it. Heart-shaped, cold and hard, it was garnet, she thought, smooth and rounded.

Her fiancé, taller than her by four heads, tugged her back. "Don't scrabble in the gutter. Disease down there."

She slid it into her pocket for safety and took her fiancé's hand.

Once inside, pressed up against the wall with her glass of cheap wine, she showed him the small red heart she'd found; perfect it was, smooth-edged, ruby redness making her hungry for jewels.

He touched it, placing it in his huge palm. It looked like a blemish in his hand, shiny scar tissue.

"Why did you pick junk out of the gutter? You don't know where this has been." But she did know, she knew very well that this had been given as a necklace in love and torn off in anger. All of that was in the stone. She squeezed it in her palm and knew the young girl who'd owned it and lost it.

A fight broke out around them. Her fiancé smiled, hitching at his pants. He said she was so proper, so smart, he liked to see her in the rough, in the middle of it.

She hated him, felt it powerfully and so blindingly she failed to step aside as a body came towards her, knocking her sideways and smashing her into a table full of glasses.

She didn't faint from blood loss. Never had fainted; her brain didn't have the shut down facility.

Knowing most of the people in the bar to be drunk, she got to her knees, assessed the most gushing wound and applied pressure to it. It was in her thigh but not too far up. The gash on her head bled furiously but would stop. The others were closer to pressure points

"Ambulance coming," the bartender told her. "Are you all right?"

"I'll be fine," she said, reassuring him. Being kind.

Her fiancé knelt beside her but his weak face made her angry. She was done with him, over him; the thought of kissing him made her ill.

LOOKING IN THE mirror two days later, spending an hour looking, feeling nauseous but looking anyway, unable not to look.

The stitches across her forehead. Her shoulders. Her wrist. Her thigh.

The stitches were so beautiful; neat and black, and as she looked at her naked self in the mirror, she imagined a dress with such stitches, a thin material, soft to the touch, held together with neat, black stitches.

She took up a pencil, used the back of a letter to draw the design. When she was happy with it, she showered carefully and dressed, visions of clothes in her head; pants and skirts, girl's dresses, boy's t-shirts, a whole line of clothing.

She fell asleep holding the heart. It seemed to pulse, although she knew that it was her own blood, her own beat.

That night she dreamt of a shop, her clothes hanging on racks. The shop had red walls and gently beating background music. It had candy hearts to eat while you waited and she knew that the horschair heart sat beneath the till.

When she awoke, she drove into the garment district and wandered from outlet to outlet, fingering the material and letting her eyes draw in the colors. She knew what she wanted; plumage, bird color, flower color. Fabrics soft and alluring.

In her dreams the pieces flew together, but in reality she cut the material too short, too crooked; she didn't know enough about dressmaking.

She slept full of dreams, awoke to try again, failure, failure.

"You know, the Museum runs a costume design course," Tony told her. He emailed her often; after she quit her job (who could work with all that fabric cottoning your thought process?) she'd helped him win his grant, so he took an interest in her. She'd asked him once about the old man, said, "He told me a strange story."

"Strange stories are the best kind. We haven't seen him in here for a while. He gets locked up every now and then."

He signed her up for the design course. "Make me a waistcoat or something," he said. "A vest."

So she learned the magic. Her fellow students envied her originality.

The vest she made gave Tony a sense of thinness. Confidence. He stopped asking Siri out; already he felt better than her. Too good for her. He would get thin. Very, very thin.

She found financial backing (no further training needed to figure out how to achieve that) and stitched and sewed her clothes. She sat in her own shop window dressed in loose flowing pants and, a fitted smooth top, her own design, and made her garments.

Into a rainbow skirt she stitched a nightmare stench, a fear of death. Into a soft silk scarf she sewed blurred vision, so that the wearer could not see loved ones.

She sold her clothes, dressed people in problems. She accepted the nightmares fatalistically; *there is important work here. Each shirt I sell makes a difference.*

She sold dresses to make women garrulous, speak their inner thoughts. Shirts that caused heart pain, limb ache. She sold trousers that led people to act out their base desires, their very deep and hidden fantasies.

All stitched neatly and carefully.

ONE NIGHT, SHE had an odd, waking dream; old man Carney, the teller, leaping for joy on the track at the station. She dreamt that there was something he didn't tell her; that if she died with the heart in her possession she would fall into a black, eternal pit. It was the power of the heart. There were times when the nightmares lost hold and she knew that she was in a different place because of the heart. She was devoted to it and all it meant, but the guilt, the guilt sometimes pushed through.

The next morning, a couple came into her store. He was aggressive, sexually aggressive, grabbing Siri when his wife was in the changing room. Saying, "You look fat," when his wife came out. Siri pulled on her own fingerless gloves, comfortable second skin. She reached out and placed a finger on the man's chest, stopped his heart for a beat. A beat was long enough for him to see the end, feel regret, make ten wishes.

"Be kind," she said. His lips were blue. He would recover, but more slowly than a younger man. He nodded.

He paid for his wife's dress, ("Sexy," he whispered to her) but would not look at Siri.

"You should take these, too," Siri said, handing the woman a pair of gloves.

The man said, "She doesn't wear gloves." He tried to take them from his wife's hands, but Siri stopped him.

"She'll wear these," she said.

SIRI COULDN'T SLEEP, that night, not even holding the horsehair heart. She turned on the television, the news, thinking briefly of her fiancé and his love for the empty words.

People of power on TV, men and women, good and bad. Siri took up a notebook and began to make a list of all the people to whom, one day, she might choose to tell the story of Poe's heart and pass on the gift of nightmares.

———————————————— ✻ ————————————————

"THE TELL-TALE HEART" *is my favorite Poe story because of the rising panic, the growing madness, the rhythm running through it.*

On a recent trip to Philadelphia, we visited a House Where Poe Lived, and I trod on a squeaky floorboard near his front door. I thought, "Is this where he imagined the body to be buried?"

I learned that Poe had disappeared just before his death, and I wondered where he was for those three days.

I also visited a flea market in New York, where the horsehair items made me feel ill. There was a butterfly hairclip wrapped tightly with discolored horsehair, and a small horsehair flywhisk, its ends split.

I traveled from city to city via train, and watched people on the various long-distance rides.

All of these elements helped me build "The Tell."

DAVID PRILL is the author of the cult novels *The Unnatural*, *Serial Killer Days*, and *Second Coming Attractions*, and the collection *Dating Secrets of the Dead*. "The Last Horror Show," from the *Dating Secrets* collection, was nominated for an International Horror Guild Award. His short fiction has appeared in *The Magazine of Fantasy and Science Fiction*, *Subterranean*, *Cemetery Dance*, and at Ellen Datlow's late lamented *SCIFICTION* web site. His story, "The Mask of '67," was published in the 2007 World Fantasy Award-winning anthology *Salon Fantastique*, edited by Ellen Datlow and Terri Windling. Another story, "Vivisepulture," can be found in *Logorrhea: Good Words Make Good Stories* (John Klima, editor). He lives in a small town in the Minnesota north woods.

THE HEAVEN AND HELL OF ROBERT FLUD

by David Prill

BEFORE HE MET the farmer's daughter, the traveling salesman ran into a fellow traveler at a drinking hole named Heaven and Hell in the sleepy corn-fed township of Swedenborg, Minnesota.

"Bob Flud, encyclopedias," said the traveling salesman, quaffing his suds.

"Nicholas Klimm, Klimm's Wonder Elixir," said the other, wiping his sweaty bald pate with a magician-sized white handkerchief. "Cures everything from eczema to excessive nervous agitation."

"I have neither. Life is excessively swell if anything."

"Your complexion is perhaps a touch sallow."

"It's the lighting in this Heaven and Hell."

"The thirst for knowledge, then, is present even in this rustic enclave."

"That's what I'm about to find out. Just drove over from Watonwan County this morning. It's been a slow week, but I've dreamed up some new pitches I'm going to throw."

"I wish you better fortune than I have experienced. Several districts have yet to be introduced to the Wonder Elixir, but thus far doors have been shut in my face with alarming regularity."

"This is all the Wonder Elixir I need," said Flud, tipping back his glass with fervor.

"And the knowledge of a thousand encyclopedias is contained within," said Klimm, tapping his temple.

They toasted. "Here's to my thirst and your brains," said Flud.

"Indeed."

Flud drained his glass and set it down on the bar. He peeled a bill from a roll, slapped it down by the empty glass, suds still sudsing deep within, and gave the proprietor a nod. "Save a stool for me in Heaven, bud. I'll be needing it again."

"You got it."

Flud turned to his counterpart. "See you on the road, pal."

"I look forward to it, best wishes, etcetera."

"Likewise."

Bob Flud left Heaven and Hell, heading for his green DeSoto. It was a thirsty-looking street, the late summer sun unforgiving. He wished he had more time to drink and shoot the breeze, but Watonwan had been a wasteland, sales-wise, so he needed to make up for it here.

Settling into the car, he spread the wrinkled road map across the dashboard. Pretty stark country, this Swedenborg Township. Miles of bean fields between here and the next collection of taverns they called a town. He was tempted to skip it and make for a more cosmopolitan destination like Mankato, but sometimes these out-of-the-way burgs produced surprises. He recalled a week last summer in northwestern Iowa when he had three hits in a row, one farm after the other, bang, bang, bang. Volume B, for Beautiful. Volume B, for Bank. A real Babe Ruth day. Afterwards he examined his sales technique in hopes of recapturing the magic, but he never could unearth what he had done differently on those calls.

Maybe there was something special about me that day, he thought, wrestling the map into submission and starting the car. Maybe I was believable, or I just looked like a sad character who as good churchgoing folk they felt compelled to help. Or maybe my tongue was pure silver that day. Or they just got a good price for their corn at the co-op that week.

Flud drove past a parched ball field where some kids were having a pick-up game. He felt a melancholy twinge, for his own quickly fading youth, for the settled life he sometimes wished he led. Someday. It didn't work out the first time, with Jean, but he was older now, more learned in the quirks of the world, more cautious with his heart. He didn't mind his life. Previously he had been chained to a desk at an insurance agency, took six months before he could cut his way to freedom. He liked being on the move, meeting new people, seeing new things...

Corn fields on both sides of the car now.

Beans.

Alfalfa.

New things.

Mankato, tomorrow, if he didn't get a nibble today...

HIS FIRST TWO encyclopedia-bereft households were a miss and a miss. Talk about cold calls. These people must been raised at the North Pole. The next prospect wanted only volume T, for the article on tractors. Flud tried to politely explain to the gentleman farmer that sets couldn't be split, but the fellow wouldn't be budged from his position, even when presented with the sorrowful scenario of another family buying a set of encyclopedias that skipped from Skeleton to Universe.

Flud was ready to skip from Swedenborg to the next bar down the road, but preached patience to himself. Every stop was a fresh opportunity, a chance to begin anew. Just do your job and keep your emotions out of it.

THE FARM, FROM a distance, seemed like any other spread on this isolated country road. However, as he drew closer, it filled Flud with a deep sense of desolation. It looked abandoned. The crops were withered, the buildings in disrepair. Yet the fact that there were crops at all, and that cows grazed in a fallow pasture, meant that it was still a working farm.

Even though the days still had some summer in them, the trees in the grove on the north side of the farmyard, left there to shelter the buildings from dangerous winter gales, were stripped bare, looking like they belonged in Halloween country.

Flud slowed, his attention caught by a herd of sheep gathered in a tight group in a roadside field on the north end of the grove.

Flud stopped. Although his window was partially open, he cranked it down the rest of the way.

The sheep.

Their mouths were opening, and closing.

No sound was coming from them. Not a single bleat.

Just mouths.

Opening.

And closing.

It was a peculiar thing. Flud remembered a sales call he once made to a house in a large city. There was a dog in the fenced yard, a German Shepherd. It opened its mouth as if to bark, but there was no sound, just silence. A mouth opening, and closing. The owner said the dog was a nuisance barker, so he had its vocal chords cut.

Prospects didn't look good, admittedly. On the verge of not making the final turn that would take him to the farmyard, Flud reminded himself of that odd duck who lived in the roadside shack on the way to Butternut. Happened a couple years ago. Flud wasn't even pitching; his radiator did the geyser bit and he just wanted to find a phone. The man in the shack babbled about baseball and the Apocalypse, but once Flud spilled about his business, the duck ordered two sets of encyclopedias, paid cash in advance.

So yes, Flud made the turn, at the mailbox that said "Platzanweiser."

The driveway descended gradually off the main road, past the white farm house, then into a circle that looped around the farmyard, past the granary, barn, chicken coop, the stark empty branches of the grove hanging over the roof, the shuttered brooder house, and back to the farm house again.

Flud parked in the shade at the bottom of the driveway, alongside a dying flower garden, the entrance to the circle. He gathered up his sample volumes, brochure packet, and order book, and left the car.

The farmyard was silent. Not summer quiet. Not the quiet of peaceful, lazy hammock days. Silent. The silence of mouths opening, and closing. The silence of a barnyard occupied by mute chickens and tongue-tied hogs.

Flud had seen dilapidated farms before, but this was different. The granary, workshop, corn crib, barn, the others, weren't simply falling apart; they were decaying, like roadkill.

The barn for instance, had lost most of its red luster. A pale greenish substance spiderwebbed across it now, mold or some other form of life that suggested decline. Most older barns sagged or caved in on themselves, but not this one. It seemed sturdy enough. It just looked... diseased.

Flud proceeded to the farm house. Going along the ancient stone walk that led to the dwelling, he began to whistle, then just let the air out quietly, feeling like he was doing something wrong. The house bore signs of a more subtle decay. Hairline cracks around the unclean windows. A strange gathering of black mushroom-like growths at the base of the brick chimney. The sunlight didn't seem to penetrate the interior of the house. It was twilight inside.

A small weather-worn box hung on the door frame. A clock with a moving wooden hour hand, a doll-figure above the clock and the words "We'll Be Back At..." A tiny knob on a miniature door. Flud opened it, recoiled slightly when a spider scooted away.

He drove an image from his mind of a larger arachnid lurking behind the greater door. Knocked.

Waited.

Again.

Flud turned and headed back into the farmyard. In cases like this he typically found the owner working in one of the out buildings, or busy in the fields.

Sidestepping a grouping of cluckless chickens, Flud scoped out the coop, wiping the webs from the filthy windows, moving along to the chicken wire door. Wooden roosts in the middle of the floor occupied by molting, disordered hens, wooden nests on each side wall. A rooster strutting along the dirt floor, beak opening, and closing. How to wake up in the morning when the rooster does not crow? Then on to the barn. The side door was open. A meowless tomcat skittered between a stack of hay bales. Flud took a tentative step inside and called out, "Hello! Anybody home?" His voice sounded harsh, unwelcome, alien even to him.

He wandered further down, to the hog house, where the dumb pigs jostled for a spot in the shadows alongside the tainted building, the only sound their heavy bristly bodies thumping down onto the cracked earth.

The granary next, which sat alongside a narrow creek. Like the other structures, discolored and decrepit. He climbed the steps and reached for the latch that would enable him to slide the door open along its rollers, then saw that it was padlocked.

"Get off my land."

Flud dropped his samples. It wasn't so much the tone or content, but the fact that there was a voice on this voiceless plot of earth at all.

He turned.

And dropped his brochures and order book.

A farmer, in blue overalls, work boots, faded green feed company cap. Across his eyes was a piece of glass. Not eyeglass. Red glass. A narrow band, not curved, held in place by baling wire.

"Uh, excuse me, ah, Mr. Platzanweiser, isn't it?" said Flud, coming down the steps and picking up his sample volumes and brochures from the parched grass. "Is the, uh, lady of the house in?"

Silence.

"Bob Flud's my name," he recited, back up. "You know I was just talking to your neighbors down the road, the Sufflows, nice folks, and they were saying what a fine family you had and how much they thought your lives could be improved, ah, with the gift of learning." Jeepers it's tough when you can't make eye contact. "Now I just happen to represent the world-renowned Canning Encyclopedia Company, and for a very modest monthly payment you can own a full set of encyclopedias, from A to Z. If you order today you will receive, free of charge, the Official Canning Atlas of the World, see the entire globe from the comfort of your favorite easy chair, and if you—"

"I said get off my land."

"Think of the opportunities for your children to expand their—"

"Ain't no children here."

"But just think of the opportunities for you and your wife to—"

The farmer took a step forward. "Ten seconds."

Flud was on his way before the countdown began. "Thank you for your time, sir, and best of luck to you on this most glorious summer day."

Flud glanced back as he reached the DeSoto. The farmer stood rooted, facing the door to the locked granary, the late afternoon sun glinting off his ruby red visor, facing the door as if the salesman were still there. A moment passed, and then the farmer turned and walked with a stiff gait in the direction of the barn.

Climbing into the car, Flud unloaded his stuff on the passenger seat, put the key into the ignition, and hesitated. He dug through the pile. His order book appeared to be missing. Must have forgotten it when the friendly farmer made me jump, he thought.

Flud left the car again and made for the granary.

When he spotted the order book, he knelt down, brushed the dirt off it, and rose...

"You heard it too, didn't you?"

Flud found himself facing the shielded farmer again.

"Heard it..."

"You came back. You heard it. You heard it, too."

Flud's instincts kicked in, seeing a deceased sale unexpectedly sit up on the slab.

"Sure, sure, pal, I heard it."

"Wasn't cow or cat or sheep or pig or chicken."

"No..."

"You heard it. Stay for supper. Tell me what you heard. Chicken supper."

Flud looked at the red glass, unable to see the eyes behind.

"You heard me, didn't you?" the farmer asked.

A sale, possibly. Another odd duck. Cash in advance.

"I'd be happy to join you for supper, Mr. Platzanweiser."

THE FARMER COLLARED the hen and hauled her over to the stained stump in the grove. He positioned her neck on the stump, her mouth opening and closing, the bird strangely rigid in his grip. He brought the ax up high and then down hard. The head went flying, the scene painted in red. The body, blood spurting from its neck stump, landed on its feet and dashed madly through the grove, disappearing into a thicket of wasted weeds. The farmer corralled another candidate, the ax a blur, pinning her down before she could flee, scaly yellow feet going through the motions of escape anyway.

The farmer plucked her, white feathers riding the air currents like snow, then dressed her and took her out to dinner. Inside the house, a pot was boiling on a wood-fired stove, and this is where the hen was laid to rest.

The farmer and the traveling salesman rested on the porch while supper cooked, the farmer softly playing a harmonica.

A strange melody, haunting, ripe with a pure and unbecoming splendor, as naked in emotion as the farmer was occluded in conversation.

He finally stopped playing, the last note trailing off into the early evening haze.

"You sure know how to handle that thing," said Flud. "Never heard anything like it."

The farmer tucked the mouth organ into the vest pocket of his overalls and said, "It's the only music I can take anymore. The rest—squeezebox, fiddle, washboard—like knives in my head, knives."

"That's too bad," said Flud.

"You're probably wonderin' about my glasses. Took it from a welder's mask. Can't stand the light, any kind of light. I'm sensitive to everything these days."

"You should see a doctor maybe. Long trip into town, though. You know, there's a lot of information contained in a single volume of an encyclopedia. You might pick up something that could help you with your condition."

This was met with silence, which extended into chicken, potatoes, carrots, all cooked into profound blandness.

Flud was beginning to feel uncomfortable with the silence. He was afraid if he talked at his usual clip, or pushed his pitch with too much vigor, the farmer's sensitivity would make any sale impossible. Could he close this sale without speaking? Maybe if he just shoved the order book at him, he would sign. Supper would be over soon, so he had to act quickly. Get the conversation going again, let him do the talking, keep leading him down the path to Canning Encyclopedia Heaven.

"So," said Flud, picking at his meal, the image of the headless hen escaping into the woods like the late edition in his mind, "have you farmed here long then?"

"Platzanweisers have plowed and planted our land for generations. I was born on our land, and I will die on our land, as it should be. I haven't set foot outside our land in twenty years. The land sustains; the land is life."

Have you looked around this joint lately? Flud thought, while nodding sympathetically.

The farmer abruptly left the table, the kitchen itself, out of sight, boots on steps.

Flud pushed back his chair, taking the opportunity to snoop around. There was a heaviness in the house, as if the dim light itself was pressing down on him. Nothing out of the ordinary among the dusty bric-a-brac and simple stick furniture. On a writing desk, a faded family photo in a tarnished frame. The farmer and a younger female: wife, daughter, or sister. No betrayal of their relationship to the camera. A stoic pose in front of the farm house, faces grim, sky leaden, heavy. But in the background, the garden flourished, flowers in bloom, beautiful even in black and white.

When Flud heard the thud, thud, thud on the steps, he retreated back into the kitchen, although he didn't sit down. His mind was working, trying to get an angle, but when the farmer reappeared, the problem solved itself.

"Encyclopedia," said Platzanweiser. "You have them with you?"

Sale!

"Sure do. Always carry samples with me."

"Do you have... S?"

"Why yes, I think I do. Just wait here. Don't go anywhere." He laughed self-consciously at his joke, and then hurried out to the car.

When he returned, the farmer was seated on a wooden rocker in the living room.

"Every volume features a genuine gold-tooled binding, handsome Italian leather cover, matching marbled end papers—"

"Read to me," said the farmer.

Flud fumbled with the book. "Uh, read to you?"

"You have S?"

"Yes."

"Read to me about... Sin."

The customer is always right, thought Flud, fanning the pages. Suddenly, reflexively, he clapped the book shut and eyed his watch. "I'm sorry, I have to leave," said Flud. "I'm late for an appointment in town. Here's a brochure. Feel free to give me a call if you decide you would like to purchase a set of encyclopedias, all the letters of the alphabet, for your very own. Thank you for your time and good night."

Flud hustled outside, his breathing shallow. The atmosphere in the house had produced a feeling of panic, anxiety, apart from the farmer's last request.

No sale was worth this, thought Flud, hurrying over to his car, the sun beginning to melt into the corn fields on the horizon, shadows more bold now, arms of darkness reaching across the yard. He climbed in, again dumped his materials on the passenger seat and gave the key a twist.

The engine tried to turn over, but didn't fire up.

Again, weaker.

Once more, a whisper.

Flud removed the key, not wanting to flood the car.

He waited a minute, two minutes, and gave it another go.

The spark had gone.

Flud slugged the dashboard and got out of the car, lifting the hood. He peered at the inner workings of the DeSoto, leaning close, strange, seeing a pale green mold-like substance throughout the engine area.

How could this be? he wondered. How could this be? He was afraid to touch it. He got a stick and tried to scrape it off, but there was so much. Flud did his best and then went around and tried starting the car again.

Dead.

Flud pulled out the key and looked toward the old house.

"SHE WON'T START," Flud told the farmer, who already had the back door open.

"Probably got damp. Happened to my tractor a while back."

"Could I use your phone? I'll call into town."

"Don't have a phone. Never saw a need for one."

"Can you drive me into town then?"

"In what?"

"You don't have a car?"

"Broke down years ago."

Flud glanced out at the accelerating darkness. Twilight seemed to give in too easily to the fullness of the dark hours. The wind picked up, carrying an unreasonable chill.

"I'll walk to one of the neighbors."

"This time of night, in these parts, walk up to a house unannounced and you're just as likely to get greeted by a shotgun blast as a..."

The farmer broke off, cocking his head slightly. He suddenly grimaced, bending over, moaning pitifully, clamping his hands to his ears, retreating, stumbling back into the kitchen.

Flud followed him in, the screen door banging shut behind him.

"What is it? What's wrong?"

The farmer knelt on the floor, head bowed. "Just shut the door, boy," he said with a strained voice.

Flud closed the inside door, and the sound of the latch bringing the farmer back to his feet. His eyes were still hidden; the welding goggles gave up nothing.

The farmer didn't speak, just shuffled into the living room, wearily lowering himself into his rocker. Flud sat down on a hard chair that was positioned against the oil stove.

Breathing steadied now, the farmer said, as if a prayer, "The land sustains; the land is life."

Flud felt shadows fall.

"She was born on our land; she was meant to die on our land, as I am, as it should be."

"What do you mean? Who are you talking about? The woman in the picture?"

"Adeline."

"The woman in the picture. Your wife? Your sister? Your daughter?"

The red visor turned his way, and dipped slightly. "Yes. Adeline."

Shadows crawled.

"What happened?"

"An accident. She was in the granary, the feed pouring through the chute in the ceiling, everyday farm work. Something got stopped up. She climbed into the bin to clear it..." His hand went to his visor and he lifted it. The eyes were still red. Bloodshot, swollen.

"It's like drowning. The grain is no different than water."

"I'm sorry," said Flud. "When did this happen?"

"Never saw a need for one."

"What?"

"Broke down years ago."

Flud couldn't make sense of him.

Visor back in place. "You heard it, didn't you?"

"I... I'm not sure."

"You heard her cries, from the granary. Her cries. You heard them, too."

Flud heard the wind, the wind and the old house, the protestations of straining wood, inside and out, and nothing more.

* * *

"You can sleep in the upstairs bedroom," said the farmer. "Hasn't been used in years. It was my room when I was a boy."

Flud thanked him for his hospitality, the emotion in the pit of his stomach far removed from his surface civility.

He's a batty old-timer who hears voices, Flud told himself, turning back the covers. Nothing of the boy remained here. A crack ran from the window-side wall, along the faded flowered wallpaper, across the ceiling, ending at the door frame.

Just grab what sleep you can and maybe hitch a ride back into town with the mailman, or walk to the next farm and make a call, bribe them if necessary.

Flud sat on the edge of the bed, the stiff stained curtains sleepwalking in the wind, offering glimpses of the impenetrable night, like a black wall beyond. He stretched out on the musty chenille bed spread, grateful to be locked away, thankful for a silence that wasn't overflowing with distress.

Then: a sound from within the walls, from downstairs, from somewhere. A harmonica. Playing a heavyhearted refrain.

From this distance, it was soothing.

Flud felt his body relax, his mind settle into an easy space.

Flud slept.

The wind rose sharply, the house's laments transforming to shouting as someone burst into Flud's bedroom. The farmer caught Flud by the shoulders, jostled him, shook him, rousted him.

"Do you hear it? Do you hear it? Adeline! She was buried alive! Can't you hear her cries, her hands clawing at the grain, the grain pouring down her throat? Can't you hear it?"

Flud groggily pushed back the farmer, scrambling out of bed.

"You crazy old man, there's nothing to hear, nothing, nothing!"

"You said you heard it, you heard it too!"

"I never heard anything, I just wanted a sale. You think your sister or wife or whatever your inbred family calls it is buried alive in the granary and is calling out to you? Fine, then I'm going to give you the gift of learning, now!"

Flud stormed out the door, taking the stairs in three bounds. The farmer was after him, tugging at him, begging him to stop. Flud broke free, charging out the screen door and into the farmyard. He didn't look back.

Halfway to the granary, something came out of the grove, at a dead run. Something white.

Lacking something, what?

The no-headed chicken frantically sprinted through the yard, blood no longer spraying from its neck stump. Yet it persevered. A real Horatio Alger story. It seemed to be zeroing in on Flud, using some kind of unnatural radar, then abruptly veered off and dashed between the hog house and the corn crib, disappearing again into darkness.

Even though the granary was padlocked, the door was rotted and the wood broke apart easily. Flud heaved open the door along its creaking rollers.

A trickle of light tiptoed in. Flud joined it.

Mice fled across the warped wooden floor.

The interior of the granary had a large empty area in the middle, flanked on the left by a huge feed bin and on the right by two smaller bins.

Not surprisingly, it was quiet as church in the granary. No voices, no cries for help, no one buried alive. This made Flud feel better, as if he had swung the night back around to his own version of reality. Getting out of that suffocating house had helped, too.

Flud stood up straight, eyes adjusting to the darkness, and looked around the granary. The equipment hadn't been in operation for a long while, taken over by the dust of disuse. It smelled like grain, the rancid variety.

Going over to the big bin, the mountain of grain rising halfway to the ceiling, Flud reached in and scooped up a palmful of grain, and let it run through his fingers. It was a pleasing feeling, so he did it again, reaching deeper into the pile. Once more, and that was when his hand touched something solid.

Flud frowned. What was it? A bin divider? A piece of equipment that accidentally fell into the heap?

The object was smooth, cool.

Flud moved his fingers across its surface, until they slipped into a pair of holes. How in the world did a bowling ball get in there? he thought.

Flud pulled.

Heavy with grain, the object came out slowly, slowly.

Flud kept pulling.

Finally it was free.

The traveling salesman met the farmer's daughter. Or was it his sister?

Fingers in eye sockets.

The skull he held in his hands was one of the few things on this farm that wasn't taken over by mold.

Flud knelt and gently set it down on the floor, then thrust his hands into the bin again. Compulsively. Again and again. More smooth, solid objects, long and short, curved and straight.

When he was done Flud gazed at the pile of her for a moment, then ran. Ran crazily, this way and that, like a chopping-block chicken, back to the house.

"She's dead! She's dead!" Flud screamed as he tore up the stone walk and arrived at the greater door, to the farmer, whose red visor was missing. "There's nothing left, you old fool! She's been dead for years! There aren't any voices, no cries for help, nothing, she's dead, dead, do you hear me dead!"

The farmer, eyes bulging now, looked at Flud plainly and said in a calm voice, "Don't you hear it?"

Flud gaped at him.

The farmer shut his eyes and his face got all twisted up, just twisted and not plain at all.

"Listen to me, Platzanweiser," said Flud. "It's over. Adeline is dead. She's been dead a long time. Just bones in there, I saw them with my own eyes."

The farmer's eyes suddenly opened wide. He was looking at Flud, really seeing him, fixed on him, for the first time since he arrived. "There's only two of us here so it must be you. It isn't cows or sheep or pigs making that sound, must be you, stop it, stop saying help me, help me, stop screaming for your life, yes I fixed it so the grain would bury you in that bin, you shouldn't have tried to leave, we can never leave, we were born on our land and we will die on our land, we are bonded together forever, brother and sister, husband and wife, father and daughter forever, it was you all along, the voices have to be coming from somewhere, no cows and sheep or pigs, quiet, quiet, quiet, no more voices!"

The farmer grabbed Flud by the shoulders and shoved him backwards, down the steps, down, down, the back of the salesman's head thudding heavily against the stone walk, a heavy darkness taking him down, down, down.

THERE WERE NO sounds, too many smells.

Up, the traveling salesman woke. Dizzy, swimming in a semiconscious state, hurt in his limbs, his head, his throat.

Especially his throat.

He felt like he was being watched.

Opened his eyes.

Chickens stared at him in the dim space, eye-to-eye. A filthy floor. The smell burned his nostrils.

He tried moving away, but something snatched his ankle and wouldn't let go. His bound hands traveled along his bare leg, knee, shin, ankle, the chain. Heavy chain. Thick enough for farm work. Wound around a beam on the back wall, chained to the building itself.

The traveling salesman felt cold. He wondered what happened to his clothes.

Dirty floor, dirty chickens. Still dressed.

Foul sunshine filtered through the dollhouse-like windows.

A noise at last.

From out there, beyond the chicken wire door.

A car door, slamming.

Through the chicken wire, the salesman could see the farmyard, the circle.

A car, not his own. The DeSoto had departed.

Two men standing at the end of a stone walk.

The farmer, no longer wearing his red visor.

Another man, bald, gesticulating with a green bottle. His face was animated.

Klimm's Wonder Elixir.

Cures everything.

From eczema to excessive nervous agitation.

The knowledge of a thousand encyclopedias is contained within.

Nicholas Klimm, my friend!

He would help; they were brothers in the art of selling, fellow travelers. They would have a beer and a good laugh at Heaven and Hell after this day was over.

My friend.

The farmer appeared to shake off the sales pitch with a smile, as if indicating his excessive nervous agitation had already been cured.

The traveling salesman smiled, too, as he opened his mouth to call out to his friend...

> S is for sin.
> For silence.
> Mouths opening.
> And closing.

After the elixir salesman left, the farmer strode over to the chicken coop, bucket in hand.

He went inside. As he gathered the eggs, he noticed that several members of his quiet brood had become non-productive, not laying a single egg, due to illness or... injury. He still had to pay for their feed, so that was money out of his pocket.

Tonight, there would have to be a culling.

MY FIRST ENCOUNTER *with Mr. Poe came on a Halloween afternoon at a grade school in Bloomington, Minnesota, back in the 1960s. One of the teachers led us without explanation into a dark room and shut the door. Strangely, the only light came from a small blue bulb in the corner. The teacher began to read to us, his face illuminated by that dim blue light, the presence of which I soon began to understand. This wasn't the usual* Little House on the Prairie *milk-and-cookies story time, this was "The Tell-Tale Heart," in all its lurid glory.*

It was a powerful, thrilling experience, and either later that year or the next I wrote a pair of ghastly horror stories for Parents Visitation Night, and dutifully taped them to the wall outside my classroom with the other artwork. One had the creative title,

"Midnight Horrors." They were, in fact, "inspired by Poe," as only a young boy can be inspired.

A bit older now, and we come to "The Heaven and Hell of Robert Flud." More inspiration, thanks to "The Fall of the House of Usher," my favorite of all his tales. Going from Gothic to American Gothic. I have some rural roots, and Usher always reminded me of the occasional odd duck you find in America's tucked away places. Isolated, a bit weird, peculiar family relationships, possibly never traveled more fifty miles from the place he was born. Just a general sense of slow suffocation. More sad than horrible in reality.

Hopefully teachers are still reading Poe to grade schoolers, and aren't put off by overprotective parents with their intellectual bicycle helmets in hand. Read Poe aloud, preferably in a dark room, the more wide-eyed kids present the better. It would make a nice birthday present for him.

Kristine Kathryn Rusch is a Hugo-winning science fiction writer. Under pen names, she also writes mysteries, romance, and mainstream fiction. What people often forget is that she got her start writing horror, first with Kevin J. Anderson, and then on her own, for Dell Abyss. She has been nominated for every major award in all the different genres and has even won a few. Her latest science fiction novel is *The Recovery Man* from Roc. To find out more, check out her website at www.kristinekathrynrusch.com

FLITTING AWAY

by Kristine Kathryn Rusch

i

IN THE END, it was his hands she vowed to remember—if, indeed, she would be able to remember anything. His hands—reaching, grabbing, pinching, pulling, clutching her neck so tightly she couldn't pry them free. She'd read somewhere that she shouldn't struggle, that she had to let him think she was dead.

But not struggling was dying. Her body fought on its own, her own hands tugging his fingers, trying to pull them away, while her feet kicked at nothing.

He was everywhere and nowhere, his legs not where they should be, his hands on her throat, but ripping her clothes too, and his face too close. She should have been remembering his face, sweat-covered, eyes too bright— avid—his mouth slightly open, sending onion breath across her skin.

He was strong—too strong—and in the end, blackness dotting her vision, her chest burning for air, her neck hurting so badly that she wondered if he'd broken it, in that last moment of consciousness, she realized she'd been doing it wrong.

She should have kneed him in the balls, shoved her hands into his stomach, gouged his eyes. Instead, she held his wrist as he killed her, and she knew if she survived, she would have nightmares about this moment forever.

God, she thought as she slipped into the darkness. *I wanted it to mean something.*

But even in that moment—the moment just before death, when all humans were supposed to achieve perfect clarity—she wasn't sure if she had been thinking of her death or her life.

ii

SHE WAS ONLY thirty. She had never really thought about her death before, at least not consciously. Oh, maybe fleetingly, when she'd stepped off a curb and a car, coming around the corner, had to swerve to miss her. She'd put a hand to her rapidly beating heart and think, *That was close.*

And then she'd finish crossing the street, the incident forgotten the moment her shoe touched the other curb.

She was a cautious woman, though. She always told friends when she would arrive some place and she rarely missed. If she was going to be late, she called ahead.

Before she moved to New York City, she took a self defense class, and after she arrived, she took a course on urban living that focused on survival tactics for dangerous situations.

The door on her apartment had three locks, and the building had a state-of-the-art security system.

Which was why it was odd that she was here, now, with a man's hands on her throat and her life squeezed out of her.

Although she was having trouble defining *here.* She wasn't far from home near her favorite jogging trail by the Hudson. It had gotten dark early, although it was never really dark in the city. Usually she saw half a dozen other joggers, but on this night she'd seen none.

Not that it mattered. She had been with Bryan.

Bryan.

Her mind flitted away from contemplation of him. Instead, she worried about her definition of "here." Since she could no longer feel his hands around her throat, no longer felt the urge to fight.

Instead, she was floating above the path, looking at the water which reflected a thousand street lights, and seemed murky all the same.

She had read somewhere—oh, she had read countless things: the mark of someone who really had no life—that during severe trauma the mind separated from the body, leaving a feeling of dislocation.

Only she didn't feel dislocated. She felt lost.

She made herself go back to her last real thought—at least the last one she could remember: that she was a cautious woman. Which made it sadder, then, that she was here, dying, at the hands of the man she had chosen to keep her safe.

Jogging partners, she'd said to him. *That's all.*

He lived just down the hall in her building. She'd seen him dozens of times before she talked to him, wearing a suit and tie or an NYPD t-shirt with well-loved blue jeans. He'd looked safe enough.

She'd even Googled him, and found nothing. Then she used a service—one of those $50 find-everything-in-the-public-records services—and made sure he didn't have a restraining order or some kind of criminal past.

He had a degree from Johns Hopkins. He was an attorney, for God's sake. He had been married once, divorced now, no children—his ex having relocated to Nebraska.

Clean. Spotless. Safe.

Until he choked the life out of her.

She blinked, made herself float down, saw the body—her body—crumpled on the path. He was trying to drag her, but it wasn't working. Finally he used those muscles of his, the ones she'd admired so in his NYPD t-shirt, and picked her up.

Then he tossed her into the river.

iii

THE COLD GREASY water brought her back into herself. She sank, already breathless from the way he had crushed her neck.

Think.

Think.

Think.

Let out one small bubble of air and follow it upwards.

She did, surfacing, splashing, suddenly afraid he was there, looking for her. What could he do? He didn't have a gun and it was too far for him to try to get her.

She didn't look up, didn't want to see him.

She tried to yell for help and couldn't—only a strange, painful wheeze came from her throat. She tried to remember from the jogs where the land met the river, and she couldn't. She never really looked, never really noticed.

Her breath whistled. It was shallow, barely enough to survive on.

He could be waiting at that spot where the land met the river. He could get her.

She rolled on her back so she could float, listening to her breath whistle, deciding that was reassuring enough. As long as she heard the rasp, felt the burn, she was still alive.

The river had eddies and currents and they would take her away from here.

She didn't know where or how, but away.

Somewhere safe.

iv

OF COURSE, THERE was nowhere safe. Not really.

The cold was making her teeth chatter. She had to get out soon, but she couldn't—not yet. She just looked up at the night sky. Or what she could see of the night sky, hidden as it was by the lights of the city.

Once upon a time, people came to the edge of the river to stargaze.

Long ago and far away.

The city'd been dangerous then, too. She'd read about it. She'd studied the entire place before she came. She was afraid of it, but she figured a woman had to face her fears or they would overtake her.

Make her into someone she was not.

Her first memory of this place was the news coverage of the Central Park Jogger—a woman who had been jogging alone (shouldn't have done that, the newsmen said) through a dangerous part of the Park (she should have known it wasn't safe, the newsmen said) when four boys attacked her, raped her, and beat her nearly to death.

At least, they thought it was four boys. Then. She had a vague memory that later someone proved it wasn't those boys, but she wasn't sure.

It didn't matter, really.

Because the only thing that separated the Central Park Jogger from all the other victims of rapes and beatings that year was that she was some kind of upscale investment banker or doctor or something—the kind of woman who shouldn't have gotten hurt. The kind that should have been left alone.

Like her.

Only a stranger didn't assault her.

Bryan did.

Bryan.

Her mind flitted away.

The chances are that you will get threatened, her urban living instructor said. *Be the strong one. Do not threaten in return. Walk away. Laugh. Pretend you have a friend nearby. If none of that works, then give the mugger your purse. If he wants more, fight. Fight with everything you have. Fight to the death if you have to. He won't fight that hard. You're the one with something at stake.*

She had fought. She had fought and she had done it wrong. Forgotten all her training in her wish to take a breath.

Like now.

Rasp in.

Whistle out.

And float.

Float away...

v

"CHRIST ON A crutch."

A voice above her, male. She tried to hide, but couldn't move. Her body—she couldn't feel it. Numb? Gone? Had she separated out of it again?

No. That whistle. That rasp. Still in it.

"She's alive."

"Call 911." Another voice. Also male.

God, a gang of them. In the river? No. She heard rustling, not like clothing, but like feet in sand or dirt. Then a car not far away, horns even farther away.

The city, going on.

Three beeps, and the second male, voice moving away from her. "Yeah. Look, I found a woman..."

Her eyes were gummed shut. It hurt to swallow. That was the only pain she felt, in her throat. And it smelled. Fish and rot and oil.

Hands touching her. Moving her. Wrapping her in something.

This time, she wouldn't go without a fight. She flattened her hand, jerked it upwards, trying to hit him with the heel.

"Jesus, lady, I'm just trying to help."

The exertion made her cough. Try to cough. Wish she could cough. She tasted blood.

That hand, that hand of hers that could move. She had to will it to pry her own eyes open.

The man above her wasn't Bryan. He was too old. His hair was gray. He had bloodshot blue eyes and a drinker's nose.

"Who done this to you, hon?" he said gently. "Who done this?"

Her lips formed "Bryan," but she couldn't say the word. No sound emerged except the whistle. Then she tried to cough again, blood trickling down her throat.

She was choking, choking on her own blood.

He put a hand behind her back and she pushed at him, but weakly, no strength at all. And no feeling in her limbs. They were like rubber. Toy limbs.

"I'm helping, I'm helping," he said. "You gotta breathe, hon. Relax, okay? Relax. You're gonna be fine."

It was a lie. One of those kind lies other people told you when you were not going to be fine, not ever going to be fine.

"What're you doing?" The second guy came back. He was clutching a cell phone in his right hand. He was beefy, made even beefier by the cable-knit sweater he wore over work pants and heavy boots. "They said not to touch her."

"Like I know that," the first guy said. "You were the one talking to them. She's choking here. I didn't take that CPR crap at the office. Did you? You gotta clear the passageways, right? Make sure she can breathe?"

"She's breathing," the second guy said. But he sounded doubtful.

She felt doubtful. The whistling had stopped. The rasping too. And she could feel that trickle of blood gathering deep inside.

She wanted them to help and she didn't want them to help and she wanted to run and she wanted to tell them to watch out for Bryan, he could be here, anyone could be here, there was nowhere safe, but she couldn't find the words, she couldn't find the air, she couldn't make a sound.

Noise scares them, her self defense teacher said. *Screaming or a whistle or a loud "What the fuck are you doing?" It'll startle them, make them stop, even for a moment. Then you can get away. Noise is your biggest ally.*

Noise. She couldn't make any.

"She's crying," the first guy said. "Hon, you'll be okay. Honest. You'll be fine."

"You wrapped her in your coat." The second guy sounded accusing, but he crouched, put a gentle hand on her shoulder. "They said you shouldn't touch her. Crime scene, you know."

She shook her head. *The crime scene wasn't here*, she wanted to say. Upriver. Or was it down? How long had she floated? How far had she come?

"Shut up about the crime scene." The first guy glared at his buddy. "Can't you see she's scared?"

"Shit, *I'm* scared," the second guy said. "Nothing like this has ever happened to me."

To him? She looked at him. He was crouched beside her, so big that he could have broken Bryan in half. Nothing had happened to him. Nothing except the inconvenience of calling 911.

"Who do you think she is?" the second guy asked.

"Can you tell us who you are, hon?" the first guy asked. "Are there people we should call?"

People. Yesterday she would have said *Call Bryan. He's got all the numbers*. He was the only one in the building who did because she trusted him. She trusted him and believed in him and when she'd told him—

Her mind flitted away.

And suddenly, there were EMTs and stretchers and lights. From inside the ambulance, the siren sounded like a buzzer—less disturbing, she supposed.

The men were gone—the first guy and the second guy (she never learned their names)—and her mouth hurt. She had a vague memory of someone trying to put a tube down her throat, but it didn't work and they'd cut a hole.

But she could breathe now at least, even though she didn't feel air through her nostrils. She reached up, tried to touch her throat and one of the EMTs—a woman, thank god, a woman—caught her hand and put it down again.

"She's conscious."

"Let's keep her that way until we get to the hospital. Let them decide how to handle this."

How to handle what? She couldn't ask. Her mouth felt odd. Her nose, breathless. And yet she was breathing. Lots of air through her aching chest.

She was shivering too. Cold and prickly as the numbness in her limbs was easing.

"You're going to be all right," the woman EMT said, and there was that lie again. "We're taking you somewhere safe."

The second lie, worse than the first. There was nowhere safe.

Didn't they know that?

vi

THEY WHISKED HER inside—industrial greens and blues, fluorescent lights and the sound of cart wheels on tile, but no smells. There should have been smells, dozens of them, and she couldn't identify any.

As they took her into one of those so-called rooms—really, a space separated from another space by an inadequate curtain—a nurse came up beside her, clipboard in hand.

"I know you can't talk, sweetheart," she said in a gentle voice.

Can't talk? She didn't know that. Not for sure. But she had suspected it. Just like she suspected a lot of things. Like the reason she couldn't feel her feet, the reason she couldn't stop shivering, the reason those men had looked on her with such incredible pity.

"But," the nurse was saying, "can you write down your name for me, maybe an address? Maybe even the name of a family member or a friend?"

She nodded and someone propped up the back of the bed. It was hard to grip the pen, her fingers wouldn't bend—they were a bluish gray color, something she'd never seen on her own fingers before.

She saw the space for name and pressed the pen against it, thinking, *it's right there, right there* her name, everyone remembers their name, right?

And the only name she could recall, the only name was Bryan.

Bryan.

Her mind tried to flit and she held it, just for a moment.

If she could remember Bryan, she could remember his address, where he lived, right? That would help, at least.

She slipped the pen down, wrote down an address in a shaky hand, scratched out the apartment number, then went back to the name.

Name.

Bryan.

And then she was gone.

vii

MAYBE YEARS MAYBE months maybe hours later, she opened her eyes—no longer gummed—and smelled (smelled!) disinfectant and the faint odor of tobacco mixed with perfume. Two women stood over her, official looking, identifying themselves as NYPD.

They told her they'd already done a kit (rape kit?) and had taken what they could for evidence. They explained all kinds of things that she didn't really want to listen to—skin beneath her fingernails, fingerprints on her neck, a footprint imprinted on one thigh.

They called her Miss Walker. Nicole Walker. That was it. That was her name. She remembered now.

Nicole Walker, originally from Poughkeepsie, moved to a one-bedroom paid for by her salary as an accountant (with some help from her parents) while she wrote her little stories and plays.

Her head was restrained by something plastic. The plastic thing was what smelled of disinfectant. There was tape alongside her mouth, and a tube inside it that the tape held in place. The shaking had stopped, but her entire body hurt.

They'd found her. From the apartment address?

"Who did this to you?" the nearest woman asked. She was forty-something, with frown lines and gray roots on black hair, a color that didn't suit her.

"We know you can't talk," the other woman said. "We have this."

She took a white board, set it beneath Nicole's left hand. Not her right. Why not her right? Most people were right handed, right? That's what they should have done.

She tried to lean forward, to see her right hand, and couldn't. She couldn't move her upper body at all.

"They don't want you moving much," said the first woman. Her voice was sympathetic. Her eyes were dead.

How many times had she seen something like this? How many times could a person see this without losing empathy, without losing the ability to feel at all?

"Just try to write," said the second woman. "I know it's hard."

The pen was fat—a marker. She could feel the coolness of the white board against her left palm, the fat pen stuck between her fingers. She could just see its end, but she couldn't see the board at all.

"Who did this?" the first woman asked again. "Do you know?"

Her mind wanted to flit. But it couldn't. It didn't dare. If they found her apartment, then they'd find Bryan and they'd think he was a friend. The only one she talked to in the building. The only one with her emergency numbers. The one her friends were supposed to call if she had gone missing.

She wrote:

B R Y A N

"Bryan hurt you?" the first woman asked.

Nicole nodded—or tried to.

"Okay, okay. Don't try to move," the first woman said as the second woman asked, "Are you sure?"

She wrote:

Y E S

But she wasn't sure if she had written that over the word "Bryan" or not. She didn't care. They seemed to understand.

"Bryan who?" the second woman asked.

And, before she could catch it, Nicole's brain flitted—this time to the water, and Bryan's voice:

What the fuck did you just say?

And when she came back, the women were gone. She would have thought she had imagined them, except the room smelled faintly of Magic Marker.

viii

It took six surgeries to repair her neck. She was lucky, the doctors said. The attack hadn't damaged her spine.

But her voice box was gone. Really and truly gone. They couldn't repair it. She got one of those electronic voices that chain smokers got, and she was told she should be grateful.

Grateful. Grateful that she had survived.

The water alone would have killed most people, one of the doctors had told her. *You had presence of mind*. But if she had had presence of mind, she would have fought back properly.

Grateful. Grateful that she had friends who offered to care for her after her last surgery.

But she couldn't face them, not every day, not waiting on her in a way that she would never, ever be able to pay back.

Grateful. Grateful that she still had parents who were willing to take her in, even though she had privately vowed never to return to that podunk town, that claustrophobic house.

She spent most of her days on their couch—a leather reclining number that had replaced the soft 1980s high-back that she'd stayed on most of her childhood.

She watched the big screen television, got to know Oprah and Ellen and half a dozen soaps. Her father ordered movie channels for her and watched with her, never saying much. He hadn't said much since he first saw her, in that hospital bed, her head strapped into place so she wouldn't damage her neck any farther.

She still wore a brace. She might have to wear it for the rest of her life. Jogging was out of the question, even if she wanted to do it again. Movement was difficult. Talking embarrassed her. Eating was hard.

Yet she should be grateful.

And in some ways, she was.

Grateful she didn't have to return to that apartment.

Grateful she didn't have to face him—at least not yet. Maybe not ever.

The detectives had been blunt: *It's a tough case. It's your word against his. The river destroyed most of the evidence. There were no witnesses to the attack, and to make matters worse, you were friends before it happened. He's a well respected young attorney with no priors. You're...*

An accountant, she had finished for the detective, but she had known what the detective meant.

You're a young woman, a dreamer, someone who had moved to the city hoping to become someone else.

Well, that worked, hadn't it? She was someone else now, someone she never wanted to be, a physically handicapped woman with so many medical bills she'd never be able to pay them. She might be able to go back to work, when she could safely sit in a chair hunched over numbers or work on a computer without straining her back.

But she had worked long enough, hard enough, to know that her very appearance would make getting a new job difficult. Who wanted an accountant who sounded like a machine? Particularly if the accountant had to deal with collections.

Her life, the one she had known, was over. She had to start again. When she could. When Ellen and Oprah and the soaps stopped being compelling.

When she allowed herself to think.

When she allowed herself to remember.

ix

SHE HAD PRESSED charges. And there had been some evidence, however minor. His DNA (damaged) under her fingernails, scratches on his face and wrist. He had said they had come from a night of rough sex. She, of course, denied it.

Then there was his handprint on her throat. His hand, reproduced in bruises, on her skin. Without fingerprints, without much more than size and shape.

The bruise on her thigh from a size 13 men's shoe.

And that was all. That was the extent of the physical evidence.

Aside from the crime scene photos—meaning her body as it had washed up—and the sympathy she would elicit in a jury.

At least, that was what the young female prosecutor was telling her. The woman had driven all the way to Poughkeepsie to visit her, looking like a lost Manhattanite in the wilds.

Her skirt was too short, her make-up too heavy, her hair so stylish that people probably noticed it as she drove by. Her voice was lovely when she wanted it to be, and Nicole found herself watching the woman's throat as she spoke.

Nicole sat in her father's chair, wearing new sweats that her mother had found, sweats large enough to fit around the brace that ran down her entire torso.

She knew how she looked, even now, months later. The bruises had faded, except around the surgical scars, but no one saw those since they were wrapped in gauze. The brace, the gauze around her throat, the stupid electronic voice box, and the fact that she still couldn't walk unaided made her into some kind of freak.

People didn't meet her gaze, not even the prosecutor—Janet? Janice? Joann?—Nicole couldn't remember and she didn't really try. She just waited until the woman looked at her, actually looked at her, instead of dryly reciting facts about a case that until today had just been a possible problem on paper.

"There are some hints in his past," JadeJaneJoyce said to her now, "but they're probably inadmissible. We'd have to get former girlfriends to testify and almost all of them have disappeared."

That, Nicole would have said once, was almost as good as a confession. But she didn't. She now knew better than to use that flat electronic voice for all but the most important sentences.

"So I'm here to walk you through that night, to see what you do remember. If we can get the full story now, we might be able to find more evidence, or maybe a witness or two. Can you do that? Can you walk through the crime with me?"

Nicole clenched her fingers against the armrests. She didn't remember much. Just what she had forced herself to remember—his hands, reaching, grabbing, pinching, pulling, clutching her neck so tightly she couldn't pry them free. That knowledge that she was dying, that she was contributing to her own death by fighting him wrong, and being unable to stop that automatic reaction—the panic that came from not being able to breathe, not being able to think.

"The doctors say I have partial traumatic amnesia." She wasn't used to the electronic voice either. In her memory, her own voice had been as musical—more musical—than JoyJillJolene's. "I remember the attack. I remember Bryan's face. I remember falling into the river. I don't remember much else."

Because her mind still flitted away from it. She didn't pass out any longer or lose time, but she did find herself contemplating the pattern on the couch or an ad on television every single time she tried to remember the events leading up to the attack.

"All we need to know," JocastaJerriJanna said to her, "is what set him off. All we've been able to gather is that you were on a routine jog with him, something you'd done a dozen times, and then he was attacking you."

His voice, filled with fury: *What the fuck did you just say?*

And no time. No time to respond.

His hands—reaching, grabbing, pinching, pulling, clutching—

Her mind flitted away.

"Nicole?" JeanJenniferJodi said to her. "Are you all right?"

No, of course she wasn't. She was wearing a brace for God's sake, speaking with an electronic voice, clutching her father's chair because she no longer had the wherewithal to have her own chair.

But she needed to be grateful. Grateful, because, as her mother had said, women had been attacked on that spot for centuries (*think of it*, her mother had said. *Centuries. There are reports of dead girls in the river since New York was New Amsterdam*), and those girls had all died. But modern medicine had saved her. *Modern medicine and her own damn gumption*, her father had said with something like pride. Gumption. In other words, she was too stubborn to die.

"Nicole?" JosieJackieJune said.

Nicole nodded. The fewer words the better. The nod meant: *I'm fine.* Then she added, "I'll try," in that horrible new voice of hers.

I'll try.

And for the first time, she would.

x

IT TOOK CONCENTRATION not to flit. Concentration and a willingness to pay attention. What was it that made her change channels, set down a book, close the newspaper? What made her walk away from her mother or shut off the radio? What made her look away?

Of course, there was nowhere safe. Not really.

That thought brought her back to the river and the cold, smelly water, oily against her skin.

Nowhere safe.

Why had she cared about safe? At that moment, when she was dying, what made her think of safety?

She was here, dying, at the hands of the man she had chosen to keep her safe.

Safe. She had thought Bryan was safe. She had researched him, observed him, learned all she could about him—although not as much as JuneJamie-Jade because then she would have seen the pattern of the missing girlfriends, the ones who fled.

The ex who had moved all the way to Nebraska.

What had Nicole said to him that night? They were jogging. She could remember that—or maybe she was remembering another trail, another jog. Under the lights, the river sparkling, the trail opening around them.

She felt safe because Bryan was with her. She wasn't alone like the Central Park Jogger, like all those other women—the ones attacked throughout the centuries. She wasn't alone, and she knew how to defend herself, and she was young and strong and she felt safe.

And then his voice, filled with fury: *What the fuck did you just say?*

What *had* she said?

She had researched him—not because she wanted to date him. She didn't. She liked him, but not that way. He was nice, but not—

Her mind flitted.

Nice, but not—

Flitting.

She made herself breathe. Focus.

Nice, but not someone she wanted to date. She'd said that up front. The day she first asked him to jog with her.

I'm not looking for a boyfriend. All I want is a friend.

I understand, he said with a smile. His smile really was lovely. Warm and sympathetic.

Which'll make him hell in front of a jury, the prosecutor—Judith, her name was Judith. Judith Melman—said. *He'll smile and they'll love him and they'll think how can such a bright, reasonable, attractive man hurt this woman? She must have misremembered. In the trauma, she must have confused him with someone else.*

But Nicole hadn't confused him with anyone else. The therapist, the one the hospital sent to talk with her when the amnesia became clear, said that the memories she had—what few she had—were real. The key was recovering the others in her own time.

The others, the therapist had said, *were somehow harder to accept than the attack itself.*

Because he was safe. He had been safe.

Her mind started to flit, and she held it, willed it in place.

She trusted him. Believed in him.

They had been jogging, talking about a case of his, the first real win on his own. Then he'd put a hand on her arm—lightly, just a touch, really, friend to friend—and he had said,

How about dinner on Friday?

A celebration? she asked, looking at the lights. Like diamonds floating on the blackness of the river. A thousand diamonds.

Yes, he said.

With friends? she asked, happy to met his friends, finally. People outside her own narrow circle.

With friend, he said, emphasizing the last word.

It took her a minute. She felt a little cold. *A date?*

Yes.

Didn't he remember their conversations? Why did men always do this, transform something fun into something awkward?

Thank you, she said, *but no. I'm not interested—*

In dating, she was going to say. I'm not interested in dating anyone right now. It's not you. It's that I'd like to establish myself first, and then maybe...

But she didn't get to any of it. His light touch turned into a grip, his genial expression into a scowl, his voice into something filled with fury.

What the fuck did you just say?

She responded calmly to a man she trusted, a man she considered her friend. *I said no.*

He slammed her against a tree, so fast she didn't have time to catch herself. Then his hands—reaching, grabbing, pinching, pulling, clutching—

And before she had a moment to think, to reflect, to *respond*, she was dying.

Dying.

And if it had been even twenty years earlier, she would have. She would have died.

So she was grateful, grateful, grateful that she had survived.

xi

IN THE END, she didn't testify. She sat in the court, behind the prosecution—not Judith, but the senior prosecutor, a man named Rutherford—and acted as an exhibit of what one man's fury could do.

The other women spoke, the ones they could find, the ones they promised to protect.

Their stories were the same.

All I said was no...

and then his hands were on my throat...

he looked so mad, I thought he would kill me...

but some woman [man] [kid] screamed...

and he let go...

He let go.

But he hadn't let go of Nicole. He had squeezed until he thought her dead, and then he had the presence of mind to toss her in the river.

To hide the evidence, Rutherford said.

Rutherford said other things—or brought in people to say them for him—like

It's a pathology peculiar to men, similar to stalking... maybe he did stalk, although he's bright enough to know that stalking is now a crime... the word 'no' from a woman he's attracted to is a trigger...

like

He's a particularly smart offender. He knows better than to leave evidence in his wake...

like

If you set him free, it's only a matter of time before he does this again. And the next woman will die. Guaranteed.

Guaranteed.

xii

SHE DIDN'T LOOK at him throughout the whole trial, not even at the end, when the jury came back with some lesser charge. Assault? Second degree?

She couldn't remember. She didn't want to remember.

She no longer wanted to think about him.

She needed to be grateful.

Grateful she could go back to her couch and not think. Flit through the channels, watch Ellen and Oprah and the soaps, and concentrate on getting better.

If there was such a thing as better in a world where she could no longer trust, no longer feel safe.

And then she chided herself:

She couldn't expect safe. No one could.

Safety was an illusion, like the diamonds on the river, sparkling in the distance, hiding something cold and greasy and terribly, terribly dark.

I LOVE POE. *In my other life, I'm a mystery writer (Kris Nelscott for the novels), and Poe is the father of the mystery. So I chose "The Murder of Marie Roget" since I knew others would do "Murders in the Rue Morgue." Poe wrote Marie Roget to answer his critics that in "Rue Morgue" he had cheated. They said he set up the puzzle and then solved it, which wasn't hard. So he had Dupin try to solve a fictionalized version of an existing case. My first two attempts at this were mysteries, but Ellen wanted horror. So I looked at the story again, and found this: "This is an ordinary, although an atrocious, instance of crime. There is nothing particularly outré about it." This is Poe talking to his critics. It's also true. What happened to Marie Roget (Mary Rogers in the real world) happens to women all the time. And to me, that's horrifying.*

LUCIUS SHEPARD was born in Lynchburg, Virginia, grew up in Daytona Beach, Florida, and lives in Vancouver, Washington. His short fiction has won the Nebula Award, the Hugo Award, the International Horror Writers Award, the National Magazine Award, the Locus Award, the Theodore Sturgeon Award, and the World Fantasy Award.

His latest books are a non-fiction book about Honduras, *Christmas in Honduras*; a short novel, *Softspoken*; and a short fiction collection, *The Iron Shore*. Forthcoming are two novels: tentatively titled *The Piercefields* and *The End Of Life As We Know It*, and two short novels: *Beautiful Blood*, *Unknown Admirer*, and *The House of Everything and Nothing*.

Kirikh'quru Krokundor

by Lucius Shepard

Had it not been for my affair with Dr. Nubia Borregales, I might not have embarked upon the study of history, that most fabulist of disciplines, and would certainly never have traveled to St. Gotthard. My interests lay in determining the larger movements of time, in great tidal shifts and patterns, whereas she was fascinated by small, apparently idiosyncratic events, claiming these localized bubbles were released from a current that undercut the flow of what we perceived as history and thus were more revealing of its actual nature. To my mind, places like St. Gotthard were aberrations, curious human footnotes, exceptions that proved the rule… though the specifics of that rule as yet elude me.

When I met Nubia I was a graduate student in the University of Miami's Department of Latin American Studies and she was thirty-one, a rising star in the academic world. She had just published her first book (an account of her immersion in *candomble* voodoo intermixed with the history of a temple in Belem) to raves from the academic community and a surprising degree of commercial success. Venezuelan by birth, her features betrayed a mixed Spanish and Indian heritage. She was on the plain side of pretty, her nose too hawkish and prominent, her mouth too wide, with an average figure (a few pounds overweight, as they say on singles websites) and a puffy face rendered forgettable and nerdish by wire-rimmed glasses and an aversion to make-up. However, her charismatic personality and quick mind more than compensated for this. She overwhelmed me, evincing a voracious sexuality unequalled by any woman I had known. We were involved for nearly four years, at which point she dropped me without a word of explanation, breaking off all contact, and moved on to an affair with a teaching assistant. Following the completion of my doctorate, I moved on as well, to an assistant professorship at Portland State, where I embarked upon a tenure track at that green and pleasant, yet undeniably second-rate institution.

It had been six years since I'd spoken to Nubia, seven since our relationship ended, but for all intents and purposes I was still in her life, still obsessed, and I wasted uncountable hours trying to determine what had happened, going over details again and again. I could have written books analyzing her behavior. I could have taught seminars on her body language, her attitudes toward other women (put simply, she would turn on them less quickly than she would a man), and her preference in hand soaps. Of course I tracked her career—it would have impossible to do otherwise. Four consecutive best sellers and frequent appearances as a TV pundit had earned her the envy of academia and, naturally, its scorn. Her work was now dismissed as sensationalist and superficial, and scurrilous stories were told about her omnivorous sexual appetites and casual cruelty, particularly as it related to grad students and TAs; thus when the department secretary informed me that Nubia was waiting in my office, she did so in a suggestive tone.

Nubia was standing by my desk, a jacket over one arm, gazing at the campus through the branches of the fir that shaded my window. I had observed changes in her during a recent appearance with Larry King, yet seeing her close at hand, I was stunned by her transformation. Gone was the chunky, schoolgirlish drone who had worn baggy T-shirts and thrift shop skirts, and hacked off her hair in lieu of a visit to the salon; in her place stood a slim, stylish brown-skinned woman with long, lustrous black hair, dressed in tailored slacks and a frilly cream-colored blouse that made her look like an orchid rising from a stem. The years had pared away the baby fat and she presented the image of a comely, confident Latina. As far as I could tell she'd had no work done. Her prominent nose was still her worst feature, yet it seemed to suit her now, to be emblematic of a vital and commanding presence, the sort of presence, I imagined, that attracts women to rich and powerful men.

"Jon!" she said, hurrying to embrace me. "You look wonderful! It's so good to see you!" She was wearing perfume. That, too, was a change.

I disengaged from her, said, "Nubia," and took a seat. "How can I help you?"

She gave no sign of being put off by the coolness of my reception; she settled into the chair opposite me and began telling me about her upcoming trip to St. Gotthard. I listened with half an ear, astonished by the depth of emotion she had dredged up in me, and when she was done, remaining civil, I inquired what this had to do with me.

"I'd like you to join me," she said. "As a colleague. If a book comes of Saint Gotthard, and I think one will, I want you to co-author it. I reserve the right to edit the final draft, but only as regards style. You'll agree, I think, that I'm a more polished writer than you."

I responded angrily, but she cut me off.

"I'm sorry for the way I treated you," she said. "I was young. I thought severing our relationship would be less painful than a measured retreat."

"That's a lie," I said. "You hopped into bed with someone else the next day. For all I know, you were sleeping with him before we broke up."

"The reason I slept with Ben was to underscore my decision. I didn't want you to have any doubts about it. If you recall, I didn't stay with him long."

"I'm astonished you remember his name, there've been so many."

She examined her nails.

"You were arrogant and cowardly," I went on. "And self-absorbed. That's why you handled things the way you did. Now you waltz in here and throw me a bone. Is this some kind of make-up call?"

After a pause she said, "I'm not going to discuss this now. I will, if you insist, but not now."

"Why not now? Isn't seven years long enough to come up with an explanation?"

"Everything you say is true. I am self-absorbed and arrogant. I was happy enough with you, but happiness was interfering with my work. I had career concerns. Departmental concerns."

"Bullshit," I said.

"Do you know how much flak I took about my personal life from McIntyre? He wanted to fire me. But I'm not getting into this. You're too emotional. If you accept my proposal, we'll have an opportunity to talk things through."

She stood and came around to my side of my desk and perched on the corner, her perfume mixing with the smell of the evergreens.

"You're partly right about this being a make-up call, but that's not germane," she said. "I value your opinions, even though we're diametrically opposed in our approach. I see the book as a dialogue between us, both on a professional and personal level. Perhaps in writing it we'll become friends again. At the least it should be an exhilarating experience."

She had no reason to play me, yet I knew I was being played. She wanted me to touch her, to make some rapprochement—that was why she positioned herself so near—but while I felt a flicker of interest, it didn't rise to the level of arousal. I was both relieved and saddened that she no longer had that affect on me.

"Come on, Jon," she said, trying to jolly me. "Don't stick me with some tedious old man for a co-author."

"I'll think about it."

Anger clouded her face. She went to her chair and retrieved her jacket. When she turned to me again, she was smiling.

"This is a lovely campus, but it's so small," she said as she slipped into the jacket. "I can see it suits you, though."

I ignored the slight.

"I'm at the Monaco until tomorrow," she said. "You need to get past our personal history and focus on your career. If you work through your pique, give me a call."

I detected a hint of injury in her voice, but I remembered what an accomplished actress she was, how skilled at manipulation, and this gave me cause for doubt. Nevertheless, the idea that I could hurt her, though satisfying on a petty level, bred the surprising notion that I didn't particularly enjoy it.

She started for the door.

"Wait," I said.

THE SETTLEMENT OF St. Gotthard had been established in an Andean valley in Venezuela in 1863 by a splinter Moravian sect, which until that time had been based in Switzerland. The word "established" gives rise to the impression of a settlement carved from the wilderness, but the Moravians occupied buildings already in place. The valley and all within it had been bequeathed to the sect twenty years previously, along with a hefty endowment, by Odell Remarque, a wealthy German eccentric and voluptuary who had expended a significant part of his fortune in seeking out the most beautiful spot on earth (the one qualification of the bequest was that the Moravians maintain the land, the buildings thereon and all they contained exactly as Remarque left them). The criteria governing his search are unclear, though he is on record as saying that he was not interested in a glorious vista, feeling that such would tend to become oppressive over time—this appeared to legislate against an Andean site, but Remarque was satisfied and sent in landscapers, engineers, and builders to tailor the valley to his precise tastes.

Unlike most religious émigrés, the Moravians had been neither persecuted nor oppressed in their native land; rather they came to Venezuela in order to evade the influence of the modern world and to further their charitable ambitions. They were a small sect, less than a thousand souls, yet exhibited the energy of a much larger body, traveling widely throughout the country, setting up schools and clinics in dozens of locales. As the decades passed, however, they gradually withdrew from these stations and the tradition of good works they embodied, and in 1928 they severed connections with the outside world, eliminating all but a single line of communication with the Venezuelan government, a bank account from which a yearly tax was withdrawn. The Interprovincial Board of the North American church sent emissaries to determine what had transpired. Some failed to return and those who did reported that the colony had fallen away from the Covenant for Christian Living (a document containing the fundamental precepts of the faith) and that their sole concern seemed to be the securing the valley against intruders. They had fortified the massive river gate that Remarque had constructed so as to provide a dramatic entrance into his fabulous preserve, and were engaged in rendering other routes into the valley impassable.

Remarque did not permit the use of photographic equipment in his domain and the Moravians continued this proscription; thus only a few old pictures of the valley existed, most showing the cluster of fantastic buildings topped by minarets and Gothic spires, lifting from a great plaza at the center of a forest. Recent satellite images gave evidence that brush had overgrown the plaza, the buildings had fallen into disrepair and the surrounding land, no longer tended, had returned to the wild—this apparent abandonment provided Nubia with the ammunition she needed to petition the government for permission to enter the valley. She availed herself of her family's political connections and wangled the use of a huge CH-47F Chinook helicopter to transport our expedition to St. Gotthard... at least that was how she explained it; but after watching her flirt with bureaucrats, I wondered mean-spiritedly if she had used a more intimate means of persuasion.

St. Gotthard was a lifelong obsession of Nubia's and, though she was unable to experience it as Remarque had intended, passing along the river and through the gate, she was thrilled by the prospect of breaching this forbidden place. For my part, I was less interested in the place than the project. The book, as Nubia envisioned it, was to contain no reference to our previous relationship, yet in it we would be characters who clearly had a history. Adventure and a hint of romance in an exotic setting would add a novelistic element to engage the pop sensibility and enable a general readership to put up with the drier sections. I had some reservations, but when I weighed the rectitude of scholarship and the rebukes of my colleagues against a potential audience with Oprah Winfrey, it was no contest.

There were to be seven in our party, including two grad students from the University of the Andes and two Venezuelan soldiers sent to report on our findings. Our videographer was Taylor Mendenhall, a young instructor at Miami, blond and good-looking in a morally straight-and-true, Sears catalogue sort of way. At a mixer in Nubia's suite at our hotel in Merida, the jumping-off place for the expedition, Taylor drew me aside and pointed to Claudia Pozzobon, one of the students, a diminutive, busty woman with a milky complexion and black hair, who was chatting with a government official.

"Claudia's kind of hot," he said. "She's got a Christina Ricci thing going on."

"I guess... yeah." I tipped my head, as if to gain a better perspective on Claudia, who was laughing at something the official said. "Happier, though."

"Huh?"

"Claudia seems happier. Christina Ricci usually plays downer roles."

"The word is Nubia's doing her."

"Ricci?"

"No, man! Claudia."

I snagged a glass of champagne from a passing waiter. "Nice."

"Doesn't it bother you? I hear you and Nubia were hot and heavy back in the day."

"Where'd you hear that?"

"Around the department. Nubia's the stuff of legend at Miami."

I knocked back the champagne and made a non-committal noise.

Taylor stared grimly at Nubia, hemmed in against the bar by several men. "Well, it bothers me."

No doubt he was bursting to tell me about his involvement with her. As a charter member of the Victims of Nubia, I had a responsibility to listen; but I wasn't in the mood. I excused myself, grabbed another glass of champagne, and went over to a window offering a view of the city and the mountains beyond. Merida was built on a plateau formation—it appeared that the land had been chewed off by something big and toothy, leaving deep canyons on three sides. The poorest barrios were closest to these drop-offs, some of the tiny white houses clinging to the edge. A yellow cable car inched along above the canyons, suspended against the backdrop of the Cordillera Occidental, a northern arm of the Andes, its rumpled slopes gone a dull Pomona in early summer, rising to snow peaks sixteen thousand feet high.

"It's beautiful, isn't it?" said Claudia, coming up beside me; her head reached to just above my elbow.

"I think it looks forbidding," I said.

She glanced up at me, perplexed.

"Scary," I said. "Ominous."

"Yes, I understood. But I don't understand why you think it's forbidding."

"The Andes are mysterious. Mountain fastnesses, deserted cities." I pretended to shudder. "Incan ghosts."

Macyory Abuin, the other student, eased up behind Claudia and whispered to her. Claudia responded in Spanish that she wasn't ready to leave.

If I hadn't been drunk, I wouldn't have spoken to Macyory. She was a timid soul and rarely spoke herself. At twenty-one, she was several years younger than Claudia, and deferred to her in most circumstances. She was thin, albeit a bit broad in the beam, and pale (not so pale as Claudia), yet her features had the vaguely Asiatic cast of the indigenous Indians: almond-shaped eyes and a broad nose, a full mouth and thick black hair. Her compacted silences reminded me of Nubia, but then I saw something of Nubia in every woman. When I asked Macyory if she was at all daunted by the prospect of entering St. Gotthard, rather than, as I expected, lowering her eyes and giving an uncommunicative answer, she said, "In situations such as this, it's best to keep fear in one's mind."

"What's there to be afraid of?"

"For me it's the isolation, being connected to civilization by so thin a thread."

"We have the army to protect us," I said.

"The army!" Claudia sniffed. "Now you're making a joke."

Nubia called to Claudia and she hurried to join the group at the bar. To my surprise, Macyory lingered at the window.

"The army is not concerned with us," she said. "They have their own interests."

"And what would those be?"

"If Saint Gotthard has been truly abandoned, they will seize everything of value."

"That should make them happy."

"Oh, yes. Certainly," she said. "But if they discover something of great value, they may not want any witnesses."

WE SET OUT for St. Gotthard three days later, flying in the shadow of Andean peaks, past montane forests, over glacial lakes and spectacular canyons, following the course of a tributary of the Chama River until we reached the head of the valley and the massive bronzed river gate, its surface etched with images of strange half-human figures, more appropriate to a sybarite's retreat (which it once had been) than to a religious colony. Despite the tangled vegetation that overgrew the work of Remarque's landscapers, I could imagine how the valley had appeared to a guest entering along the river—it poured between the banks of a narrow gorge, a stretch that widened into a crystalline pool; then it narrowed again, bearing the new arrival beneath arches formed by the epiphyte-laden boughs of trees with dense, dark crowns and thick gray trunks; then the trees thinned out, admitting to a view of rolling hills. The watercourse went through a series of such drastic alternations, moving from claustrophobic gloom to inspiring vistas, the surrounding terrain obscured by granite cliffs carved with glyphs, by giant ferns that formed a plumed aisle, and by lumpish hills whose crests had been sculpted into quaint troll-like shapes. These last flattened out, giving way to an undulant terrain of green bamboo and creeks that sprang from the naked rock to splash down among tumbled boulders the size of cottages. At length the river spilled into a basin at whose nearer reach stood a dock fashioned of ebony planks upon which the guest could stand and contemplate the glory of St. Gotthard: a circular band of forest that enclosed four improbable buildings, their roof ornaments and spires lifting high above the trees. They expressed a bizarre mingling of architectures: Tibetan and Byzantine and Gothic, and something best described as a nineteenth century futurism. From a remove they blended into an aesthetically pleasing whole, yet once we drew near they seemed at odds with one another, a tawdry grouping of the sort one finds crammed into a corner of a theme park, pretending to be skyscrapers and ancient pyramids and the like. The forest occupied the lower, gentler slopes of a mighty hill and beyond the hill lay the central massif of the Cordillera Occidental, a towering range whose sharp peaks were wisped by fumes of cloud, offering the impression that they were venting steam, furious at our intrusion.

We circled the plaza while our pilot, Captain Abreu, announced our arrival over a loudspeaker to whoever might not have heard the sound of our approach; but no one came forth to greet us. As I've said, the plaza was overgrown with bushes and young trees, the paving stones barely visible beneath weeds, and offered no place for the Chinook to land. The captain hovered at a height of ten feet and, after dumping tents and other camping equipment out the door, we climbed down by means of a metal ladder. Once the Chinook had passed out of hearing, seeking a landing site beyond the forest, silence descended over the area, broken by the flow of wind. Sgt. Perdomo, a squat, taciturn Indian with a jowly face and acne-scarring on his cheeks, oversaw the others as they made camp in front of the largest building, a structure whose façade had the massive doors and decorative conceits of a Gothic cathedral, but was more like a castle in its overall design. The doors were cracked open—Nubia and I pushed through the brush that fronted them and slipped inside.

I anticipated that we would find a chamber of considerable size opening off the foyer, with a vaulted ceiling lost in shadow; but the room we entered, though large, had more the atmosphere of a private club (or a hotel lobby minus the reception desk). It had been left vulnerable to the elements for many years. Shafts of light penetrated the dimness, falling from high, narrow windows, revealing a carpet so mired in filth that I could scarcely make out its color scheme (an Arabic design of dull red, cream, and inky blue); patches of mildew all but obscured the wall hangings. Overstuffed leather chairs and mahogany drink tables were set about in an orderly fashion, but their surfaces were dappled with fungal growths and animal droppings. In the middle of the room, a ruined fountain leaked a dribble of rusty water, contributing to the smell of dampness and decay. The basin and the statue that had formed its centerpiece were shattered. Chunks of marble lay everywhere, some twenty and thirty feet from the fountain, as if they had been hurled. Nubia was holding one such chunk when I came up, and was looking down at hundreds of yellow blossoms scattered about the basin: blooms of the golden rain tree (I had observed several specimens in the plaza), relatively fresh, no more than a day old.

"Looks like someone's around," I said.

Nubia made a derisive noise. "You think?"

She handed me the marble fragment. It had been broken from the statue's face: a hollowed eye and a portion of the forehead.

"Given Remarque's sensibilities, I expect he furnished the place with statuary that offended the Moravians," I said. "I don't think we can infer anything other than the fact that they must have objected to it."

"Then why not simply remove the statue? The flowers are clearly an offering. I think we can *infer* that something has gone very wrong here."

"You so want this to be a mystery," I said.

"The entire population vanished. That's not a mystery?"

"I doubt it's the lurid one you're hoping for. They may not have liked living here and erected homes in the forest. They're probably watching us, deciding what to do."

"Doesn't that suggest something's wrong?"

"It suggests that they're unaccustomed to visitors."

Nubia took back the marble shard. "I'd forgotten how reasonable you can be."

"That's why I'm here, isn't it? To play yang to your yin... or is it the other way around?"

She moved away, stooping to examine another chunk of marble.

"Opposition's always been a huge part of our relationship," I said. "Contrariness. Which makes it even odder, the way you dumped me. I would have thought you'd relish one last argument."

Nubia went to a knee, examining another shard. "I wonder if we could reassemble the face? I'd like to see it."

"You're still not talking to me? I'm still too emotional? I'm going to keep being emotional until we air this out. I was so fucked up when you dumped me, I nearly lost my grant."

"It might make an interesting cover for the book."

"Damn it, Nubia!"

"Maybe a title as well: *The Shattered Face.* What do you think?"

I watched her picking among the scraps of marble and felt anger rising in me like mercury in a hot glass stick.

"All right," I said. "But we're not leaving until I get an explanation. One that goes deeper than you were worried about your damn career."

Without looking up, Nubia asked, "Would you mind fetching Claudia? She's clever at puzzles."

ONCE CAMP WAS established, the group split up to investigate the buildings. They had been erected in a formation shaped like a V with one stroke left unfinished, and from a distance they had appeared clumped together, though in actuality they were set thirty-five or forty yards apart. The Castle was at the point of the V and the building I chose to investigate was on its right: an oversized Tibetan temple with whitewashed walls and ornately carved lintels. From its roof sprouted a stubby tower with a brass finial at the top. The interior was disappointingly plain: a hundred or more rooms furnished in a utilitarian manner: desks, chairs, antique office equipment. Dust and mold were thick on every surface. In the desks and cabinets I discovered papers. Bills, letters addressed to various Moravian functionaries from companies in Merida and, inside a metal box, legal documents, some of extreme age—these I took with me. I would have explored the tower, but a locked door blocked my path.

It wasn't until dinner that anyone expressed concern over Captain Abreu, who had not returned. Some thought was given to searching for him, but Sgt. Perdomo pointed out that it would be foolhardy to look for him at night. If he didn't return by morning, he, the sergeant, would go after him. The conversation turned to the four buildings. Each was in a ruinous state comparable to the Castle, except for the Hotel, a pyramidal structure with slit windows, whose walls (holed as from a bombardment) offered glimpses into several bedchambers furnished with outmoded bondage devices. Of the four, the building we called Pleasure Dome was the least damaged. It occupied a position behind and to the right of the Temple, and was modeled after a mosque, with minaret-like towers at each corner and a dome of glass panels. Taylor told us it contained three main rooms: an assembly hall, a basement whose door he had been unable to force, and, enclosed by the dome, a garden that had overgrown its borders, now more thicket than garden. He had noticed white objects in among the leaves—statuary, he believed—and said it would be necessary to cut back the vegetation in order to be sure.

With our pilot missing, the surrounding shrubs compressed into crouching shadows, dwarfed by the walls of the Castle—I felt on edge, yet I also felt challenged by the situation, as if I were accustomed to an adventurous life and not a wilting academic. Instead of being put off by the babble around me, my normal reaction to groups, I eagerly interacted with the others (excepting Nubia) and, when it came time to retire, I was sorry to abandon the camaraderie I'd found around the campfire. I had not been in my tent long, reading by battery lamp, when Nubia pushed aside the flap. She had on baggy shorts and a T-shirt, and was carrying the box of documents I had retrieved from the Temple. Without preamble, she asked if I had examined them.

"Briefly," I said, offended by her abrupt entrance. "Why?"

"I want you to see something."

"Can't it wait?"

She sat beside my sleeping bag, opened the box and held out a yellowed piece of paper. I gave an annoyed sigh and sat up. Someone had scribbled variant spellings of two words in ink on the face of the document, the most common being half-a-dozen repetitions at the bottom of the page, as if this were the spelling that had been settled on: Kirikh'quru Krokundor.

I gave an indifferent shrug. "What is it?"

"I don't know. I Googled the words and their elements, but none of the results relate to anything that has a connection to St. Gotthard."

"It was probably someone goofing around."

She handed me a second page, a contract signed by someone named A. Kuenzy—but Kuenzy had first signed another name to the page, one he or she had crossed out yet which was still recognizable: Kirikh'quru Krokundor. The document was dated August 16, 1928, the year in which the Moravians had broken off contact with the outer world.

"Now we know who was goofing around," I said. "The guy must have spaced while signing the contract."

"Could be," Nubia said. "It doesn't make any linguistic sense—it reminds me of the names my kid invents for characters in his role-playing games."

"You have a kid?"

"Gerardo." She tucked a stray curl behind her ear and smiled. "I adopted him several years ago. He's staying with my mother."

This evidence of humanity (she had never before expressed any maternal feelings) softened my attitude toward her. As if this erosion of anger had cleared wax from my ears, I heard the scuttling of nocturnal creatures in the brush, the wind keening fitfully, all the night sounds. She began outlining our duties for the following morning, not with her usual brusque tone, but putting the schedule out there for me to approve. She glanced at me now and then, and not to see whether I was paying attention. She seemed reluctant to look away. Her nipples were erect, pushing against the fabric of the T-shirt, and there was a flush on her cheeks. Occasionally she touched my hand. Warmth suffused my body, causing me to feel dull and drugged, and I felt a stirring in my groin. I had it in mind to tip her face up to be kissed, but then remembered how deeply I despised her—I was amazed that I could have forgotten even for a second. Though I continued to have an acute awareness of her body, her scent, I decided that my arousal must be vestigial, the remnant of an old chemistry I was unable to purge because she had denied me a proper resolution. I wanted to make love to her no less, but it would have been the mother of all grudge-fucks. She may have picked up on a subtle change in the emotional climate, for her manner grew brisk and, after a minute or so, acting flustered, she returned to her tent, leaving me, as she had years before, in a state of frustration.

THE NEXT MORNING I went to wake Taylor, thinking to get a head start on what promised to be a grueling day; but he was not in his tent. I speculated with a degree of amusement as to whose tent he might be in; then I grabbed a machete and headed for the Pleasure Dome in accordance with Nubia's schedule, knowing she would send him along in due course. Mildewed maroon carpeting covered the wide stairway leading up from the bottom floor and the bas-reliefs on the plaster walls were in good repair. They depicted men and women engaged in foreplay and, as the stair wound upward, in sexual congress. I wondered how the Moravians had related to these images. They were not prudes, but I doubted they would have been comfortable with them. I wondered, too, not for the first time, at Remarque's motives in deeding St. Gotthard to the sect. Had he intended it as an affront to their sensibilities? Had he hoped the reliefs would have a debasing effect? And if the latter were so, had his tactic succeeded?

At the top of the stairs were double doors; past the doors, steps led down into the garden whose vegetation yielded an unexpectedly clean, dry smell. I heard rustling in the undergrowth, as of rodents. Citrus trees and bougainvillea and bamboo flourished amid a tangle of anonymous shrubs, and I saw something white that might have been one of the statues mentioned by Taylor; but what held my attention were the glass panels of the dome, at least half of them intact. Lead mullions sectioned the panels into irregular shapes and these shapes had varying degrees of opacity. The mullions were thin, difficult to make out against the gray backdrop of morning, making it appear that translucent clouds had invaded a circular patch of sky and were shifting about, a trippy effect that brought to mind the early stages of a psychotropic drug experience. As if the sight had infected my eyes, patches of opacity shifted across the leaves as I pushed deeper into the garden.

I followed the path that Taylor had cut the previous day—the severed branches still oozed sap—and heard an unmistakably human outcry. It occurred to me that whoever had scattered flowers by the broken fountain might be the source of the cry. I eased forward and heard a softer cry. Through a gap in the leaves I spotted Claudia Pozzobon reclining on a bench of white stone, her shorts and panties about her ankles, her top pushed up to expose her gelatinous breasts. She rubbed her fingers between her legs, one hand braced on the moss-fettered thigh of a statue, a subhuman figure with tusk-like teeth—it leaned over the bench, as if deeply interested in what Claudia was doing. I had a gynecological view of the proceedings and my initial thought was to withdraw; yet I kept watching, attentive as a hound, for several seconds. I might have stayed longer if Claudia had not spoken.

"*Come mi bollo!*" she said in a fierce whisper. "*Mas! Como eso! Ay, mas!*"

Half-believing that she'd spotted me, I retreated. I had the suspicion that someone was watching me watch her and this increased my pace. I paused on the landing, worried that if she *had* seen me, she might tell the others. I decided to wait for her, to pretend that I was coming up the stairs. When she burst through the doors, she displayed no surprise on seeing me and asked if I'd been spying on her. I didn't think I could pull off a lie.

"Look," I said. "I heard a noise, I was curious. I'm sorry. It was only for a second."

"It's okay," she said. "If I caught you at it, I'd probably peek, too. Are you sure you weren't there longer?"

"I wasn't spying on you! All right?"

"Whatever. I could have sworn someone was watching me the whole time."

"If you thought someone was watching, why didn't you stop?"

"I liked the idea." She gave me a sidelong look. "It must just have been those creepy statues, eh?"

"This is no place I'd choose to get friendly with myself."

"How old are you? Thirty? For such a young guy, you're extremely repressed." She put a hand on her hip. "I was horny. I'm sharing a tent with Macyory and she's gay. I don't want her to get the wrong idea."

"I thought…"

"What?"

"I thought you were gay."

"Sometimes… but I'm not attracted to Macyory."

"But you're attracted to Nubia."

"Are you kidding? She's too old for me. We flirt, but that's just girl stuff. Did Taylor say something? Is that where you're hearing this? He's all obsessed—he thinks everybody is after her. Maybe he's right." She shook her head in bewilderment. "I don't get what it is about her. Men lose their minds when she's around."

I made no comment.

"You too, eh?" said Claudia.

"Here we are, in the midst of all this beauty and mystery, and we're having a stupid high school conversation."

"What should we talk about? Beauty and mystery?" Claudia's mouth tightened with disdain. "Bor-ing!"

AT MID-MORNING A heavy rain sluiced over the surface of the dome, blurring its cloudy definition, and Taylor joined me in hacking and slashing at vines and branches. I told him I'd stopped by his tent and asked where he had been—he said he must have been taking a piss. He was in a sullen mood and we worked without speaking, managing to clear two groupings of statues and benches. One statue was of a nude faceless woman with anatomically precise musculature, its hands outspread as if bestowing a blessing upon the bench beneath. The other grouping consisted of three statues and the remains of a wooden couch sufficiently wide to support four or five reclining bodies. The statues were half-again life-size, unfinished… or else their subjects had been unfinished, partial faces emerging from smooth white stone, hunched over the couch as if preparing to snatch up someone with a club-like three-fingered hand. This unsettling tableau firmed up my notion that the theme of the garden had something to do with a kinship between Eros and terror. It must have been, I thought, a kink of Remarque's. I had done some research on him before leaving on the trip and had found a sketchy biography, mentions of his business dealings, his promiscuity, his friendship with various disreputable characters, actors and criminal types, but nothing that commented on him in depth.

Around noon, leaving Taylor at work, I went to get something to eat. Nubia and Macyory were sitting in Nubia's tent, peering glumly out at the rain through the open flap. They had made sandwiches. The tent was spacious, with room for a writing desk and a cot, on which the two women sat, and I pulled the desk chair about so I could face them. To piss off Nubia, I asked if I was interrupting something. "No!" she said crabbily. I plucked a sandwich from the table and told them what we had found.

"Taylor's still hacking away," I said. "But I think all we'll find is more of the same. My time would be better spent trying to get into the tower. Or the basement of the Pleasure Dome."

"Abreu is still missing," said Nubia. "I sent the sergeant to find him."

Sitting next to each other emphasized their Indian blood. They might have been cousins joined in a depressed unity.

"Are we in trouble?" I asked.

"Probably not," Nubia said, and Macyory added, "Nothing's definite, but it's not good news."

"We're in trouble, then?"

Nubia made a noise like a cat sneezing. "Do you have to always seize upon the worst case scenario?"

Macyory ran a hand consolingly along her leg, leaving it resting on her upper thigh; then she laid her head on Nubia's shoulder and shut her eyes. This casual intimacy intrigued me.

"We'll be fine," said Nubia, speaking more to Macyory than to me.

I removed the wrapping from my sandwich and lifted a corner of the bread—a BLT. I had a bite and said, "Suppose Abreu *and* Perdomo don't come back. Wouldn't it be wise to have a contingency plan?"

"If we don't report in, they'll send another helicopter," said Nubia.

"Oh, yeah!" I said with heavy sarcasm. "We can depend on the Venezuelan army to act with customary swift efficiency.

"What's your point?"

"No point." I had another bite. "Simply wondering if you had a plan other than to run screaming into the forest."

The rain fell harder, sending up splashes like ricochets from the ground outside, drumming on the tent, causing me to raise my voice.

"Where's Claudia?" I asked.

"In the Castle," Macyory said. "She's trying to put that face together."

She and Nubia interlaced their fingers. I withheld comment, a rare moment of restraint. After finishing my sandwich, I unwrapped a second one. As I ate I took note of Nubia's listlessness, assuming this was due to worries about Abreu's continued absence; yet the women seemed less concerned with the captain than with one another. Macyory made eye contact with Nubia whenever possible and arranged her features into an imploring look when she succeeded. I decided to let them work out their problem, whatever it was, and made for the Temple, thinking I'd have a go at the locked door; but my energy was low and I made for the Castle instead.

Gray light from the windows dressed the room in a thick dusk. Claudia was on all fours beside the broken fountain; she had cleared a space on the floor and upon it, lit by a battery lamp, lay the product of her labors: a marble face less than half-complete. Part of the throat was joined to a section of the jaw, and a portion of the opposite cheek was fitted to a second eye. She had assembled most of the forehead, too, and had placed a piece of the nose underneath them. Without a mouth and chin, it was hard to determine whether the face was male or female. Arranged on a patch of rotted, reddish carpet, it had a barbaric quality.

"What do you think?" she asked, coming to her knees.

"Nubia will be happy. It'll make a good cover illustration as is."

Claudia regarded her work, tipping her head to one side. "It's a young girl or a boy with feminine eyes. See how large they are? How the lashes are accentuated?"

"You're probably right."

"Of course the mouth could make it look more adult or more masculine. Now it looks almost elfin."

A feeling of unease stole over me. The room, with its moldy stench and mildewed wall hangings, the tables and stained leather chairs, and the faint sound of the fountain... Nothing moved, but I had a sense that something had been moving a split-second before, or else it had slipped away beyond a dimensional gate and was peering at us still.

"I can't find any of the mouth," Claudia said. "Do you really think this will satisfy Nubia?"

"Hmm-hmm."

"Are you listening to me?"

"I'm sorry," I said. "This place creeps me out. Yeah, she'll be delighted." She stood and dusted herself off. "I need a break."

I continued to search for evidence of things not seen. Claudia stepped close to me; the tips of her breasts grazed my shirtfront.

"Want to take a break with me?" she asked.

I had no doubt what she meant and I started to say it would be inappropriate and I didn't get involved with students and I didn't feel that way, the stock responses; but then, suddenly, I did feel that way. Her scent and her stare melted my inhibitions. The thinnest strand of false morality held me back.

"Don't you think I'm too old for you?" I asked, making a feeble stab at humor.

"Let's find out." I hesitated and she made a peevish sound. "Do I have to convince you?"

"It's not that. I don't want to be walked in on."

"There's a room in back with a couch that's fairly clean," she said pertly. "Clean enough, anyway."

SEX WITH CLAUDIA was the sort of sex that gives you a hangover. It lacked all but a scant emotional component, yet we shared a peculiar clinical unity. I knew everything she wanted and she seemed unerringly to know my wants as well. As we progressed the sex grew rougher, but this was in keeping with our needs. She nipped my neck and chest, locked her teeth in my shoulder and raked my sides with her nails. I believe I marked her as well. Afterward I smelled like her and she smelled like me. She offered a perfunctory kiss and went back to work. I returned to camp (noticing that the flap of Nubia's tent was closed) and lay down on my sleeping bag. Usually I was scrupulous about using protection, but the fact that I hadn't used any with Claudia worried me not in the least. I dozed off thinking about her body.

I woke around four. The rain had stopped, Nubia's tent flap was still down and the sun was trying to break through. I dug an apple out of stores and ate it sitting in a camp chair beside dead coals of the previous night's fire. The sun gave up, the temperature dropped. It promised to be a chilly night. Nubia came out of her tent. She pulled up a chair, but said nothing. Her hair was mussed and she looked groggy. We talked about the book and then she asked what I'd been up to that day.

"Not much," I said. "Like everyone else, I've been dogging it."

"Nobody's dogging it!"

"Right. Claudia's putting together a face and Taylor's chopping brush and God knows what Macyory's doing. You better crack the whip, because they don't seem real motivated. They're more interested in each other than in St. Gotthard. Me, too. I just had a close encounter with Claudia."

It took a second for her to decipher my meaning. "Congratulations," she said frostily.

"It wasn't like that," I said. "It was... odd."

"Odd how?"

I told her about stumbling across Claudia in the garden, about our conversation afterward and what had happened earlier that day.

"I don't think she was even into me," I said. "It's like she's addicted to sex."

"You must have enjoyed it."

"I realize academics are a horny bunch and Claudia's attractive, but this was freakish. I wasn't in the mood and then, wham!"

Wind scattered petals from a rain tree along the paving stones. I thought how strange it was to be there among these ruins, these enormous, moronic monuments to fucking.

"Why tell me about it?" she asked. "Are you trying to injure me?"

"I doubt that's possible."

Her sigh held a note of exasperation, of condescension, as if she were saying, "Oh, you pitiful child!" The attitude this implied—that she was being forbearing—uncorked my anger.

"God, I detest you," I said.

"I understand that."

"No, you don't understand. You couldn't possibly understand. You've got a PhD in self-deception. If the stories about you are true, and I'm sure they are, what you did to me, you've done to other guys... and women, too."

"You shouldn't believe everything you hear."

"It's your M.O. Where relationships are concerned, you're a sociopath. A serial rapist."

"You're being ridiculous!"

"You violate your lovers emotionally. You display no sign of conscience, or if you do, it's barely enough to inspire the occasional 'I'm sorry.' But you only say 'I'm sorry' when you want to prolong the rape. You're a pathological narcissist. You can't accept that anyone could sustain a low opinion of you, though you have a low opinion of yourself. At least you used to. Hanging out with Doctor Phil must have boosted your self-esteem."

"I'm not going to listen to this," she said.

"You said we'd talk. Well, let's talk. We can do it later, when everyone's around, or we can have a chat now. Either way is fine with me, but I won't be put off much longer."

Half out of her chair, she sat back. "Fine. Go ahead."

I felt a pulse in my temple as I struggled to recall my train of thought.

"You cut people off at the knees and watch them bleed out. You contrive a scenario that justifies what you're doing, but the pain you cause is the only thing that matters. How you perceive the situation, how you felt about it at the time, is irrelevant."

"I loved you, Jon."

"You've convinced yourself of that, I'm sure. It's half the kick. All that drama feels so authentic. You feel the pain, but it's a good, crunchy pain. It gives you a taste of what the poor slob you've sliced up is going through."

She was tearing up, but I didn't care. I understood that what I wanted was not an explanation, but a chance to say these things.

"The crying is a terrific special effect," I said. "I always wondered why it was so much more persuasive than the rest of your repertoire, and I think I've figured it out. Before you came to Miami, I bet guys fucked you over routinely. You weren't that pretty, and you were a brain. That's a buzzkill for high school guys. You probably had to do tricks to get laid. I'm sure they laughed at you. Maybe they passed around dirty pictures of you. Whatever they did, it was cruel. You probably cried a lot, but you learned how to manipulate people. By the time you earned your degree, you were ready for some payback. Your pathology's a form of compensation. Like the *In Cold Blood* guy. Perry Smith. He told Capote the Clutter family had never done anything to hurt him, not like all the other people in his life. He said he thought the reason he'd killed them was simply because he felt someone had to pay. You haven't killed anyone, but the principle's the same."

"You're blaming me for your obsession," she said, wiping her eyes. "A normal human being, someone balanced... they would have cut their losses."

"It's my fault now? I shouldn't have put my neck in the way of your ax? Because I'm not *normal,* that excuses you?"

"I'm not trying to avoid blame."

"That's exactly what you're doing. You're telling me because my involvement with you was deeper than your involvement with me, it means I'm neurotic. Abnormal. And you think that lets you off the hook somehow?"

"What I'm trying to get across is that however despicable I am, the fact remains you have a problem with obsession. You better deal with it or you're going to be unhappy for a long time."

"Well, that's what I'm doing. Dealing with it. I'm talking to the cunt who denied me the opportunity to deal with it when dealing with it would have been material."

She fixed her eyes on a distant point and adopted a stoic expression. "Name-calling's helpful."

I watched her for some seconds and then pointed at her forehead. "What's it like in there? All gray and gloomy? Every now and then a sizzle of electricity, a sky full of flapping things illuminated by a short circuit? I may not be normal, but to rationalize things the way you do, you've got to be batshit!"

"Is this helping you? Wouldn't a discussion be preferable?"

"Sure. If you're going to contribute some emotional truth. Something less general than protesting that you loved me." I paused to work at a sliver of food trapped between my teeth. "You know, I used to daydream about hurting you, but I guess I'm not that kind of guy."

"You don't think this is hurting me?"

"I don't know. Is it? If so, it's not hurting enough. I engaged in some violent fantasies. That's par for the course, I suppose, for people who've been raped. But you've chosen your victims well. Wimps. Kids. Lonely professors. Otherwise you might have wound up chained in some maniac's basement, begging Jesus to let you die."

I stood and she looked at me sharply, as if to make certain I posed no physical threat. I had more to say, but I perceived her then not as a woman, but as a peculiar bug with breasts whose bite had weakened me. I wanted nothing more to do with her.

Her voice followed me as I walked to my tent. "I hope this has been therapeutic, Jon."

* * *

I LIVED THROUGH a long wasted dream that night and my mind was still fogged with anger when I stepped out into a sunny morning. Nubia and the others were gathered around Sgt. Perdomo. Though she deserved every abusive word I'd delivered, I felt diminished by the exercise and didn't want to face her. But Taylor called to me and as I walked up he said, "Abreu's okay. He's sick, but the Moravians are taking care of him."

"The Moravians?" I looked to Perdomo. "You've seen them?"

"The captain is recovering at their village," Perdomo said. "A little dysentery. In two or three days he will be well."

"Where's the village?"

"Up in the hills." Perdomo waved at the green slopes above and smiled. "He is receiving excellent care."

I had never observed a smile on Perdomo's heavy-jowled face. From the outset he had radiated antipathy toward our party, especially toward the Americans. This attitude was doubtless related to the Chavez regime's issues with the United States and his general behavior was typical of an Army lifer, ill at ease and sullen in the company of civilians. Now he was positively beaming and, another peculiarity, his speech was hoarse and somewhat stilted. When Macyory asked him the name of the village, he said, "Kirikh'quru. It's a strange name, don't you think?"

Nubia studied him. "I've seen that name used in association with the word 'Krokundor.' Do you know what it means?"

Perdomo shook his head. "I only know the name of the village."

"I want you to take me there."

"It's far, the village, and I need to rest," Perdomo said. "I walked most of the night."

"You made it there and back in a day."

"With respect, I can cover rough terrain much quicker than you."

"Make a map," suggested Taylor, and then to Nubia: "I'll go with you."

"The Moravians are a reclusive people," said Perdomo. "They took the captain in because he was sick, and they let me see him because I am his friend. They don't want to meet with you."

"They told you that?" Nubia asked.

"Yes. When I go to collect Captain Abreu, I'll take you with me. Perhaps they will have grown more amiable."

"Why won't they meet with us?" asked Claudia.

"They have adopted our ways and live as we used to live," Perdomo said. "They wish to be left alone by those they consider impure."

Macyory and Taylor chimed in with simultaneous questions, and Nubia said, "We've imposed on Sergeant Perdomo enough. We should let him rest."

The sergeant inclined his head.

"I do have one last question. You are Chama, correct?"

Perdomo said, "Yes."

"The Chama live in the north, clustered around Merida. I assume that when you referred to the Moravians having adopted 'our ways,' you were referring to another tribal group?"

"I used 'our ways' in the sense of the general Venezuelan culture. I wasn't referring to a specific tribe."

"Of course," Nubia said.

AFTER BREAKFAST I located a small clearing off to the side of the Pleasure Dome offering an unobstructed of the Andes. The black rock of their flanks showed in cruel relief and the snowy peaks looked deadly sharp against the sky, capable of penetrating its blue skin. Sunlight fired the surface of the glass dome, its brightness making me squint, and I had an image of its heyday, of cool, shaded bowers, lovers coupling under the pupilless eyes of the statues.

"Catching a break?"

Nubia emerged from the brush and stood waiting for a reply. When none came, she kicked away some vegetable litter, and sat down facing me. Cicadas struck up a droning. "I have something to discuss with you," she said. "Can you put your feelings on hold?"

"Maybe," I said.

"Sergeant Perdomo seemed more voluble than usual, don't you think?"

I wanted to disagree, to reignite our old argument, but I said, "Yeah, little bit."

"More voluble and more fluent. I don't buy his story. The Moravians may live in a nearby village, and they may be taking care of Abreu. But he's hiding something. When I said the Chama lived in the north, he agreed with me. The Chama have settlements all along the river system. Remarque bought this land from them."

"He might not know about the settlements," I said. "He's not an educated man."

"He'd know. The Chama have a strong tradition of oral history."

A bird whizzed past overhead, a flash of green and yellow, and gave a shrill cry.

"Another thing," she said. "Two nights ago in your tent, my body reacted to you. I wanted you to make love to me. I attributed the reaction to nostalgia, yet I knew you wanted me, and..."

She looked down at her knees. I tracked the curve of her inner thigh into the shadow of her loose-fitting shorts and imagined running my hand along her thigh, into that shadow.

"I'm not sure how I got out of your tent without jumping you," she went on. "Then the next morning, Macyory told me she'd slept with Taylor."

"I thought she was gay."

"So did Macyory. She was confused and I consoled her."

"And that's when I found you together at lunch?"

She nodded. "After you left Macyory and I... we got busy. No matter what you've heard, I'm not a lesbian. Not until yesterday." She batted at a fly trapped in her hair. "People's wires are getting crossed. It's not so far afield that you can't explain it rationally. Out in the wilds, freed from normal restraints. But you and Claudia, Macyory and Taylor, me and Macyory. And now Perdomo. If it were just one thing, I could accept that explanation. But taken all together, something's not right."

"We're under stress," I said. "Especially you and me."

"You think this is a stress reaction? Come on!"

"What do you think it is?"

"I don't know! I hoped you'd be able to help me put it in perspective."

"It's weird, but this is a weird situation. Truthfully I'm more concerned about the helicopter."

"Perdomo says it's in good shape. If you believe his story, I guess you should believe him about that."

She hung her head, prodded a leaf on the ground beside her hip. I lifted my eyes to the dome. The light shifting across its glass surface reminded me of the opaque shapes I'd seen the previous day. I thought to mention them, but didn't want to prolong the conversation.

"Right now I feel like I did the other night," she said. "I'd do you in a heartbeat. Which seems unlikely in light of your diatribe last night. That was a potent anti-aphrodisiac." She left room for a response and then asked, "Are you feeling anything similar?"

"Nope."

"Then why've you been staring at my crotch? Is my voice coming from down there?" She appeared to be searching for something she could throw. "Damn it, Jon! Can't you be honest? I'm not trying to seduce you."

"All right. I feel something."

"Well...?"

"Well, what?"

"Do you have an opinion on what might be happening?"

"What the fuck do you want me to say? A mysterious force is making us crazy for sex? If we discard the rational, that's the only option left. Let's say that's true. Let's say an airborne poison or a witch doctor's curse or whatever is coercing us to screw ourselves stupid, and we're going to disappear like the Moravians. If you're right, we can't count on anything Perdomo told us, so we don't have a pilot. We can wait for help to come from Merida... or take a little hike along the river. That's the way to go as far as I'm concerned. We're all such accomplished outdoorsmen."

"I saw boats when we flew over the lake," she said. "They may still be serviceable."

"You've considered leaving? Before now, I mean?"

"I'm responsible for Claudia and Macyory and Taylor. I have to consider their welfare."

"This wasn't a good idea," I said after a pause.

"Coming to St. Gotthard?"

"Coming to St. Gotthard. Inviting me along. What did you have in mind? You must have been hoping for some specific outcome between us."

"If I was," she said, "I'm not anymore."

I KEPT APART from people for most of that day, strolling in the forest that encircled the buildings until I became spooked by things I saw along the dim avenues leading off among the moss-furred trunks. The forest was of the sort such as can be found anywhere in northern Europe (oaks and hawthorn and other species transplanted from Germany), and I felt almost at home in the gloom beneath the thick canopy. But I began to encounter life-sized statues of smiling men and women, fully clothed, normal in every respect, who had been magicked into stone mid-stride as they hurried toward St. Gotthard: some glanced over their shoulders as if encouraging their slower comrades in the race to pleasure; others pressed forward eagerly, bearing gifts in their hands. Moss covered the marble, but someone had taken pains to clean their faces and, when I looked deeper into the forest, past roots thick as crocodile tails, beneath low-hanging limbs, and behind gauzy veils of spiderweb, I caught sight of tiny white ovals suspended in mid-air, the green of their torsos and legs invisible against the myriad greens of the backdrop.

I came upon one statue that sounded an intentionally sinister note: a beautiful woman with eyes bulging from her aghast face, breasts swelling from her nightgown, a noose about her neck, the marble rope cunningly affixed to an oak branch. Her hands grasped the rope and she strained to touch the earth with her toes, making it appear that were she to relax, she would strangle. The message embodied by the statue was, I thought, that there were rules even in this licentious place, and he or she who broke them would meet with Remarque's justice. He, after all, had been the lawgiver in his domain. This started me thinking about the man—I wondered whether his decision to build in the valley had been informed solely by an appreciation of its beauty, or if the force that was afflicting us had influenced him to a degree. If such were the case, considering our state of distraction after only three days, the Moravians wouldn't have been able to carry out their good works for a period of sixty years. But what if the effect had been muted in Remarque's day and something had occurred during the Moravians' residency that amplified the force?

I bounced these questions around and decided that the idea of a mysterious force was ludicrous. I had been thinking like a fantasist, tailoring reality to fit the template of a fiction. Reality was not that neat, beset by quirky, random weathers, and I persuaded myself that this little sexual storm would pass, proving to have been a curious coincidence of stress and hormones, irrelevant to any matter of significance. But as I threaded my way through the brush in late afternoon, I saw Taylor sitting on the steps of the Pleasure Dome, shirtless, his muscular torso gleaming with sweat. I was so taken by the sight, I didn't register the thoughts running through my brain; yet when I realized I'd been wondering how his skin would feel against mine, I was mortified by their tenor and by the image I presented, leering from behind a bush, and hurried back to camp. Once inside my tent, I had no lingering desire to caress Taylor's bare chest, but the incident was a powerful indicator that some unknown force *was* affecting us: the transitions I'd experienced with Claudia and Nubia had involved the same abrupt mood swings. I tried to analyze my feelings during the homoerotic episode, but was unable to filter out my heterosexual aversion. I took three Benadryl and conked out on my sleeping bag.

I woke before first light, feeling (thanks to a dream in which I was tag-teamed by Claudia and Nubia) more secure in my sexuality. No one else was up and rather than waking them I decided to plumb one of the obvious mysteries of St. Gotthard. Taking a flashlight and a hatchet, I walked over to the Pleasure Dome, intending to break into the basement; but the flashlight failed to dispel the spooky atmosphere of the interior and I sat outside, waiting for sunrise. The sky above the peaks paled to gray, then to rosy pink, and I saw Perdomo moving through the brush alongside the Castle. I thought he was hunting for a place to piss, but he kept going, moving with a peculiar jerky gait, stopping now and again to gaze up at the sky. I lost sight of him and, the sky having lightened further, I went about my business.

Shadows filled the stairwell leading to the basement, but there was sufficient light to work. The wood of the door had swollen and I was unable to force it. I began chopping with the hatchet, the blows loud as gunshots in all that silence, and opened a gash in the upper panel. Foul air rushed out—the door must have been sealed for a very long time. I shined the light through the hole and made out a portion of wall and floor, both of naked rock. I attacked the door with renewed vigor and, after a minute or two, succeeded in creating a gap large enough to slip through. Beyond the door lay a narrow corridor, like an adit in an old mine, angling left and downward. If the Moravians' purpose had been to construct a basement, I wondered why they hadn't excavated the ground directly beneath the Pleasure Dome. By my reckoning, the tunnel was leading me out under the plaza. The air grew fouler as I proceeded. Though it was cold and damp, I stripped off my T-shirt and wrapped it about the lower half of my face. A hundred feet farther along, the corridor opened onto a cavern. The light did not penetrate to the opposite wall, but the scraping of my soles set up reverberations that told me I had entered a vast enclosure.

As I went I swept the light across the ground. Stalagmites bloomed from the darkness like pale, stubby phantoms, the tallest reaching to my waist. The occasional high-pitched cry came to my ears. Bats disturbed by the light. I hated bats. I had gone about seventy or eighty feet when the floor began to slope downward at a steep angle. Pausing, I shined the light ahead. At the bottom of a defile, a scattering of gray sticks was ranged about a fissure in the cavern floor. I had a shriveling feeling in my gut, but continued my approach to within a few yards. Dozens of human skeletons surrounded the fissure, some lying together, one atop the other and in side-by-side embraces, in every manner of sexual attitude. I played my light across the mingled bones. There were more than a hundred skulls, perhaps as many as two hundred. Pieces of jewelry glinted among them, but I could see no evidence of clothing. Assuming they had been here since the late twenties (at the longest), I would have expected to find shreds of fabric; it appeared the Moravians had come naked into the cavern, drawn to the fissure by something within, and died while having sex. Panicking, I lurched back a step, slipped in a declivity and sat down hard. My panic did not lessen, but I knew it would be pointless to run. The thing that had caused this was no longer in the fissure. The Moravians had freed it when they excavated the basement. Now it was loose in St. Gotthard, influencing us, stimulating our sexuality, albeit not to the extent that it had the Moravians. The skeletons spoke to an uncontrollable impulse. They must have been driven into an orgiastic frenzy that superseded the need for nourishment.

I sat by the lip of the fissure, gripped by despair, staring at the skeletons' pitted skulls and intertwined limbs, and realized I was seeing my future, all our futures. Finally I roused myself and made my way back through the cavern, along the corridor, and out onto the steps of the Pleasure Dome. A flotilla of white clouds trawled across the peaks and the leaves in the brush covering the plaza trembled in a breeze, each cupping a glint of sunlight, and the massy crowns of the forest trees… they, too, glittered, trembling as though in joyous agitation. It was possible at that moment to believe that St. Gotthard *was* the most beautiful spot on earth, a landscape whose separate elements enabled a perfect balance between the small and the majestic. Yet no force of beauty could dispel what I had witnessed or discredit what I then believed—however pleasing to the eye was the face presented by the world, the corruption that lay beneath was a truer face, be it the inner awfulness of men and women, or the secrets yielded by a cavern in the Andes.

As I pushed through the bushes on my way to tell the others, I ran across Perdomo lying in my path. I made a detour around him, but then he moaned and struggled to sit up. I asked if he was all right and he stared up at me dumbly.

"Are you all right?" I asked again.

"What… ?" He cast about as if searching for something and then glared at me. "Did you take my rifle?"

"It's back at camp."

He tried to stand and fell back. "*A lo verga!* I feel like shit! How did I get here?"

"Don't you remember?"

"No, I..." He put a hand to his brow.

"What do you remember?"

He didn't answer; I repeated the question.

"The forest," he said. "And those fucking statues. The helicopter."

"You found it?"

Perdomo nodded. "I radioed Merida and told them about Abreu. I said we needed another pilot."

"Are they sending one?"

Another nod.

"When... when are they sending him?"

"Tomorrow or the day after, they said."

"When did you radio them?"

"I'm not sure."

"Was it in the morning? The morning after Doctor Borregales told you to find Captain Abreu?"

"I think... yes."

The sun was nine o'clock high. If the army had sent a helicopter at first light, we might expect it in an hour or two. I wondered what the chances were that they had acted in a timely fashion.

"What else do you remember?" I asked.

"The village. They left a trail that was easy to follow."

"They? The Moravians? You followed their trail and that's where you found the captain?"

Bewildered, Perdomo asked, "How do you know this?"

"You told us. You returned two days ago and said Abreu had dysentery and the Moravians were taking care of him. You don't recall that?"

"Two days! It's not possible."

"What's the last thing you remember?"

Perdomo ran a hand through his hair. "The captain was unconscious, lying in a hammock. In a *casita*. They said they had given him some medicine and he would sleep for hours. Then I went outside and they were waiting. They were naked, men and women both."

"Are you certain they were Moravians?"

"Their skins were dark from the sun, but their faces... they were gringos. There were hundreds of them. They crowded close, telling me how fortunate I was." A frightened look erased his confusion. "Something happened to me!"

"What?"

"I became dizzy." Perdomo put the tips of his fingers to his face, an oddly feminine gesture. "I can't remember."

After three or four more questions, none of which he could answer, I helped him up. Once on his feet, he shook me off and again expressed a desire to be reunited with his rifle. The surly Perdomo had returned, but that didn't relieve my concerns about the smiling Perdomo who had replaced him for two days. I let him lead the way as we crossed the plaza toward camp.

Nubia's tent flap was closed. I called to her and heard movement inside. She poked her head out, buttoning her blouse, squinting in the bright sunlight, and asked what time it was. Before I could answer, Claudia stepped from the tent and, hard on her heels, Macyory. Taylor emerged a moment later, looking rumpled and sheepish.

"Anyone else in there?" I asked. "A couple of dwarves, maybe? Barnyard animals?"

Scowling, Nubia said. "What do you want?"

I told her what I had found in the Pleasure Dome and what Perdomo (sitting cross-legged beside the dead campfire, happy with his rifle) had confided in me. Nubia ordered Taylor to have a look in the cavern.

"You think I'm lying?" I said.

"I think it's wise to verify your findings." She finished buttoning her blouse and went over to Perdomo.

Claudia, with Macyory at her shoulder, asked if there was anything they should do, and I said, "You can tell me what went on last night in Nubia's tent."

"Isn't it obvious?"

"It's obvious you had a foursome. What's not so obvious is how it came about."

She folded her arms and looked at the ground.

"Claudia and Taylor started making out," said Macyory. "We were sitting around talking and they just went at it. And then Nubia joined in."

"Without any preamble?"

"I wanted to kiss him," Claudia said with a touch of defiance. "So I did."

"I thought Nubia would say something," said Macyory. "But instead she kissed Claudia."

"What about you?" I asked.

"I felt hurt," she said. "But then Claudia began kissing me. It was strange, because I know she doesn't like me that way."

A flush came into Claudia's face, but she said nothing.

"Do you remember what happened after that?" I asked. "Was there anything out of the ordinary?"

Macyory hesitated, and I said, "This is no time to be reticent."

"I'm not very experienced, but last night I understood how to please Claudia... and everyone."

When Taylor returned from the Pleasure Dome, we gathered by the Coleman stove and tried to hash things out. We agreed that the most reasonable course of action was to wait for the helicopter, yet we disagreed on every other point. Taylor argued that whatever had killed the Moravians and was affecting us must be environmental, a gas, a poison escaped from the fissure.

Nubia said it was too erratic to be environmental and I said it seemed less erratic than opportunistic, afflicting couples when they were alone... until last night, anyway. Perhaps the fact that it had gone to such extremes, seizing upon four people at once, was evidence that it had grown stronger. Claudia stubbornly refused to admit that anything was out of the ordinary. She argued that the Moravians might have died as the result of poison or gas, but that a natural poison would have dissipated after so many years, and therefore could not have affected us. She added in a snotty tone that I must lead a sheltered life, indeed, to consider a foursome extreme. As to Perdomo's blackout (he kept apart from us, declining to participate in the discussion), Macyory blamed it on some psychological defect. It reminded Nubia, however, of instances of possession such as she had witnessed in Brazil. When I remarked that I'd never heard of a case of possession lasting for two days, she replied that the fact I hadn't heard of it didn't invalidate the notion.

We had been talking for about an hour when Perdomo came over to us, carrying his rifle and pack, and told us he was leaving.

"It's no good here," he said. "I will send another message when I reach the helicopter."

"Remember what happened the last time you went for a walk," I said, and Claudia chimed in, "You're supposed to protect us."

"From what?" Perdomo gestured with his rifle. "From something in the air? A ghost? I have things in here..." He tapped the side of his head. "Things that are not mine."

"What sort of things?" Nubia asked.

"Feelings," he said. "They are not my feelings. I can't sit here and do nothing."

Nubia asked him to explain what he meant by "not my feelings," but Perdomo clammed up. She urged him to stay one night more, saying that he couldn't run from his thoughts and there were things he could do here to keep busy. He could investigate the tower, for starters. She employed her wiles and Perdomo relented. He took my hatchet and headed for the tower, while Nubia went off to the Pleasure Dome to inspect the skeletons. The rest of us remained sitting, eyeing each other as if wary of a sudden sexual attack.

THAT NIGHT THERE were clouds and a sprinkling of stars, but a lopsided moon sailed clear of them, casting a cold ivory brilliance over St. Gotthard, a ghastly form of daylight that imbued the ruins with a splendor they did not deserve. Painted with moonlight, the scene lost its aura of a seedy Las Vegas—the buildings might have been relics of an ancient civilization that had aspired to nobility yet fell before its aspirations could be achieved. The Castle, its grandiose façade simplified by moon shadow, seemed the eidolon of the principle upon which that civilization was founded. Etched sharply in the windless air, the brush looked like intricate black sculpture; the round-ed shapes of our tents glowed whitely like the eggs of a mythological creature half-buried in the earth.

I kept watch, comforted by the fire's conversational crackling. Everyone else was in their tents, even Perdomo. His exploration of the tower had unearthed nothing of value, proving that sometimes a locked door is mere-ly a locked door. He lent me his rifle and taught me how to operate the safety and went to bed. I sat with it across my knees, but before long I set it on the ground—holding it made me edgy. I took solace from the thick Andean silence, but my mind wouldn't settle, flying from anxiety to anxi-ety. When Nubia came out of her tent, dragging her sleeping bag, I was relieved to have company. The ruddy light scrubbed the lines from her face, and her physical attitude, sitting with hands held above the fire, her hair tied back, made me think of a stoic young priestess coaxing a spirit forth from the flames. After an awkward silence she said, "I'm truly sorry about what I did to you."

"It's okay," I said, surprised to hear those words issue from my mouth. She must have been surprised as well; she looked at me askance and said, "Are you forgiving me?"

"It's not a question of forgiveness. Maybe it's just I had a chance to say some things. I—" I shook my head. "I'm all talked out, okay."

"You said some things that were hard to bear. You were entitled to say them, but they were harsh."

"They wouldn't have been as harsh if I'd had the opportunity to say them years ago."

She started to respond, but I cut in. "We've both said harsh things. Maybe we should be satisfied with this much progress and move on from here."

"If that's what you want." She pulled the sleeping bag up around her knees. Sap popped in the fire. "I've been reconfiguring my ideas about the book."

"You still think there's a book in this?"

"We can't be certain about anything we've learned, so it can't be a book with any scholarly pretensions. Maybe a novel."

"A novel? I don't see it."

"The other day you were saying Remarque must have been fixated on some connection between Eros and terror. It got me thinking about the Greek and Roman cults of Eros."

"I don't remember telling you that."

"You did... right before you went off on me. Anyway, there was a lot of kinky stuff attaching to those cults. We might take the tack that Eros wasn't a god, but a life form. A parasite with the power to enhance the human biological impulse. Or to increase suggestibility. People think about sex all the time, so increased sexual activity would be one of its main effects."

"You're crazy if you believe people would read a novel based on that premise."

"Sex sells."

"Maybe," I said. "But if this parasite did to the world what it did to the Moravians, there wouldn't be any world left."

"Not necessarily. We have Perdomo's testimony, dubious as it is, that some of them survived. Suppose the parasites were actually symbiotes and they were dying out because of advances in medicine or something in our diet that made us resistant. The only place they could survive were backwaters where those advances weren't in play. Some became trapped in a cave in St. Gotthard and went dormant. When the Moravians tunneled into the cave and set them free, they were desperate for the sustenance we provide and they went too far. Once they'd replenished themselves, they sustained the remainder of the colony."

"Wouldn't the Moravians be immune?"

"We could cover that by saying they were only partly immunized against the parasite... the symbiotes. In the 1860s when the Moravians came to St. Gotthard, pasteurization was just becoming widespread. We can use something like that. We can say the Moravians had developed partial immunities that didn't kill the symbiotes, but made them ill. They adapted. They mutated. When we happened along, they had a similar problem with our more complete immunities, and now they're adapting to them. That would explain why they've been slow to affect us. It's a pulpy idea, but we can ground it in our relationship and throw in historical detail to de-emphasize the pulp elements."

"I doubt I could pull off a novel."

"Remember the comments I made on your papers at Miami? 'Cut back on the purple prose.' With a novel, the purpler the better, at least in certain passages."

We discussed it some more, refining the concept, tailoring it to fit the facts as we knew them, sometimes tailoring the facts, and then she said, "Mind if I sleep here? You can wake me in an hour or two and I'll stand watch."

"Yeah, all right."

"You don't sound sure."

I saw in my mind's eye the skeletons in the cavern, the desolate product of an inhuman passion. It did no good to think about it.

"Jon?"

"Go on, get some sleep."

She snuggled deeper into the sleeping bag and turned on her side. Soon her breathing grew deep and regular. The rhythms of her breath lulled me and I sat up straight and attempted to focus on practical matters. What we would do if the helicopter failed to arrive? If Perdomo left it might be best to leave with him. Staying in St. Gotthard offered no security. Nubia stirred and murmured something. I remembered that she talked in her sleep and I pricked up my ears; but she said no more.

I must have dozed off, for I heard a voice repeating my name and sat up, confused and bleary-eyed. Nubia stared past my shoulder, her mouth open. Following the direction of her gaze, I saw three figures on the opposite side of the fire, two youngish women and a bald man who, judging by his unkempt gray beard, was in his fifties. Painted by the flickering light, they were naked and in poor physical condition, filthy and covered with insect bites, scarcely recognizable as human beings, more like mangy animals drawn to our fire. The women were slack-breasted and severely under-weight; their hair was matted and the taller woman's pubic hair overgrew portions of her thighs and belly. Their skins showed brick red yet, as Per-domo testified, their haggard faces were Caucasian. They carried no weapons, but I scrambled up, snagged a burning branch from the fire and swung it menacingly, sending a trail of sparks through the air.

"We mean you no harm," said the taller of the women in Spanish.

I was not reassured. Remembering the rifle, I started to reach for it, but Nubia restrained me.

"You are of St. Gotthard?" she asked.

"No longer," said the man. "We are of Kirikh'quru."

"Kirikh'quru Krokundor?"

In ragged unison, the two women echoed Nubia, as if the words were part of a litany.

"Indeed." The man smiled, revealing a mouth half-full of rotten teeth

"Why did you hide from us?" I asked.

The woman who had spoken previously said, "We had business to attend." And her sister, who was wider-hipped, a dirty blonde, said, "We've been waiting for this moment."

The man farted, continuing to smile.

Over their heads I thought I saw opaque shapes whirling against the moonstruck façade of the Castle—they were gone before I could be certain of them.

"Come back tomorrow when we're less tired," I said.

"No," said Nubia. "Please, sit. I have so many questions."

"Be patient," said the man, and the blonde woman said, "First we must bear witness."

"Bear witness to what?" Nubia asked.

"A miracle!"

The leering relish with which she said this alarmed me. I snatched up the rifle and trained it on them.

"Jon!" Nubia attempted to shove the barrel aside, but I fended her off.

"I don't trust their fucking miracle," I said, and thumbed back the safety.

I don't remember falling. The next I knew, I was gazing up at the pitted ivory moon, feeling drugged and sluggish. A drum was beating close by and I realized it was my heart. There were other sounds, but I couldn't unscram-ble them. An instant before I lost consciousness, I had the intimation of an androgynous, childlike face, similar to one Claudia had assembled on the floor of the Castle. I didn't see it, not exactly, but seemed to know its lineaments like those of my own face.

When I regained my senses, the sun was high and I was naked, lying closer to the tents than where I had fallen. My vision rippled. With an effort, I propped myself on an elbow. Nubia, also unclothed, stood nearby, her arms folded, watching Macyory and Claudia fondling and licking the tall woman, squirming in the dirt between her legs like animals, and Perdomo… he was engaged with the blond woman while the bearded man was attempting to penetrate him from behind. Together they made a blithering, grunting stew of sound that disoriented me further. I couldn't gather it all in. Unsteady, I leveraged myself into a sitting position and saw Taylor lying by the entrance to Nubia's tent. I crawled over to him. He wasn't breathing, his mouth was open, and a faint cloudiness showed in his eyes. There was no blood, no apparent wound, but I knew he was dead.

A sense of detachment gripped me, suppressing any emotional reaction I might have had. An ant emerged from the thatch of his hair. I watched with interest, tracking its progress across his forehead and cheek, wondering whether it would enter his mouth. Then a hand clutched my shoulder. The tall woman kneeled beside me, pressing her breasts against my arm. Her smell was gamey and overripe, her smile a horrid display of inflamed gums and discolored teeth tilted like gravestones in soft earth. Yet when she pressed my hand between her furred thighs, I wanted her… though wanted is too tame a word for the overpowering lust that caused me to push her down beside Taylor's corpse and mount her.

When I make love to my wife nowadays, that memory will at times surface from the urgency of the act, and I will turn from her and lie with both hands clasped to my head, trying to squeeze it out as though it were an abscess. I have many memories of that day (I had sex with everyone at the campsite, with multiple partners) yet none so degrading as that one. The tall woman and I bucked and humped, bumping into Taylor's corpse, rolling atop it, our hands brushing his skin, locking in his hair, as though engaged in a grotesque ménage a trois. She grimaced beneath me, grating noises issued from her throat, and her legs spasmed and stiffened, banging against my sides like shutters loose in a gale. I pinned her by the throat to stop her from smiling, yet the smile remained undimmed.

Zombie-fucking. That was how the hours passed. I was mindful of nothing but the flesh. Later that afternoon, I was sharing Macyory with Perdomo when I heard the beat of helicopter rotors. I knew what this signaled, but I continued battering away at Macyory until a soldier pulled me away. I tried to climb atop her again and he knocked me aside. Surrendering to exhaustion, I watched soldiers separating the bearded man, Claudia and the Moravian women. They shouted, shoving the Moravians to one side, and posted a guard over them. Others provided blankets. I didn't notice the cold until a blanket was draped across my shoulders, and then I sat shivering and miserable. People said things to me that I couldn't understand—it was as if they were speaking in ape or ocelot—and ordinary objects had no meaning. I could not have told you the function of a cooking pot or a comb. I crossed glances with Macyory and we both quickly looked away—I supposed she felt, as did I, traumatized, caught between shame and lust. Claudia, her head bowed, appeared to have dwindled under her blanket to the size of a child. Only Nubia seemed to have survived unscathed. She was talking with an officer who squatted beside her, displaying no hesitancy in manner, no sign of trauma; yet when she stood and walked with him, she was stiff-legged and faltered more than once, having to grasp his arm for support.

The soldiers cleared brush, enough for the helicopter (a Chinook identical to the one that had brought us) to land. Once our party was aboard, it lifted off and a second helicopter settled to the ground, discharging more soldiers. I saw them moving into the brush surrounding the campsite, and then we were too high, angling north away from St. Gotthard. Through the side window I had a final glimpse of the buildings rising above the forest, saw the great glass dome glinting orange with the late sun and the spires of the Castle afire in that glow, regaining a purity and nobility that was never truly theirs. And then they were gone. I leaned back and closed my eyes, receding into a dim, enervated state. When I opened them again I saw Nubia staring at me fixedly. I thought she was seeing through me, beyond me, to some interior place, but then she wetted her lips and seemed to focus and smiled. I at first took strength from that smile, but it stuck on her face, unwavering, reminding me of the Moravian woman's smile, and I turned my face to the wall, finding in the dull green metal a solace she could not offer.

WHAT HAPPENED IN St. Gotthard had so circumstantial a character or, to use Nubia's word, allusive, it's tempting to accept the explanation given by the Venezuelan government: an unknown environmental agent caused both the Moravians and our party to experience delirium. There is no way of testing this theory, however. The buildings in St. Gotthard were demolished by aerial bombardment, access to the valley is prohibited, and the Moravians have been relocated. In Latin America, "relocation" is sometimes a euphemism for a more sinister fate, and investigations by various human rights organizations (prodded into action by Taylor's parents and the Interprovincial Board of the Moravian Church) failed to disclose the site of their new village. Captain Abreu and Sergeant Perdomo have apparently been "relocated" as well, for nothing has been heard from them since. As for the rest of us, we were flown to Merida, interrogated, and returned to our places of residence. That we were not "relocated" is due, I understand, to the influence of Nubia's family. The government's decisive and, it would seem, brutal resolution of the incident is typical of governments everywhere in reaction to a perceived threat; yet I cannot grasp what threat they perceived. Perhaps they believed that they could utilize the "environmental agent" as a weapon, or perhaps... I don't know. It may reflect their general policy toward all unfathomable things.

I tried to contact the others, seeking their interpretation of the events. Macyory and Claudia would not speak to me, and when I called Nubia's parents at their home in Merida, where she was recuperating, she, too, refused; but her father got on the phone and told me that he was concerned by Nubia's mental state, saying she acted cold and distracted much of the time. I told him not to worry, it would pass, and kept to myself the fact that I had similar moods.

I settled back into my routine at Portland State and, with the passage of time, managed more-or-less to put St. Gotthard from mind, though I continued to have moments when I felt aloof from the world, and experienced fugues that my girlfriend (soon to be my wife) described as being periods during which I "went away." In spite of these passages, I enjoyed my work, I married, I began to thrive. Four years after my return, as I browsed the new releases in Powell's Books, one of the book jackets jumped out at me. Superimposed on a black backdrop was a partially reconstructed face of white marble, the same androgynous, elfin face (or its duplicate) that Claudia had assembled on the floor of the Castle. The book was called *The Shattered Face* and the author was Dr. Nubia Borregales. A card was taped to the shelf beneath the book, announcing that Dr. Borregales would be signing at Powell's on Thursday following her lecture at Lincoln Hall.

I bought a copy and, skimming it in my office, was startled to discover that the basis of the book was our conversation about the novel we proposed to write. It followed our basic blueprint—a symbiotic life form (the kro'kundor) that stimulated human sexuality for its own ends had emerged from a cavern in St. Gotthard. Yet there were two salient differences. Nubia conceived of the symbiotes as being the living tools of a dominant entity, a powerful and perhaps immortal creature, an Eros-type figure, whom she called the Child and whom the Moravians had called Kirikh'quru. The kro'kundor acted as an interface that enabled Kirikh'quru to connect with humanity, serving as amplifiers of his will. The second difference was that the book was not a novel. It purported to be a record of Nubia's interaction with the Child. She claimed that the Child had possessed her and now spoke through her. With typical exuberance, the jacket copy labeled her "a true prophet of the Third Millennium." A temple devoted to her teachings on sexual health had been built in the Dominican Republic.

I had made a concerted effort to sever my ties with Nubia, to reject those shreds of our relationship that had survived the expedition, and I had been aware of none of this. Upon reflection, I realized her evolution from pop historian/archaeologist to New Age guru was a natural progression, the perfect culmination of her character arc. I searched for more details on the

Internet and came across an article on New Age cults that mentioned Nubia and reported on disturbing rumors concerning her temple in the DR, rumors of disappearances and orgiastic rites that resulted in bloodshed. I discounted the article—misinformation is the chief currency of the Internet—yet I could not discount it entirely. Taylor's death had been in no way allusive.

Thursday afternoon, I sat in the rear of the hall and watched Nubia's performance. It was patently a performance. Dressed in dark brown slacks and a silk blouse; her face transformed by dramatic make-up into the semblance of a Hindu queen; she paced the stage like a rock star for over two hours, microphone in hand, delivering an impassioned plea for (so I understood it after deciphering her quasi-intellectual twaddle) more and better fucking, occasionally lapsing into a trance during which her body language became stiff and awkward, and she spoke in a raspy voice, disgorging messages from the Child. A bulky man trailed behind her, ready to catch her should she swoon, as sometimes happened after these possessions. The audience, composed in the main of suburban housewives, with a smattering of gays and college-age heterosexuals (and a group of hecklers who were quickly ushered out), laughed at Nubia's jokes, kept a respectful silence when the Child held the floor, and burst into prolonged applause at the end. Nubia stood center-stage, arms upraised, eyes closed, as though she were absorbing a beatific energy.

I waited until the crowd around her thinned before making an approach and caught her as she was leaving through a side exit, shouldering aside her publicist, a young guy wearing a black shirt and slacks who sought to shield her from me by interposing his body. The mask of make-up couldn't disguise signs of fatigue, but all in all she looked the same as when she had visited me in my office. This time there was no embrace.

"I wondered if you'd come," she said.

"Wouldn't have missed it for the world." I held the door for her and followed her out into the late afternoon sun. "It was more entertaining than Cirque du Soleil."

A half-smile. "Is there some place close where we can get a drink?"

The publicist murmured something about the signing.

"We have almost two hours!" she snapped. "I'll be there!"

I led her away from the remaining autograph seekers and we drove to the Virginia Café, a downtown bar with a woodsy ambiance not far from Powell's and, at that hour, hosting a mere handful of customers. We sat in a booth near the front. A waitress with multiple piercings brought our drinks. Nubia tapped my ring finger and asked if I were truly married or if the ring was just to ward off co-eds.

"It takes more than that," I said. "Some are quite determined. Resisting them requires moral rectitude."

She laughed, a slight, ridiculing laugh.

"I resisted you in St. Gotthard," I said. "That's the gold standard of resistance."

A puzzled expression crossed her face and then, amused, she said, "Of course! You wouldn't remember. You were with the Child."

"Don't start that crap with me!"

"You don't believe me? That's why I wouldn't talk to you when you called at my parents'. I thought you wanted to get back together."

"Why would I want that? What reason would I have? According to you, I have no memory of us fucking."

I must have spoken loudly—a man at the bar turned to stare at us.

"You have to understand," Nubia said. "I was confused when I got back to Merida. It took me a long time to grasp what was going on."

"You're talking about the Child now? Your imaginary friend confused you?"

"Let's just drop it."

"No, please. I want to hear."

She concentrated on setting down her glass so that it fit precisely to the circle of moisture it had made on the table. "The Child passed from you to me while we were making love..."

"It's been a decade since we made love."

"Very well. While we were fucking!"

The man at the bar stared again, as did the bartender.

"What exactly is the Child?" I asked. "I'm not saying I'll believe you, but for the record what is it? You skate around the topic in the book. You give a lot of embellishment but not much substance."

"I don't know what it is. Over the years I've picked up a few things. It's old... and empty. And it wants adoration. It demands celebrants, people having sex to celebrate its presence. But I don't understand why. I have the idea it's frivolous, that sex is just something it likes." She paused. "It's intelligent, but I think its memory is failing. It may be senile."

"How do you know that? I assume it knocks you out of the driver's seat when it takes over."

"I get bursts of memory that aren't mine. I see people... short, with Mediterranean features and complexions. Ancient cities and buildings, only the colors are bright and there's no sign of age or decay. But it doesn't appear to retain any recent memories. The Moravians, for example. It doesn't have many memories of them. Just tatters." She fingered the rim of her glass. "At any rate, I've seen enough to know that Eros was no god, not as we imagine gods."

"I've read your speculations."

"They're not speculations."

"Aren't you ashamed? Peddling this garbage... hustling fools. Does money mean that much to you?"

"Do you think I enjoy this?" She slapped the table, rattling the glasses. "I don't have a choice! I told you it wants celebrants. This is how it goes about getting them. It likes me. I suit it. Literally. It wears me like a goddamn suit whenever it wants." Anger emptied from her face and she lowered her head, fussing with a cocktail napkin. "It tried everyone else first. Macyory, Claudia... It killed Taylor. That happens sometimes. There's some kind of incompatibility and they die." She tore a strip off the napkin. "It's always close to me. If I make a move it doesn't like, it takes control."

Her rapid shifts in mood, from amused to ruminative to angry to depressed... I thought them evidence of mental difficulty or very bad acting. She had always been the cause of my troubles, the source of my delirium, and whatever her condition I wanted no more to do with her. I had a sudden desire for my wife's company. I pulled out my wallet and dropped a twenty on the table.

"Maybe one day it'll find somebody it likes better," she said. "That's all I can hope for. I hope it's soon, because if it isn't... there'll be nothing left of me. It's corroding me, erasing me."

I slid out of the booth.

She asked, "What are you doing?"

"Leaving."

"Don't!" She caught at my sleeve. "Stay a little longer. It's so rare I get the chance to talk to anyone."

"Either you're insane or you're a criminal," I said. "Maybe you're both. I don't propose to waste time figuring it out."

I started for the door and she seized my wrist. Her face was no longer distraught, but calm. Something seemed to stir inside my skull. Confused by that sensation, I shook her off and made for the street. Outside, amid the clamor of traffic and the voices of passers-by, I hesitated, held in place by our old connection—but its hold had weakened. I strode toward the parking structure where I had left the car.

"Jon!"

Nubia's voice was raspy, strained, as if it had taken a supreme effort to produce that single syllable. She stood in front of the bar and, though she was about thirty feet distant, I felt her as if she were beside me, a cold, aloof presence spearing me with dagger eyes. She came forward, one stiff-legged, halting step, then another. I glanced overhead, half-expecting to see opaque shapes flurrying. She took a third step, braced with a hand against the building, and I fled, not running, but walking fast, desperate to get away from her, whatever she was, Eros incarnate or a lesser form of affliction. At the corner I turned back. Nubia had fallen and several pedestrians had closed in about her. A man in a gray T-shirt stooped and took her elbow, preparing to help her stand.

In the parking structure I sat in the car, my hand on the ignition, trying to find some clue, some lie or misstep that would prove the matter one way or the other. It was possible that Nubia was the ultimate victim of St. Gotthard and in need of rescue, but every element of her story was unbelievable, and that it was *our* story, *our* invention, made it more so... though even that could be explained away by the supranatural influence of the Child. I switched on the engine, listened to it idle, staring at the designation of the parking slot on the grimy cement wall: B-8. Bingo, I thought. Now what? Shrill laughter echoed behind me—a couple walking to their car. Minutes ticked by. My cell played a dervish snatch of Elvis Costello, a speeded-up version of "Watching The Detectives." It was my wife, asking if I wanted to pick up a movie and some take-out from the Indian place. I said I would and was cheered, knowing I would soon be drowned in the extraordinary illusion of ordinary comforts.

"How was the lecture?" she asked.

"What you'd expect. We had a drink afterward. It was..." I searched for words to describe the encounter. "Pretty terrible. Sad. She's gone now."

After a silence she said, "Where are you?"

"Parking structure."

"You okay?"

"Yeah, I just... I still can't work it out. I thought talking to her would help, but it didn't. It..." I made a frustrated noise.

"How long have you been there? In the parking structure?"

"Not long, I don't think." I looked at my watch, but could make no sense of the dial. "I don't know."

"Jon?"

I felt exhausted and dazed and frail, as I had when the soldiers rescued us from St. Gotthard. Staring at the watch, dazzling gold and crystal, an incomprehensible thing, brought tears to my eyes. "I don't know."

"Jon," my wife said firmly. "Come home."

POE'S "THE DOMAIN *of Arnheim*" *concerns a wealthy man who spends a good portion of his life searching for the most beautiful place on earth. It strikes me as a fragmentary work, since it merely states this as fact, gives a slender bit of character development, and then describes the place he found and how he developed it. I was intrigued by its incompleteness and I wondered what such a place would be like today after years of human occupation. What would be left and how would the place be used? I wondered, too, if a wealthy man who spent so much time and money on such a trivial aim could have a good character. Poe paints him as a dilettante, a lover of beauty, but to my mind such a man would be indulgent at the least, and it was more likely that his indulgence, when magnified by wealth and eroded by small-mindedness, would veer into the perverse.*

Suzy McKee Charnas is a born and raised New Yorker. After two years in Nigeria with the Peace Corps, she taught in private school in New York and then worked with a high school drug-abuse treatment program. In 1969 she married and moved to New Mexico, where she began writing fiction full-time.

Her first novel, *Walk to the End of the World*, was a Campbell award finalist. The cycle of four books that sprang from *Walk* ended in 1999 with *The Conqueror's Child*, which won the James P. Tiptree Award. Her SF and fantasy books and stories have also won the Hugo award, the Nebula award, and the Mythopoeic award for young-adult fantasy. Her play *Vampire Dreams* has been staged several times, and a collection of her stories and essays, *Stagestruck Vampires*, was published in 2004.

She lectures and teaches about SF, fantasy, and vampires whenever she gets the chance to, most recently in a writing workshop at the University of New Mexico. Her website is at www.suzymckeecharnas.com

LOWLAND SEA

by Suzy McKee Charnas

MIRIAM HAD BEEN to Cannes twice before. The rush and glamour of the film festival had not long held her attention (she did not care for movies and knew the real nature of the people who made them too well for that magic to work), but from the windows of their festival hotel she could look out over the sea and daydream about sailing home, one boat against the inbound tide from northern Africa.

This was a foolish dream; no one went to Africa now—no one could be paid enough to go, not while the Red Sweat raged there (the film festival itself had been postponed this year till the end of summer on account of the epidemic). She'd read that vessels wallowing in from the south laden with refugees were regularly shot apart well offshore by European military boats, and the beaches were not only still closed but were closely patrolled for lucky swimmers, who were also disposed of on the spot.

Just foolish, really, not even a dream that her imagination could support beyond its opening scene. Supposing that she could survive long enough to actually make it home (and she knew she was a champion survivor), nothing would be left of her village, just as nothing, or very close to nothing, was left to her of her childhood self. It was eight years since she had been taken.

Bad years; until Victor had bought her. Her clan tattoos had caught his attention. Later, he had had them reproduced, in make-up, for his film, *Hearts of Light* (it was about African child-soldiers rallied by a brave, warm-hearted American adventurer—played by Victor himself—against Islamic terrorists).

She understood that he had been seduced by the righteous outlawry of buying a slave in the modern world—to free her, of course; it made him feel bold and virtuous. In fact, Victor was accustomed to buying people. Just since Miriam had known him, he had paid two Russian women to carry babies for him because his fourth wife was barren. He already had children but, edging toward sixty, he wanted new evidence of his potency.

Miriam was not surprised. Her own father had no doubt used the money he had been paid for her to buy yet another young wife to warm his cooling bed; that was a man's way. He was probably dead now or living in a refugee camp somewhere, along with all the sisters and brothers and aunties from his compound: wars, the Red Sweat, and fighting over the scraps would leave little behind.

She held no grudge: she had come to realize that her father had done her a favor by selling her. She had seen a young cousin driven away for witchcraft by his own father, after a newborn baby brother had sickened and died. A desperate family could thus be quickly rid of a mouth they could not feed.

Better still, Miriam had not yet undergone the ordeal of female circumcision when she was taken away. At first she had feared that it was for this reason that the men who bought her kept selling her on to others. But she had learned that this was just luck, in all its perverse strangeness, pressing her life into some sort of shape. Not a very good shape after her departure from home, but then good luck came again in the person of Victor, whose bed she had warmed till he grew tired of her. Then he hired her to care for his new babies, Kevin and Leif.

Twins were unlucky back home: there, one or both would immediately have been put out in the bush to die. But this, like so many other things, was different for all but the poorest of whites.

They were pretty babies; Kevin was a little fussy but full of lively energy and alertness that Miriam rejoiced to see. Victor's actress wife, Cameron, had no use for the boys (they were not hers, after all, not as these people reckoned such things). She had gladly left to Miriam the job of tending to them.

Not long afterward Victor had bought Krista, an Eastern European girl, who doted extravagantly on the two little boys and quickly took over their care. Victor hated to turn people out of his household (he thought of himself as a magnanimous man), so his chief assistant, Bulgarian Bob, found a way to keep Miriam on. He gave her a neat little digital camera with which to keep a snapshot record of Victor's home life: she was to be a sort of documentarian of the domestic. It was Bulgarian Bob (as opposed to French Bob, Victor's head driver) who had noticed her interest in taking pictures during an early shoot of the twins.

B. Bob was like that: he noticed things, and he attended to them.

Miriam felt blessed. She knew herself to be plain next to the diet-sculpted, spa-pampered, surgery-perfected women in Victor's household, so she could hardly count on beauty to secure protection; nor had she any outstanding talent of the kind that these people valued. But with a camera like this Canon G9, you needed no special gift to take attractive family snapshots. It was certainly better than, say, becoming someone's lowly third wife, or being bonded for life to a wrinkled shrine-priest back home.

Krista said that B. Bob had been a gangster in Prague. This was certainly possible. Some men had a magic that could change them from any one thing into anything else: the magic was money. Victor's money had changed Miriam's status from that of an illegal slave to, of all wonderful things, that of a naturalized citizen of the U.S.A. (although whether her new papers could stand serious scrutiny she hoped never to have to find out). Thus she was cut off from her roots, floating in Victor's world.

Better not to think of that, though; better not to think painful thoughts.

Krista understood this (she understood a great deal without a lot of palaver). Yet Krista obstinately maintained a little shrine made of old photos, letters, and trinkets that she set up in a private corner wherever Victor's household went. Despite a grim period in Dutch and Belgian brothels, she retained a sweet naiveté. Miriam hoped that no bad luck would rub off on Krista from attending to the twins. Krista was an *East* European, which seemed to render a female person more than normally vulnerable to ill fortune.

Miriam had helped Krista to fit in with the others who surrounded Victor—the coaches, personal shoppers, arrangers, designers, bodyguards, publicists, therapists, drivers, cooks, secretaries, and hangers-on of all kinds. He was like a paramount chief with a great crowd of praise singers paid to flatter him, outshouting similar mobs attending everyone significant in the film world. This world was little different from the worlds of Africa and Arabia that Miriam had known, although at first it had seemed frighteningly strange—so shiny, so fast-moving and raucous! But when you came right down to it here were the same swaggering, self-indulgent older men fighting off their younger competitors, and the same pretty girls they all sniffed after; and the lesser court folk, of course, including almost-invisible functionaries like Krista and Miriam.

One day, Miriam planned to leave. Her carefully tended savings were nothing compared to the fortunes these shiny people hoarded, wasted, and squabbled over; but she had almost enough for a quiet, comfortable life in some quiet, comfortable place. She knew how to live modestly and thought she might even sell some of her photographs once she left Victor's orbit.

It wasn't as if she yearned to run to one of the handsome African men she saw selling knock-off designer handbags and watches on the sidewalks of great European cities. Sometimes, at the sound of a familiar language from home, she imagined joining them—but those were poor men, always on the run from the local law. She could not give such a man power over her and her savings.

Not that having money made the world perfect: Miriam was a realist, like any survivor. She found it funny that, even for Victor's followers with their light minds and heavy pockets, contentment was not to be bought. Success itself eluded them, since they continually redefined it as that which they had not yet achieved.

Victor, for instance: the one thing he longed for but could not attain was praise for his film—his first effort as an actor–director.

"They hate me!" he cried, crushing another bad review and flinging it across the front room of their hotel suite, "because I have the balls to tackle grim reality! All they want is sex, explosions, and the new Brad Pitt! Anything but truth; they can't stand truth!"

Of course they couldn't stand it. No one could. Truth was the desperate lives of most ordinary people, lives often too hard to be borne; mere images on a screen could not make that an attractive spectacle. Miriam had known boys back home who thought they were "Rambo." Some had become killers, some had been become the killed: doped-up boys, slung about with guns and bullet-belts like carved fetish figures draped in strings of shells. Their short lives were not in the movies or like the movies.

On this subject as many others, however, Miriam kept her opinions to herself.

Hearts of Light was scorned at Cannes. Victor's current wife, Cameron, fled in tears from his sulks and rages. She stayed away for days, drowning her unhappiness at parties and pools and receptions.

Wealth, however, did have certain indispensable uses. Some years before Miriam had joined his household, Victor had bought the one thing that turned out to be essential: a white-walled mansion called La Bastide, set high on the side of a French valley only a day's drive from Cannes. This was to be his retreat from the chaos and crushing boredom of the cinema world, a place where he could recharge his creative energies (so said B. Bob).

When news came that three Sudanese had been found dead in Calabria, their skins crusted with a cracked glaze of blood, Victor had his six rented Mercedes loaded up with petrol and provisions. They drove out of Cannes before the next dawn. It had been hot on the Mediterranean shore. Inland was worse. Stubby planes droned across the sky trailing plumes of retardant and water that they dropped on fires in the hills.

Victor stood in the sunny courtyard of La Bastide and told everyone how lucky they were to have gotten away to this refuge before the road from Cannes became clogged with people fleeing the unnerving proximity of the Red Sweat.

"There's room for all of us here," he said (Miriam snapped pictures of his confident stance and broad, chiefly gestures). "Better yet, we're prepared and we're *safe*. These walls are thick and strong. I've got a rack of guns downstairs, and we know how to use them. We have plenty of food, and all the water we could want: a spring in the bedrock underneath us feeds sweet, clean water into a well right here inside the walls. And since I didn't have to store water, we have lots more of everything else!"

Oh, the drama; already, Miriam told Krista, he was making the movie of all this in his head.

Nor was he the only one. As the others went off to the quarters B. Bob assigned them, trailing an excited hubbub through the cool, shadowed spaces of the house, those who had brought their camcorders dug them out and began filming on the spot. Victor encouraged them, saying that this adventure must be recorded, that it would be a triumph of photojournalism for the future.

Privately he told Miriam, "It's just to keep them busy. I depend on your stills to capture the reality of all this. We'll have an exhibition later, maybe even a book. You've got a good eye, Miriam; and you've had experience with crisis in your part of the world, right?"

"La Bastide" meant "the country house" but the place seemed more imposing than that, standing tall, pale, and alone on a crag above the valley. The outer walls were thick, with stout wooden doors and window-shutters as Victor had pointed out. He had had a wing added on to the back in matching stone. A small courtyard, the one containing the well, was enclosed by walls between the old and new buildings. Upstairs rooms had tall windows and sturdy iron balconies; those on the south side overlooked a French village three kilometers away down the valley.

Everyone had work to do—scripts to read, write, or revise, phone calls to make and take, deals to work out—but inevitably they drifted into the ground floor salon, the room with the biggest flat-screen TV. The TV stayed on. It showed raging wildfires. Any place could burn in summer, and it was summer most of the year now in southern Europe.

But most of the news was about the Red Sweat. Agitated people pointed and shouted, their expressions taut with urgency: "Looters came yesterday. Where are the police, the authorities?"

"We scour buildings for batteries, matches, canned goods."

"What can we do? They left us behind because we are old."

"We hear cats and dogs crying, shut in with no food or water. We let the cats out, but we are afraid of the dogs; packs already roam the streets."

Pictures showed bodies covered with crumpled sheets, curtains, bedspreads in many colors, laid out on sidewalks and in improvised morgues—the floors of school gyms, of churches, of automobile showrooms.

My God, they said, staring at the screen with wide eyes. Northern Italy now! So *close*!

Men carrying guns walked through deserted streets wearing bulky, outlandish protective clothing and face masks. Trucks loaded with relief supplies waited for roads to become passable; survivors mobbed the trucks when they arrived. Dead creatures washed up on shorelines, some human, some not. Men in robes, suits, turbans, military uniforms, talked and talked and talked into microphones, reassuring, begging, accusing, weeping.

All this had been building for months, of course, but everyone in Cannes had been too busy to pay much attention. Even now at La Bastide they seldom talked about the news. They talked about movies. It was easier.

Miriam watched TV a lot. Sometimes she took pictures of the screen images. The only thing that could make her look away was a shot of an uncovered body, dead or soon to be so, with a film of blood dulling the skin.

On Victor's orders, they all ate in the smaller salon, without a TV.

On the third night, Krista asked, "What will we eat when this is all gone?"

"I got boxes of that paté months ago." Bulgarian Bob smiled and stood back with his arms folded, like a waiter in a posh restaurant. "Don't worry, there's plenty more."

"My man," said Victor, digging into his smoked Norwegian salmon.

Next day, taking their breakfast coffee out on the terrace, they saw military vehicles grinding past on the roadway below. Relief convoys were being intercepted now, the news had said, attacked and looted.

"Don't worry, little Mi," B. Bob said, as she took snaps of the camouflage-painted trucks from the terrace. "Victor bought this place and fixed it up in the Iranian crisis. He thought we had more war coming. We're set for a year, two years."

Miriam grimaced. "Where food was stored in my country, that is where gunmen came to steal," she said.

B. Bob took her on a tour of the marvelous security at La Bastide, all controlled from a complicated computer console in the master suite: the heavy steel-mesh gates that could be slammed down, the metal window shutters, the ventilation ducts with their electrified outside grilles.

"But if the electricity goes off?" she asked.

He smiled. "We have our own generators here."

After dinner that night Walter entertained them. Hired as Victor's Tae Kwan Do coach, he turned out to be a conservatory-trained baritone.

"No more opera," Victor said, waving away an aria. "Old country songs for an old country house. Give us some ballads, Walter!"

Walter sang "Parsley Sage," "Barbara Ellen," and "The Golden Vanity."

This last made Miriam's eyes smart. It told of a young cabin boy who volunteered to swim from an outgunned warship to the enemy vessel and sink it, single-handed, with an augur; but his Captain would not to let him back on board afterward. Rather than hole that ship too and so drown not just the evil Captain but his own innocent shipmates, the cabin boy drowned himself: "He sank into the lowland, low and lonesome, sank into the lowland sea."

Victor applauded. "Great, Walter, thanks! You're off the hook now, that's enough gloom and doom. Tragedy tomorrow—*comedy* tonight!"

They followed him into the library, which had been fitted out with a big movie screen and computers with game consoles. They settled down to watch Marx Brothers movies and old romantic comedies from the extensive film library of La Bastide. The bodyguards stayed up late, playing computer games full of mayhem. They grinned for Miriam's camera lens.

In the hot and hazy afternoon next day, a green mini-Hummer appeared on the highway. Miriam and Krista, bored by a general discussion about which gangster movie had the most swear words, were sitting on the terrace painting each other's toenails. The Hummer turned off the roadway, came up the hill, and stopped at La Bastide's front gates. A man in jeans, sandals, and a white shirt stepped out on the driver's side.

It was Paul, a writer hired to ghost Victor's autobiography. The hot, cindery wind billowed his sleeve as he raised a hand to shade his eyes.

"Hi, girls!" he called. "We made it! We actually had to go off-road; you wouldn't believe the traffic around the larger towns! Where's Victor?"

Bulgarian Bob came up beside them and stood looking down.

"Hey, Paul," he said. "Victor's sleeping; big party last night. What can we do for you?"

"Open the gates, of course! We've been driving for hours!"

"From Cannes?"

"Of course from Cannes!" cried Paul heartily. "Some Peruvian genius won the Palme D'Or, can you believe it? But maybe you haven't heard—the jury made a special prize for *Hearts of Light*. We have the trophy with us—Cammie's been holding it all the way from Cannes."

Cameron jumped out of the car and held up something bulky wrapped in a towel. She wore party clothes: a sparkly green dress and chunky sandals that laced high on her plump calves. Miriam's own thin, straight legs shook a little with the relief of being up here, on the terrace, and not down there at the gates.

Bulgarian Bob put his big hand gently over the lens of her camera. "Not this," he murmured.

Cameron waved energetically and called B. Bob's name, and Miriam's, and even Krista's (everyone knew that she hated Krista).

Paul stood quietly, staring up. Miriam had to look away.

B. Bob called, "Victor will be very happy about the prize."

Krista whispered, "He looks for blood on their skin; it's too far to see, though, from up here." To Bob she said, "I should go tell Victor?"

B. Bob shook his head. "He won't want to know."

He turned and went back inside without another word. Miriam and Krista took their bottles of polish and their tissues and followed.

Victor (and, therefore, everyone else) turned a deaf ear to the pleas, threats, and wails from out front for the next two days. A designated "security team" made up of bodyguards and mechanics went around making sure that La Bastide was locked up tight.

Victor sat rocking on a couch, eyes puffy. "My God, I hate this; but they were too slow. *They could be carrying the disease.* We have a responsibility to protect ourselves."

Next morning the Hummer and its two occupants had gone.

Television channels went to only a few hours a day, carrying reports of the Red Sweat in Paris, Istanbul, Barcelona. NATO troops herded people into makeshift "emergency" camps: schools, government buildings, and of course that trusty standby of imprisonment and death, sports arenas.

The radio and news sites on the web said more: refugees were on the move everywhere. The initial panicky convulsion of flight was over, but smaller groups were reported rushing this way and that all over the continent. In Eastern Europe, officials were holed up in mountain monasteries and castles, trying to subsist on wild game. Urbanites huddled in the underground malls of Canadian cities. When the Red Sweat made its lurid appearance in Montreal, it set off a stampede for the countryside.

They said monkeys carried it; marmots; stray dogs; stray people. Ravens, those eager devourers of corpses, must carry the disease on their claws and beaks, or they spread it in their droppings. So people shot at birds, dogs, rodents, and other people.

Krista prayed regularly to two little wooden icons she kept with her. Miriam had been raised pagan with a Christian gloss. She did not pray. God had never seemed further away.

After a screaming fight over the disappearance of somebody's stash of E, a sweep by the security squad netted a hoard of drugs. These were locked up, to be dispensed only by Bulgarian Bob at set times.

"We have plenty of food and water," Victor explained, "but not an endless supply of drugs. We don't want to run through it all before this ends, do we?" In compensation he was generous with alcohol, with which La Bastide's cellar was plentifully stocked. When his masseuse (she was diabetic) and one of the drivers insisted on leaving to fend for themselves and their personal requirements outside, Victor did not object.

Miriam had not expected a man who had only ever had to act like a leader onscreen to exercise authority so naturally in real life.

It helped that his people were not in a rebellious mood. They stayed in their rooms playing cards, sleeping, some even reading old novels from the shelves under the window seats downstairs. A running game of trivia went on in the games room ("Which actors have played which major roles in green body make-up?"). People used their cell phones to call each other in different parts of the building, since calls to the outside tended not to connect (when they did, conversations were not encouraging).

Nothing appeared on the television now except muay thai matches from Thailand, but the radio still worked: "Fires destroyed the main hospital in Marseilles; fire brigades did not respond. Refugees from the countryside who were sheltering inside are believed dead."

"Students and teachers at the university at Bologna broke into the city offices but found none of the food and supplies rumored to be stored there."

Electricity was failing now over many areas. Victor decreed that they must only turn on the modern security system at night. During daylight hours they used the heavy old locks and bolts on the thick outer doors. B. Bob posted armed lookouts on the terrace and on the roof of the back wing. Cell phones were collected, to stop them being recharged to no good purpose.

But the diesel fuel for Victor's vastly expensive, vastly efficient German generators suddenly ran out (it appeared that the caretaker of La Bastide had sold off much of it during the previous winter). The ground floor metal shutters that had been locked in place by electronic order at nightfall could not be reopened.

Unexpectedly, Victor's crew seemed glad to be shut in more securely. They moved most activities to the upper floor of the front wing, avoiding the shuttered darkness downstairs. They went to bed earlier to conserve candles. They partied in the dark.

The electric pumps had stopped, but an old hand-pump at the basement laundry tubs was rigged to draw water from the well into the pipes in the house. They tore up part of the well yard in the process, getting dust everywhere, but in the end they even got a battered old boiler working over a wood fire in the basement. A bath rota was eagerly subscribed to, although Alicia, the wig-girl, was forbidden to use hot water to bathe her Yorkie anymore.

Victor rallied his troops that evening. He was not a tall man but he was energetic and his big, handsome face radiated confidence and determination. "Look at us—we're movie people, spinners of dreams that ordinary people pay money to share! Who needs a screening room, computers, TV? We can entertain ourselves, or we shouldn't be here!"

Sickly grins all around, but they rose at once to his challenge.

They put on skits, plays, take-offs of popular TV shows. They even had concerts, since several people could play piano or guitar well and Walter was not the only one with a good singing voice. Someone found a violin in a display case downstairs, but no one knew how to play that. Krista and the youngest of the cooks told fortunes, using tea leaves and playing cards from the game room. The fortunes were all fabulous.

Miriam did not think about the future. She occupied herself taking pictures. One of the camera men reminded her that there would be no more recharging of batteries now; if she turned off the LCD screen on the Canon G9 its picture-taking capacity would last longer. Most of the camcorders were already dead from profligate over-use.

It was always noisy after sunset now; people fought back this way against the darkness outside the walls of La Bastide. Miriam made ear plugs out of candle wax and locked her bedroom door at night. On an evening of lively revels (it was Walter's birthday party) she quietly got hold of all the keys to her room that she knew of, including one from Bulgarian Bob's set. B. Bob was busy at the time with one of the drivers, as they groped each other urgently on the second floor landing.

There was more sex now, and more tension. Fistfights erupted over a card game, an edgy joke, the misplacement of someone's plastic water bottle. Victor had Security drag one pair of scuffling men apart and hustle them into the courtyard.

"What's this about?" he demanded.

Skip Reiker panted, "He was boasting about some Rachman al Haj concert he went to! That guy is a goddamn A-rab, a crazy damn Muslim!"

"Bullshit!" Sam Landry muttered, rubbing at a red patch on his cheek. "Music is music."

"Where did the god damned Sweat start, jerk? Africa!" Skip yelled. "The ragheads passed it around among themselves for years, and then they decided to share it. How do you think it spread to Europe? They brought it here on purpose, poisoning the food and water with their contaminated spit and blood. Who could do that better than musicians *'on tour?'*"

"Asshole!" hissed Sam. "That's what they said about the Jews during the Black Plague, that they'd poisoned village wells! What are you, a Nazi?"

"Fucker!" Skip screamed.

Miriam guessed it was withdrawal that had him so raw; coke supplies were running low, and many people were having a bad time of it.

Victor ordered Bulgarian Bob to open the front gates.

"Quit it, right now, both of you," Victor said, "or take it outside."

Everyone stared out at the dusty row of cars, the rough lawn, and the trees shading the weedy driveway as it corkscrewed downhill toward the paved road below. The combatants slunk off, one to his bed and the other to the kitchen to get his bruises seen to.

Jill, Cameron's hair stylist, pouted as B. Bob pushed the heavy front gates shut again. "Bummer! We could have watched from the roof, like at a joust."

B. Bob said, "They wouldn't have gone out. They know Victor won't let them back in."

"Why not?" said the girl. "Who's even alive out there to catch the Sweat from anymore?"

"You never know." B. Bob slammed the big bolts home. Then he caught Jill around her pale midriff, made mock-growling noises, and swept her back into the house. B. Bob was good at smoothing ruffled feathers. He needed to be. Tensions escalated. It occurred to Miriam that someone at La Bastide might attack her, just for being from the continent on which the disease had first appeared. Mike Bellows, a black script doctor from Chicago, had vanished the weekend before; climbed the wall and ran away, they said.

Miriam saw how Skip Reiker, a film editor with no film to edit now, stared at her when he thought she wasn't looking. She had never liked Mike Bellows, who was an arrogant and impatient man; perhaps Skip had liked him even less, and had made him disappear.

What she needed, she thought, was to find some passage for herself, some unwatched door to the outside, that she could use to slip away if things turned bad here. That was how a survivor must think. So far, the ease of life at La Bastide—the plentiful food and sunshine, the wine from the cellars, the scavenger hunts and skits, the games in the big salon, the fancy-dress parties—had bled off the worst of people's edginess. Everyone, so far, accepted Victor's rules. They knew that he was their bulwark against anarchy.

But: Victor had only as much authority as he had willing obedience. Food rationing, always a dangerous move, was inevitable. The ultimate loyalty of these bought-and-paid-for friends and attendants would be to themselves (except maybe for Bulgarian Bob, who seemed to really love Victor).

Only Jeff, one of the drivers, went outside now, tinkering for hours with the engines of the row of parked cars. One morning Miriam and Krista sat on the front steps in the sun, watching him.

"Look," Krista whispered, tugging at Miriam's sleeve with anxious, pecking fingers. Down near the roadway a dozen dogs, some with chains or leads dragging from their collars, harried a running figure across a field of withered vines in a soundless pantomime of hunting.

They both stood up, exclaiming. Jeff looked where they were looking. He grabbed up his tools and herded them both back inside with him. The front gates stayed closed after that.

Next morning Miriam saw the dogs again, from her balcony. At the foot of the driveway they snarled and scuffled, pulling and tugging at something too mangled and filthy to identify. She did not tell Krista, but perhaps someone else saw too and spread the word (there was a shortage of news in La Bastide these days, as even radio signals had become rare).

Searching for toothpaste, Miriam found Krista crying in her room. "That was Tommy Mullroy," Krista sobbed, "that boy that wanted to make computer games from movies. He was the one with those dogs."

Tommy Mullroy, a minor hanger-on and a late riser by habit, hadn't made it to the cars on the morning of Victor's hasty retreat from Cannes. Miriam was doubtful that Tommy could have found his way across the plague-stricken landscape to La Bastide on his own, and after so much time.

"How could you tell, from so far?" Miriam sat down beside her on the bed and stroked Krista's hand. "I didn't know you liked him."

"No, no, I hate that horrible monkey-boy!" Krista cried, shaking her head furiously. "Bad jokes, and pinching! But now he is dead." She buried her face in her pillow.

Miriam did not think the man chased by dogs had been Tommy Mullroy, but why argue? There was plenty to cry about in any case.

Winter had still not come; the cordwood stored to feed the building's six fireplaces was still stacked high against the courtyard walls. Since they had plenty of water everyone used a lot of it, heated in the old boiler. Every day a load of wood ash had to be dumped out of the side gate.

Miriam and Krista took their turns at this chore together.

They stood a while (in spite of the reeking garbage overflowing the alley outside, as no one came to take it away any more). The road below was empty today. Up close, Krista smelled of perspiration and liquor. Some in the house were becoming neglectful of themselves.

"My mother would use this ash for making soap," Krista said, "but you need also—what is it? Lime?"

Miriam said, "What will they do when all the soap is gone?"

Krista laughed. "Riots! Me, too. When I was kid, I thought luxury was change bedsheets every day for fresh." Then she turned to Miriam with wide eyes and whispered, "We must go away from here, Mimi. They have no Red Sweat in my country for sure! People are farmers, villagers; they live healthy, outside the cities! We can go there and be safe."

"More safe than in here?" Miriam shook her head. "Go in, Krista, Victor's little boys must be crying for you. I'll come with you and take some pictures."

The silence outside the walls was a heavy presence, bitter with drifting smoke that tasted harsh; some of the big new villas up the valley, built with expensive synthetic materials, smoldered slowly for days once they caught fire. Now and then thick smoke became visible much further away. Someone would say, "There's a fire to the west," and everyone would go out on the terrace to watch until the smoke died down or was drifted away out of sight on the wind. They saw no planes and no troop transports now. Dead bodies appeared on the road from time to time, their presence signaled by crows calling others to the feast.

Miriam noticed that the crows did not chase others of their kind away but announced good pickings far and wide. Maybe that worked well if you were a bird.

A day came when Krista confided in a panic that one of the twins was ill.

"You must tell Victor," Miriam said, holding the back of her hand to the forehead of Kevin, who whimpered. "This child has fever."

"I can't say anything! He is so scared of the Sweat, he'll throw the child outside!"

"His own little boy?" Miriam thought of the village man who drove out his son as a witch. "That's just foolishness," she told Krista; but she knew better, having known worse.

Neither of them said anything about it to Victor. Two days later, Krista jumped from the terrace with Kevin's small body clutched to her chest. Through tears, Miriam aimed her camera down and took a picture of the slack, twisted jumble of the two of them. They were left there on the driveway gravel with its fuzz of weeds and, soon after, its busy crows.

The days grew shorter. Victor's crowd partied every night, never mind about the candles. Bulgarian Bob slept on a cot in Victor's bedroom with a gun in his hand: another thing that everyone knew but nobody talked about.

On a damp and cloudy morning Victor found Miriam in the nursery with little Leif, who was on the floor playing with a dozen empty medicine bottles. Leif played very quietly and did not look up. Victor touched the child's head briefly and then sat down across the table from Miriam, where Krista used to sit. He was so clean shaven that his cheeks gleamed. He was sweating.

"Miriam, my dear," he said, "I need a great favor. Walter saw lights last night in the village. The army must have arrived, at long last. They'll have medicine. They'll have news. Will you go down and speak with them? I'd go myself, but everyone depends on me here to keep up some discipline, some hope. We can't have more people giving up, like Krista."

"I'm taking care of Leif now—" Miriam began faintly.

"Oh, Cammie can do that."

Miriam quickly looked away from him, her heart beating hard. Did he really believe that he had taken his current wife into La Bastide after all, in her spangly green party dress?

"This is so important," he urged, leaning closer and blinking his large, blue eyes in the way that (B. Bob always said) the camera loved. "There's a very, very large bonus in it for you, Miriam, enough to set you up very well on your own when this is all over. I can't ask anyone else; I wouldn't trust them to come back safe and sound. But you, you're so level-headed and you've had experience of bad times, not like some of these spoiled, silly people here. Things must have gotten better outside, but how would we know, shut up in here? Everyone agrees: we need you to do this.

"The contagion must have died down by now," he coaxed. "We haven't seen movement outside in days. Everyone has gone, or holed up, like us. Soldiers wouldn't be in the village if it was still dangerous down there."

Just yesterday Miriam had seen a lone rider on a squeaky bicycle pedaling down the highway. But she heard what Victor was *not* saying: that he needed to be able to convince others to go outside, convince them that it was safe, as the more crucial supplies (dope, toilet paper) dwindled, that he controlled those supplies, that he could, after all, have her put out by force.

Listening to the tink of the bottles in Leif's little hands, she realized that she could hardly wait to get away; in fact, she *had* to go. She would find amazing prizes, bring back news, and they would all be so grateful that she would be safe here forever. She would make up good news if she had to, to please them; to keep her place here, inside La Bastide.

But for now, go she must.

Bulgarian Bob found her sitting in dazed silence on the edge of her bed.

"Don't worry, Little Mi," he said. "I'm very sorry about Krista. I'll look out for your interest here."

"Thank you," she said, not looking him in the eyes. *Everyone agrees*. It was hard to think; her mind kept jumping.

"Take your camera with you," he said. "It's still working, yes? You've been sparing with it, smarter than some of these idiots. Here's a fresh card for it, just in case. We need to see how it is out there now. We can't print anything, of course, but we can look at your snaps on the LCD when you get back."

The evening's feast was dedicated to "our intrepid scout Miriam." Eyes glittering, the beautiful people of Victor's court toasted her (and, of course, their own good luck in not having been chosen to venture outside). Then they began a boisterous game: who could remember accurately the greatest number of deaths in the *Final Destination* movies, with details?

To Miriam they looked like crazy witches, cannibals, in the candlelight. She could hardly wait to leave.

Victor himself came to see her off early in the morning. He gave her a bottle of water, a ham sandwich, and some dried apricots to put in her red ripstop knapsack. "I'll be worrying my head off until you get back!" he said.

She turned away from him and looked at the driveway, at the dust-coated cars squatting on their flattened tires, and the shrunken, darkened body of Krista.

"You know what to look for," Victor said. "Matches. Soldiers. Tools, candles; you know."

The likelihood of finding anything valuable was small (and she would go out of her way *not* to find soldiers). But when he gave her shoulder a propulsive pat, she started down the driveway like a wind-up toy.

Fat dogs dodged away when they saw her coming. She picked up some stones to throw but did not need them.

She walked past the abandoned farmhouses and vacation homes on the valley's upper reaches, and then the village buildings, some burned and some spared; the empty vehicles, dead as fossils; the remains of human beings. Being sold away, she had been spared such sights back home. She had not seen for herself the corpses in sun-faded shirts and dresses, the grass blades growing up into empty eye sockets, that others had photographed there. Now she paused to take her own carefully chosen, precious pictures.

There were only a few bodies in the streets. Most people had died indoors, hiding from death. Why had her life bothered to bring her such a long way round, only to arrive where she would have been anyway had she remained at home?

Breezes ruffled weeds and trash, lifted dusty hair and rags fluttering from grimy bones, and made the occasional loose shutter or door creak as it swung. A few cows—too skittish now to fall easily to roaming dog packs—grazed watchfully on the plantings around the village fountain, which still dribbled dispiritedly.

If there were ghosts, they did not show themselves to her.

She looked into deserted shops and houses, gathering stray bits of paper, candle stubs, tinned food, ball-point pens. She took old magazines from a beauty salon, two paperback novels from a deserted coffee house. Venturing into a wine shop got her a cut on the ankle; the place had been smashed to smithereens. Others had come here before her, like that dead man curled up beside the till.

In a desk drawer she found a chocolate bar. She ate it as she headed back up the valley, walking through empty fields to skirt the village this time. The chocolate was crumbly and dry and dizzyingly delicious.

When she arrived at the gates of La Bastide, the men on watch sent word to Bulgarian Bob. He stood at the iron balustrade above her and called down questions: what had she seen, where exactly had she gone, had she entered the buildings, seen anyone alive?

"Where is Victor?" Miriam asked, her mouth suddenly very dry.

"I'll tell you what; you wait down there till morning," Bulgarian Bob said. "We must be sure you don't have the contagion, Miriam. You know."

Miriam, not Little Mi. Her heart drummed painfully. She felt injected into her own memory of Cammie and Paul standing here, pleading to come in. Only now she was looking up at the wall of La Bastide, not down from the terrace.

Sitting on the bonnet of one of one of the cars, she stirred her memory and dredged up old prayers to speak or sing softly into the dusk. Smells of food cooking and woodsmoke wafted down to her. Once, late, she heard squabbling voices at a second floor window. No doubt they were discussing who would be sent out the next time Victor wanted news of the world and one less mouth to feed.

In the morning, she held up her arms for inspection. She took off her blouse and showed them her bare back.

"I'm sorry, Miriam," Victor called down to her. His face was full of compassion. "I think I see a rash on your shoulders. It may be nothing, but you must understand—at least for now, we can't let you in. I really do want to see your pictures, though. You haven't used up all your camera's battery power, have you? We'll lower a basket for it."

"I haven't finished taking pictures," she said. She aimed the lens up at him. He quickly stepped back out of sight. Through the viewfinder she saw only the parapet of the terrace and the empty sky.

She flung the camera into the ravine, panting with rage and terror as she watched it spin on its way down, compact and clever and useless.

Then she sat down and thought.

Even if she found a way back in, if they thought she was infected they would drive her out again, maybe just shoot her. She imagined Skip Reiker throwing a carpet over her dead body, rolling her up in it, and heaving her outside the walls like rubbish. The rest of them would not approve, but anger and fear would enable their worst impulses ("See what you made us do!").

She should have thought more before, about how she was a supernumerary here, acquired but not really *needed*, not *talented* as these people reckoned such things; not important to the tribe.

"Have I have stopped being a survivor?" she asked Krista's withered back.

In the house Walter was singing. "Some Enchanted Evening!" Applause. Then, "The Golden Vanity."

Miriam sat with her back against the outside wall, burning with fear, confusion, and scalding self-reproach.

When the sun rose again she saw a rash of dark blisters on the backs of her hands. She felt more of them rising at her hairline, around her face. Her joints ached. She was stunned: Victor was right. It was the Red Sweat. But how had she caught it? Through something she had touched—a doorknob, a book, a slicing shard of glass? By merely breathing the infected air?

Maybe—the *chocolate*? The idea made her sob with laughter.

They wouldn't care one way or the other. She was already dead to them. She knew they would not even venture out to take her backpack, full of scavenged treasures, when she was dead (she threw its contents down the ravine after the camera, to make sure). She'd been foolish to have trusted Bulgarian Bob, or Victor either.

They had never intended to let the dove back into the ark.

She knelt beside Krista's corpse and made herself search the folds of reeking, sticky clothing until she found Krista's key to the rubbish gate, the key they had used to throw out the ashes. She sat on the ground beside Krista and rubbed the key bright on her own pant-leg.

Let them try to keep her out. Let them try.

Krista was my shipmate. Now I have no shipmates.

At moonrise she shrugged her aching arms through the straps of the empty pack and walked slowly around to the side alley gate. Krista's key clicked minutely in the lock. The door sprang outward, releasing more garbage that had been piled up inside. No one seemed to hear. They were roaring with song in the front wing and drumming on the furniture, to drown out the cries and pleadings they expected to hear from her.

Miriam stepped inside the well yard, swallowing bloody mucus. She felt the paving lurch a little under her.

A man was talking in the kitchen passageway, set into the ground floor of the back wing at an oblique angle across the well yard. She thought it was Edouard, a camera tech, pretending to speak on his cell as he sometimes did to keep himself company when he was on his own. Edouard, as part of Security, carried a gun.

Her head cleared suddenly. She found that she had shut the gate behind her, and had slid down against the inside wall, for she was sitting on the cool pavement. Perhaps she had passed out for a little. By the moon's light she saw the well's raised stone lip, only a short way along the wall to her left.

She was thirsty, although she did not think she could force water down her swollen throat now.

The paving stones the men had pried up in their work on the plumbing had not been reset. They were still piled up out of the way, very near where she sat.

Stones; water. Her brain was so clogged with hot heaviness that she could barely hold her head up.

"Non, non!" Edouard shouted. "Ce n'est pas vrai, ils sont menteurs, tous!"

Yes, all of them; menteurs. She sympathized, briefly.

Her mind kept tilting and spilling all its thoughts into a turgid jumble, but there were constants: *Stones. Water.* The exiled dove, the brave cabin boy. Krista and little Kevin. She made herself move, trusting to the existence of an actual plan somewhere in her mind. She crawled over to the stacked pavers. Slowly and with difficulty she took off her backpack and stuffed it with some of the smaller stones, one by one. Blood beaded black around her fingernails. She had no strength to pull the loaded pack onto her back again, so she hung it from her shoulder by one broad strap, and began making her painful way toward the well itself.

Edouard was deep in his imaginary quarrel. As she crept along the wall she heard his voice echo angrily in the vaulted passageway.

The thick wooden well-cover had been replaced with a lightweight metal sheet, back when they had had to haul water by hand before the old laundry pump was reconnected. She lifted the light metal sheet and set it aside. Dragging herself up, she leaned over the low parapet and peered down.

She could not make out the stone steps that descended into the water on the inside wall, left over from a time when the well had been used to hide contraband. Now... something. Her thoughts swam.

Focus.

Even without her camera there was a way to bring home to Victor all the reality he had sent her out to capture for him in pictures.

She could barely shift her legs over the edge, but at last she felt the cold roughness of the top step under her feet. She descended toward the water, using the friction of her spread hands, turning her torso flat against the curved wall like a figure in an Egyptian tomb painting. The water winked up at her, glossy with reflected moonlight. The backpack, painful with hard stone edges, dragged at her aching shoulder. She paused to raise one strap and put her head through it; she must not lose her anchor now.

The water's chill lapped at her skin, sucking away her last bit of strength. She sagged out from the wall and slipped under the surface. Her hands and feet scrabbled dreamily at the slippery wall and the steps, but down she sank anyway, pulled by the bag of stones strapped to her body.

Her chest was shot through with agony, but her mind clung with bitter pleasure to the fact that in the morning all of Victor's tribe would wash themselves and brush their teeth and swallow their pills down with the water Victor was so proud of, water pumped by willing hands from his own wonderful well.

Head craned back, she saw that dawn pallor had begun to flush the small circle of sky receding above her. Against that light, black curls of the blood that her body wept from every seam and pore feathered out in secret silence, into the cool, delicious water.

"Lowland Sea" is *one of those stories that wove itself together all on its own, using bits and scraps resurgent from months, no, years of watching the world and other people's art.*

One basic strand was a novel I'd recently read about a woman tracking down her supposedly-dead actress-mother at the Cannes film festival. I liked the protagonist's "outsider" status looking in on an alien mini-culture. This connected with the persistence of reports on the upsurge in modern slavery, particularly sexual slavery; news stories about the abuses of children that poverty, sexism, and war bring with them; and the nightly footage of shattered villages and dusty, flyblown refugee camps.

The original stimulus, of course, was Edgar Allan Poe's wonderful "The Masque of the Red Death." Taking off from that little masterpiece of horror was irresistibly easy. What better version of arrogant aristocracy than our current culture of movie celebrity? What more gruesome incarnation of the merciless and class-blind horror of plague than a mutated form of Ebola? And what more satisfying resolution than disaster at the hands of a person purchased from the world of struggle, oppression, and routine exploitation that so many of the rich casually build their wealth upon?

Oh oh, there I go opening myself up to charges that I've written not a tasty "escapist" horror story but a propaganda screed!

I don't think so; after all, late in the process there appeared some of those magical-feeling serendipities that happen when you've been dealing with a real story that wanted telling—little grace notes that turn up along about draft number twelve (or later), each one a small, bright reward for the work and also its validation, in a funny way.

It's like this: I knew I was all right with this story when my Christmas present from one of the grandkids turned out to be The Moviegoer's Companion, *a small book of invaluable details to help sharpen the verisimilitude of my filmic revelers; and then again there was that moment when it dawned on me that Noah's dove* and the doomed cabin boy just touch each other, wing-tip to wing-tip in passing, in a way that strikes a soft, melancholy chord much richer and more satisfying than anything I could have consciously planned.

Those are the times that I really *love* my job.

JOHN LANGAN is the author of *Mr. Gaunt and Other Uneasy Encounters* (Prime 2008). His stories have appeared in *The Magazine of Fantasy & Science Fiction*. He lives in upstate New York with his wife and son.

Technicolor

John Langan

Come on, say it out loud with me: "And Darkness and Decay and the Red Death held illimitable dominion over all." Look at that sentence. Who says Edgar Allan Poe was a lousy stylist? Thirteen words—good number for a horror story, right? Although it's not so much a story as a masque. Yes, it's about a masque, but it is a masque, too. Of course, you all know what a masque is. If you didn't, you looked it up in your dictionaries, because that's what you do in a senior seminar. Anyone?

No, not a play, not exactly. Yes? Good, okay, "masquerade" is one sense of the word, a ball whose guests attend in costume. Anyone else?

Yes, very nice, nicely put. The masque does begin in the sixteenth century. It's the entertainment of the elite, and originally, it's a combination of pantomime and dance. Pantomime? Right—think "mime." The idea is to perform without words, gesturally, to let the movements of your body tell the story. You do that, and you dance, and there's your show. Later on, there's dialogue and other additions, but I think it's this older sense of the word the story intends. Remember that tall, silent figure at the end.

I'm sorry? Yes, good point. The two kinds of masque converge.

Back to that sentence, though. Twenty-two syllables that break almost perfectly in half, ten and twelve, "And Darkness and Decay and the Red Death" and "held illimitable dominion over all." A group of short words, one and two syllables each, takes you through the first part of the sentence, then they give way to these long, almost luxurious words, "illimitable dominion." The rhythm—you see how complex it is? You ride along on these short words, bouncing up and down, alliterating from one "d" to the next, and suddenly you're mired in those Latinate polysyllables. All the momentum goes out of your reading; there's just enough time for the final pair of words, which are short, which is good, and you're done.

Wait, just let me—no, all right, what was it you wanted to say?

Exactly, yes, you took the words out of my mouth. The sentence does what the story does, carries you along through the revelry until you run smack-dab into that tall figure in the funeral clothes. Great job.

One more observation about the sentence, then I promise it's on to the story itself. I know you want to talk about Prospero's castle, all those colored rooms. Before we do, however, the four "d"s. We've mentioned already, there are a lot of "d" sounds in these thirteen words. They thread through the line, help tie it together. They also draw our attention to four words in particular. The first three are easy to recognize: they're capitalized, as well. Darkness, Decay, Death. The fourth? Right, dominion. Anyone want to take a stab at why they're capitalized?

Yes? Well... okay, sure it makes them into proper nouns. Can you take that a step farther? What kind of proper nouns does it make them? What's happened to the Red Death in the story? It's gone from an infection you can't see to a tall figure wandering around the party. Personification, good. Darkness, Decay, (the Red) Death: the sentence personifies them; they're its trinity, its unholy trinity, so to speak. And this godhead holds dominion, what the dictionary defines as "sovereign authority" over all. Not only the prince's castle, not only the world of the story, but all, you and me.

In fact, in a weird sort of way, this is the story of the incarnation of one of the persons of this awful trinity.

All right, moving on, now. How about those rooms? Actually, how about the building those rooms are in, first? I've been calling it a castle, but it isn't, is it? It's "castellated," which is to say, castle-like, but it's an abbey, a monastery. I suppose it makes sense to want to wait out the Red Death in a place like an abbey. After all, it's both removed from the rest of society and well-fortified. And we shouldn't be too hard on the prince and his followers for retreating there. It's not the first time this has happened, in literature or life. Anyone read *The Decameron*? Boccaccio? It's a collection of one hundred stories told by ten people, five women and five men, who have sequestered themselves in, I'm pretty sure it's a convent, to wait out the plague ravaging Florence. The Black Death, that one.

If you consider that the place in which we find the seven rooms is a monastery, a place where men are supposed to withdraw from this world to meditate on the next, its rooms appear even stranger. What's the set-up? Seven rooms, yes, thank you, I believe I just said that. Running east to west, good. In a straight line? No. There's a sharp turn every twenty or thirty yards, so that you can see only one room at a time. So long as they follow that east to west course, you can lay the rooms out in any form you like. I favor steps, like the ones that lead the condemned man to the chopping block, but that's just me.

Hang on, hang on, we'll get to the colors in a second. We need to stay with the design of the rooms for a little longer. Not everybody gets this the first time through. There are a pair of windows, Gothic windows, which means what? That they're long and pointed at the top. The windows are opposite one another, and they look out on, anybody? Not exactly: a chandelier hangs down from the ceiling. It is a kind of light, though. No, a candelabrum holds candles. Anyone else? A brazier, yes, there's a brazier sitting on a tripod outside either window. They're, how would you describe a brazier? Like a big metal cup, a bowl, that you fill with some kind of fuel and ignite. Wood, charcoal, oil. To be honest, I'm not as interested in the braziers as I am in where they're located. Outside the windows, right, but where outside the windows? Maybe I should say, What is outside the windows? Corridors, yes, there are corridors to either side of the rooms, and it's along these that the braziers are stationed. Just like our classroom. Not the tripods, of course, and I guess what's outside our windows is more a gallery than a corridor, since it's open to the parking lot on the other side. All right, all right, so I'm stretching a bit, here, but have you noticed, the room has seven windows? One for each color in Prospero's Abbey. Go ahead, count them.

So here we are in this strange abbey, one that has a crazy zig-zag suite of rooms with corridors running beside them. You could chalk the location's details up to anti-Catholic sentiment; there are critics who have argued that anti-Catholic prejudice is the secret engine driving Gothic literature. No, I don't buy it, not in this case. Sure, there are stained-glass windows, but they're basically tinted glass. There's none of the iconography you'd expect if this were anti-Catholic propaganda, no statues or paintings. All we have is that enormous clock in the last room, the mother of all grandfather clocks. Wait a minute...

What about those colors, then? Each of the seven rooms is decorated in a single color that matches the stained glass of its windows. From east to west, we go from blue to purple to green to orange to white to violet to—to the last room, where there's a slight change. The windows are red, but the room itself is done in black. There seems to be some significance to the color sequence, but what that is—well, this is why we have literature professors, right? (No snickering.) Not to mention, literature students. I've read through your responses to the homework assignment, and there were a few interesting ideas as to what those colors might mean. Of course, most of you connected them to times of the day, blue as dawn, black as night, the colors in between morning, noon, early afternoon, that kind of thing. Given the east-west layout, it makes a certain amount of sense. A few more of you picked up on that connection to time in a slightly different way, and related the colors to times of the year, or the stages in a person's life. In the process, some clever arguments were made. Clever, but not, I'm afraid, too convincing.

What! What's wrong! What is it! Are you all—oh, them. Oh for God's sake. When you screamed like that, I thought—I don't know what I thought. I thought I'd need a new pair of trousers. Those are a couple of graduate students I've enlisted to help me with a little presentation I'll be putting up shortly. Yes, I can understand how the masks could startle you. They're just generic white masks; I think they found them downtown somewhere. It was their idea: once I told them what story we would be discussing, they immediately hit on wearing the masks. To tell the truth, I half-expected they'd show up sporting the heads of enormous fanged monsters. Those are relatively benign.

Yes, I suppose they do resemble the face the Red Death assumes for its costume. No blood splattered on them, though.

If I could have your attention up here, again. Pay no attention to that man behind the curtain. Where was I? Your homework, yes, thank you. Right, right. Let's see... oh—I know. A couple of you read the colors in more original ways. I made a note of them somewhere—here they are. One person interpreted the colors as different states of mind, beginning with blue as tranquil and ending with black as despair, with stops for jealousy—green, naturally—and passion—white, as in white-hot—along the way. Someone else made the case for the colors as, let me make sure I have the phrasing right, "phases of being."

Actually, that last one's not bad. Although the writer could be less obtuse; clarity, people, academic writing needs to be clear. Anyway, the gist of the writer's argument is that each color is supposed to take you through a different state of existence, blue at one end of the spectrum representing innocence, black at the other representing death. Death as a state of being, that's... provocative. Which is not to say it's correct, but it's headed in the right direction.

I know, I know: Which is? The answer requires some explanation. Scratch that. It requires a boatload of explanation. That's why I have Tweedledee and Tweedledum setting up outside. (Don't look! They're almost done.) It's also why I lowered the screen behind me for the first time this semester. There are some images I want to show you, and they're best seen in as much detail as possible. If I can remember what the Media Center people told me... click this... then this...

Voila!

Matthew Brady's *Portrait* of Edgar, taken 1848, his last full year alive. It's the best-known picture of him; were I to ask you to visualize him, this is what your minds' eyes would see. That forehead, that marble expanse—yes, his hair does make the top of his head look misshapen, truncated. As far as I know, it wasn't. The eyes—I suppose everyone comments on the eyes, slightly shadowed under those brows, the lids lowered just enough to suggest a certain detachment, even dreaminess. It's the mouth I notice, how it tilts up ever-so-slightly at the right corner. It's hard to see; you have to look closely. A strange mixture of arrogance, even contempt, and something else, something that might be humor, albeit of the bitter variety. It wouldn't be that much of a challenge to suggest colors for the picture, but somehow, black and white is more fitting, isn't it? Odd, considering how much color there is in the fiction. I've often thought all those old Roger Corman adaptations, the ones Vincent Price starred in—whatever their other faults, one thing they got exactly right was Technicolor, which was the perfect way to film these stories, just saturate the screen with the most vibrant colors you could find.

I begin with the *Portrait* as a reminder. This is the man. His hand scraped the pen across the paper, brought the story we've been discussing into existence word by word. Not creation *ex nihilo*, out of nothing, creation... if my Latin were better, or existent, I'd have a fancier way to say out of the self, or out of the depths of the self, or—hey—out of the depth that is the self.

Moving on to our next portrait... Anyone?

I'm impressed. Not many people know this picture. Look closely, though. See it?

That's right: it isn't a painting. It's a photograph that's been tweaked to resemble a painting. The portrait it imitates is a posthumous representation of Virginia Clemm, Edgar's sweetheart and child bride. The girl in the photo? She'll be happy you called her a girl. That's my wife, Anna. Yes, I'm married. Why is that so hard to believe? We met many years ago, in a kingdom by the sea. From? "Annabel Lee," good. No, just Anna; although we did meet in the King of the Sea Arcade, on the Jersey shore. Seriously. She is slightly younger than I am. Four years, thank you very much. You people. For Halloween one year, we dressed up as Edgar and Virginia— pretty much from the start, it's been a running joke between us. In her case, the resemblance is striking.

As it so happened, yes we did attend a masquerade as the happy couple. That was where this photo was taken. One of the other guests was a professional photographer. I arranged the shot; he took it, then used a program on his computer to transform it into a painting. The guy was quite pleased with it; apparently it's on his website. I'm showing it to you because... well, because I want to. There's probably a connection I could draw between masquerade, the suppression of one identity in order to invoke and inhabit another, that displacement, and the events of our story, but that's putting the cart about a mile before the horse. She'll like that you thought she was a girl, though; that'll make her night. Those were her cookies, by the way. Are there any left? Not even the sugar cookies? Figures.

Okay, image number three. If you can name this one, you get an "A" for the class and an autographed picture of the Pope. Put your hand down; you don't know. How about the rest of you?

Just us crickets...

It's just as well; I don't have that picture of the Pope anymore. This gentleman is Prosper Vauglais. Or so he claimed. There's a lot about this guy no one's exactly sure of, like when he was born, or where, or when and where he died. He showed up in Paris in the late eighteen-teens and caused something of a stir. For one winter, he appeared at several of the less reputable *salons* and a couple of the—I wouldn't go so far as to say more reputable—maybe less disreputable ones.

His "deal?" His deal, as you put it, was that he claimed to have been among the quarter of a million soldiers under Napoleon Bonaparte's personal command when, in June of 1812, the Emperor decided to invade Russia. Some of you may remember from your European history classes, this was a very bad idea. The worst. Roughly a tenth of Napoleon's forces survived the campaign; I want to say the number who limped back into France was something like twenty-two thousand. In and of itself, being a member of that group is nothing to sneeze at. For Vauglais, though, it was only the beginning. During the more-or-less running battles the French army fought as it retreated from what had been Moscow, Vauglais was separated from his fellows, struck on the head by a Cossack's sword and left for dead in a snow bank. When he came to, he was alone, and a storm had blown up. Prosper had no idea where he was; he assumed still Russia, which wasn't too encouraging. Any Russian peasants or what have you who came across French soldiers, even those trying to surrender, tended to hack them to death with farm implements first and ask questions later. So when Prosper strikes out in what he hopes is the approximate direction of France, he isn't what you'd call terribly optimistic.

Nor is his pessimism misplaced. Within a day, he's lost, frozen and starving, wandering around the inside of a blizzard like you read about, white-out conditions, shrieking wind, unbearable cold. The blow to his head isn't helping matters, either. His vision keeps going in and out of focus. Sometimes he feels so nauseated he can barely stand, let alone continue walking. Once in a while, he'll see a light shining in the window of a farmhouse, but he gives these a wide berth. Another day, and he'll be closer to death than he was even at the worst battles he saw—than he was when that saber connected with his skull. His skin, which has been numb since not long after he started his trek, has gone from pale to white to this kind of blue-gray, and it's hardened, as if there's a crust of ice on it. He can't feel his pulse through it. His breath, which had been venting from his nose and mouth in long white clouds, seems to have slowed to a trickle, if that. He can't see anything; although, with the storm continuing around him, maybe that isn't so strange. He's not cold anymore—or, it's not that he isn't cold so much as it is that the cold isn't torturing him the way it was. At some point, the cold moved inside him, took up residence just beneath his heart, and once that happened, that transition was accomplished, the temperature outside became of much less concern.

Technicolor

There's a moment—while Vauglais is staggering around like you do when you're trying to walk in knee-high snow without snowshoes, pulling each foot free, swiveling it forward, crashing it through the snow in front of you, then repeating the process with your other foot—there's a moment when he realizes he's dead. He isn't sure when it happened. Some time in the last day or so. It isn't that he thinks he's in some kind of afterlife, that he's wandering around a frozen hell. No, he knows he's still stuck somewhere in western Russia. It's just that, now he's dead. He isn't sure why he hasn't stopped moving. He considers doing so, giving his body a chance to catch up to his apprehension of it, but decides against it. For one thing, he isn't sure it would work, and suppose while he's standing in place, waiting to fall over, someone finds him, one of those peasants, or a group of Russian soldiers? Granted, if he's already dead, they can't hurt him, but the prospect of being cut to pieces while still conscious is rather horrifying. And for another thing, Prosper isn't ready to quit walking. So he keeps moving forward. Dimly, the way you might hear a noise when you're fast asleep, he's aware that he isn't particularly upset at finding himself dead and yet moving, but after recent events, maybe that isn't so surprising.

Time passes; how much, he can't say. The blizzard doesn't lift, but it thins, enough for Vauglais to make out trees, evergreens. He's in a forest, a pretty dense one, from what he can see, which may explain why the storm has lessened. The trees are—there's something odd about the trees. For as close together as they are, they seem to be in almost perfect rows, running away into the snow on either side of him. In and of itself, maybe that isn't strange. Could be, he's wandered into some kind of huge formal garden. But there's more to it. When he looks at any particular tree, he sees, not so much bark and needles as black, black lines like the strokes of a paintbrush, or the scratches of a pen, forming the approximation of an evergreen. It's as if he's seeing a sketch of a tree, an artist's estimate. The black lines appear to be moving, almost too quickly for him to notice; it's as if he's witnessing them being drawn and re-drawn. Prosper has a sudden vision of himself from high above, a small, dark spot in the midst of long rows of black on white, a stray bit of punctuation loose among the lines of an unimaginable text.

Eventually, Vauglais reaches the edge of the forest. Ahead, there's a building, the title to this page he's been traversing. The blizzard has kicked up again, so he can't see much, but he has the impression of a long, low structure, possibly stone. It could be a stable, could be something else. Although there are no religious symbols evident, Prosper has an intuition the place is a monastery. He should turn right or left, avoid the building— the Russian clergy haven't taken any more kindly to the French invaders than the Russian people—instead, he raises one stiff leg and strikes off towards it. It isn't that he's compelled to do so, that he's in the grip of a power that he can't resist, or that he's decided to embrace the inevitable, surrender to death. He isn't even especially curious about the stone structure. Forward is just a way to go, and he does.

As he draws closer, Vauglais notices that the building isn't becoming any easier to distinguish. If anything, it's more indistinct, harder to make out. If the trees behind him were rough drawing, this place is little more than a scribble, a jumble of lines whose form is as much in the eye of the beholder as anything. When a figure in a heavy coat and hat separates from the structure and begins to trudge in his direction, it's as if a piece of the place has broken off. Prosper can't see the man's face, all of which except the eyes is hidden by the folds of a heavy scarf, but he lifts one mittened hand and gestures for Vauglais to follow him inside, which the Frenchman does.

And... no one knows what happens next.

What do I mean? I'm sorry: wasn't I speaking English? No one knows what happened inside the stone monastery. Prosper writes a fairly detailed account of the events leading up to that point, which is where the story I'm telling you comes from, but when the narrative reaches this moment, it breaks off with Vauglais's declaration that he's told us as much as he can. End of story.

All right, yes, there are hints of what took place during the five years he was at the Abbey. That was what he called the building, the Abbey. Every so often, Prosper would allude to his experiences in it, and sometimes, someone would note his remarks in a letter or diary. From combing through these kinds of documents, it's possible to assemble and collate Vauglais's comments into a glimpse of his life with the Fraternity. Again, his name. There were maybe seven of them, or seven after he arrived, or there were supposed to be seven. He referred to "Brother Red," once; to "The White Brother" at another time. Were the others named Blue, Purple, Green, Orange, and Violet? We can't say; although, as an assumption, it isn't completely unreasonable. They spent their days in pursuit of something Vauglais called The Great Work; he also referred to it as The Transumption. This seems to have involved generous amounts of quiet meditation combined with the study of certain religious texts—Prosper doesn't name them, but they may have included some Gnostic writings.

The Gnostics? I don't suppose you would have heard of them. How many of you actually go to church? As I feared. What would Sr. Mary Mary say? The Gnostics were a religious sect who sprang up around the same time as the early Christians. I guess they would have described themselves as the true Christians, the ones who understood what Jesus's teachings were really about. They shared sacred writings with the more orthodox Christians, but they had their own books, too. They were all about *gnosis*, knowledge, especially of the self. For them, the secret to what lay outside the self was what lay inside the self. The physical world was evil, a wellspring of illusions and delusions. Gnostics tended to retreat to the desert, lead lives of contemplation. Unlike the mainstream Christians, they weren't much on formal organization; that, and the fact that those Christians did everything in their power to shunt the Gnostics and their teachings to the margins and beyond, branding some of their ideas as heretical, helps explain why they pretty much vanished from the religious scene.

"Pretty much," though, isn't the same thing as "completely." (I know: such precise, scientific terminology.) Once in a while, Gnostic ideas would resurface, usually in the writings of some fringe figure or another. Rumors persist of Gnostic secret societies, occasionally as part of established groups like the Jesuits or the Masons. Which begs the question: Was Vauglais's Fraternity one of these societies, a kind of order of Gnostic monks? The answer to which is—

Right: no one knows. There's no record of any official, which is to say, Russian Orthodox, religious establishment: no monastery, no church, in the general vicinity of where we think Prosper was. Of course, a bunch of Gnostic monastics would hardly constitute anything resembling an official body, and so might very well fly under the radar. That said, the lack of proof against something does not count as evidence for it.

That's true. He could have been making the whole thing up.

Transumption? It's a term from classical rhetoric. It refers to the elision of a chain of associations. Sorry—sometimes I like to watch your heads explode. Let's say you're writing your epic poem about the fall of Troy, and you describe one of the Trojans being felled by an arrow. Let's say that arrow was made from the wood of a tree in a sacred grove; let's say, too, that that grove was planted by Hercules, who scattered some acorns there by accident. Now let's say that, when your Trojan hero sinks to the ground, drowning in his own blood, one of his friends shouts, "Curse the careless hand of Hercules!" That statement is an example of transumption. You've jumped from one link in a chain of associations back several. Make sense?

Yes, well, what does a figure of speech have to do with what was going on inside that Abbey?

Oh wait—hold on for a moment. My two assistants are done with their set up. Let me give them a signal... Five more minutes? All right, good, yes. I have no idea if they understood me. Graduate students.

Don't worry about what's on the windows. Yes, yes, those are lamps. Can I have your attention up here, please? Thank you. Let me worry about Campus Security. Or my masked friends out there will.

Okay—let's skip ahead a little. We were talking about The Transumption, a.k.a. The Great Work. There's nothing in his other references to the Abbey that offers any clue as to what he may have meant by it. However, there is an event that may shed some light on things.

It occurs in Paris, towards the end of February. An especially fierce winter scours the streets, sends people scurrying from the shelter of one building to another. Snow piles on top of snow, all of it turning dirty gray. Where there isn't snow, there's ice, inches thick in places. The sky is gray, the sun a pale blur that puts in a token appearance for a few hours a day. Out into this glacial landscape, Prosper leads half a dozen men and women from one of the city's less-disreputable *salons*. Their destination, the catacombs, the long tunnels that run under Paris. They're quite old, the catacombs. In some places, the walls are stacked with bones, from when they were used as a huge ossuary. (That's a place to hold the bones of the dead.) They're also fairly crowded, full of beggars, the poor, searching for shelter from the ravages of the season. Vauglais has to take his party deep underground before they can find a location that's suitably empty. It's a kind of side-chamber, roughly circular, lined with shelves full of skull piled on skull. The skulls make a clicking sound, from the rats shuffling through them. Oh yes, there are plenty of rats down here.

Prosper fetches seven skulls off the shelves and piles them in the center of the room. He opens a large flask he's carried with him, and pours its contents over the bones. It's lamp oil, which he immediately ignites with his torch. He sets the torch down, and gathers the members of the *salon* around the skulls. They join hands.

It does sound as if he's leading a séance, doesn't it? The only difference is, he isn't asking the men and women with him to think of a beloved one who's passed beyond. Nor does he request they focus on a famous ghost. Instead, Vauglais tells them to look at the flames licking the bones in front of them. Study those flames, he says, watch them as they trace the contours of the skulls. Follow the flames over the cheeks, around the eyes, up the brows. Gaze into those eyes, into the emptiness inside the fire. Fall through the flames; fall into that blackness.

He's hypnotizing them, of course—mesmerizing would be the more historically-accurate term. Under the sway of his voice, the members of the *salon* enter a kind of vacancy. They're still conscious—well, they're still perceiving, still aware of that heap of bones burning in front of them, the heavy odor of the oil, the quiet roar of the flames—but their sense of their selves, the accumulation of memory and inclination that defines each from the other, is gone.

Now Prosper is telling them to think of something new. Picture the flesh that used to clothe these skulls, he says. Warm and smooth, flushed with life. Look closely—it glows, doesn't it? It shines with its living. Watch! watch—it's dying. It's growing cold, pale. The glow, that dim light floating at the very limit of the skin—it's changing, drifting up, losing its radiance. See—there!—ah, it's dead. Cool as a cut of meat. Gray. The light is gone. Or is it? Is that another light? Yes, yes it is; but it is not the one we have watched dissipate. This is a darker glow. Indigo, that most elusive of the rainbow's hues. It curls over the dull skin like fog, and the flesh opens for it, first in little cracks, then in long windows, and then in wide doorways. As the skin peels away, the light thickens, until it is as if the bone is submerged in a bath of indigo. The light is not done moving; it pours into the air above the skull, over all the skulls. Dark light is rising from them, twisting up in thick streams that seek each other, that wrap around one another, that braid a shape. It is the form of a man, a tall man dressed in black robes, his face void as a corpse's, his head crowned with black flame—

Afterwards, when the half-dozen members of the *salon* compare notes, none of them can agree on what, if anything, they saw while under Vauglais's sway. One of them insists that nothing appeared. Three admit to what might have been a cloud of smoke, or a trick of the light. Of the remaining pair, one states flat-out that she saw the Devil. The other balks at any statement more elaborate than, "Monsieur Vauglais has shown me terrible joy." Whatever they do or don't see, it doesn't last very long. The oil Prosper doused the skulls with has been consumed. The fire dies away; darkness rushes in to fill the gap. The trance in which Vauglais has held the *salon* breaks. There's a sound like wind rushing, then quiet.

A month after that expedition, Prosper disappeared from Paris. He had attempted to lead that same *salon* back into the catacombs for a second— well, whatever you'd call what he'd done. A summoning? (But what was he summoning?) Not surprisingly, the men and women of the *salon* declined his request. In a huff, Vauglais left them and tried to insert himself into a couple of even-less-disreputable *salons*, attempting to use gossip about his former associates as his price of admission. But either the secrets he knew weren't juicy enough—possible, but I suspect unlikely—or those other *salons* had heard about his underground investigations and decided they preferred the comfort of their drawing rooms. Then one of the men from that original *salon* raised questions about Prosper's military service—he claimed to have found a sailor who swore that he and Vauglais had been on an extended debauch in Morocco at the very time he was supposed to have been marching towards Moscow. That's the problem with being the flavor of the month: before you know it, the calendar's turned, and no one can remember what they found so appealing about you in the first place. In short order, there's talk about an official inquiry into Prosper's service record—probably more rumor than fact, but it's enough for Vauglais, and he departs Paris for parts unknown. No one sees him leave, just as no one saw him arrive. In the weeks that follow, there are reports of Prosper in Libya, Madagascar, but they don't disturb a single eyebrow. Years—decades later, when Gauguin's in Tahiti, he'll hear a story about a strange white man who came to the island a long time ago and vanished into its interior, and Vauglais's name will occur to him, but you can't even call that a legend. It's... a momentary association. Prosper Vauglais vanishes.

Well, not all of him. That's right: there's the account he wrote of his discovery of the Abbey.

I beg your pardon? Dead? Oh, right, yes. It's interesting—apparently, Prosper permitted a physician connected to the first *salon* he frequented to conduct a pretty thorough examination of him. According to Dr. Zumachin,

Vauglais's skin was stubbornly pallid. No matter how much the doctor pinched or slapped it, Prosper's flesh remained the same gray-white. Not only that, it was cold, cold and hard, as if it were packed with ice. Although Vauglais had to inhale in order to speak, his regular respiration was so slight as to be undetectable. It wouldn't fog the doctor's pocket mirror. And try as Zumachin might, he could not locate a pulse.

Sure, Prosper could have paid him off; aside from his part in this story, there isn't that much information on the good doctor. For what it's worth, most of the people who met Vauglais commented on his skin, its pallor, and, if they touched it, its coldness. No one else noted his breathing, or lack thereof, but a couple of the members of that last *salon* described him as extraordinarily still.

Okay, back to that book. Actually, wait. Before we do, let me bring this up on the screen...

I know—talk about something completely different. No, it's not a Rorschach test. It does look like it, though, doesn't it? Now if my friends outside will oblige me... and there we go. Amazing what a sheet of blue plastic and a high-power lamp can do. We might as well be in the east room of Prospero's Abbey.

Yes, the blue light makes it appear deeper—it transforms it from ink-spill to opening. Prosper calls it "*La Bouche*," the Mouth. Some mouth, eh?

That's where the design comes from, Vauglais's book. The year after his disappearance, a small Parisian press whose biggest claim to fame was its unauthorized edition of the Marquis de Sade's *Justine* publishes Prosper's *L'Histoire de Mes Aventures dans L'Etendu Russe*, which translates something like, "The History of My Adventures in the Russian," either "Wilderness" or "Vastness." Not that anyone calls it by its title. The publisher, one Denis Prebend, binds Vauglais's essay between covers the color of a bruise after three or four days. Yes, that sickly, yellow-green. Of course that's what catches everyone's attention, not the less-than-inspired title, and it isn't long before customers are asking for "*le livre verte*," the green book. It's funny—it's one of those books that no one will admit to reading, but that goes through ten printings the first year after its appears.

Some of those copies do find their way across the Atlantic, very good. In fact, within a couple of months of its publication, there are at least three pirated translations of the green book circulating the booksellers of London, and a month after that, they're available in Boston, New York, and Baltimore.

To return to the book itself for a moment—after that frustrating ending, there's a blank page, which is followed by seven more pages, each showing a separate design. What's above me on the screen is the first of them. The rest—well, let's not get ahead of ourselves. Suffice it to say, the initial verdict was that something had gone awry in the printing process, with the result that the *bouche* had become *bouché*, cloudy. A few scholars have even gone so far as to attempt to reconstruct what Prosper's original images must have been. Prebend, though—the publisher—swore that he'd presented the book exactly as he had been instructed.

For those of us familiar with abstract art, I doubt there's any great difficulty in seeing the black blot on the screen as a mouth. The effect—there used to be these books; they were full of what looked like random designs. If you held them the right distance from your face and let your eyes relax, almost to the point of going cross-eyed, all of sudden, a picture would leap out of the page at you. You know what I'm talking about? Good. I don't know what the name for that effect is, but it's the nearest analogue I can come up with for what happens when you look at the Mouth under blue light—except that the image doesn't jump forward so much as sink back. The way it recedes—it's as if it extends, not just through the screen, or the wall behind it, but beyond all that, to the very substratum of things.

To tell the truth, I have no idea what's responsible for the effect. If you find this impressive, however...

Look at that: a new image and a fresh color. How's that for coordination? Good work, nameless minions. Vauglais named this "*Le Gardien*," the Guardian. What's that? I suppose you could make an octopus out of it; although aren't there a few too many tentacles? True, it's close enough; it's certainly more octopus than squid. Do you notice... right. The tentacles, loops, whatever we call them, appear to be moving. Focus on any one in particular, and it stands still—but you can see movement out of the corner of your eye, can't you? Try to take in the whole, and you swear its arms are performing an intricate dance.

So the Mouth leads to the Guardian, which is waving its appendages in front of...

That green is bright after the purple, isn't it? Voila "*Le Récif*," the Reef. Makes sense, a cuttlefish protecting a reef. I don't know: it's angular enough. Personally, I suspect this one is based on some kind of pun or word play. "*Récif*" is one letter away from "*récit*," story, and this reef comes to us as the result of a story; in some weird way, the reef may be the story. I realize that doesn't make any sense; I'm still working through it.

This image is a bit different from the previous two. Anyone notice how?

Exactly: instead of the picture appearing to move, the light itself seems to—I like your word, "shimmer." You could believe we're gazing through water. It's—not hypnotic, that's too strong, but it is soothing. Don't you think?

I'll take your yawn as a "yes." Very nice. What a way to preface a question. All right, all right. What is it that's keeping you awake?

Isn't it obvious? Apparently not.

Yes! Edgar read Prosper's book!

When? The best evidence is sometime in the early eighteen thirties, after he'd relocated to Baltimore. He mentions hearing about the green book from one of his fellow cadets at West Point, but he doesn't secure his own copy until he literally stumbles upon one in a bookshop near Baltimore's inner harbor. He wrote a fairly amusing account of it in a letter to Virginia. The store was this long, narrow space located halfway down an alley; its shelves were stuffed past capacity with all sizes of books jammed together with no regard for their subject. Occasionally, one of the shelves would disgorge its contents without warning. If you were underneath or to the side of it, you ran the risk of substantial injury. Not to mention, the single aisle snaking into the shop's recesses was occupied at irregular intervals by stacks of books that looked as if a strong sneeze would send them tumbling down.

It's as he's attempting to maneuver around an especially tall tower of books, simultaneously trying to avoid jostling a nearby shelf, that Edgar's foot catches on a single volume he hadn't seen, sending him—and all books in the immediate vicinity—to the floor. There's a huge puff of dust; half a dozen books essentially disintegrate. Edgar's sense of humor is such that he appreciates the comic aspect of a poet—as he styled himself—buried beneath a deluge of books. However, he insists on excavating the book that undid him.

The copy of Vauglais's essay he found was a fourth translation that had been done by a Boston publisher hoping to cash in on the popularity of the other editions. Unfortunately for him, the edition took longer to prepare than he'd anticipated—his translator was a Harvard professor who insisted on translating Prosper as accurately as he could. This meant an English version of Vauglais's essay that was a model of fidelity to the original French, but that wasn't ready until Prosper's story was last week's news. The publisher went ahead with what he titled *The Green Book of M. Prosper Vauglais* anyway, but he pretty much lost his shirt over the whole thing.

Edgar was so struck at having fallen over this book that he bought it on the spot. He spent the next couple of days reading and re-reading it, puzzling over its contents. As we've seen in "The Gold Bug" and "The Purloined Letter," this was a guy who liked a puzzle. He spent a good deal of time on the seven designs at the back of the book, convinced that their significance was right in front of him.

Speaking of those pictures, let's have another one. Assistants, if you please—

Hey, it's Halloween! Isn't that what you associate orange with? And especially an orange like this—this is the sun spilling the last of its late light, right before all the gaudier colors, the violets and pinks, splash out. You don't think of orange as dark, do you? I know I don't. Yet it is, isn't it? Is it the darkest of the bright colors? To be sure, it's difficult to distinguish the design at its center; the orange is filmy, translucent. There are a few too many curves for it to be the symbol for infinity; at least, I think there are. I want to say I see a pair of snakes wrapped around one another, but the coils don't connect in quite the right way. Vauglais's name for this was "*Le Coeur*," the Heart, and also the Core, as well as the Height or the Depth, depending on usage. Obviously, we're cycling through the seven rooms from "The Masque of the Red Death;" obviously, too, I'm arguing that Edgar takes their colors from Prosper's book. In that schema, orange is at the center, three colors to either side of it; in that sense, we have reached the heart, the core, the height or the depth. Of course, that core obscures the other one—or maybe not.

While you try to decide, let's return to Edgar. It's an overstatement to say that Vauglais obsesses him. When his initial attempt at deciphering the designs fails, he puts the book aside. Remember, he's a working writer at a time when the American economy really won't support one—especially one with Edgar's predilections—so there are always more things to be written in the effort to keep the wolf a safe distance from the door. Not to mention, he's falling in love with the girl who will become his wife. At odd moments over the next decade, though, he retrieves Prosper's essay and spends a few hours poring over it. He stares at its images until they're grooved into the folds of his brain. During one long afternoon in 1840, he's sitting with the book open to the Mouth, a glass of water on the table to his right. The sunlight streaming in the windows splinters on the water glass, throwing a rainbow across the page in front of him. The arc of the image that's under the blue strip of the bow looks different; it's as if that portion of the paper has sunk into the book— behind the book. A missing and apparently lost piece of the puzzle snaps into place, and Edgar starts up from the table, knocking over his chair in the process. He races through the house, searching for a piece of blue glass. The best he can do is a heavy blue jug, which he almost drops in his excitement. He returns to the book, angles the jug to catch the light, and watches as the Mouth opens. He doesn't waste any time staring at it; shifting the jug to his right hand, he flips to the next image with his left, positions the glass jug over the Guardian, and... nothing. For a moment, he's afraid he's imagined the whole thing, had an especially vivid waking dream. But when he pages back to the Mouth and directs the blue light onto it, it clearly recedes. Edgar wonders if the effect he's observed is unique to the first image, then his eye lights on the glass of water, still casting its rainbow. He sets the jug on the floor, turns the page, and slides the book closer to the glass.

That's how Edgar spends the rest of the afternoon, matching the designs in the back of Vauglais's book to the colors that activate them. The first four come relatively quickly; the last three take longer. Once he has all seven, Edgar re-reads Prosper's essay and reproaches himself as a dunce for not having hit on the colors sooner. It's all there in Vauglais's prose, he declares, plain as day. (He's being much too hard on himself. I've read the green book a dozen times and I have yet to find the passage where Prosper hints at the colors.)

How about a look at the most difficult designs? Gentlemen, if you please...

There's nothing there. I know—that's what I said, the first time I saw the fifth image. "*Le Silence*," the Silence. Compared to the designs that precede it, this one is so faint as to be barely detectable. And when you shine a bright, white light onto it, it practically disappears. There is something in there, though; you have to stare at it for a while. More so than with the previous images, what you see here varies dramatically from viewer to viewer.

Edgar never records his response to the Silence, which is a pity. Having cracked the secret of Vauglais's designs, he studies the essay more carefully, attempting to discern the use to which the images were to be put, the nature of Prosper's Great Work, his Transumption. (There's that word again. I never clarified its meaning vis à vis Vauglais's ideas, did I?) The following year, when Edgar sits down to write "The Masque of the Red Death," it is in no small part as an answer to the question of what Prosper was up to. That answer shares features with some of the stories he had written prior to his 1840 revelation; although, interestingly, they came after he had obtained his copy of the green book.

From the looks on your faces, I'd say you've seen what the Silence contains. I don't suppose anyone wants to share?

I'll take that as a "No." It's all right: what you find there can be rather... disconcerting.

We're almost at the end of our little display. What do you say we proceed to number six? Here we go...

Violet's such a nice color, isn't it? You have to admit, some of those other colors are pretty intense. Not this one, though; even the image—"*L'Arbre*," the Tree—looks more or less like a collection of lines trying to be a tree. Granted, if you study the design, you'll notice that each individual line seems to fade and then re-inscribe itself, but compared to the effect of the previous image, this is fairly benign. Does it remind you of anything? Anything we were discussing, say, in the last hour or so?

Oh never mind, I'll just tell you. Remember those trees Vauglais saw outside the Abbey? Remember the way that, when he tried to focus on any of them, he saw a mass of black lines? Hmmm. Maybe there's more to this pleasant design than we'd thought. Maybe it's, not the key to all this, but the key trope, or figure.

I know: which means what, exactly? Let's return to Edgar's story. You have a group of people who are sequestered together, made to disguise their outer identities, encouraged to debauch themselves, to abandon their inner identities, all the while passing from one end of this color schema to the other. They put their selves aside, become a massive blank, a kind of psychic space. That opening allows what is otherwise an abstraction, a personification, to change states, to manifest itself physically. Of course, the Red Death doesn't appear of its own volition; it's called into being by Prince Prospero, who can't stop thinking about the reason he's retreated into his abbey.

This is what happened—what started to happen to the members of the *salon* Prosper took into the Parisian catacombs. He attempted to implement what he'd learned during his years at the Abbey, what he first had perceived through the snow twirling in front of his eyes in that Russian forest. To manipulate—to mold—to...

Suppose that the real—what we take to be the real—imagine that world outside the self, all this out here, is like a kind of writing. We write it together; we're continuously writing it together, onto the surface of things, the paper, as it were. It isn't something we do consciously, or that we exercise any conscious control over. We might glimpse it in moments of extremity, as Vauglais did, but that's about as close to it as most of us will come. What if, though, what if it were possible to do something more than simply look? What if you could clear a space on that paper and write something *else*? What might you bring into being?

Edgar tries to find out. Long after "The Masque," which is as much caution as it is field guide, he decides to apply Prosper's ideas for real. He does so during that famous lost week at the end of his life, that gap in the biographical record that has prompted so much speculation. Since Virginia succumbed to tuberculosis some two years prior, Edgar's been on a long downward slide, a protracted effort at joining his beloved wife. You know, extensive forests have been harvested for the production of critical studies of Edgar's "bizarre" relationship with Virginia; rarely, if ever, does it occur to anyone that Edgar and Virginia might honestly have been in love, and that the difference in their ages might have been incidental. Yet what is that final couple of years but a man grieving himself to death? Yes, Edgar approaches other women about possible marriage, but why do you think none of those proposals work out?

Not only is Edgar actively chasing his death, paddling furiously towards it on a river of alcohol; little known to him, death has noticed his pursuit, and responded by planting a black seed deep within his brain, a gift that is blossoming into a tumor. Most biographers have remained ignorant of this disease, but years after his death, Edgar's body is exhumed—it doesn't matter why; given who Edgar was, of course this was going to happen to him. During the examination of his remains, it's noted that his brain is shrunken and hard. Anyone who knows about these things will tell you that the brain is one of the first organs to decay, which means that what those investigators found rattling around old Edgar's cranium would not have been petrified gray matter. Cancer, however, is a much more durable beast; long after it's killed you, a tumor hangs around to testify to its crime. Your guess is as good as mine when it comes to how long he'd had it, but by the time I'm talking about, Edgar is in a pretty bad way. He's having trouble controlling the movements of his body, his speech; half the time he seems drunk, he's stone cold sober.

There's something else. Increasingly, wherever he turns his gaze, whatever he looks at flickers, and instead of, say, an orange resting on a plate, he sees a jumble of black lines approximating a sphere on a circle. It takes him longer to recall Vauglais's experience in that Russian forest than you'd expect; the cancer, no doubt, devouring his memory. Sometimes the confusion of lines that's replaced the streetlamp in front of him is itself replaced by blankness, by an absence that registers as a dull white space in the middle of things. It's as if a painter took a palette knife and scraped the oils from a portion of their picture until all that remained was the canvas, slightly stained. At first, Edgar thinks there's something wrong with his vision; when he understands what he's experiencing, he speculates that the blank might be the result of his eyes' inability to endure their own perception, that he might be undergoing some degree of what we would call hysterical blindness. As he's continued to see that whiteness, though, he's realized that he isn't seeing less, but more. He's seeing through to the surface those black lines are written on.

In the days immediately prior to his disappearance, Edgar's perception undergoes one final change. For the slightest instant after that space has uncovered itself to him, something appears on it, a figure—a woman. Virginia, yes, as he saw her last, ravaged by tuberculosis, skeletally thin, dark hair in disarray, mouth and chin scarlet with the blood she'd hacked out of her lungs. She appears barefoot, wrapped in a shroud stained with dirt. Almost before he sees her, she's gone, her place taken by whatever he'd been looking at to begin with.

Is it any surprise that, presented with this dull white surface, Edgar should fill it with Virginia? Her death has polarized him; she's the lodestone that draws his thoughts irresistibly in her direction. With each glimpse of her he has, Edgar apprehends that he's standing at the threshold of what could be an extraordinary chance. Although he's discovered the secret of Prosper's designs, discerned the nature of the Great Work, never once has it occurred to him that he might put that knowledge to use. Maybe he hasn't really believed in it; maybe he's suspected that, underneath it all, the effect of the various colors on Vauglais's designs is some type of clever optical illusion. Now, though, now that there's the possibility of gaining his beloved back—

Edgar spends that last week sequestered in a room in a boarding house a few streets up from that alley where he tripped over Prosper's book. He's arranged for his meals to be left outside his door; half the time, however, he leaves them untouched, and even when he takes the dishes into his room, he eats the bare minimum to sustain him. About midway through his stay, the landlady, a Mrs. Foster, catches sight of him as he withdraws into his room. His face is flushed, his skin slick with sweat, his clothes disheveled; he might be in the grip of a fever whose fingers are tightening around him with each degree it climbs. As his door closes, Mrs. Foster considers running up to it and demanding to speak to this man. The last thing she wants is for her boarding house to be known as a den of sickness. She has taken two steps forward when she stops, turns, and bolts downstairs as if the Devil himself were tugging her apron strings. For the remainder of the time this lodger is in his room, she will send one of the serving girls to deliver his meals, no matter their protests. Once the room stands unoccupied, she will direct a pair of those same girls to remove its contents—including the cheap bed— carry them out back, and burn them until nothing remains but a heap of ashes. The empty room is closed, locked, and removed from use for the rest of her time running that house, some twenty-two years.

I know: what did she see? What could she have seen, with the door shut? Perhaps it wasn't what she saw; perhaps it was what she felt: the surface of things yielding, peeling away to what was beneath, beyond—the strain of a will struggling to score its vision onto that surface—the waver of the brick and mortar, of the very air around her, as it strained against this newness coming into being. How would the body respond to what could only register as a profound wrongness? Panic, you have to imagine, maybe accompanied by sudden nausea, a fear so intense as to guarantee a lifetime's aversion to anything associated with its cause.

Had she opened that door, though, what sight would have confronted her? What would we see?

Nothing much—at least, that's likely to have been our initial response. Edgar seated on the narrow bed, staring at the wall opposite him. Depending on which day it was, we would have noticed his shirt and pants looking more or less clean. Like Mrs. Foster, we would have remarked his flushed face, the sweat soaking his shirt; we would have heard his breathing, deep and hoarse. We might have caught his lips moving, might have guessed he was repeating Virginia's name over and over again, but been unable to say for sure. Were we to guess he was in a trance, caught in an opium dream, aside from the complete and total lack of opium-related paraphernalia, we could be forgiven.

If we were to remain in that room with him—if we could stand the same sensation that sent Mrs. Foster running—it wouldn't take us long to turn our eyes in the direction of Edgar's stare. His first day there, we wouldn't have noticed much if anything out of the ordinary. Maybe we would have wondered if the patch of bricks he was so focused on didn't look just the slightest shade paler than its surroundings, before dismissing it as a trick of the light. Return two, three days later, and we would find that what we had attributed to mid-afternoon light blanching already-faded masonry is a phenomenon of an entirely different order. Those bricks are blinking in and out of sight. One moment, there's a worn red rectangle, the next, there isn't. What takes its place is difficult to say, because it's back almost as fast as it was gone; although, after its return, the brick looks a bit less solid... less certain, you might say. Ragged around the edges, though not in any way you could put words to. All over that stretch of wall, bricks are going and coming and going. It almost looks as if some kind of code is spelling itself out using the stuff of Edgar's wall as its pen and paper.

Were we to find ourselves in that same room, studying that same spot, a day later, we would be startled to discover a small area of the wall, four bricks up, four down, vanished. Where it was—let's call what's there—or what isn't there—white. To tell the truth, it's difficult to look at that spot— the eye glances away automatically, the way it does from a bright light. Should you try to force the issue, tears dilute your vision.

Return to Edgar's room over the next twenty-four hours, and you would find that gap exponentially larger—from four bricks by four bricks to sixteen by sixteen, then from sixteen by sixteen to—basically, the entire wall. Standing in the doorway, you would have to raise your hand, shield your eyes from the dull whiteness in front of you. Blink furiously, squint, and you might distinguish Edgar in his familiar position, staring straight into that blank. Strain your gaze through the narrowest opening your fingers can make, and for the half a second until your head jerks to the side, you see a figure, deep within the white. Later, at a safe remove from Edgar's room, you may attempt to reconstruct that form, make sense of your less-than-momentary vision. All you'll be able to retrieve, however, is a pair of impressions, the one of something coalescing, like smoke filling up a jar, the other of thinness, like a child's stick-drawing grown life-sized. For the next several months, not only your dreams, but your waking hours will be plagued by what you saw between your fingers. Working late at night, you will be overwhelmed by the sense that whatever you saw in that room is standing just outside the cone of light your lamp throws. Unable to help yourself, you'll reach for the shade, tilt it back, and find... nothing, your bookcases. Yet the sensation won't pass; although you can read the spines of the hardcovers ranked on your bookshelves, your skin won't stop bristling at what you can't see there.

What about Edgar, though? What image do his eyes find at the heart of that space? I suppose we should ask, What image of Virginia?

It—she changes. She's thirteen, wearing the modest dress she married him in. She's nine, wide-eyed as she listens to him reciting his poetry to her mother and her. She's dead, wrapped in a white shroud. So much concentration is required to pierce through to the undersurface in the first place—and then there's the matter of maintaining the aperture—that it's difficult to find, let alone summon, the energy necessary to focus on a single image of Virginia. So the figure in front of him brushes a lock of dark hair out of her eyes, then giggles in a child's high-pitched tones, then coughs and sprays scarlet blood over her lips and chin. Her mouth is pursed in thought; she turns to a knock on the front door; she thrashes in the heat of the disease that is consuming her. The more time that passes, the more Edgar struggles to keep his memories of his late wife separate from one another. She's nine, standing beside her mother, wound in her burial cloth. She's in her coffin, laughing merrily. She's saying she takes him as her lawful husband, her mouth smeared with blood.

Edgar can't help himself—he's written, and read, too many stories about exactly this kind of situation for him not to be aware of all the ways it could go hideously wrong. Of course, the moment such a possibility occurs to him, it's manifest in front of him. You know how it is: the harder you try to keep a pink elephant out of your thoughts, the more that animal cavorts center-stage. Virginia is obscured by white linen smeared with mud; where her mouth is, the shroud is red. Virginia is naked, her skin drawn to her skeleton, her hair loose and floating around her head as if she's under water. Virginia is wearing the dress she was buried in, the garment and the pale flesh beneath it opened by rats. Her eyes—or the sockets that used to cradle them—are full of her death, of all she has seen as she was dragged out of the light down into the dark.

With each new monstrous image of his wife, Edgar strives not to panic. He bends what is left of his will toward summoning Virginia as she was at sixteen, when they held a second, public wedding. For an instant, she's there, holding out her hand to him with that simple grace she's displayed as long as he's known her—and then she's gone, replaced by a figure whose black eyes have seen the silent halls of the dead, whose ruined mouth has tasted delicacies unknown this side of the grave. This image does not flicker; it does not yield to other, happier pictures. Instead, it grows more solid, more definite. It takes a step towards Edgar, who is frantic, his heart thudding in his chest, his mouth dry. He's trying to stop the process, trying to close the door he's spent so much time and effort prying open, to erase what he's written on that blankness. The figure takes another step forward, and already, is at the edge of the opening. His attempts at stopping it are useless—what he's started has accrued sufficient momentum for it to continue regardless of him. His lips are still repeating, "Virginia."

When the—we might as well say, when Virginia places one gray foot onto the floor of Edgar's room, a kind of ripple runs through the entire room, as if every last bit of it is registering the intrusion. How Edgar wishes he could look away as she crosses the floor to him. In a far corner of his brain that is capable of such judgments, he knows that this is the price for his *hubris*— really, it's almost depressingly formulaic. He could almost accept the irony if he did not have to watch those hands dragging their nails back and forth over one another, leaving the skin hanging in pale strips; if he could avoid the sight of whatever is seething in the folds of the bosom of her dress; if he could shut his eyes to that mouth and its dark contents as it descends to his. But he can't; he cannot turn away from his Proserpine as she rejoins him at last.

Four days prior to his death, Edgar is found on the street, delirious, barely-conscious. He never recovers. Right at the end, he rallies long enough to dictate a highly-abbreviated version of the story I've told you to a

Methodist minister, who finds what he records so disturbing he sews it into the binding of the family Bible, where it will remain concealed for a century and a half.

As for what Edgar called forth—she walks out of our narrative and is not seen again.

It's a crazy story. It makes the events of Vauglais's life seem almost reasonable in comparison. If you were so inclined, I suppose you could ascribe Edgar's experience in that rented room to an extreme form of auto-hypnosis which, combined with the stress on his body from his drinking and the brain tumor, precipitates a fatal collapse. In which case, the story I've told you is little more than an elaborate symptom. It's the kind of reading a literary critic prefers; it keep the more… outré elements safely quarantined within the writer's psyche.

Suppose, though, suppose. Suppose that all this insanity I've been feeding you isn't a quaint example of early-nineteenth-century pseudoscience. Suppose that its interest extends well beyond any insights it might offer in interpreting "The Masque of the Red Death." Suppose—let's say the catastrophe that overtakes Edgar is the result of—we could call it poor planning. Had he paid closer attention to the details of Prosper's history, especially to that sojourn in the catacombs, he would have recognized the difficulty—to the point of impossibility—of making his attempt alone. Granted, he was desperate. But there was a reason Vauglais took the members of his *salon* underground with him—to use as a source of power, a battery, as it were. They provided the energy; he directed it. Edgar's story is a testament to what must have been a tremendous—an almost unearthly will. In the end, though, it wasn't enough.

Of course, how could he have brought together a sufficient number of individuals, and where? By the close of his life, he wasn't the most popular of fellows. Not to mention, he would have needed to expose the members of this hypothetical group to Prosper's designs and their corresponding colors.

Speaking of which: pleasant as this violet has been, what do you say we proceed to the *piece de resistance*? Faceless lackeys, on my mark—

Ahh. I don't usually talk about these things, but you have no idea how much trouble this final color combination gave me. I mean, red and black gives you dark red, right? Right, except that for the design to achieve its full effect, putting up a dark red light won't do. You need red layered over black—and a true black light, not ultraviolet. The result, though—I'm sure you'll agree, it was worth sweating over. It's like a picture painted in red on a black canvas, wouldn't you say? And look what it does for the final image. It seems to be reaching right out of the screen for you, doesn't it? Strictly speaking, Vauglais's name for it, "*Le Dessous*," the Underneath, isn't quite grammatical French, but we needn't worry ourselves over such details. There are times I think another name would be more appropriate: the Maw, perhaps, and then there are moments I find the Underneath perfect. You can see why I might lean towards calling it a mouth—the Cave would do, as well—except that the perspective's all wrong. If this is a mouth, or a cave, we aren't looking into it; we're already inside, looking out.

Back to Edgar. As we've said, even had he succeeded in gathering a group to assist him in his pursuit, he would have had to find a way to introduce them to Prosper's images and their colors. If he could have, he would have... reoriented them, their minds, the channels of their thoughts. Vauglais's designs would have brought them closer to where they needed to be; they would have made available certain dormant faculties within his associates.

Even that would have left him with challenges, to be sure. Mesmerism, hypnosis, as Prosper himself discovered, is a delicate affair, one subject to such external variables as running out of lamp oil too soon. It would have been better if he could have employed some type of pharmacological agent, something that would have deposited them into a more useful state, something sufficiently concentrated to be delivered via a few bites of an innocuous food—a cookie, say, whose sweetness would mask any unpleasant taste, and which he could cajole his assistants to sample by claiming that his wife had baked them.

Then, if Edgar had been able to keep this group distracted while the cookies did their work—perhaps by talking to them about his writing—about the genesis of one of his stories, say, "The Masque of the Red Death"—if he had managed this far, he might have been in a position to make something happen, to perform the Great Work.

There's just one more thing, and that's the object for which Edgar would have put himself to all this supposed trouble: Virginia. I like to think I'm as romantic as the next guy, but honestly—you have the opportunity to rescript reality, and the best you can come up with is returning your dead wife to you? Talk about a failure to grasp the possibilities...

What's strange—and frustrating—is that it's all right there in "The Masque," in Edgar's own words. The whole idea of the Great Work, of Transumption, is to draw one of the powers that our constant, collective writing of the real consigns to abstraction across the barrier into physicality. Ideally, one of the members of that trinity Edgar named so well, Darkness and Decay and the Red Death, those who hold illimitable dominion over all. The goal is to accomplish something momentous, to shake the world to its foundations, not play out some hackneyed romantic fantasy. That was what Vauglais was up to, trying to draw into form the force that strips the flesh from our bones, that crumbles those bones to dust.

No matter. Edgar's mistake still has its uses as a distraction, and a lesson. Not that it'll do any of you much good. By now, I suspect few of you can hear what I'm saying, let alone understand it. I'd like to tell you the name of what I stirred into that cookie dough, but it's rather lengthy and wouldn't do you much good, anyway. I'd also like to tell you it won't leave you permanently impaired, but that wouldn't exactly be true. One of the consequences of its efficacy, I fear. If it's any consolation, I doubt most of you will survive what's about to follow. By my reckoning, the power I'm about to bring into our midst will require a good deal of... sustenance in order to establish a more permanent foothold here. I suspect this is of even less consolation, but I do regret this aspect of the plan I'm enacting. It's just—once you come into possession of such knowledge, how can you not make use—full use of it?

You see, I'm starting at the top. Or at the beginning—before the beginning, really, before light burst across the perfect formlessness that was everything. I'm starting with Darkness, with something that was already so old at that moment of creation that it had long forgotten its identity. I plan to restore it. I will give myself to it for a guide, let it envelop me and consume you and run out from here in a flood that will wash this world away. I will give to Darkness a dominion more complete than it has known since it was split asunder.

Look—in the air—can you see it?

For Fiona

WHEN I WAS *a college freshman, my English class read a selection of Poe's stories, including "The Masque of the Red Death." For "The Masque," the Professor gave us the assignment of figuring out what we thought the meaning to the story's elaborate color schema was. He spent an entire class writing our responses on the board, comparing our answers. At the end of class, we asked him what he thought. He smiled and said, "I don't know."*

Here's another attempt at an answer.

ELLEN DATLOW has been editing science fiction, fantasy, and horror short fiction for over twenty-five years. She was fiction editor of *OMNI Magazine* and *SCIFICTION* and has edited more than fifty anthologies, including the horror half of the long-running *The Year's Best Fantasy and Horror*, *Little Deaths*, *Twists of the Tale*, *The Dark*, *Inferno*, *The Del Rey Book of Science Fiction and Fantasy*, *The Coyote Road: Trickster Tales*, *Salon Fantastique*, and *Troll's Eye View: a Book of Villainous Tales* (the last three with Terri Windling). She has won the Locus Award, the Hugo Award, The Stoker Award, the International Horror Guild Award, and the World Fantasy Award for her editing. She was named recipient of the 2007 Karl Edward Wagner Award, given at the British Fantasy Convention for "outstanding contribution to the genre."